WHISPERS OF *War*

❧ BOOK THREE ❧

NAOMI FINLEY

Cover designer: Victoria Cooper Art
Website: www.facebook.com / VictoriaCooperArt

Editor: Scripta Word Services
Website: scripta-word-services.com

Reading Order for Series

Novels can be read alone or with the novella series.
The author's shorter works are best read in the suggested order.

1857–1861

∽ CHAPTER ∽
One

Livingston Plantation

TEARS CASCADED DOWN MY CHEEKS AS I TOUCHED THE FABRIC OF the tiny nightshift my son had never worn. The babe had breathed for a few precious moments before the rise and fall of his chest had ceased.

The hot summer sun enveloped the nursery I'd decorated with the hopes and dreams of happiness in the years to come. As the babe had grown inside of me, I had loved him with a fierceness observed in other mothers, equivalent with the love and protectiveness I felt for Josephine's son, Sailor.

I kissed the garment and clasped it to my chest before opening the drawer and placing it underneath the other garments, each purchased with love, care, and anticipation of my son's arrival.

A sad smile played on my heart with the memory of Bowden's elation when I told him of the pregnancy. He'd swept me off my feet and whirled me in the air before marching to the forge to tell Jimmy the news. After, he'd insisted on gathering the plantation folk to celebrate, and oh, how we'd celebrated! We had danced arm and arm with the folks in the quarters until my feet swelled and ached. The new life had signified hope and change for Livingston; the family Bowden so desperately desired.

In the months after, worry had controlled my days. What if

it sensed my nervousness and screamed, as Evie had as a babe? What if I didn't feel a connection to the child? The latter worry had become almost paralyzing. But ever dutiful and with loving devotion, Mammy and Mary Grace had tried to soothe me with the assurance that being a mother came naturally. I hadn't been so sure. Such worries seemed trivial after his birth.

Together the women had taught me much about life, and it was Mammy I'd cried out for as Ben and Bowden fought to save my son. Then, when Little Ben took his last breath, she'd pulled me to her bosom and held me as I soaked her blouse in my grief.

Afterward, days melded into weeks, and I couldn't conjure the strength to pull myself out of bed or leave my chamber. Mammy and Bowden brought food, but, full of misery and despair, I refused their efforts. Wallowing in my anguish, I begged God to take me and return my son to his father.

I walked to the bassinet sitting in the middle of the room and ran my fingers over the angel wings etched into the headboard, masterly crafted by Jimmy, and engraved as he had Ruby's.

Earlier that morning, Mammy's patience had worn thin. Storming into my chamber, she'd thrown open the drapes against my protests. "I know you hurting, angel gal, but Masa Bowden be leavin' today. And I know his heart could use some love. He hurting too. You got to 'member dat." She perched on the edge of the bed and pushed the hair out of my eyes. "You got to git outta dat bed and let de sun take a drink of ya."

Pulling myself together, I'd walked down the corridor and paused outside the nursery on the way downstairs. Since my son's death, I hadn't been inside, but my heart yearned for comfort and wholeness. I strode through the room, touching each item, losing track of time until he spoke.

"Willow, I really must go," Bowden said from behind me.

The hollow ache in his voice tugged at my heart, but I didn't turn to face him.

His boots scuffed the floorboards as he crossed the room, and the warmth of his hand on my shoulder conjured a tear and sent a shudder through me. Squeezing my eyes tight shut, I paused before turning my face to kiss his wrist. He embraced me, and I leaned back against him, soaking in the comfort of his nearness.

"Must you go?" I lay my head against his chest. The tension in my body eased at the steady beating of his heart.

"I have to," he breathed into my hair. "The banks in New York have closed, and most shipments have come to a halt. If I don't get our goods out of the harbor, we stand to lose much."

I turned to face him, trying to quell the desire to beg him to stay. "I shall miss you terribly."

He gripped my arms, eyes searching my face. "Listen…" He struggled to speak, and his eyes mirrored the pain in my soul. "Someway, somehow, we have to find a way to go on."

"I don't know how to fill the void. It feels like part of my soul is missing. Like I'll never feel whole again." I knotted his shirt in my fingers.

"I know." He brushed back a tendril of my hair and cradled my cheek in his hand. "Like you, I'm trying to figure this all out while grasping at anything to keep from crumbling."

"I'm sorry." I bit my quivering lip.

He had gotten up each day and managed the plantation and ventured into Charleston to see to operations at the docks.

"Forgive me. I wanted to be there for you. Indeed, I did…I do. I will try harder."

He enfolded my hand in his. "There is no need to apologize. I cast no blame. No parent is equipped to lose a child."

Many nights, I had pondered Reuben's—alias Silas—belief

that my mother had cursed his family. When I'd been overcome with grief, I'd wondered why darkness overshadowed our family. Would heartache and loss continue to follow us?

"Somehow, with the loss of him, it's guilt that takes precedence over my sorrow," Bowden said.

"Guilt? But there was nothing you and Ben could do. It was out of your hands. You can't blame—"

"It isn't that. I'm fully aware we are only men, not miracle workers."

"Then what troubles you so?" I placed his hand over my heart.

His words came out thick and weighted with a truth that no amount of comfort could erase. "How can I grieve for the loss of one son when I've inflicted the humans I held in bondage with this same pain? I sold their children without a second thought. Like an angel of death, I sowed my lands with their blood and misery."

I'd witnessed the bitterness and shame that chased him, and each day lashed his soul.

He shook his head as if to dislodge the melancholy seizing his thoughts, and feigned a smile. Leaning down, he placed a tender kiss on my lips before straightening and scooping an arm around my shoulders. "Knox awaits. He is taking me to catch the steamer."

"Will you see Kipling while you're in New York?" I asked as we descended the back steps of the veranda.

"I'm unsure. I have much to discuss with Saul and Ruby about the building of the black school. Our funding will help get their ambitions off the ground."

"Please give her my love and congratulations on the baby. I've meant to send her my well wishes." There was enough self-blame between the pair of us, so I stifled the guilt chewing at me over my selfishness and shortcomings as a friend. "Did Mammy give you the gifts to take to her?"

"That she did."

We rounded the side of the house to find the private carriage ready. At the open door of the buggy, Bowden released me. "Promise me that you will take care of yourself while I'm gone. I should be back in two weeks."

"I will manage. You needn't worry."

He kissed me again, and all too soon he pulled away. "We really must go." He turned to scan the grounds until his gaze fell on Knox, who sat on the front veranda with legs outstretched and boots resting on the railing. "You ready?"

"Waiting on you." Knox pushed to his feet and strode across the veranda to the steps.

"I expect you will keep my wife out of trouble while I'm gone," Knox said with a grin.

A light laugh escaped me. "I can't make promises." I marveled at how good it felt to laugh, and the magic Knox had over people. I caught Bowden's smile out of the corner of my eye.

Knox shrugged. "I figured it was worth the effort."

"You know how it is when two stubborn women get together." Bowden gave my shoulders a playful squeeze. I'd missed the lightheartedness between us and I made myself a promise: upon his return, I'd see to it that we spent more time laughing.

"Let's get on our way. Whitney will be fuming if I miss the evening meal." He feigned a frantic look. "Don't dally, Knox. Put your feet down. Empty the chamber pot. Gather the wood. A fellow gets married, and his daily duties become a full ledger that will keep him hopping for the rest of his days." His face split with an ear-to-ear grin.

"I have no sympathy for you. You knew the woman you

were marrying and you chased her anyway." Bowden slapped his friend's back.

Laughter erupted from the pair, and I joined in their merriment; the clouds of the day somehow faded. The desire to feel whole again gripped me, and I put my mind to the task.

"I wonder where he is?" Bowden said.

"I right here, Masa Bowden," a breathless voice said. Jimmy dashed into the front yard, polished and gleaming in a dark suit. His fingers fumbled with the felt bowler hat he held while his eyes flitted around the grounds as though reconsidering his decision. "You certain we ain't gonna drown on dat big boat? I mean, I wants to see my gal and my grandbaby, but I skeered de boat go down 'fore I git to see dem."

"Plenty of ships travel the Atlantic and safely reach their destinations without sinking. You've nothing to worry about," I said.

"Ef you say so, Missus Willie." He shook his head, seeming unconvinced.

"I've never seen you look more handsome." I touched his arm. "Ruby will be delighted with the surprise. I only wish I could be there to see her face and kiss the baby."

"She will understand. You gots to take care of you now." He regarded me as if I were fragile, and to be honest, lately, I'd felt like it. But it didn't sit well with me. The people of Livingston needed me.

"I'm fine." I squirmed under the men's gazes.

"You and de masa had a great hurt. You don't need to be strong dis time. We take care of you, ef'n you let us."

"Thank you." I patted his arm, my heart expanding with love and gratitude.

Over his shoulder, I spotted Mammy marching toward us in her take-charge kind of way. We all stood a little straighter at her approach.

"Let's get on the road," Bowden said.

"Don't you worry 'bout a thing, Masa. Missus Willow be in good hands while you gone," Mammy said.

Bowden smiled at her. "I can't think of more capable hands."

She stretched to her full five feet and beamed. "As long as I 'round, de missus never be alone."

"Dat makes two of us," Jimmy said.

Bowden pecked my cheek and lips before boarding the carriage, and Jimmy climbed in beside him. Knox closed the door and clambered onto the driver's seat.

Mammy and I stepped back and waved as the carriage lurched forward. Bowden turned and waved while Jimmy sat, board stiff, staring straight ahead. My chest felt empty as they exited the gates. The next weeks would be long and empty without them.

Mammy trudged back inside, and I turned to follow.

A small voice stilled my footsteps. "Missus."

Turning to Sailor, a beautiful boy of four, I smiled. "Well, hello."

His blended parentage was evident in his lighter-toned skin and kinky textured hair. His coffee-brown eyes scoured my face. "Are you still sad?"

The innocence of his question tugged at me, and I placed a hand on his shoulder. "A little, but I'm happier now that you're here."

A broad smile revealed gleaming white teeth. "Mammy said I need to let you be. But I miss you."

"Mammy means well. I'm happy to see you." I dabbed his nose with my finger. "Where is Evie?"

"In de house. Her mama said she can't play today."

An image of Mary Grace and Gray's daughter flashed in my mind. The girl had more sass and attitude than folks would deem acceptable in a Negro, but it was her spunk I admired most. A mirror vision of Mammy.

As of a year ago, I had moved Sailor into the house, and he resided in the living quarters with the other house folks. The danger of raising the child as though he were white was great, but I wouldn't let him remain a ward of the quarters. Bowden had agreed that we should do what was best for the boy. Rumors had spread amongst the good folks of Charleston that Ben, or Bowden, had bred the boy with a slave. Although such vulgarity irked me, it was a cover and protection for the boy we were willing to endure.

"Well, her mama must have had her reasons." I encircled his shoulders with my arm and led him toward the front steps.

His brow furrowed, then he said, "Missus Willow?"

"Hmm?"

"Wid Masa and Jimmy gone, who gwine to take me fishing?"

"They won't be gone long. Only a few weeks. I expect you can wait until they return."

His face fell but he didn't put up a fuss.

"All right, you run along and see if Mammy needs any help shucking peas."

"Yes, ma'am."

I waited until he disappeared around the corner of the house before ascending the steps.

"He is a beautiful boy," Mary Grace said as she walked out onto the veranda.

"He is." I crossed my arms and leaned against a column and regarded her.

"I see the battle in your face. You still question if you are doing right by him." Mary Grace had learned to live with her grief over the death of Gray and focused all her attention and free time in raising Evie and Noah, her adopted son from the swamp massacre.

"Keeping a mother from her child isn't right," I said.

"But you know what her husband would do if he discovered she bore a son with a Negro."

I recalled the luncheon I'd had with Josephine in the spring. A yellow bruise had marred her cheekbone, and another was revealed beneath her cuff as she reached for a teacup.

I rubbed my temples before regarding the woman who'd been like a sister to me. "But perhaps knowing of him would give her hope."

"What does Masa Bowden say?"

"He shares your outlook."

"I know that look in your eyes. You would defy him."

"Only if I thought I was doing the right thing. I know what my heart tells me. Especially after what I've lost. I know her pain, and telling her the truth may relieve the heartache."

Her brows drew together. "You best give it more time before you react. You're still grieving."

"Then I'd never say anything." I looked at her, feeling bleak. "If she decides to claim him, the hole in my heart will deepen, and I'm not sure I could bear that."

She touched my wrist, and her eyes softened. "I understand all too well. But life does go on, and you find a way to get up each morning."

"It's just that Bowden was so excited about the baby." I choked back the emotions. "We both were."

"I know." Her voice thickened.

Sensing the return of the melancholy, I tried to shake it off and turned my thoughts away. "What has Evie done now, to earn her a day in the house?"

"She took it upon herself to give the weaver's boy a shiner."

"Maybe he deserved it?"

She folded her arms across her chest and pursed her lips. "Because he said she looked like a boy with her shorn head?"

I giggled and shrugged.

A lice infestation in the quarters had required that most of the children's hair be shorn; even some womenfolk had decided it was easier to shave their heads than administer the endless, but necessary, combing for nits and lice. *"I pick cotton all day. Ain't 'bout to pluck critters all night,"* I'd overheard a woman say as she'd passed under my chamber window that morn.

Mary Grace's scowl deepened.

I threw my hands in the air. "All right, maybe she was in the wrong."

"The child doesn't take after her father or me. She has more spirit than I can handle."

"Spirit will do her good in life. Look at your mama." I nudged my head to the parlor window, where I'd spotted Mammy standing with a hand on her hip, her other hand wagging sass at a house servant. "I wonder what the poor girl did?" I said, our heads tucked together as they'd often been when we were children.

"You know Mama. If chores aren't done right, we are all gonna hear about it," she said out of the corner of her mouth.

We shared a chuckle, and I left Mary Grace to her work and headed inside.

∽ CHAPTER ∽
Two

TILLIE HELPED ME GET READY FOR THE LUNCHEON AT JOSEPHINE'S townhouse in Charleston. I slipped into a chemisette before donning a blue afternoon dress. As I exited the privacy screen my cage crinoline caught, and Tillie bounded forward to grab the screen before it crashed to the floor.

"I do declare, the designers that make these crinolines must all be men," I said with a huff. "I'd like to see them move around in these horrible garments. I mean, can they add any more rows of flounces to the bottoms?" I eyed her plain cotton frock with envy.

A soft giggle came from Tillie.

I looked at her with a sheepish grin. "I suppose I shouldn't be complaining. Do tell me, how is your husband?"

Her face brightened with the glow of a newlywed. "Oh, he fine, Missus Willow."

I gestured at her middle. "And the babe? It grows strong?"

Months prior, Tillie and Pete, radiating hope and love, had come to Bowden and me with news she was with child, and had requested permission to marry. I had been immersed in grief and secretly begrudged her happiness, and the wrongness of my jealousy vexed me. Upon my weeping confession to Bowden one evening, he had soothed me with words of tenderness: *"You mustn't be too hard on yourself."*

Tillie's slender fingers encircled the small bump protruding from her stomach, evoking a pang of envy, then sorrow, in me. I recalled how Bowden had affectionately stroked my belly in the privacy of our chamber.

"Et kicks are strong."

I cradled my stomach with the urge to have my son nestled safely in my womb. Anxiety washed over Tillie's face, alerting me to my actions, and I dropped my hands.

"I sorry, Missus," she whispered with a downcast gaze. "I know you and Masa Bowden was so happy 'bout de babe."

"No, don't. It is I who is sorry." Heavy of heart, I sat on the stool in front of my vanity. "I must ask your forgiveness."

She screwed up her face. "What for, Missus?"

"Because when you and Pete came to us about the baby, I was bitter and hurting." I leaned forward and clasped her hands. "I am happy for you, truly I am."

"I understand. We all see your pain. Pete and I wondered ef we should say anything, but we knowed soon my belly would grow and we bes' be tellin' you and de masa."

"You did right. Please accept my apology."

"Ain't nothing to forgive," she said. "But ef you need to hear et for yourself, I 'ccept your apology."

I squeezed her hand. "Thank you."

Against Bowden's wishes, I had remained at Livingston throughout the hottest months; the thought of enduring the solemn faces and intrusive interrogations by Charleston's elite and attending social gatherings plagued me with anxiety. Residing at Livingston amongst the ones I loved provided the solace I needed.

Influenza sweeping through the quarters had kept Ben and Kimie busy from morning to night. Hoping to contain the illness, house folk kept to the house. I yearned to be in Ben's company, and the yearning grew each time I stood on the back veranda and observed him making rounds in the quarters. Sometimes, seeing me, he'd pause and wave, but he was too far away for me to catch a smile or reassuring word.

"Any update on Pete's condition?"

"Masa Ben said de fever broke, and he hopes he be on de mend by week's end." Longing for her man shone in her face.

"I'm happy to hear that. He has responsibilities waiting on him." I dropped my eyes to her stomach and smiled.

Tillie returned a bright smile. "Dat he does, Missus."

I lifted the straw bonnet, embellished with extravagant silk flowers and ribbon trim, from the vanity. At Bowden's insistence, I had made the impulsive purchase during our wedding journey to Texas to visit his brother, Stone. After placing the hat on my head, Tillie inserted pins to ensure it remained in place.

"Missus."

"Yes." I beheld her in the looking glass.

"I believe de Lard will bless you and de masa wid another babe. I knowed et won't replace de li'l masa, but He fill de void in your heart. You will see."

Tears welled in my eyes. "I hope you are right."

I yearned for Bowden's return and the comfort his presence brought. His strength and tenderness had become a great assurance in our few years of marriage. And for that, I gave thanks.

I again heard Mammy's words in my head: *You can either luk at de world lak et owe you somepin', or you can be grateful for what you got and count de extra blessings de Lard seed fit to bestow on you. Reckon dis crazy life feels better dat way.*

Her wisdom continued to inspire me to see the world through her eyes. Born into a life of privilege, I knew my hardships paled in comparison to the daily suffering of others. The folks in bondage at Livingston kept me reevaluating the world through a different eyeglass. Their sufferance, and the denial of their liberty, never ceased to weigh on me.

"I have a request of you." I retrieved a parasol and a light covering to ward off any breeze. "While I'm gone, would you help Mary Grace empty the nursery and put the things in storage?"

"Ef you sho', Missus." Uncertainty pleated her brow.

"I believe it will be for the better." I touched her arm on my way out.

~ CHAPTER ~
Three

A S I STEPPED OUT ONTO THE VERANDA, I NOTICED A RIDER coming up the lane. Shielding my eyes, I recognized the auburn mane bouncing beneath a wide-brimmed bonnet. I descended the stairs and walked to Parker, who waited with my driver by an open carriage.

"Afternoon, Missus." He had grown into a strapping man with muscles built during his time at sea. Our ships moored in Charleston harbor, and he'd come home on leave from Captain Gillies to see his pa, Owen, the plantation's head cooper.

"Good afternoon to you." I took his outstretched hand and stepped into the carriage. Seating myself, I arranged the fabric of my dress before opening the silk parasol.

"I was wondering, ma'am, ef you might have a word wid Kimie." Over the years, Kimie's childhood affections for Parker had never wavered, and he'd become taken with her.

"About what?"

He rested his weight on his cane. "Well, she ain't bin sleeping. She determined not to lose another person. Masa Ben has tried to git her to rest, but she stubborn as any 'oman I ever saw."

I offered a reassuring nod and a small smile. The innocence of young love warmed my heart. "I will speak to her."

He grinned and smacked his leg with enthusiasm. "Thank you, Missus. I knowed I could count on you."

I arched a brow. "I said I will speak to her, but I can't make any promises that she will heed my words."

"Ef anyone can talk sense into her, et be you." He stepped back as Whitney reined her horse to a stop beside the carriage. "Good day, Missus Tucker."

"Parker," she said, her voice clipped. "I wasn't aware you were back. But, then again, I haven't seen much of my sister lately. Where is the girl?"

"Down at de hospital in de quarters." His eyes flitted back and forth, and pearls of sweat beaded his brow. Whitney had that effect on people, and if she knew her younger sister's feelings for Parker had become something more, I wasn't sure which one of them she'd go after first.

He swallowed hard and summoned the courage to make his plea once more while avoiding Whitney's intrusive stare. I secretly praised him. "'Member what I ask, Missus."

"I will," I said.

He turned on his heel and hobbled off.

"Are you going to tell me what that was all about?" Whitney asked.

"Perhaps." I shrugged. "Well, don't dally, let's be on our way." I offered her a taste of her own typically curt manner. When she sat unmoving on her mount, staring after Parker, I said, "Are ya coming?"

"I didn't ride over here to visit myself." Sarcasm was second nature to her. Whereas civil people strive for a gracious reply, Whitney preferred not to waste a wit of consideration on people's "tender feelings," as she referred to them.

She dismounted, and a stable boy raced to take her horse. Once she sat across from me, the driver slapped the reins, and our carriage lurched forward.

"Was it just me, or did Parker seem uneasy around me?" she said.

My laugh came out as a snort that took both of us by surprise. "You'd think you'd be used to that by now. Your brash mannerisms aren't for everyone."

"I have no time for the sensitive lot."

"I'm simply making an observation."

She scoffed and rolled back her shoulders with an upward tilt of her nose. "I will never fit into elite society, nor do I care to."

I smirked. "Are you referring to a sailor as elite society?"

She glared at me and shifted in her seat to peer out over the fields as we rode along.

I decided to change the subject and avoid starting the morning off on the wrong foot. "Are you aware that Parker and Kimie fancy each other?"

"No. Do they?" She stared straight ahead, as a look of confusion turned to hurt. "Why wouldn't she tell me?"

No matter how hard she tried, the tough exterior she put forth didn't fool me; I recognized the vulnerability that hovered under the surface of Whitney Tucker.

"Maybe because she feared your reaction. Kimie has been in love with him for years."

"How did I miss that?"

"You aren't the most observant when it comes to love. Why, I recall the torture you put Knox through to make you commit."

"Because I never saw myself as the marrying type." Her nose returned to its prior position.

"Parker shared his concern that she is working herself too hard."

"My sweet my little sister. She doesn't get the do-gooder spirit from me." She graced me with a sideways glance.

"Don't we know it."

She gave me a dirty look but resisted a reply to my gibe.

"The one thing I'm very aware of when it comes to Kimie is that she is stubborn. She won't listen to me. You should send a message to the quarters and instruct her yourself."

"I'll do that upon my return."

Our driver drove the carriage past the slave market on our way to Josephine's. The auctioneer's voice echoed from the sales lot where men came to purchase Negroes, cattle, and mules. Public selling of slaves had been banned the previous year, but the demand for Negroes to work our lands and in our homes continued. Bids rose, and the excitement of the crowd turned my stomach.

"Maybe I'm not ready for an outing." I blotted the sweat from my brow with a handkerchief. A wave of lightheadedness hit me.

"You do look a tad bit pale." Whitney pulled a fan from her handbag and waved it in front of me. I welcomed the light breeze.

She looked over my shoulder in the direction we'd come. "Sometimes it seems the world has gone mad. Men selling men. Blacks hunting down their own and returning them to their masters for a profit. Look at Preston Brooks's attack on Senator Sumner in the Senate Chamber. The senator had to take leave from his senate duties because of his injuries. Word is he may not return for some time."

I recalled the incident between Senator Sumner of Massachusetts and Representative Preston Brooks of South Carolina, who had severely beaten the senator with his cane after Sumner delivered a speech attacking the institution of slavery.

"Yet South Carolinians have deemed Brooks a hero and returned him to Congress," I said. "It's maddening, I tell you. Men like David Atchison, who claims that Northerners are abolitionist tyrants and Negro thieves, only add to the brewing hate between Southerners and Northerners. Then we have fanatics like John Brown. People won't soon forget what happened at Pottawatomie Creek." I shuddered at the stories of the brutality that Brown and his sons had unleashed on the five pro-slavery men.

"Pastor Abel's endless sermons defending the morality of slavery through extensive Biblical justification quells my desire to attend Sunday services," she said. "He uses his pulpit to infuse personal views into the congregation. Corruption at its worst if you ask me."

"I couldn't agree more."

Our conversation ended as our carriage stopped in front of Josephine's townhouse.

Nerves fluttered in my stomach, as they often did when I engaged with Josephine. I lifted the bronze knocker, but the door swung open before I had a chance to knock.

"Mrs. Armstrong and Mrs. Tucker," Josephine's butler greeted us. "The missus is expecting you. She's waiting in the garden."

He bade us enter, and we followed him down the corridor to the back of the home and through double glass doors into the courtyard. Summer blossoms of various shades filled the gardens and climbing roses weighted latticework trellises. The intoxicating scent of jasmine wafted on the afternoon air.

Josephine, clad in a veiled hat and an ivory gown with a small blue print, meandered the garden paths. The butler signaled us with a white-gloved hand to wait, then went to address the lady of the house. "Missus, your guests have arrived."

Josephine turned. "Thank you," she said, and he took his leave. She strode toward us with outstretched arms and embraced Whitney, then me. "It is refreshing to see faces that bring me joy."

I questioned her choice of a veiled hat for tea, and if I knew Whitney the way I did, I figured she was wondering the same.

"Please come and join me." She swept a hand toward a small table draped with a freshly pressed white linen tablecloth and crowded with white platters of refreshments. In the center, next to the vase of peonies, sat a pitcher of mint julep. As we seated ourselves, two slave boys of seven or so came out and stood nearby to air us with palmetto fans.

"I was surprised to hear you weren't staying in town throughout the hot months." Josephine filled a crystal glass and handed it to me.

"You know how people can be," I said. "Gossiping behind fans and eyeing me with pity. I wasn't ready to deal with them."

"Will your husband be joining us?" Whitney asked.

When Josephine's parents had found out about her relationship with a Negro slave, and that she'd birthed a child, they'd arranged a marriage between her and a man much her senior.

"No, he is back at Bentwood bedding his wench, I suspect. Two or three mulattos have been born in the quarters since we wed. Slaves' whisperings say they are his." She looked at me. "I suppose we women have no choice but to turn a blind eye on such things."

Her reference to the rumors of Bowden possibly being Sailor's father twisted my stomach. I took a sip of my drink, then, as much as it pained me to do so, I said, "I suppose so."

"If my husband's lust is satisfied with quarter wenches, it saves me from having to submit," she said with indifference. "I care not what my husband does as long as he stays far away from me. But I can't imagine you feel the same." She directed her question at me. "The love between you and Bowden is something women aspire to in a marriage."

"Yes, well, rumors are rumors for a reason." The topic

fatigued me. "It's chatter that keeps bored and unhappy people entertained and focused on matters other than those in their own households."

She laughed but went on to fill us in on the happenings in Charleston. "Did you hear that Lucille is engaged to her cousin? I suppose he is the only one that would have her."

"Don't tell me it's the cousin with the too-large ears?" Whitney said.

"That's the one. Edwin Meyer," Josephine said. "No respectable gentleman of Charleston would have her, due to her reputation."

What had gotten into Lucille? Her lewd behavior and frolicking with men was no secret, but it was as if her parents had no clue about her promiscuous ways—or they chose to look the other way. Josephine and she had never rekindled their friendship, and Josephine was better off for it.

"It's a shame how she conducts herself," I said with a downcast gaze. "I can't help but feel sorry for her." She had become a laughingstock, and the subject of most conversations.

"It's all her doing. I don't feel the least bit sorry for her," Josephine said. "Besides, it's Edwin's money that persuaded her, after her pa's dealings with the railroad and his funds being seized. He's lost his wealth and almost lost the plantation. My husband said Edwin agreed to purchase the family estate and help Lucille's father if she would accept his offer to marry. But marriage won't stop her fornicating." Although her expression was hidden behind the veil, there was no denying the disgust in her voice. "Guard your husbands, ladies, because she's made her attempts on mine. Not that I care—another woman in his bed would save me from my wifely duties."

Josephine's misery in her loveless marriage was no secret among her friends, but each year she retreated deeper into herself, finding no joy in the world. The one person that could bring her happiness was the one I feared losing the most.

"Did he harm you again?" I conjured up the courage to ask.

Whitney paused mid-motion in reaching for a tea biscuit, and Josephine stiffened at my question.

After a minute or two, she lifted the veil to reveal the ugly yellowed bruise on her cheekbone. "It is much better than it was. I'd hoped it would be gone by the time you came for a visit."

"But why hide what we already know?" I asked.

"Because it's humiliating. I never dreamed this would be my life." She shooed away the fanning boys before scanning the perimeter for eavesdroppers. In a low voice, she said, "If I hadn't just given birth, I'd have escaped with Jethro. But I'd only have slowed him down. Foolishly, I'd hoped when he reached freedom he'd send word, but with the Fugitive Slave Act, it isn't safe. I suppose it's best this way. You both must think poorly of me—copulating with a Negro and all. I am forever grateful to each of you for your friendship and for keeping my indiscretions between us."

I took another long drink before setting the glass on the table. My hand shook, and my prior bout of lightheadedness returned with a vengeance.

"Willow, are you all right?" Josephine covered my hand with hers. "You look pale."

"I-I'm fine."

"Do accept my apologies. Talk of this must bring up all the pain and loss you have recently suffered. How careless of me." Tears swelled in her eyes.

"My heart grieves for you," I said. "I too think of that day, and because of my part in it, I feel guilty—"

"Oh, poppycock." She waved a hand in dismissal. "There's nothing to feel guilty about. It's because of you that Jethro made it to freedom. Unless you are referring to your decision to not turn him in." She tensed. "Please tell me it isn't so?"

"It's not that," I said with a gulp. "It's…"

"Willow has been pushing herself too hard." Whitney's chair scraped back on the garden stones. "You must rest. If you will excuse us, Josephine, I think it's best if I take her home." She gripped my arm and tried to pull me up.

Although I appreciated her concern for me, and her attempts to save me from the inevitable, she couldn't protect me from what needed to be done.

"No!" Something snapped in me, and I slammed the table with my fist. "Sit down." I felt fearful, verging on panic, but the loss of my son and the pain of it pushed me forward. "I have something to confess. Something I've hidden for far too long."

Whitney dropped into her chair, looking stunned at my outburst. She eyed me, and then Josephine, warily. "Please, Willow, reconsider. You aren't thinking clearly," she implored me.

"Maybe not. But my heart can't take this anymore." I peered at Josephine through my tears. "I've wronged you. And after I tell you what has weighed on my heart all these years, you will hate me, and I won't blame you, but it's time you know."

Josephine gathered my hands in hers and stroked the tops of them with her thumbs. "I'm sure it isn't that bad. You have become a dear friend to me, but if it eases your conscience, please tell me."

"Very well." I took a few deep breaths. "I know where your son is."

"What?" She dropped my hands. "How is that possible? Jethro gave him to someone who would care—" She stopped as it dawned on her. "You?"

I bobbed my head. "I was on the veranda when I saw him leave the babe at our door."

"But why did he choose you? Or Livingston, for that matter?" Her brow puckered. "Maybe he was aware of the talk of how you manage your slaves."

"What talk?" Whitney straightened.

"That she doesn't whip her slaves, and they are treated with fairness," Josephine said. "But—wait." She leaped to her feet, and her chair crashed backward onto the stones. She gripped the table to steady herself. "The boy. The mulatto child rumored to be Bowden's or your uncle's. Is he—"

"Shh." Whitney yanked her back down. "Keep your voice down."

"Your son resides at Livingston. I've ensured Sailor has received the care I would give my own child. He is a beautiful boy." Silent tears cascaded down my cheeks and thickened my voice. "He is very loved."

She blanched. "Sailor? That's what you called him?"

I nodded.

"I can't believe this." Her jaw quivered.

"I'm sorry. I wanted to tell you. To ease the suffering and yearning I witnessed each time we met. But Jethro made me promise to protect the boy and you. It's been killing me to keep it from you." I lowered my gaze from her searching eyes. "The guilt has been consuming me not only for your anguish but for my own selfish needs."

"Whatever do you mean?" she said.

Nausea clenched my stomach. "I've been so afraid of losing him. You see, I-I've come to care for the child."

She gasped. "But he is colored."

"He is a child," I said with a stubborn determination to still the defensiveness roiling within me. Fighting through the fog in my head, I forced myself to think wisely, to avoid revealing my abolitionist views.

She sat with her lips pursed, but her gaze looked past me as though time had stolen her thoughts. "I must see him." She met my gaze.

"Do you think that is wise?" Whitney said. "Surely you know the danger if your husband or family found out the child still draws breath." I elevated a hand to silence her.

"I've thought long and hard about what I'd do if I found out where my son is. The only way I could sleep at night is believing and putting faith in Jethro, that he found someone who'd care for and love our child. The thought of him coming of age to work in the fields has grieved me."

But not as a fan boy forced to forgo a childhood so that his owner wouldn't suffer from the heat? Ridicule fired within me, but I bit my tongue to keep silent.

She continued. "And the likelihood of him being sold away—unbearable. But I pushed away such thoughts and dwelt on visions of my son living happy and content."

Why your son and not the millions of other enslaved children? Her blindness to her hypocrisy angered me. What of her dismissal of the wenches her husband bedded to save herself? The ways of the South were so ingrained in her she failed to see the fallacy of her concerns, and how deeply embedded they were.

"I do not wish to jeopardize him, and I fully understand the importance of keeping his identity hidden. The question is, why do you continue to help me? I'm indebted to you for your help with Jethro, a crime that's punishable if you were caught."

"Then let's not talk about it so openly," Whitney said hotly. "Such talk endangers everyone, and I do not intend to swing from a rope."

Josephine ignored her and directed her question at me. "Does Bowden know?"

"He does, but you mustn't worry; he won't see you or the child harmed."

She relaxed in her chair, and a tender smile touched her mouth. "Do you think I could see him?"

An uneasy fear stole my breath.

"I would never tell him who I am. I just need to see him for myself."

"Very well. We will arrange a time." I stood.

"May the Lord bless you richly, Willow Armstrong." She walked us to the door, and as we stepped out, I turned to find her standing with her eyes closed and face raised to the sky. For the first time in years, happiness haloed her.

I tried to calm the anxiety in my gut. Had I done the right thing in revealing the child's whereabouts? My heart told me yes, but my mind swirled with fear of what it meant for Sailor...and me.

✧ CHAPTER ✧
Four

Bowden

THE CARRIAGE PULLED TO A STOP OUTSIDE OF ASTOR HOUSE, one of the luxurious hotels in Lower Manhattan, which occupied a full block. Built with blue-gray granite in Greek Revival style, its entrance was flanked by two vast columns. Lights from the lobby and guest rooms above illuminated the boardwalk.

"Shall we?" I said to James, who leaned forward to take a gander at the hotel.

"I don't know, Mr. Armstrong." He'd forgone "masa," as I'd instructed him to do while in the North. "Et sho' do luk fancy. Dose folkses ain't gonna lak me dirtying up de place."

"This is one of the few hotels that will allow slaves. They won't accommodate free blacks, but have quarters for men such as yourself."

His brow puckered. "Don't seem right."

"I couldn't agree more. But what *does* make sense these days?"

The driver opened the door and I disembarked, followed by James. I opened my coat to retrieve payment from my pocketbook and thrust it into the hand of the scowling driver. I arched a brow at his demeanor. "Is there an issue, sir?"

"We don't take too kindly to the stench of you. Coming

down here and bringing your niggers with you." His lip curled with disgust. "The greedy people that own this place may seek to cater to you wealthy Southerners, but the rest of us won't be so accommodating." He climbed up onto the carriage and unstrapped our trunks. "Seeing as you brought your slave with you, why don't you get him to carry your belongings." He pushed our luggage over the side. James and I jumped out of the way to avoid being struck.

I gritted my teeth and swallowed the sarcasm on the tip of my tongue. And with the grace expected of a Southern gentleman, I bowed at the waist and said, "Thank you for your Northern hospitality."

The driver mumbled a profanity before taking his seat and flicking the reins. We stood staring after the departing carriage.

"Welcome to New York." I extended my hands to the heavens and gave James a cheeky grin.

"Swell fellow," James said with a grunt.

"He will be the first of many." I clapped a hand on his shoulder before bending to retrieve a trunk. James took care of the other.

Inside, he waited with our luggage while I checked in at the front desk.

"Good day, sir, how can I help you?" The lanky gentlemen behind the desk regarded me over spectacles perched on the tip of his long nose.

"I'm looking for a room for three nights," I said

The man eyed me before looking past me to where James stood, wide-eyed, admiring the imperial ceilings and chandeliers of the lobby. His expression grew taut. "Can I have your name, sir?"

"Armstrong, Bowden Armstrong." I removed my hat and tucked it in the crook of my arm.

"Welcome to Astor House." His smile was false; the glint in his eyes revealed he was hired to perform a service, and like the carriage driver, he held no use for *my kind*.

A polished man who glistened from his oily complexion to his dark slicked-back hair appeared beside the clerk and offered me a brilliant smile. "Good day, sir. I am the hotel manager. Have you stayed with us before?"

"No, sir. This will be the first."

He gave me his full attention. "We hope to make your stay enjoyable. And as I'm sure you are aware, we have accommodations for your slave."

I nodded.

"I'll have the porter deliver your luggage to your room." He moved from behind the desk and came to stand beside me. "During your stay, I hope you will take advantage of our private dining room, where businessmen, politicians, and professionals often visit for lunch."

"Perhaps I will." I tilted my head in polite acknowledgment.

The manager left me in the hands of the clerk, and when we'd finished, I went to inform James of the arrangements.

"I will send a message to your daughter and inform her of our arrival," I said.

"Dat be good, Ma—" James caught himself. "Mr. Armstrong, sir."

I expected we'd face hostility during our stay in New York, but James referring to me as his master would set an unnecessary target on our backs. If Willow hadn't insisted I bring James to meet his grandchild, I would have made the journey alone.

"I'll meet you outside at six. We will have our dinner amongst friends tonight."

"Dat we will, sah." A broad smile expanded on his weathered face.

Later, after scanning the lobby for James, I approached the doors to exit the hotel and the doorman stood with his back to me, neglecting to open the door. Stepping outside, I soon became aware of laughter and taunting voices. I noticed the amused look on the doorman's face as he stood, engrossed by a pair of men some feet down the boardwalk.

"Sahs, please. I ain't meant no harm."

I recognized James's voice. My heart leaped. I took a second gander at the men and spotted him in the shadows, cornered by them as they prowled around him. I dodged folks to get to him. Ruby and Willow would never forgive me if he was harmed in any way.

"What's that you say, cotton picker? I can't hear ya," one man said in an exaggerated Southern drawl while jabbing James in the chest. He reached up and swiped his hat off his head.

"Sah, I say…" James watched the man grind his hat into the boardwalk with his foot.

"We done heard what you said, you damn nigger." The other man shoved him from behind.

I lunged forward and grabbed the thicker of the pair by the collar and heaved him backward.

"Hey, what the—" he sputtered.

"Leave him be," I said.

"Aw, here we go. Look, darkie, we found your masa," the other man said, grinning wickedly through an unruly ginger beard. "You can't function without him, can ya? Don't have any smarts at all." His eyes flashed. "Spent all your life in his field with your arse in the air."

"James, come," I said.

James took up a position beside me, his keen eyes trained on the men, his hands ready at his sides. I'd come to appreciate the character of the blacksmith. His love and loyalty toward Willow were unwavering, and to me, as her husband, he'd shown respect that went beyond slave to master. I sensed he'd risk striking a white man to get us out of the tight situation.

I released the man I still held and gave him a shove toward his friend. "We don't want any trouble. Let us be on our way."

The man spun back around and shouted at the onlookers. "I think my friend, Hank, and I should show this cotton picker and his nigger what we think of the trash from the South." He circled me a couple times before he swooped in to attack. But I was ready. Raising an arm to block his blow, I landed a hook on his face. He fell back with a growl, and I ducked the swing from Hank.

The hotel manager rushed up, with the doorman on his heels. Winded, he glared at the pair. "You men had better take your leave before you find yourselves in a jail cell for the night."

The men halted their advance and shared a look. "Very well." The burly fellow flicked a finger at the blood dripping from a gash over his left eyelid. His eye was starting to swell. "We will go, but be warned, cotton picker." His other eye glinted coldly at me. "Men like John Brown will put an end to Southern breeders, and no kept niggers will stop them." He spat at our feet.

I gritted my teeth to hold back the remark on the tip of my tongue. Despite the stand the high and mighty Northerners took, their dependence on the South's cotton to supply their factories remained.

After the men left, I straightened my cravat and jacket. James retrieved our hats from the boardwalk.

"I'm sorry, Mr. Armstrong," the hotel manager said. "Are you all right?"

"Yes. I thank you for intervening." I held out a hand.

He grasped it and signaled a hansom cab with the other. "You be on your way, and for the inconvenience, and the bad mood you may have after the poor behavior of those men, your fare is on us."

I offered my thanks and walked toward the cab.

"I'll have your job for this," the manager said to the doorman. "Dislike them or not, our Southern acquaintances keep you in a job."

I gestured for James to climb in and followed.

As we rode down the street, I regarded him as he sat stiffly on the seat beside me. "There is nothing to worry about," I said.

"Et a hard thing to stand back, unable to lift a hand to help dose you care 'bout or dose in need, jus' 'cause you black." He brushed the dirt from his trousers with vigorous strokes.

"I understand your frustration. You did well under the circumstances."

"I warn't 'bout to take et much longer. Ef I seed dose men were gonna git de upper hand, I would've stepped in. I ain't 'bout to let Missus Willie lose another one she loves. No, sah. Dat gal bin through 'nuf."

"Your love for my wife is admirable and deeply appreciated," I said. "Now, how about we focus on persons more deserving of our thoughts, like Ruby and that new grandbaby of yours."

Teeth gleamed in the darkness. "Yes, sah. I think dat be a right smart thing to do."

❦ CHAPTER ❦
Five

Oliver Evans

THE PREY DELIVERS ITSELF INTO YOUR HANDS. THE TIME IS NOW. END him, the clamoring voices shrieked.

I held back the velvet curtain, observing the brawl occurring outside of the Astor House from inside the hired carriage. I clutched the cigar tighter between my teeth.

It had been years, but the resentment for Bowden Armstrong and his wife had never diminished. The cocky bastard revealed his stupidity by bringing a nigger with him. He had defied death at my hands and married the woman whose fortune I'd sought to acquire.

"What is it, darling?"

The silky, seductive voice pulled me from the scene unfurling outside. Her perfume tantalized my senses, and I set my jaw at the influence Madame Amelie Laclaire had over me. From the moment I walked into her cathouse and she peered at me across the bar, she had captured my attention. A fiery-haired seductress cloaked in silks, with creamy flesh spilling from her bodice. It hadn't been her beauty that fascinated me, but her ability to govern people with a smile or a flick of her hand. Men and women alike unraveled under her spell, and a woman like her in one's pocket was an asset I had sought to obtain.

Women were odd creatures. The more a man pushed them

away, the harder they fought to win his attention. My thoughts shifted to the feisty Southern belle who had been the exception. Every day since I'd escaped the posses fixed on hanging me for murdering Charles Hendricks and the Widow Jensen, I'd salivated and planned my revenge.

"Nothing to concern yourself with," I said, with more hostility than I'd intended.

She is too close, the voices warned.

I flexed my fingers on the seat, and the muscles in my neck cramped as I struggled to assert authority over the nattering.

"It doesn't appear to be nothing." She pouted, and leaned forward to stroke my inner thigh with a laced-gloved hand. "Perhaps we can find a more suitable place so that I can relieve you of your tension."

I removed the cigar and gripped her face, and she winced from my grasp but said nothing. Covering her full, rouge-stained lips with mine, I wrapped an arm around her waist and crushed her delicate frame against me. Her bones popped, and my euphoria at her frailty heightened my passion. But again, she didn't pull from my grasp; instead, she moaned with pleasure, and I succumbed to the lust that never waned between us.

Aware of the games she played with men, I had proceeded with caution in approaching her, but her mastery over foolhearted humans had intrigued me. I, on the other hand, would never fall victim to her. There was but one puppet master—me. However, no woman had ever intoxicated me as she had, and I fought against the bouts of vulnerability that arose in her presence. Defenselessness was an emotion I refused to experience again. For now, she held purpose. Domination would forever be mine, and I wasn't against snapping her pretty little neck.

She forced her tongue into my mouth, and I bit down

slightly, eliciting a whimper. I smiled in triumph, and my tongue, a fervent conqueror, gained control. Seizing the back of her neck, I pulled her tighter.

When I released her she touched slender fingers to her mouth, as if it was tender from our kiss. "I do declare, Oliver Evans, you have a way of leaving a woman breathless and aching."

She referred to me by the alias I'd acquired from the husband of my late wife, Elizabeth Evans, a wealthy woman from Maine who'd been twenty years my senior and recently widowed before our encounter. She'd been the first of my victims after I'd fled to the North. I had wooed her, then endured her withered flesh next to mine for three insufferable months before I rid myself of her in a shallow grave. I left town with her fortune and under the identity of her late husband.

I sank back against the seat and inhaled another puff of the cigar while admiring Amelie.

She fixed her lopsided feathered hat and smoothed the bodice of her gown. The theater had been packed that night. Women had regarded her with displeasure while their gentlemen's eyes had widened with appreciation for a woman many knew on a personal basis, and others admired from afar. She could entertain as many men as she liked; I cared not, because no one would own her as I did.

One night, after we had fallen back against the linens, perspiring and panting from copulating, she'd made her first mistake. Lost in her ardor, she had revealed her secret. I exhaled, recalling how I'd manipulated her trust, and in doing so, mastered her. If she ever endeavored to defy me, I would not hesitate to destroy the great Madame Laclaire.

From the corner of my eye, I noticed a cab pull up outside of the hotel, and moments later, pull away. Peering at the shadows where the altercation between Armstrong and the men had taken place, I discovered they had vanished.

Fool. You let him get away.

Silence.

Striking the roof, I signaled the driver to leave. My thoughts returned to Charleston and the face of the woman who taunted me in my dreams. On the seat, my hand balled into a fist and the nails bit into my flesh.

One day, you will see the Armstrongs' hearts cease beating. Victory will be ours, the voices crowed.

Yes. The day would come when I would bathe in their blood and behold Willow's beloved Livingston Plantation engulfed in flames. But I wouldn't stop there. I would see the Hendricks name forever tarnished and their enterprises in ruins. My master plan had given me patience in the matter.

A day of reckoning was coming, but until then, I would bide my time...

∽ CHAPTER ∽
Six

Ruby

A CARRIAGE PULLED UP OUT FRONT, AND I LAY MY DAUGHTER IN her bassinet before walking to the window to peer down at the street. The driver opened the door and Bowden exited. I started to turn away when someone stepped out behind him. Papa? My chest pounded. What in heaven's name?

I tiptoed from the nursery and closed the door before darting down the corridor. Downstairs, I raced past the parlor but halted when I spotted Saul sitting, reading the paper.

"Come, dear husband. Bowden has arrived, and he's brought Papa with him!"

He grinned and lowered his paper. "You must contain yourself, or you will burst from excitement."

I frowned at the lack of surprise on his face. "You knew he was coming."

"I received a letter from Mr. Armstrong saying that if he could convince James to come, he'd bring him, at the request of Willow."

I rested my hands on my hips and scowled. "And you didn't tell me?"

"It was to be a surprise."

I clapped my hands under my chin. "I can't believe you

didn't let on. You're the worst at surprises. Come, we mustn't make them wait. Besides, it's been far too long."

He strode to my side and dropped a kiss onto my temple. "You, my darling, are most beautiful when your eyes are alight with passion."

My love for Saul had blossomed into a love I never thought possible. My affections for Kipling had dulled in comparison. I suppose I'd always love him in some way, but Saul had been good to me. We'd never had a lot, but love and respect continued to bond us.

The rap of the door knocker echoed in the foyer. I laced my fingers with Saul's and pulled him toward the door. "I shall not wait another minute." With a deep chuckle, he allowed me to lead him to the door.

Aisling, the young Irish woman I'd found near death in the slums of Five Points, entered the foyer. Orphaned soon after her arrival in New York, she'd taken to stealing to survive, as Will and I had done. We could hardly afford to pay her, but she had nowhere to go. So an arrangement was made, and we exchanged room and board for duties around the house. Our friends had thought us crazy, bringing her into our home, but I thought of my mother, and if she hadn't found me and brought me home, I likely would have become another casualty of Five Points.

I'd given up my position at the newspaper office, but my work with the Anti-Slavery Society continued, and when I was away from home, Aisling cared for our daughter.

"Please prepare tea and refreshments to be served in the parlor. We have important guests tonight," I said. "And then you can have the evening off. I know of a certain young man that would be delighted to sit a moment in your company."

"Yes, Mrs. Sparrow." Her cheeks grew rosy, and she curtsied before disappearing down the hall to the kitchen.

I opened the front door, and Bowden removed his hat with a grin that made his eyes glisten.

"Mr. Armstrong, it's our utmost pleasure to welcome you to our home," I said.

"I assure you, the pleasure is mine." He stepped aside graciously and plucked Papa from his shadow. "I have someone who has journeyed far to see you."

Papa removed his hat and stood looking awkward but smart in his dark suit. "Hello, how ya doing, gal." His eyes took in Saul's height, which intimidated even the whites. "Yes, sah. Well, I'll be." A look of approval softened his taut features.

"Come in." I stepped aside. "You must tell us all about Willow, Mary Grace, and the others. What about young Kimie? How is she?"

"Ruby darling, you must let our guests settle in before you pelt them with questions." Merriment shone in Saul's eyes.

"Forgive me," I said.

"It's quite all right." Bowden crossed the threshold. "Kimie isn't so young anymore, and she's been a real blessing to Ben and the quarter folks. All she talks about is Florence Nightingale and how she led a group of female nurses to the Crimea a few years back. Knox says he wished he had the funding to send her off to Nightingale's programs in British hospitals, but with farmers struggling to sell their crops extra funds are becoming scarce."

"Kimie has passion on her side. She will do well." I took their hats and hung them on pegs by the door. "Saul brought home the drawings for the new school today."

Saul smiled at me and capped Bowden's shoulder with a hand. "Shall we retire to the parlor and take a look?"

"I'm most eager," Bowden said, and the pair walked on ahead.

"Let me git a luk at you, gal," Papa said when we were alone.

I held out my arms for his inspection. I noted the dampness in his eyes.

"Well, I be. Motherhood luk mighty fine on ya."

My heart leaped at his praise. "Do you want to see her?"

"'Bout to split wid excitement." The tenderness in the man before me hugged my heart. I looped my arm through his. He offered a small smile, and calloused fingers patted my arm. We climbed the stairs and walked down the hallway to my daughter's room.

"We ain't gonna wake her, are we?" he whispered.

"It doesn't matter. It isn't every day a slave can travel the ocean to see his granddaughter," I said.

He nodded. A bead of sweat trickled down the side of his face.

"It will be fine. You mustn't worry. She is just a baby."

"Et ain't dat I worried 'bout. Babes are so fragile, I plumb skeered I drop her."

I opened the door and moved to light a lantern on the dresser, and then another on a stand by the rocking chair. Soon a warm glow filled the nursery. Mother and I had decorated the room in pale yellow and pink. A white-painted bassinet wreathed in pink silk and white fabric sat in the middle of the room.

I took Papa by the hand and led him to the cradle. We peered down at my chubby daughter, wrapped in a cream afghan knitted by the ladies from the Anti-Slavery Society of New York.

Papa inhaled as he gazed at the babe. "Well, ain't dat somepin'. Lak a li'l angel, ain't she?"

I smiled. "Yes."

"Reminds me of you when you were a babe. Many a night, I prayed dat de Lard would grant us wid a boy, but instead he gave me you. And although back den I was skeered of what et meant to have a gal in a world dat deems no justice for a slave, dese days I mighty happy I got you."

Tears welled in my eyes, and I quickly brushed them away. There was so little time, and I wasn't about to waste the moments I had with tears. "Do you want to hold her?"

"I think et bes' we don't wake her." He wiped his palms on his pants.

I leaned forward and scooped the baby up before he could protest further.

He stepped back, his eyes flitting left and right. "Now wait one minute. I jus' a clumsy ol' blacksmith. Dese hands ain't used to delicate things. Why, I ain't touched a babe since you were a wee one."

"She won't break," I said. "Take a seat. I'll be right beside you, and if you decide you're uncomfortable, I'll take her."

He nodded, and without another word, took a seat. He cautiously held out his arms. "Now, do et real easy lak."

I placed the baby in his arms, and his cheeks puffed out with the breath he was holding.

"See? You're a natural. Nothing to worry about at all."

He released the air from his lungs in a gasp. My daughter stretched and struck her tiny fist at the heavens, and a tenderness washed over Papa's face. "My, my...purty li'l thing she be." His thumb stroked the babe's unruly curls. "What you say you called her again?"

"Mercy."

"Yes," he cooed. "Might be dat Miss Rita's Lard found mercy and returned you to me. Never thought I'd be off de plantation, sitting in a house my gal owns and holding my grandbaby. Guess an ol' fool lak me gotta find some kind of goodness in dat." Silent tears fell over his weathered cheeks. He touched Mercy's hand with a finger, and her fingers flexed and encircled his. Instant love radiated from Papa's face, and I knew at that moment that our goodbye would be much harder this time around.

Some time later, Papa lay Mercy back in her bed, then removed a small wooden rocking horse from his pocket. "I made dis for her, so she can know dat though I be far, I be thinking of her." He placed it in the corner of the bassinet.

"I'm sure she will treasure it always."

We left the room, and as we walked down the corridor, I asked, "How is Willow?" The concern over my friend's loss had weighed on my heart since I'd received the news.

"She having a hard time. Reckon losing de babe left a hole in her heart. Doesn't leave her chamber most days." His voice cracked. "De gal don't deserve to suffer so. She a good woman and she done so much for so many. Times lak dese is when I question Miss Rita's God and why he let things lak dis happen." He shook his head.

His insight into Willow's grieving only deepened the ache in my soul for the woman he'd fathered in his heart. I envied the time she spent with him and the years slavery had robbed him and I of, but each day I was grateful he had her protection and love.

"And Bowden?" I lowered my voice on the landing as we came to a stop. "How is he holding up?"

"Throws himself into work. Menfolk different dan womens. But he hurting jus' de same. Missus Willie 'bout de strongest woman I know next to Miss Rita, but dis loss did somepin' to her. I reckon 'cause, lak most of us, we luked at de babe as a new start. De li'l masa was to be the next generation of masas dat believed all humans be equal. He was hope. And when you a slave, dere ain't much hope."

He approached the first step to descend, and I gripped his arm. "Are you happy, Papa?"

He paused and twisted to eye me. "Can a slave ever truly be happy?" He shrugged. "I don't rightfully know. Suppose I don't understand what true happiness be. But ef dis be my lot in dis life, I reckon property on Livingston be de closest thing dere is to happiness for a slave."

His words grieved me. "You know, all you have to do is say the word and the Armstrongs or we would find a way to get you to Canada."

He clucked his tongue and waved a hand in dismissal. "Folkses say dat in Canada white stuff called…s-snow falls from de heavens. In some places et up to your waist overnight, and dey say et real cold." He shivered at the thought. "No sirree, dese ol' bones ain't made for dat weather. My home be in de South wid Missus Willie."

I laughed and patted his arm as we descended the stairs.

The men stood as we entered the parlor. "Well, James, what do you think?" Bowden extended his arms in a grand sweep, anticipation evident on his face.

"She a mighty fine baby, Masa Bowden, sah." Papa's shoulders rolled back. "Mighty fine. I thank you for bringing me."

Aisling strolled into the room carrying a tray of tea. She placed it on the table before us, then picked up the teapot and filled a cup.

"If you don't mind." Bowden opened his satchel and withdrew a bottle of brandy. "I thought we could have a toast to the arrival of a healthy babe to carry on the Sparrow name and James's legacy."

Papa gawked at Bowden, mouth agape, clearly struggling to conceal his emotions. Aisling hurried to a cabinet in the corner of the parlor, withdrew glasses, and placed them on the table.

Bowden poured an inch in each glass and handed one to each of the men, then raised his. "To Saul and Ruby: May love guide their footsteps and words throughout these next years. May Mercy bring you all the love you so richly deserve. James," he centered his gaze on Papa, "may your family continue to grow and fill your life with joy."

"Thank you, Masa." Tears glistened in Papa's eyes as he lifted his glass and emptied the contents.

I lifted my teacup.

"Mrs. Sparrow, is there anything else you require?" Aisling asked.

"No, thank you. You may go and enjoy your evening."

After she was gone, Bowden looked at me. "I do hope we will have the privilege of meeting the Stewarts during our visit."

"Yes, certainly. My parents have requested we join them tomorrow evening at their home." I glanced at Papa for his reaction.

"I sho' lak to meet dese folkses who bin so good to my gal. Lak to thank dem," he said.

My heart surged with happiness. I'd dreamed of the day, since I'd been reunited with Papa, of him meeting my parents.

"Splendid." Bowden grinned before turning his attention to my husband. "Do tell me, where did your family originate? Have you always lived in the North?"

Saul entwined his fingers, resting them on his stomach. "I've lived in the North all my life, but my granddaddy was born in slavery. When I was a boy he told me the story of how he landed in New York. He stood on the dock by the harbor, his face elevated to the sky as he breathed in the air of freedom. The cheeps of a sparrow perched on the railing overlooking the Hudson River drew his attention. The little critter sat there and eyed my granddaddy, unafraid and curious. But at the blowing of the horn of an approaching steamer, he took flight, and as Granddaddy watched him until he disappeared, he decided to take the surname Sparrow."

"Many slaves acquire a surname upon reaching freedom," I said. "Some take new first names as well, as most don't have the names given to them by their parents, but the ones appointed by their masters."

Bowden lifted the snifter of brandy to his lips and took a sip before holding the glass to stare into the liquid as though he were preoccupied.

Thinking it better to change the subject, I said, "I do hope to visit Livingston again, but with all the unrest in our country we hesitate to travel south."

"People speak of war as though it is something to take lightly," Saul said. "Talk of Americans fighting fellow Americans—it's ludicrous."

Bowden leaned forward to rest his elbows on his knees, his expression grave. "A great unrest has settled over our country, and if something isn't done about it, war will come. And with it, brothers will turn on brothers. It does not bode well for the North, or the South."

"And if there is to be a war, what side would you be fighting for?" Saul folded his hands under his chin.

Bowden straightened and leaned back in his chair. "I am a Southerner. Although I don't support slavery and would give my life to right the wrongs I've done, I'd be forced to fight for land and country."

"Kipling said if there is to be a war, he would be forced to fight with the North." My nerves hummed at the thought of war. Mercy was only a few months old, and the turmoil threatening the country kept me awake at night.

"The whites have a choice in the matter of which side they'd stand united with, while we black Northerners and Southerners," Saul gestured at Papa, "remain in chains, unable to defend our homes or families. This is our country as much as it is theirs. I was born and raised in America, yet I have no rights or say in what happens." He jabbed at his chest with building passion. "When will justice come to *all* Americans? Look at the Supreme Court's decision over Dred and Harriet Scott. 'Blacks are not citizens,' they say. Are we not people? Are we not American citizens? Who are they to say we can't enter suits in a court of law? What does this mean for the future of us and our children?"

The scar on Bowden's face reddened as his grip tightened on the snifter. "The injustices in this country will be our undoing."

"No disrespect to you," Saul said to Bowden, "but James, as a man enslaved to the South, what is your opinion?"

Papa sent a nervous glance at Bowden, who spread his hands wide. "You're as free to speak as any man."

Sadness pulled at Papa's visage. "I reckon et be a mighty sad day, dat for sho'. But lak de rest of ya, some things bother me when I git to thinking 'bout what be happening."

"Like what?" Bowden asked.

"Et folkses lak young Masa Jack and dese Northerners. Though dey say dey ain't all right wid slavery, dey still view de world as whites and blacks. Ef a day come dat de country be at war, I reckon my heart be torn between de home and people I love in de South and my gal and her family here in de North," Papa said.

The melancholy that filled the streets had overtaken the evening, and in hopes of veering our visit to more pleasant matters, I said, "The frame has gone up for the new school."

Bowden's face brightened. "That's splendid news. In the downturn of the economy and all the talk of war, it's good to have a sign of hope for people."

"Is it a wise decision to continue?" I asked. "Willow wrote that business is down, and you've all sunk tremendous funding into the cause."

"Allowing our slaves to escape, or providing them passage to freedom, has come at a high cost, but no amount of money can replace what is right and what is wrong. The folks at Livingston who expressed their desire to stay on and aid in our cause earn coin for a future we can only hope for. Endless efforts have been put into teaching folks skills and providing them with a quality life, regardless of the circumstances. But all of our efforts don't change the fact that they're slaves and we're their masters. Although the numbers have dropped, the end of our exports of cotton to Europe has put a strain on our finances. The expense of caring for the people at Livingston is high, but we must do what is right for them."

"And you and Missus Willie do dat," Papa said. "Don't seem to matter ef we free in de North or de promised land or a slave in de South, 'cause we still black. Until change comes in folkses' minds and hearts, no war gwine to change a thing."

"Unfortunately there is truth in what you speak." Bowden dropped his gaze to the floorboards.

As the evening progressed, the events happening around the world and our concerns hung in the room like a massive cloud.

When I slipped into bed next to Saul that evening, I scooted into the curve of his arm and rested my cheek on his chest. "Do you think war will come?" I played with a tendril of hair on his chest.

"I don't know." He kissed my hair before resting his chin on the top of my head. "But if it does, there is nothing you or I can do to stop it."

"I hate that Mercy has to grow up in a world where people judge each other by the color of their skin. What gives men the impression that one color is better than another?"

The rich silkiness of his voice deepened. "Humankind has always been driven by power and greed. The weak are trampled under the strong."

"We may be black, and most of us born into slavery, but we aren't weak." Defensiveness vibrated in my chest. "Too many slaves have fallen under the impression that they're incapable of surviving beyond their master's house. A mentality carved by masters into their thinking since birth."

"All we can do is continue to help those we can to gain freedom and start a new life."

I fell asleep that night thinking of the limitations of freedom, and what it meant to be black in a world drowning in prejudice.

CHAPTER
Seven

Willow

AT BREAKFAST ONE MORNING SOME WEEKS AFTER BOWDEN returned home, Mammy set a platter of hot buttermilk biscuits on the table as Tillie filled my cup with coffee before moving on to Bowden. My eyes were drawn to her protruding stomach, and although I'd made a conscious decision to move on, some days my shortcomings consumed me. That morning, the familiar sadness tightened my chest, and although I'd fought to keep it hidden, the warmth of Bowden's hand covered mine. I glanced at him, and the tenderness in his eyes told me I hadn't succeeded.

"Josephine's coming today to take care of the little matter we spoke of." I slathered butter over a buttermilk biscuit.

"Is she?" He frowned. "Are you certain this is wise?" He eyed Tillie and Mammy and gestured for them to leave the room.

I waited until we were alone. "After losing Little Ben, the guilt of keeping the truth from her was too much. It was bad enough to witness her pain all these years, but I managed to keep quiet. After our loss, though, I realized just how much pain she was in. It wasn't right; I should have told her from the start."

He added cream to his coffee before forking a sausage. "You speak from your heart; it's the thing I admire most about you.

But you know as well as I, in her delicate state, if she'd known, she may have acted irrationally. You honored Jethro's wishes; there can be no blame placed."

I rested a hand on his wrist. "Thank you for trying to see good in me, and for loving me regardless. But you're wrong and you know it. At first, yes, it was about helping them, but then it became about me. With losing Father, and the pressures of running this place, I found comfort in the child and welcomed the distraction. I was aware of this, but I never protected my heart. I love that little boy. And may God forgive me, but the thought of losing him eats me up inside."

"It is better the child was loved and cared for than the alternative. What is done is done."

I studied him, considering his undying love and devotion and its blindness.

"And no, I do not say these things because my love for you blinds me," he said with a grin.

I gaped. His ability to read my most intimate thoughts continued to astound me.

"I know you, and I know your heart could never harm another." He leaned in and kissed my cheek before capturing my watery gaze with his. "This pain we feel will ease with time. One day we will be blessed with another child."

I rose and went to him, capturing his face in my hands as his arms encircled my waist. I kissed him, and he returned it with enough passion to make my head spin. Breathless, we pulled apart, and I smiled down at him with satisfaction. His beautiful eyes captured my soul. "I love you, Bowden Armstrong, with all that I am."

"And I, you," he said.

When I released him and returned to my seat, he said with a chuckle, "Don't you wish you'd agreed to marry me earlier?"

I shook my head in amusement and clicked the back of my spoon on the shell of the hard-boiled egg resting in the silver holder on my plate.

"I am meeting Sam at his office to go over the sale of the Rhode Island estate," he said.

"I can't believe we are selling it. I hate to see it go, but if we are to implement change, then we have no other choice."

"We are fortunate to have enough to do so. Times are changing, and I worry it may not always be the case."

"Do you think these murmurs of war could come to fruition?" I leveled a worried gaze at him.

"No one knows for certain, but there is cause to be concerned."

We continued in conversation about his duties at the office, and maintenance of the grounds and outbuildings at Livingston before he laid his napkin on the table and stood. "I must go. Do you think you will be fine handling this matter without me?"

I nodded and rose to meet his embrace.

After he was gone, I sat thinking of what war could mean for Livingston and the South. My reflections turned to my loved ones in the North, but I swiftly pushed them away and concentrated on Josephine's arrival.

Her private carriage rode in to Livingston shortly before noon, and I walked out onto the front veranda to greet her.

"Good day, Josephine." I descended the stairs as her driver helped her out.

She stood under a blue silk parasol, her eyes wandering the grounds as though she were trying to spot her son.

"I trust your ride was enjoyable." I pushed down the nerves that had been swirling in my stomach all morning, and reassured myself that I was doing right by the child and Josephine. But...what if she took Sailor and went on the run? I'd be powerless to stop her; the boy was hers, after all. The inner battle left me wishing I had been born without a conscience.

She wore a tight expression as she looked at me. "It seemed dreadfully long today."

"Come, join me in the music room for some refreshments." I took her arm as she lowered her parasol with shaking hands. "It will all be fine. You needn't worry." But would it? I gulped back my own worry.

Her eyes searched mine, as though she were trying to summon the courage I feigned. "Perhaps a drink will calm my nerves."

"You're in luck. Miss Rita makes some of the best cordial you'll ever put your lips to." I exuded cheerfulness for both our sakes.

Inside, we settled into gold embroidered armchairs overlooking the gardens. She removed lace gloves and laid them beside her. Time passed with light chatter, but as the objective of the day loomed, I nodded at Mary Grace, who stood just inside the threshold, waiting on further instructions. At my signal, she turned and left.

"Do you think he will like me?" Josephine said, openly vulnerable.

"You have nothing to fear." I gave her a consoling smile. "He is a loving child."

"Much like his father." Her gaze grew far away, and a tenderness enveloped her face. "I've never been overly warm or approachable until Jethro. He changed me."

"Love does that to a person," I said with a light laugh. "I never saw myself having children until I married Bowden."

"There are no proper words that can be said for your loss. All I can say is, I understand your pain," she said.

I glanced at my hands, where they lay in my lap. "I know."

We sat quietly for a moment, two women intertwined in the ache of what motherhood had cost us. "For what it's worth, I am truly sorry."

"It is only you who holds any ill feelings," she said. "I can't begin to thank you for what you've done. And for the rest of my days, I will be grateful."

I swallowed back tears, and the burden of my guilt lightened. If she could grace me with forgiveness, perhaps there was no place for the guilt I carried.

The sound of footsteps in the hallway silenced our conversation, and Josephine adjusted herself in her seat to peer at the door. "I'm scared," she breathed.

My response stayed on my lips as Mary Grace and Sailor entered the room.

"Missus Willow!" He pulled his wrist free of Mary Grace's hand and bounded toward me. "I've bin askin' to come see you, but Mammy said no." He appeared none too pleased as he came to stand in front of me.

I smiled and stroked his wooly curls. "We have a special guest. Why don't you introduce yourself?" I peered over his head at Josephine, who sat gawking at the child with awe. It was as though she'd stepped back into the past.

Sailor spun around. "Oh, hello. "I'm Sailor. Who you be?" He stared with curiosity at his mother.

"I-I'm Josephine."

"Os-iphine." He tested the name. "Do you have any children? Missus Willow won't let me play wid de other children."

"Oh." She looked from him to me with inquiring eyes.

"We had an outbreak of influenza in the quarters," I said.

She returned her gaze to the boy. "Missus Willow knows best."

"Do you got children?" he asked again.

She hesitated, and we shared a glance. I held my breath. "No, I don't have children," she said, and I slowly released the air constricting my lungs.

"Don't you like dem?" He cocked his head.

A small smile played on her lips. "Of course."

"Why don't you got any?"

I touched his arm to stop his inquiries, but Josephine lifted a hand to stop me, appearing undisturbed by his invasive questioning. "Someday I hope to."

He smiled at that. "Dat's good." The platter of cookies captured his attention.

Josephine leaned forward and plucked one from the platter and held it out to him. "Would you like one?"

Sailor's eyes grew wide, and he nodded vigorously.

"Take it." Josephine gestured at him with the cookie.

He looked to me. I smiled and nodded. He grinned and snapped up the cookie. "Thank you, ma'am."

Tears pooled in Josephine's eyes as she watched her son devour the cookie. Her fingers lifted from her lap and then settled again as she fought the urge to reach out and touch him.

Sailor coughed between mouthfuls.

"Mary Grace, please bring the child something to drink," I said.

"Yes, Missus." Mary Grace curtsied and scurried off.

"Sailor has a sweet tooth," I said.

Josephine cleared her throat, suppressing the emotions twisting her face. "Is this true?"

He bobbed his head.

Josephine smiled and placed a hand on his thin shoulder. "I too have a sweet tooth."

"Missus Willow do too," he said between mouthfuls. "Guess dat makes us all the same." He circled his finger at the three of us.

"Do you like us being the same?" Josephine asked.

"Sho' do." He rolled back his shoulders.

"Can I ask you a question?" Josephine directed her question at Sailor but glanced at me as if asking my permission. I gestured for her to continue. "Do you like it here?"

My chest tightened and I regarded her nervously.

He frowned at her. "What you mean?"

"Are you happy?"

He pushed the last bite into his mouth and gave her a nod, but his attention returned to the cookies. The tautness in Josephine's shoulders eased. I handed him one. "This is the last."

Mary Grace returned and handed a glass to Sailor. He swallowed a big gulp and wiped his lips with his sleeve.

"Why don't you run along and play now. It was nice to meet you, Sailor." Josephine stroked his arm, and his gaze locked on her hand.

"You gwine come again?"

"Would you like that?"

"Yessum," he said.

She laughed.

He grinned, but confusion played on his face, as though he wasn't sure what was so funny. However, Josephine's joy was obvious. The child had managed to delight his mother. My heart swelled as I observed the pair.

After Mary Grace and Sailor left the room, Josephine said with amusement, "I'm not sure if it was me he liked or the cookies."

"Both, I'm sure," I said.

"I wish he could see him." Sadness enveloped her. "He is so much like his father. You were right; he is a beautiful boy, in heart and appearance."

"What will you do now?" I asked.

"I don't seek to disrupt what you have given the child, but I do have a request."

Tightness gripped my throat as I waited for her to continue.

"Do you suppose I could see him again?"

I released a breath. "Of course. Anytime you wish."

Later, as I walked her to the carriage, she paused and turned. "I can't begin to express my gratitude for what you've done—"

I lifted a hand to stop her, then gently gripped her forearms, my gaze capturing hers. "Our secret has been a comfort to me. I love him, and as long as he resides at Livingston, Sailor will never want for anything."

"Yes, I can see that." She glanced down at her hands. "No one can ever know that he is mine. I don't trust what my husband or father would do. He is the child I've heard about," she said as though validating it to herself.

"You mean the bastard child of my husband or my uncle?" I said without skipping a beat.

"Yes."

"He's the only mulatto child at Livingston."

"You endure what people are saying to protect him?"

"Bored tongues will always have reason to talk," I said, resuming our stroll to the carriage. "The boy is safe and his identity unknown, and we intend to keep it that way."

"I owe—"

"No!" I stopped in my tracks. "Please," I said in a gentler tone. "I won't hear it again. I did what needed doing, that is all."

"Is it true?"

"What?" My brows lowered as I studied her.

"That you're a Negro-lover?" She hurried to explain. "I mean, you've shown a fondness for them since we were children."

"Call me tenderhearted." I turned and we continued down the path to the carriage. "I don't like to see anyone abused or treated unfairly." No matter the bond we shared over the child, I wouldn't risk divulging my true passions and views on slavery.

"Life would have been more comfortable if I hadn't been weak and fallen in love with a Negro. My folks have never looked at me the same way. And if my husband were to find out I bedded a Negro, his abuse would be relentless."

"Why do you stay?"

"Leave and go where? My parents would disown me, so I couldn't go home. I'd be penniless."

"But you'd be free. You could go find Jethro and be happy."

"A white woman with a black man? I think not. I love him, but there would never be any happiness in this life for us. We would be ostracized for our relationship. Besides, now that I know where my son is, I could never leave. It gives me comfort to know that I can see him, and to have a piece of Jethro always."

"You would see him in the arms of another?" I asked.

"If not with me, I hope he can find love again and that at least one of us can be happy." She leaned in and pecked my cheek, then pulled back and offered a small smile. "Thank you for your friendship. I'd best be going before my husband returns home to find me gone."

I stood unmoving, deep in thought, in the front yard long after she'd gone. Until a small hand slipped into mine, and I looked down to find Sailor peering down the lane.

"Why don't you and I go for a little walk?" I said.

He squinted up at me. "Can I bring a fishing pole?"

I laughed. "Yes, and perhaps we can ask Jimmy to join us."

He let out a whoop of glee and darted off in the direction of the forge as I turned to wander inside and fetch a shawl. The thought of spending the afternoon in Jimmy and Sailor's company added a skip to my step.

CHAPTER
Eight

SUMMER FADED INTO AUTUMN, AND HARVEST WAS UPON US. Wagons piled with cotton lined the perimeters of the fields, and the nostalgic melodies of the quarter folks reverberated throughout the morning. I filled a bucket with some water and handed it to Sailor and Evie; they staggered under its weight.

I reached to steady the bucket but Sailor rocked back, pulling Evie along with him. He flicked his tongue over his upper lip in determination. "We got et. Come on," he said to Evie, and they trotted off toward the field hands.

I watched the children totter down the line as folks called out praise. I wiped my brow with the back of my hand and walked to the end of the wagon, and paused as I overheard two field hands.

"No use gathering cotton ef Masa can't find nobody to buy et," a woman said.

"My Clara say et ain't any better at de Andrepont Plantation." I heard worry in the man's words. "Says de barns got heaps of de masa's white gold. From what I hear, cotton still ain't moving, and slaves need to worry 'bout dat too."

"Why should you care ef her masa's cotton sells?" she said.

"'Cause, you damn fool, ef her masa's cotton don't sell soon, he may take to selling slaves, and ef dat happens, I might not see Clara and de chillum again."

"Maybe you ask Masa Bowden to put in a word, dat ef

Clara's masa decide he luking to sell slaves, he consider de masa first."

"No matter how good de masa and de missus bin, money only goes so far. Can't be 'pectin' dem to be givin' handouts to every slave dat need helpin'. Especially wid times lak dey be." The chatter faded as they returned to the fields.

The conversation stayed with me over the next hours as I helped the children and the water girls quench the thirst of laborers.

Later, the children and I returned to the house. As we entered the foyer, I pushed back my wide-brimmed bonnet, letting it dangle from its ribbons around my neck before peeling off my leather gloves. Exhaustion shone on the children's faces, and the heat of the morning sun glistened on their foreheads. "You run along and see if you can find a bite to eat. You did good today." I used the hem of my pinafore to wipe the sweat from my face.

After their running footsteps had faded down the corridor, I entered the parlor to find Mary Grace standing on a ladder, rehanging freshly laundered drapes. Bowden and I had purchased the navy and gold damask curtains when we'd journeyed to England in search of my father's daughter. Although Father had several acquaintances, we still hadn't located anyone with information about Callie.

After Father's death, the staff at his townhouse had been left with no choice but to secure work elsewhere after their wages stopped arriving. Only a stableman had stayed to take care of the animals, with hopes the family would come. Bowden and I had questioned him on my father's comings and goings, and people he associated with, but the man seemed to know very little. He said Father's groomsman, Julius, might have known more, but he'd passed some time ago. He went on to say that Father was a private man and didn't entertain in his home, often meeting his colleagues and business associates elsewhere. I'd asked for the name of his driver, but the man said Father had hired a carriage for his outings.

We had returned home, frustrated and empty-handed. I'd concluded that the whereabouts of Callie would always be a mystery.

Mary Grace balanced on the ladder while eyeing me. "You know what the fine ladies and gentlemen of Charleston will say if they catch you out in the fields as though you're a watering wench."

I waved a hand and plopped down on the settee. "I care not what the Charleston chinwags say. I dread that the social season is approaching. It's bad enough I'm forced to endure charity work and feign an interest in their meddlesome conversations. I do miss the days when Whitney lived here; at least then I had her to join me at these events. She made them nervous and I found pleasure in watching them squirm. Although I did find myself bracing at what would come out of her mouth. But now she isn't welcome in most social circles and events that require my attendance."

Mary Grace laughed, shaking her head. "The hardships of a mistress."

I scowled and stood. "Listen, I'm heading in to town to pick up supplies—"

"Surely that is a job one of Jones's men could handle."

Indignation clenched my hands into fists. "I do not wish to be handled like a delicate doll that will break at any moment. If I am to go on, I must keep myself busy. Sitting cooped up in this house, crocheting and cross-stitching, will never keep my mind occupied. Besides," I eased my tone at the wide-eyed way she regarded me, "Jones and his men are busy with the harvest, and it will do me good to leave here for a bit."

"It's just that—"

"That what?" I walked to the bottom of the ladder and peered up at her. "I know your intentions are good, but I'm fine. Most days I find joy, and little by little, the pain lessens. You all needn't worry about me."

She nodded uncertainly.

"I'm going to town," I said firmly, "and I'd like your company."

"Can you hand me that last curtain?" She nudged her head toward the settee where it was draped.

I obliged and held the curtain up for her. She handed me the rod, and I helped her feed the drape along its length.

After Gray's death, I never thought the light would come back into her eyes, but young Noah and Evie had given her a purpose to continue on. Her resilience was admirable and remarkable. Although I'd never known my mother, or had female relatives to inspire me, it was with Mammy and Mary Grace that I established the feminine bond. Daily they taught me what we women were capable of and what it meant to be a mother. I had hoped to implement their lessons of love and devotion on my son. Instead, it was Josephine's son that walked in my shadow and filled my heart with love and joy. Evenings, when I pulled him onto my lap to read to him, the warmth of his body and sweet voice replenished the void in my soul. I'd grown even more attached to that little boy than I'd been in the past, so much that my loved ones eyed me with concern. The white blood in his veins became more evident each day. I doted on the child and sought to give him a life of quality, where he knew what it was to be loved.

"All done." Mary Grace climbed down the ladder. She untied her pinafore and pulled it over her head. "Let me fetch my bonnet and a coat, and I'll meet you out front."

I followed her out into the foyer, and Mammy entered from the warming kitchen. "What you two up to now?" She regarded us with suspicion.

Mary Grace and I glanced at each other and smiled. "Don't you be worrying about nothing, Mama. Missus Willow asked me to accompany her to town."

"Playing when you should be working." Mammy planted a fist on her ample hip and gave Mary Grace a look of disapproval. "Missus got you spoiled rotten. You need to stay here on dis plantation where you safe." She turned her authoritative gaze on me, and I straightened as though she was the mistress of the place. "Can never tell who is out luking to harm two purty gals on de road. Dat why you got married, Missus, so a man take care of ya, and do all de running."

"Bowden has his hands full with Hendricks Enterprises and the cause. And with the recent expansion of new stations, we will see him less than before."

"I don't lak et one bit. Masa Bowden always gone. Masa Ben spending all his time in de quarters. He hardly comes for a meal at de big house."

It had been decided that Ben would take over the sick hospital at Livingston, and we'd seen a vast improvement in the quarter folks' health. Neighboring plantations sent for him when their families and slaves became ill, and in helping them, his work became a valuable resource for gathering information to aid our cause. Contentment had radiated from him, until my son's death. Although he tried to hide it, I knew he blamed himself that his namesake had only lived mere hours. At first he'd refused to return to the quarters, saying if he couldn't save his own grandson, he wasn't fit to be a doctor. However, when influenza broke out, Bowden had begged him to return to the hospital.

I stroked Mammy's arm. "I miss them too. But long before

Ben returned and I married Bowden, I had you all. And you're as dear to me as always."

The last years with Bowden had been more than I ever dreamed possible. Our numbers at Livingston had thinned drastically, and many faces had come and gone, either moving along to the road to freedom, or age and sickness had taken them.

"I don't lak et. De grounds becoming scarcer by de day. All de folkses leaving and gwine to Canada or running off to make et on deir own. Soon dere be no one left." Mammy's shoulders slumped. "Dose folkses lak family, and wid dem gone, et gonna take de spirit right outta de place."

"I know, and I feel the emptiness too," I said with a sigh. "But we couldn't hold them against their will. It would go against our moral beliefs."

She narrowed her eyes. "I ain't for nigras kept in bondage. Et foreign territory out dere. Most ain't bin far from de property lines of de plantation. Lakly git lost, or worse, caught. What ef someone catches dose on de run, and dey so skeered dey snitch on you and de masa? Put us all in danger. 'Fore I worried 'bout Mary Grace and you. Now I got two grandbabies to worry 'bout too. When white folkses git an idea in deir heads dat a nigger got any sense or might rebel, dey go crazy. You can't forgit what happened out in dem swamps."

"Your fears are valid. We all fear the same things. But those that have chosen to remain at Livingston to aid in the cause are aware of the risk and the protocol, should a threat arise," I said. "Let Bowden and I worry about Livingston and people's safety. These are your years to enjoy those grandbabies."

"A mama don't stop worrying. Till de Lard calls me home, and I'm reunited with Big John, I be watching 'round evvy corner for someone luking to harm de ones I love."

"All right." I threw my hands up. "You win. I know there isn't any use in telling you differently when you have your mind made up."

"And we don't know anyone else like that, now do we?" Mary Grace winked at me before striding down the hallway to the back door.

Mammy and I stared after her.

"Motherhood is good for her," I said.

"Dat et be. I wish Big John could see my gal now," Mammy said.

"We've tried to locate him, but with your previous master's passing and his wife's frail memory, it proved to be useless. The servants said Mr. Adams made him a breeder after you were sold, and that he took a second wife and fathered a son with her. When Mrs. Adams fell on hard times, she sold the boy, and soon after, Big John ran off."

"Lakly dead." Tears welled in Mammy's eyes.

I stroked her arm as my mind raced to images of the slave catchers and the howling of bloodhounds. I shivered.

"Most lakly don't remember me anyhow." Melancholy enveloped her and she heaved a deep sigh.

I encircled her shoulders with my arm. "Trust me, Mammy. No one would forget you."

She smiled through her tears. "You reckon?"

"It is a fact." I squeezed her tighter and kissed her brow.

"De Lard sought to bless me when he gave me you, angel gal. Yes, he surely did."

"The blessing was all mine." I released her and walked to the stairs, saying over my shoulder, "I trust you will see things are in order in our absence."

"You can bet on et."

I paused as Tillie entered the corridor, slopping a pail of water and carrying cloths to scrub the floor.

"Now gal, what did I tell you 'bout lugging dat water all de way from de river in your condition." Mammy marched toward her.

"I don't mind, Miss Rita. I got to earn my keep wid a new mouth coming." She looked like a mouse that had caught the eye of a cat.

Mammy removed the bucket from Tillie's hand and set it down before lifting the hem of her frock. "Luk at de size of dose ankles. Gonna split wide open ef you keep gwine on lak you ain't heavy wid chile."

"But, Miss Rita, plenty of slaves have given birth 'fore and dey ain't ever had special treatment," she said meekly.

"Well, dis here ain't any ol' plantation," she said firmly. "Dis place owned by Missus Willow and Masa Bowden and dey luking to help. Ain't dat right, Missus Willow?"

I rested my hand on the banister and smiled down at them. "Why don't you put your feet up for a spell and we'll assign someone else to wash the floors."

"Ef you say so, Missus," Tillie said, appearing none too sure.

Later, I retrieved my bonnet from the hall table, slipped on my waist-length cape, and walked out onto the veranda. Mary Grace sat waiting for me on the driver's seat of a wagon in front of the house. I spotted Sailor asleep on the porch swing. "Poor little tyke is plumb worn out," I said to myself as I hurried past.

In the yard behind the general store, Mary Grace and I stood speaking with Miss Smith while men loaded our supplies into the bed of the wagon.

"With this economic downturn, I have an abundance of supplies." Miss Smith gestured to the tall piles of products in burlap sacks. "The railroads aren't transporting goods, and the farmers are left with crops they can't sell. I worry about what will happen."

"And with good cause, I'm afraid," I said. "The docks are overloaded with cotton with the mills closing down in New England. And now, with Europe refusing imports from the US, Bowden fears it'll become much worse."

Mary Grace stood close, and although she kept her eyes lowered, her face grew taut with concern about developments in the United States. Freedom for all had become a united effort for everyone at Livingston, but those who understood the whisperings and events occurring across our country knew enough to be troubled.

"Yes, and with all this talk of South Carolina seceding from the Union flooding the streets and every conversation, this can't be good for the businesses of the South." Miss Smith's lips formed a thin line.

"Bowden and Ben believe it is all just getting started," I said.

Miss Smith's helper strode up to us and removed his hat. "You all set, Missus Armstrong."

"Much obliged," I said.

He nodded and jogged off to help the next customer.

"I need to get these supplies back to Jones." I slipped on my riding gloves and bid Miss Smith a good day.

Some miles outside of Charleston, I glanced at the rumbling gray curtain overhead. "I don't like the looks of the sky. The roads will become treacherous if the storm releases before we reach Livingston."

Mary Grace lifted the collar of her coat to ward off the breeze. "It's moving in quick."

I urged the team to pick up its pace. "Julia writes that Isaac and his daughter made it to St. Catherines."

"That is good news," Mary Grace said. "But my heart breaks for his wife. She's devastated that he ran without her."

I thought about Mammy's words earlier that morning. "Fear's a funny thing," I said. "Most enslaved are raised and die on the plantation of their birth, too afraid to think for themselves. God gave us *all* the ability to think. Some slaves will never step out of formation because of the fear instilled in them, while others will resist the very foundation slavery is built on. Human corruption can be seen all through the ages, and if our efforts to end slavery come to fruition, it still won't stop the supremacy mentality of humanity. You can execute men like John Brown, but another will rise in his place."

"It's unnerving," she said. "What if men like that were to show up at Livingston?"

"We can't think like that. Living in fear does no one any good."

She glanced at me. "But if they did, what then?"

"I expect we would defend our home," I said.

The storm that had come out of nowhere rolled and cracked overhead; the dark clouds threatened to unleash. A mile farther down the road, the sky opened, and I blinked away the rain obscuring my vision. The road quickly turned to muck, and ruts jostled and jerked the wagon. Relentless, the downpour came harder, and my teeth chattered as my wet clothing allowed the cold to grip my bones.

Two bends in the road before home, Mary Grace pointed. "Look there. It looks like someone is in trouble."

I squinted and picked out a carriage stuck in the middle of the road. One side appeared to be lower than the other. "Looks like they have broken a wheel." I fumbled for the rifle under the seat.

Each time I spotted a carriage or a rider along the stretch of road, the memories of what had happened when Reuben—alias Silas Anderson—had approached Whitney and I, not a mile back, surfaced. His attempt on Bowden's life. The revelation that he had murdered my father, Mrs. Jenson, and her slaves. His unsuccessful ambition to ensure I suffered the same fate. The awareness that his family had murdered my mother, and that he was the brother of Rufus, the man who'd hurt Mary Grace in unspeakable ways. Although the actions of Reuben no longer took precedence in my mind and fear of his return had subsided, he still haunted me.

In my peripheral vision, I saw Mary Grace's fingers dig into the edge of the wagon seat. "You needn't worry," I said. "Whoever it may be, they most likely don't pose a threat. We'll see if they need our help. And if I get the slightest feeling that we're in danger, we'll be gone before they can act." She glanced at me and bobbed her head, but anxiety flickered in her eyes.

As we drew near, I noticed the fabric of a woman's dress as she stood looking down at a man kneeling in the mud.

I reined the team to a stop and cupped a hand around my mouth to be heard over the violence of the storm. "May we offer you a hand?"

The woman swung to look at us. Sopping dark ringlets hung beneath a burgundy-trimmed bonnet. She slopped toward us through the mud as the man rose to his feet and wiped muddied hands on his trousers. "The wheel hit a rut and broke. My brother was seeing what he could do." The woman had an English accent.

"There's nothing we can do without tools to fix it." The man joined his sister at the side of our wagon. He glanced from me to Mary Grace, his gaze hesitating on her. "Miss." He tipped his hat, and she quickly averted her gaze. "You don't happen to have any tools in that wagon, do you, ma'am?" he said to me.

"No, but perhaps we could give you a ride," I said, and Mary Grace inhaled sharply. "Where are you headed?"

"Home," the woman said. She had delicate features, a cute upturned nose, and appeared to be twenty or so.

"Where is home?" I asked.

The man took off his hat, revealing blond hair, and shook off the rain. "Our parents purchased the old Armstrong plantation."

"You don't say." My fingers tightened on the loose reins. "Am I to believe you're the long-awaited Barlows from England?"

He grinned. "Indeed, we are."

"My husband sold the property to you. We expected you some years back."

The Barlow siblings shared a glance before the sister turned green-hued eyes on me. "Mum got sick, and was unfit to travel."

Their lawyer had sent word to Sam, our family friend and a Charleston lawyer, about Mrs. Barlow's illness, and I wondered if she still yet lived.

The gentleman replaced his hat and took a step forward. "Well, let us introduce ourselves. I'm Magnus, and this is my sister Emily."

The woman's brow knitted as she regarded her brother before turning her attention back to us. "How do you do." She delivered an awkward curtsy, and almost fell back.

Magnus gripped her elbow to keep her upright. "We don't need you breaking a bone before we return home. Mum will be worried about our delay. I'm surprised she hasn't sent Dad or a stable hand out to find us." He appeared to be some years older than his sister, perhaps in his early thirties.

"I'm afraid there isn't room for all of us on the seat. If you don't mind, sir, would you climb atop the supplies?" I nodded my head at the back.

"Missus Willow, it isn't fitting." Mary Grace leaped to her

feet and stepped onto the wagon wheel to climb down. "The gentleman can have my seat."

Magnus hurried around to her side. "No, miss. You stay where you are. I'll take the back." He gently gripped Mary Grace's arm to aid her, but she recoiled from his touch. "I don't mean you any harm." He released her and, saying no more, returned to help his sister into the wagon. Mary Grace plopped down on the seat, and he clambered up onto the oiled tarp and wedged himself down between two crates.

I drove the wagon on toward the estate, keeping my eye on the lightning flashing in the distance.

❧ CHAPTER ❧
Nine

B Y THE TIME THE BRICK MANSION CAME INTO VIEW, THE COLD AND misery I felt was reflected on the faces of the others. As we neared the home, I spotted a lanky, silver-haired gentleman pacing the front gallery.

From one of the outbuildings, a stableman bounded toward us. "Miss Barlow. Mr. Barlow. We were worried about you. Your dad had me hitching his horse." His blue eyes roved over the sorry lot of us.

Magnus jumped off the back of the wagon with a splash into the water rippling down the drive. "We ran into trouble. Our carriage hit a rut and snapped the wheel clean off." He hurried to my side. "Ma'am, I think it's best if you and your friend come inside until the storm passes."

"Our plantation is nearby," I said through chattering teeth.

"You seem like a self-assured lady. I saw you keeping your eyes on the sky. You know as well as I, you'll be driving right into the lightning."

I glanced at the smoke coming out of the chimneys, and the thought of a toasty fire was downright inviting. "Mary Grace?" I glanced at her.

She shook her head. "We best get home. Everyone will be worried if we don't show up."

A crack of lightning split the sky, and Magnus tipped his head to shield his face from the rain and shouted, "They will have a lot more to worry about if that lightning hits you. Come in and dry off. Perhaps a cup of tea will soothe the chill. And as soon as the storm passes I will escort you ladies home."

"We aren't getting any drier, standing out here discussing it." Miss Barlow gave me a nudge.

"Very well." I stood. "We'll take your offer. Besides, it will be nice to get to know our new neighbors." Magnus's hands gripped my waist and swung me to the ground. I wrapped my arms around myself in a desperate effort to stave off the chill as he lifted Miss Barlow.

Mary Grace crept forward, hesitantly eyeing me, and I gave her a nod. She rested her hands on his broad shoulders as Magnus lifted her to the ground as though she were weightless. When his hands lingered on her waist a moment too long for her liking, she clawed at his hands in rising panic.

Brow furrowed, he released her. "Sorry, miss. I-I…"

"Let's get inside," Miss Barlow urged. She smiled at Mary Grace and took her arm.

I glanced at Magnus, whose gaze followed Mary Grace as Miss Barlow led her toward the steps. He stood as though mulling over what he'd done wrong. But when someone had suffered as she had, trust didn't come easily, and although she'd seemed to find content-ment, she'd never forget what the whites had stolen. Years enslaved to my family. The knowledge that she was a free black kept hidden, a decision made by Father and Mammy. Her purity. Her husband.

Magnus looked at me, and the confusion subsided as he offered an arm. "Shall we?"

I took his arm and gathered the waterlogged fabric of my skirt. We hurried to the shelter of the gallery where the elderly gentleman awaited us.

"Son?" He glanced from Magnus to Miss Barlow. "What happened?"

Magnus reiterated what he'd told the stableman. "And then Mrs. Armstrong and…I'm sorry, I didn't catch your name."

"Mary Grace, sir." She offered a small curtsy.

"Mary Grace came along and offered us a ride," he said.

"Welcome to our home." The gentleman thrust out a hand. "I'm Daniel Barlow. Thanks for your assistance."

"Pleased to meet you, Mr. Barlow," I said as his light grip sheathed my hand.

He guided us inside, where the warmth of the home greeted us, and ordered white servants to stoke the fire and bring tea. I recalled how Bowden had said the man he sold the plantation to was a lover of art and not in favor of slavery. At first glance, it appeared there was truth in what Barlow's lawyer had told Sam.

"Please forgive the chaos, as we are still getting settled," he said.

All eyes turned toward a woman in a gray afternoon gown as she swept down the walnut staircase. Her dark hair was parted in the middle and pinned at the nape of her neck.

"Ah, my darling." Mr. Barlow strode to the bottom of the stairs. "We have guests. This is Mrs. Armstrong, and her friend Mary Grace." At the mention of our names, a look of surprise crossed the woman's face. As she reached the last step, Mr. Barlow held out a hand, and she smiled tenderly at him and slipped slender fingers in his. "I'd like to introduce my wife, Isabella."

When the woman drew near, she appeared to be some years younger than her husband. Ribbons of gray lined her dark hair, but her hazelnut skin was flawless, as if not touched by age. Mrs. Barlow smiled warmly as her gaze fell to the water puddle on the floor. "We've plenty of time for introductions later. You all must get out of those wet clothes before you catch your death." She motioned to a heavyset blond woman who stood nearby, awaiting instructions. "Take our guests upstairs and provide them with dry clothing."

"Yes, Mrs. Barlow." The servant gestured for us to follow.

Upstairs, she led us into a room with open chests overflowing with bolts of fabric. Smaller trunks held sewing notions. In the center of the room sat a desk and an Isaac Singer sewing machine, and in front of a window stood an empty wooden dress form. The servant closed the door behind us and moved to the closet. "Go head and get out of those clothes before you ruin the rug."

"Are the Barlow women seamstresses?" I asked. We removed our bonnets and capes while marveling at the chests.

"Mrs. Barlow is one of the finest seamstresses in London." She returned carrying two frocks, one yellow and one light blue. After draping the dresses on a chair, she returned to the closet. While she rummaged around inside, Mary Grace and I removed our clothing.

The woman walked out holding undergarments, and peered at Mary Grace and me. She gestured at me. "These should fit." I unlaced my petticoats, and she turned her attention to Mary Grace. "Take off those bindings. I have undergarments for the both of you."

Dressed in dry clothing, we were given cloths to pat our hair dry.

"I will have the garments laundered and delivered to you," she said as we returned to the main floor. She led us to the parlor, where Mr. Barlow and Magnus stood in front of the fire, engaged in a quiet conversation. Mrs. Barlow entered the room behind us with a tray of tea and light refreshments.

My stomach rumbled as I eyed the platter of sandwiches. "We appreciate your hospitality."

Mr. Barlow set his whiskey glass down on a stand. "I must visit your plantation and introduce myself to your husband."

"I would be honored to return your hospitality. I will

speak with my husband and arrange a time that we can all dine together."

"Please, have a seat." Magnus strode forward and motioned at a gold embroidered settee.

I mumbled a thank you and took a seat as Mary Grace turned to slip into the shadows of the room, as she was accustomed to doing in the presence of whites.

"No, you must join us." Magnus summoned her with a wave of his hand. "We do not discriminate in this house." He glanced at me. "If it's all right with you, Mrs. Armstrong."

"Of course." I watched him with building curiosity. Although slavery was abolished in England, as it was in the North, racism raged in many parts of the world, regardless if people were slave owners or not. "Come, it's quite all right." I patted the seat beside me.

"I don't know, Missus," Mary Grace said.

"Please." Magnus smiled at her. "We have no slaves here. Only hired staff who moved with us of their own free will."

Boldness blazed in Mary Grace, and she looked him square in the eye with an unusual fierceness. "I'm free!"

"Please accept my apology." Magnus dipped his head. "I assumed…"

"One must never assume," Mrs. Barlow said softly as she poured tea into a cup and handed it to me.

"Mary Grace and her mother reside at Livingston, and it is as much their home as mine. Upon my mother's death she gave them their freedom papers. No matter what the law states, they are free and have chosen to remain at Livingston." Again I patted the settee, and Mary Grace seated herself. I gripped her hand to still its shaking before turning my attention back to the Barlows.

After serving tea to Mary Grace, Mrs. Barlow sat across from us on a sofa and the men took two armchairs. It was evident

Mr. Barlow had a different outlook on whites and blacks; after all, he'd married a mulatto and sired a daughter. Magnus left me puzzled because he appeared to take more after his father, and I questioned if he carried any mixed blood at all. I pondered on Miss Barlow's whereabouts, and if she'd be joining us.

"You pay no heed to the law?" Mr. Barlow asked.

"Some laws are meant to be broken," I said. "What are your views on slavery?" I glanced from Mr. Barlow to his son.

"Slavery is a greedy man's philosophy." Magnus leaned back in his chair and steepled his index fingers under his chin.

I arched a brow. "If this is your core belief, why buy a plantation in the heart of slave country?"

"The desire for change, and matters we needed to tend to in Charleston," Mr. Barlow answered, smoothing his mustache.

"We have family in the area that we wanted to check in on," Mrs. Barlow said.

I peered at her over the rim of my teacup and frowned. "Is that so? I don't believe I know of any Barlows in these parts."

"That's because it isn't the Barlow side of the family we are inquiring about." Green-hued eyes, much like her daughter's, held mine.

I squirmed under her gaze. "If you don't mind me asking—"

"Ask anything you like; we have nothing to hide." The Barlow men had let Mrs. Barlow take the lead.

Miss Barlow entered the room, and the men rose and waited until she settled beside her mother before they return to their prior positions. Mrs. Barlow reached out and patted her daughter's hand, then returned her gaze to me. "I believe, if we're to be neighbors, honesty is the best measure. We've come here to inquire about your family and to check on you," she said.

"Me?" My cup rattled as I placed it back on the saucer. "I'm afraid you've managed to confuse me, Mrs. Barlow."

"Please, call me Isabella," she said. "You see, I knew your father. In fact, we all did."

My heart leaped. "Truly?"

She smiled. "Charles was a good friend to me long before he became friends with my husband. If you care to hear my story, you will understand exactly how important he was to us and how the loss of him has shaken us all."

"Please." I leaned forward, my heartbeat pounding in my ears. If they had been friends of Father's, perhaps they would know of his daughter.

"Before slavery was abolished in England I was a slave, and my master, like many you hear about, was cruel. My mother and I suffered unspeakable abuse while enslaved in his household. It was during the last beating I received by his hand that something inside of me snapped, and determined to be free of him, I escaped. Weak from the lash, I collapsed in an alley, where Charles found me and took me to his townhouse. He cared for me until I recovered." She paused. I wanted to urge her to continue, but the pain gripping her face kept me silent. "At first he frightened me because he was so reserved and the simple fact that he was a slave master. I soon realized he was a troubled man, imprisoned by the mysteries and secrets of his past. There was an ache in his eyes that pulled at me."

I gulped at her mention of secrets from his past. Did she know about my parentage? "Father had an intimidating presence." I tried to find some connection to the bridge that unified us. "Please, continue. I must know more."

Tears glittered in her eyes, and she removed a handkerchief from her sleeve and dabbed their corners before continuing. "Charles and I both were scarred by our past, and it was what drew us together. In our friendship we found comfort, and I grew to love him. I suppose a piece of me always will." She offered an apologetic look to her husband. "Although Charles treated me with affection and kindness, he could never love me the same way he loved your mother, and I realized that part of him would never be mine. After her death he returned to London, and sometime later, our friendship turned to intimacy, and I became pregnant."

Her words faded at the mention of pregnancy. Was she the mother of Callie? If so, where was she?

"At first I never told him of the daughter we shared because I was scared. He was a slave owner, and I worried about his reaction to the news that he'd fathered a child of mixed blood. If anyone found out, it would ruin him."

"But he did find out. He mentioned a daughter in his will," I said.

"We do not know of the will, but yes, he knew of Callie. When Charles found us and I told him the truth, he made me a promise that he'd not turn his back on us." She glanced at her daughter and squeezed her hand.

"He kept that promise to Mum and me." Miss Barlow's voice shook with emotion.

"You aren't…" I gawked.

"I am Callie," she said.

A chill rushed over me, and I turned to Magnus. "But you introduced your sister as Emily."

He stirred in his seat. "I'm sorry about my dishonesty." The awkward glance they'd exchanged on the road suddenly made sense.

"But why?" I asked.

"When you stated you were Mrs. Armstrong, I knew you were *her*," he said. "I thought it best if the truth came from Mum."

I swallowed hard and glanced back at Father's lover and

his daughter, Callie. "Is it really you?" Prickles scurried over my flesh.

She bobbed her head as silent tears streaked her cheeks.

I bit down on my lip to quell mine and studied the anguished faces in the room. Each person seemed to be holding their breath. But why move all the way across the ocean instead of sending a letter?

I sat numbed by the revelation. Had I not dreamed of finding Callie? Then why did every muscle in me tense as I looked at her? She was his. Truly his. I, on the other hand, was his niece. My rambling thoughts filled me with turmoil and insecurity. I could hardly compete for the favor of a man that was dead.

"I expected it would be a lot for you to take in," Isabella said. "If you don't mind, I'll let my husband tell you how he came to purchase this place."

Mr. Barlow patted his wife's hand, and said to me, "As you're probably aware, I never had the privilege of meeting your husband. All arrangements were made through our lawyers."

"How did you find out my husband was looking for a purchaser for his estate?"

"Perhaps the history between your father and me will shed some light on how our friendship and partnership began. I first met your father at a ball in London when he was still in the business of selling and trading Negroes. I recognized an inner struggle in him. A battle between what he'd always known, and what was right."

I recalled the same struggle within my husband, years prior.

Mr. Barlow continued. "I'd wanted to help those enslaved in Cuba and Brazil find refuge in England and other anti-slavery countries. Some years later, Charles and I crossed paths again. Something had changed in him. He enlightened me on his work in America, and soon we became allies in our joint mission to help those enslaved."

"Ironic, isn't it? A slave owner, but an abolitionist," I said dryly.

"Yes, but it created the perfect disguise. He was the agent, and an important part of our group of abolitionists in Europe. The respect he'd earned in his travels because of his wisdom, his wit, and his wide pool of resources and acquaintances helped many enslaved people. You can understand the great loss to our organization with his death. Without his funding, ships, and influential appeal, our operations have stopped.

"After Charles disappeared, I inquired at the docks in London about his whereabouts and was informed of his death. But the details they provided were limited. Although his ships continued to sail into London's harbor and his trade operations continued, all efforts for our cause had ceased. Some time later, when Captain Gillies informed me that Charles had been murdered, we worried about your well-being," he said. "Your father had me swear that if anything ever happened to him, I'd find you."

A tear spilled down my cheek as Mr. Barlow spoke of Father's love for me. I glanced at Callie, and for a brief moment wondered which of us had received the best of Charles Hendricks.

"During one of my meetings with the captain, he told me of the Armstrong property and your husband's desire to sell. He also informed me of its location near Charles's plantation. The captain said that, like your mother and father, you were a soldier in the cause. I intended to pay you a visit and not only fulfill my promise to your father, but seek your alliance so our efforts to end slavery could continue. On impulse, I purchased your husband's property in the hopes of moving here and offering my services. But Isabella became ill and was near death's door, too weak to travel. We decided to remain in England until she recovered. We didn't expect so much time to pass."

"Why risk bringing your wife and Callie to a slave-owning state? You must know that will only bring hardship and judgment on you all," I said. Although Callie could pass as white, there was no denying Isabella's parentage.

"We are no strangers to judgment over our union, and we've grown accustomed to such prejudice," Isabella said.

"You must know, after I found out Father had a daughter, I went to England to search for you. On his deathbed, he told my uncle to find you. I had given up hope that we would. And now that you are here, I'm unsure what to think." My insides trembled as the shock of it all settled in.

Mary Grace covered my hand where it lay on the settee, and I looked at her and smiled through my tears. I wanted to bury my head in her shoulder, as I'd often done as a child after Father's harshness overwhelmed me and sent me fleeing to my room. The tenderness in her eyes confirmed her love and support.

"We were unsure if he had told you about me," Callie said. "He always talked of you, but no matter how many times I asked for him to bring you, he never did."

He spoke of me. My heart skipped at the knowledge.

"As a young girl, I dreamed of the games we'd play if you were to come to England." She laughed. "Every time he came to London he'd come to visit and bring me presents. Often he'd come with Dad." She motioned to Mr. Barlow. "It is through him that Mum and Dad met. They married when I was twelve, and I inherited a brother."

"Magnus," I said, glancing at him. The blond hair and blue eyes finally made sense.

"My mum passed when I was small, and she's the only mother I remember." Magnus directed a loving gaze at Isabella.

Callie went on to explain, "Mum and Charles decided that, for the safety of his work, they'd keep his identity from me until I was older. I was fifteen when the three of them sat me down and informed me that I was a Hendricks, and the girl I'd longed to be my friend was, in fact, my sister. Charles promised that, when the time was right, he'd bring you with him and tell you the truth. But life robbed him of the opportunity." She lowered her head.

"Do you resent them for keeping the secret?" I asked.

"No. I understood why they'd done it. And although I knew my father as a friend of the family and Dad's colleague, he spent as much time with me as he could, often taking me to the docks and on rides in the countryside. He loved me, and I him."

I envied her for the time she'd had with him, the bond they'd formed that I had so desperately craved.

"I understand we're strangers but I do hope we can become friends, if not share the bond of sisters." The genuineness in her smile softened my tendency to put up my guard. I returned her smile, but it soon faded as my thoughts turned to the risk of having Callie living in Charleston. If she had been a child he'd conceived with a slave from the quarters, folks would turn a blind eye. However, if people were to find out Father had sired a daughter with a freed slave from London, it would cast unnecessary suspicion and put Livingston in danger.

"I hope so too, but you must know my concerns have to be about the people of Livingston and what it would mean for our operation. If word got out that you were Father's daughter, it would threaten everything," I said.

"Coming here, we were aware of this," Callie said. "I proudly bear the Barlow name, and the Hendricks blood I carry will remain our secret."

"We will protect and stand by you as we did him." Magnus rose to his feet.

"I appreciate that." I stood, and the rest followed. Lightheadedness caught me, and I gripped the arm of the davenport to steady myself.

"Are you all right?" Isabella's touch was gentle, her eyes filled with motherly concern.

I embraced her kindness. "It's been a lot to take in. I will be fine once I get some fresh air."

"You're in luck. The storm seems to have passed, and the sun has come out." Mr. Barlow strode to the window, where the sun poured over the oak floors. I'd been so engrossed in the Barlows' revelation of Father's affairs in London that I hadn't noticed the clouds had parted, and the sky had ceased its rumbling.

"Thank you for your hospitality. We must return home."

"I will send someone to bring your wagon around," Magnus said. "Would you like me to accompany you home?" He looked from me to Mary Grace.

"That's fine; we can manage," I said.

Later, as we left the plantation behind, I glanced at Mary Grace. "I caught the young Mr. Barlow admiring you."

She huffed. "Most likely never had a Negress before."

"He doesn't strike me as such. He conducts himself as every bit the gentleman."

She twisted away and stared into the swamps, becoming silent. My thoughts returned to the Barlows, and the possibilities their arrival could bring.

CHAPTER
Ten

THE BARLOWS VISITED LIVINGSTON SEVERAL TIMES OVER THE months to come. One evening, after the men had retired to the cigar room to discuss men's affairs and Callie, Isabella, and I sat engrossed in a game of cards in the parlor, the front door opened and footsteps echoed in the foyer.

"Evenin', Masa Ben, et sho' good to see ya." Mammy's voice hummed with delight.

He chuckled. "And you as well."

"Missus Willow be in de parlor wid de ladies."

Weighted footsteps drew closer, and we stood as Mammy and Ben strolled through the doorway.

"Missus Willow, luky here, et Masa Ben in de flesh." Her dark eyes gleamed and she lifted a hand to smooth back stray hairs.

Where Mammy and my father had a relationship that was strictly business, Ben and she had a friendship that had expanded over the decades. But Mary Grace and I couldn't miss the opportunity, when it arose, to tease Mammy about the way she brightened up whenever Ben came into view. She'd scowl and say, *"He a fine man. Ain't nothing more dan dat."*

Ben smiled down at Mammy with a keen look of respect. "Thank you, Miss Rita."

"Let me take your coat." She gave his sleeve a tug. "You sit awhile and enjoy yourself. Ain't nobody gwine need ya tonight."

I watched with fondness and amusement, not putting it past her to swiftly turn someone away if they came seeking his help. Nurturing others defined Mammy; it gave her a sense of purpose. I saw how her eyes held onto the stray blond lock that fell over his forehead, and I grasped her inner struggle to refrain from flicking it back into place.

He handed her the coat, and after she left, he turned and charmed the ladies with a pleasant smile. With the influenza outbreak behind us, the weariness that had hooded his visage for months had retreated.

I strode to him and kissed his cheek. "I'm delighted to see you. Won't you join us? You've yet to meet the Barlows." I looped my arm with his and guided him toward the ladies. "Isabella, Callie, I'd like you to meet my father's brother, Benjamin Hendricks."

The conversation had yet to indicate whether or not the Barlows knew the truth about my parentage, and I'd found it unnecessary to inform them.

"Willow has told me much about you." He greeted the ladies with an outstretched hand.

Isabella placed a small dark hand in his, her face pale, as though Ben's appearance had summoned up the past. In return, he stood observing the mulatto woman who'd found her way into Charles Hendricks's heart with open intrigue.

He blinked a few times as if to block out his pondering before shifting his gaze to Callie, who eyed him warily. She was every bit her mother in appearance, but many of her mannerisms were much like Father's. Amusement touched her eyes, but rarely her mouth. She sat back and listened, and only offered her opinion or advice when necessary. But where Father had been reserved in warmth and emotion, she had inherited those traits from her mother, and for that, I was thankful.

Ben peered down at her, and a mixture of emotions played on his face. "So you're his daughter?"

"Yes, sir." Callie curtsied.

He cleared his throat. "W-we've been most eager to meet you."

Callie released a breath, as though she'd been worried about his reaction to her.

"As I'm sure Willow has told you, we'd given up hope of finding you. I couldn't believe it when she told me ya'll had purchased the Armstrong homestead. This all makes one believe in miracles, doesn't it?" he said lightly.

The tension that had been in the room moments prior vanished.

Isabella stood with her hands clasped before her, observing the conversation between niece and uncle. "Indeed," she said. "It's nice to finely meet you, Mr. Hendricks. I've heard so much about you."

He stepped back and encircled my shoulders with his arm, pulling me close. "I'm sure. Willow has a tendency to exaggerate my efforts."

"I refer to *him*." Isabella said.

Ben's smile slipped. "Yes, well, it is no secret that my brother and I never saw eye to eye."

Callie and I shared a nervous look but kept out of their exchange.

"I do not mean to conjure up old wounds," Isabella said. "But I always thought, if I could meet you one day, I'd tell you how much your brother regretted his actions."

"What's done is done. Let us leave the past where it lies, shall we?" His tone exuded composure, but his fingers gripped my upper arm.

"No," Isabella said firmly.

All eyes turned to her.

"Please, let's have a seat." Her expression was solemn.

Once we were seated, Isabella continued with what weighed on her mind. "I want you to know that I speak from a place of reverence." Ben nodded but remained silent. "We all are aware that Charles was stubborn and set in his ways. He shared with me, countless times in the last years, how he yearned to make things right between you. He spoke of his remorse and his deep love for you. Sometimes he'd reminisce how things used to be when you were younger. But as we often do with time, he took it for granted, and never got to say the things that were in his heart."

"I appreciate and accept your need to tell me my brother's desire."

"You are a remarkable man, Mr. Hendricks," Isabella said.

Ben inclined his head. "You're too kind."

"Your sacrifice was more than most could handle." Her gaze shifted to me. "Charles struggled with the secrets he kept from you. The truth of your parentage."

I sucked back a breath, my heart hammering. "You know?" I looked from her to Ben.

"Yes, from the beginning."

I gulped, uncertain if I should be relieved or concerned.

"Although I've come to see this is a truth you've chosen to keep quiet, and for the best, I'm sure. I wanted you to know it isn't something you need to hide from us," Isabella said.

I smiled in an attempt to break the awkwardness that had fallen over the room. "It created a lifetime of secrets, mysteries, and heartache," I said. "My hope is that we can reform our family and leave our children a legacy they can be proud of."

"I couldn't agree more," Callie said.

"If only he could see us now, here under one roof." Ben regarded the painting of him and Father as young men hanging on the wall. The artist had painted it after they'd returned from a morning hunt. Ben had informed me that it was done in the early days, before the struggle for the affections of my mother had divided them.

A short time later, Ben left us to join the men and our conversation turned to the Barlows' lives in England.

"It must be hard to leave your friends and family behind," I said.

"Yes, I miss my dearest friend terribly." Isabella peered at me over her hand of cards. "She's been like a sister to me, and helped raise Callie. A woman of many qualities. She'd make some gentleman very happy."

"Oh?" I raised a brow.

A sparkle lit in her eyes. "She'd be a delightful match for Benjamin."

"Is that so?"

She nodded.

"Mum!" Callie exclaimed. "I'm sure Aunt Pippa wouldn't be keen on you playing matchmaker."

Isabella clucked her tongue. "Nonsense. It's payback, I tell you."

"For what?" Callie and I said in unison.

She held out her fingers and folded each one as she spoke. "For trying to set me up with the post rider, Pastor Thomas, the Gypsy circus conductor, and above all, that dreadful Mr. Samson."

"The widowed farmer from down the way?" Callie stared in dismay.

"That's correct. His wife most likely died from depression." Isabella's nose wrinkled with distaste.

"But he was twice your age," Callie gasped. "What was she thinking?"

"You concede my point?" her mother said.

"Well, I do consider Ben to be far more delightful than this Pippa's choice in men," I said indignantly, but curiosity tugged at me. "Is there a reason she's unwed?"

"Please don't get the wrong impression of her. She's the purest soul you will ever meet."

"I reiterate my question; is there a reason—"

"It is as Mum says. Aunt Pippa is unwed because she loved but once in her life." Callie's expression grew dreamy, and I found myself leaning in as she continued. "It was young love. Aunt Pippa is the daughter of Lord Buxton, and she had fallen in love with a stable boy. Her dad refused such a lowly union. So, they defied him and ran off together. After the young man died in the cholera outbreak of '32, she refused to return to Lord Buxton's home. Mum found her on the streets, begging. She gave her a home and they've been the greatest of friends since. After Mum married Dad, she remained at the cottage where I'd grown up."

I sat mesmerized by the story.

"It is quite romantic, really." Callie's eyes gleamed with enchantment. I regarded her with some surprise. Could it be that she was a romantic at heart? I'd never thought her the type.

"She does seem like a woman of substance," I said, my mind running with images of a Lady willing to give up all for love. Romantic indeed. I wanted more than anything for Ben to find love again. Whitney and I'd often played matchmaker with women in town. We had listed the pros and cons of each single woman, and so far, I'd deemed none worthy of him.

Later that evening, as the Barlows' carriage drove down the lane, Bowden, Ben, and I stood on the veranda watching.

"Isabella says her friend Pippa may come for a visit soon," I said. "She sounds amazing. After what they told me about her tonight, I can't wait to meet her."

Bowden's brow furrowed. "What is the interest?"

"She is unmarried." I smiled.

Bowden and Ben exchanged a glance of disbelief.

"Now don't you go getting any ideas," Ben said.

"But I—"

"No. I won't hear of it. You and Whitney stay out of my affairs." He gripped my shoulder and glowered. "I won't soon forget the last catastrophe of a certain Miss Eva, which the pair of you thought was a brilliant idea."

"So we were wrong." I jutted my chin out. "We are more experienced now."

Bowden chuckled. "If the women have their way, you'll be walking across that lawn out there to wed this Miss…" He glanced at me with a sudden blank stare.

"Pippa."

Ben raised a brow. "Willow, I'm warning you. I have my hands full with patients. I have no time for a woman in my life."

As you say, I thought, while I envisioned him dressed in his Sunday best next to a glowing bride.

I closed the distance between us and linked my arm with his before holding out my other to Bowden. Once I stood between the men, I guided them back into the house. "One should make time for a companion in life."

"Says the one that I had to sling over my shoulder to marry me." Bowden threw back his head and chuckled.

"And she thinks she will have a say on who or if I marry," Ben said over my head to my husband.

In the foyer, we stopped, and I released my escorts. "I don't mean to pry." Both men lifted a brow and shared a united look that said "Sure." I scowled and folded my arms across my chest. "I just want you happy."

Ben stepped forward and kissed my forehead. "I am. Now

if you two will excuse me, I think I'll retire for the evening. I need to research a procedure I haven't done in years before Mr. Caldwell arrives tomorrow."

I stood staring after him until Bowden scooped me off my feet, stealing my breath. He grinned as he strode toward the steps with me, a rag doll in his arms. "All right, Mrs. Armstrong, enough of your prying for today."

I laid a hand on his chest as he climbed the stairs. "It's hardly prying when it comes with good intention. I want him to have the same happiness we do."

"And if someone had tried to pick a husband for you, you would have welcomed it with open arms?"

I recalled Father's attempt to arrange a marriage between Kipling and me. "Well, I…" I lightly thumped his chest with my palm. "That isn't the same."

He nodded as if to say, "If you say so." And the glimmer of amusement in his eyes agitated me all the more.

CHAPTER
Eleven

THE MORNING THE COMMOTION BROKE OUT IN THE WORK YARD, Bowden sat on the back veranda engaged in a conversation with Magnus Barlow. I stood in the doorway of the kitchen house, observing the men while cutting off pieces of apple and placing them in my mouth.

"What you spying on dose menfolkses for?" Mammy added another log to the fire.

I ignored her question and countered with one of my own. "What are your thoughts on the younger Mr. Barlow?"

"Can't get a read of a fellow from a few dinners. But I can't help but notice how he eye my gal when she 'round. Et doesn't sit well wid me at all." She came to stand beside me to get a look at the fellow in question.

"It would do her well to have a fine gentleman like him show interest in her. Who knows, perhaps he would be a good suitor for her." I munched a slice of apple.

"Oh, hush, now." She narrowed her eyes. "No white man luk at a mulatto 'oman any different dan he does a hog. Dat is unless he luking to lay wid her, and dere ain't no man ever gonna touch my gal widout my say-so." Her lips compressed, and her face hardened.

"But look how Papa cared for Isabella, how he provided for and loved Callie. And look at Mr. Barlow, he wed a mulatto."

Mammy snorted, marched to the table, and turned out the

biscuit dough onto the floured surface. "My gal and Mr. Barlow? Now I know you crazy. De whole world done gone crazy." She muttered a few inaudible words and thumped the biscuit dough harder, mashing it with the heels of her palms.

Unsure what had prompted her tangent, I turned back to watching the men.

"Ain't et a mite easier to sink your teeth into de thing?" Mammy said as I popped another slice into my mouth.

"How you choose to eat your apples is up to you," I said with more sass than sensibility. She'd stormed down to the kitchen house soon after Magnus's arrival, and everyone in her path had hurried to clear out. "What has gotten into you today?" I glanced back at her.

She stopped attacking the dough and looked up, then something in the distance caught her attention, and her lips pinched. "See dere?" She waved a hand and strode toward me while wiping her floured hands on her apron.

I turned to observe what had her wound tight. Mary Grace had stepped out onto the back veranda, and Magnus now stood. *Oh...* It dawned on me what had gotten up under Mammy's head rag.

"I understand he be a gentleman and all, but I ain't luking for him to go hurting my gal. She jus' gitting back to her old self after losing Gray. I won't have et, I tell ya."

"And it has nothing to do with your concern that he has also caught her attention?"

Mammy gave me a sour look and returned to the table to beat her frustration into the dough.

"You best take it easy on that dough, or those biscuits won't be fit to eat." I strode to a shelf and retrieved a cast iron frying pan and set it on the table beside her. I scooped a tablespoon of lard into the pan before walking to the fireplace to stoke the coals.

"Stop! Let him go." Kimie's wails reached us.

I straightened, and Mammy and I gawked at each other before bolting for the door.

"Dat Miss Kimie?" Mammy stood wide-eyed, scanning the grounds for Whitney's sister.

"I think so." I stepped out of the kitchen house. "I'd best go and see what the matter is."

I hurried in the direction of the cries and soon spotted Jack Barry straddled over someone on the ground, laying the punches to them. A crowd had gathered, and Parker's father, Owen, stood over the wrestling figures.

"Come now, Masa Jack, let him be," Owen pleaded, panic in his voice.

Kimie, her face tear-stained, caught sight of me and rushed forward. "Please, you must stop him." She grabbed my arm, pulling me toward the men.

As I drew closer, I saw the man pinned beneath the lean figure of Kimie's twin. Parker lay with his arms up, trying his best to shield himself from the blows of Jack's fists. "I'll teach you for ever touching my sister," he said between heavy breaths.

"Enough!" I grabbed Jack's collar and dodged his fist as he swung at me.

Recognition reflected in his eyes, and he blanched. "Excuse me, Mrs. Armstrong, I'm right sorry. I didn't know it was you."

My chest heaved. "Get off of him, or I'll have you removed from the property."

Jack obeyed while keeping his gaze locked on Parker. "Damn fool forgets he's a Negro."

"He did nothing wrong!" Kimie dropped to her knees beside Parker and started dusting him off. He pulled away and grabbed the cane Owen held out for him. Eyes flashing at Jack, he pulled to his feet.

"What is the meaning of this?" I crossed my arms and glared up at Jack.

He glared at Parker. "I caught him kissing Kimie behind the stables. I'm not for slavery any more than the rest of you, but I'm also not about to stand by and let no darkie kiss my sister. They need to stick with their own kind."

Parker used the back of his hand to wipe the blood from his mouth. One glance at him and anyone would know he could have taken Jack if he had wanted to, regardless of his disability. But because it was illegal to hit a white man, Parker had contained himself, a tribute to his self-control. The pride that thumped in my chest for the young man was overshadowed by the disappointment I felt over Jack's behavior. I clenched my teeth and looked back at Jack. "And you couldn't think of a better way to deal with your frustration than to resort to violence?"

"Figured I would handle it man to man." Jack stretched to his full height.

"Violence is never the answer. You'd think *you'd* understand this more than others."

My remark had the intended result. Jack winced at my reminder. "I'm not him." He rocked onto his toes. "I'll never be him! But Parker deserved what he got. And if I ever see him lay his hands or lips on Kimie again, I'll beat him good." He leveled a glare at Parker before bending to retrieve his hat on the ground. He slapped it on his leg to remove the dust and turned back to me. Regret flickered in his eyes and he opened his mouth to speak, then thought better of it and whirled and stomped off in the direction of the stables.

Bowden pushed through the crowd that had gathered. "All right, folks, back to your duties."

As people broke away, mumbling amongst themselves, Bowden looked to Parker, who blinked through the blood dripping from the gash over his brow. "You all right? Anything broke?"

"Jus' my pretty face," Parker said with a grin, trying to shuffle off his rage in front of Bowden, but I knew him better than that.

"Bowden, do you mind if I speak to Parker?"

Bowden gestured with a hand and inclined his head.

"Come," I said.

Parker walked with me, and as we broke away from the others, his amiability slipped, and his jaw locked.

"Jack was wrong in what he did."

"Is he? What is wrong is dat I'm a man jus' lak him, and I have to lay dere and take dat beating widout defending myself."

I winced. "I know—"

"No, you don't!" His chest heaved. "You never gonna know what et feels lak to be in dis skin. Never." The composure he'd presented to Bowden dissolved, and vulnerability surfaced.

"Parker." I stopped. "Listen." I tilted my head to look into his eyes, but he twisted to look out over the fields.

"Et ain't right. He humiliated me in front of de whole plantation...in front of Kimie."

My heart grieved for him and his wounded pride. No man wanted to look vulnerable or be embarrassed in front of a woman. "You have every cause to be mad." I touched his arm.

He looked at me out of the corner of his eye but refused to turn his head.

"You really love her, don't you?" I said.

"What does et matter? She white and I a darkie. Her brother will never accept et. And Mr. Knox most lakly come over here and lay another beatin' on me once Jack runs off to tell him. And I could take Jack, but her pappy is bigger dan de two of us put together."

"Bowden will speak to them both on the matter."

"Ain't no use." Parker looked at me and his face softened somewhat. "But I appreciate you none de less."

I forced a smile. "Head on down and get Ben to stitch you up."

"Yessum." He turned and hobbled off.

Kimie stood eyeing Parker, yearning for him to look at her, but he walked on past without a word. She burst into tears.

Bowden gawked from Parker to Kimie before his eyes sought me. He shrugged awkwardly.

"Oh, for heaven's sakes," I mumbled and went to his aid. "Kimie," I touched her elbow, "I'd like to speak to you."

She dropped her hands from her face. Misery gleamed in her blue eyes.

"Let's take a walk, shall we?" I said.

"You aren't cross with Parker and me, are you? Because this was Jack's doing."

"No, of course not." I steered her toward the path leading around the pond.

"Then what is it?"

"I'm concerned about the open show of affection between you and Parker. The world doesn't embrace romantic feelings between a white and a black. If the wrong person were to see you and Parker together, he could be dangling at the end of a rope." The love affair between Josephine and Jethro, and her father's rage, came to mind. Whitney and Knox could try as they might, but Jack was a young man now and they couldn't control his actions.

"But we love each other and want to be together," Kimie said.

"Are you aware of the sacrifice your love would entail? The union between a white and a black would mean a life of prejudice and hardship."

I'd seen it coming for years now, the way Kimie would come to Livingston after she'd received news that Parker had returned from the sea. She'd run off to the quarters after a quick greeting. I reckon I'd assumed she would outgrow the affections that had flourished since she was a child. But now she was a woman in all ways, with eyes only for Parker. She'd caught the eye of Wyatt Harris, the son of a banker from Charleston. If he were to catch word, or worse yet, see the couple locked in a passionate embrace, a posse would come to Livingston looking for blood.

"I don't care what people think. I love him, and he loves me." She stomped her foot.

Most days, I would consider Kimie the embodiment of pleasantness. And where Whitney was tall, brazen, and intolerant of most people, Kimie was petite, polite, and found solace and commonality amongst the quarter folks. The sisters, although opposites in many ways, had the same resilience and fierceness. The stubborn glint Kimie had in her eye matched the one Whitney would get if something weren't to her liking.

"One can't help but love who their hearts tell them, but for your sake and Parker's, you must use discretion."

"Jack thinks he can tell me who to love. He needs to scamper off and leave me be. He's always thought he could boss me around, but not anymore. I'm grown, and I won't allow it. Some days I can't wait until he goes off to Mount Royal. Then I can think for myself without his nattering in my ear."

"Jack can be difficult, but he's looking out for you like the rest of us."

"I know you all mean well, but this is my life. And I need to live it my way. Parker and I will face what comes our way."

The innocence of her love for Parker tugged at my heart. I stopped and gripped her shoulders. "I don't fault you for love. You understand that, don't you?"

"Yes, it's just…" Her eyes welled with tears. "It is unfair. What does it matter if my skin is white and his is black? When two people love each other, isn't that all that should matter?"

I choked back the emotions catching in my throat. In a perfect world, yes.

"I love him so much it hurts my very soul." Misery shone in her face. "What harm are we causing?"

"You aren't. All your frustrations are reasonable, but the path you're on is dangerous. I wish it weren't true, but it is." I hugged her, and she laid her face against my shoulder and wept.

"I just want to be with him."

"I know." I stroked her back.

She sniffled and stepped back, wiping her tears. "Whitney says I shouldn't worry about love and marriage and to invest my time and heart in nursing."

"Hogwash! Don't listen to a word your sister says. Except the nursing part." I smiled. "You're a brilliant nurse. Ben says you're a quick study and an excellent assistant."

"Truly?" Her eyes brightened with hope. "He has been the most excellent teacher. He even lets me take the lead sometimes. Whitney says I spend more time with him and in the quarters than I do at home. 'Why don't you marry Ben?' she had the nerve to say one day. Can you imagine?" She snorted. "I admire and respect him, but marry him? Why, he is old enough to be my father."

"Much too old for you. Besides, I have my eye on a certain someone for him." I winked.

"Really? Do tell." She grabbed my hands with enthusiasm.

"All right," I said with the hope of easing the melancholy in her heart. "But you must promise it'll be our secret. Because if Bowden or Ben find out that I'm still meddling in Ben's affairs, they won't be the least bit happy with me."

Kimie giggled, then said, "I won't tell a soul."

CHAPTER
Twelve

WHILE IN CHARLESTON ONE NOVEMBER AFTERNOON, I walked down to the harbor to visit Bowden at the office. Through the windowpane of the closed door, I saw him and Captain Gillies with their heads together in deep conversation. When I knocked on the door, they pulled apart and swung to look at me.

Bowden's face lacked warmth at the sight of me, and a pang of disappointment snagged my heart. He waved to grant entry and urged me to close the door before going back to talking in hushed tones to the captain. I stood awkwardly waiting, straining to eavesdrop on their conversation to no avail.

After a moment or two, the men straightened and turned to me.

"To what do we owe the pleasure?" Bowden regarded me as though his mind remained preoccupied.

"The Barlows required some supplies, and Callie asked me to come along. While they're running errands, I thought per- haps a husband could spare a few minutes for his wife," I said hopefully.

As I'd walked to the pier, the fantasy of him gathering me into his arms and kissing me passionately had captured my thoughts. I missed him terribly. Weeks had passed since he'd left on business in Maryland, only to return and become occupied with demands at the pier. He'd sent word that he'd returned, but obligations at the dock required his attention, and he'd be staying at the townhouse in Charleston until he could get away.

"I'm sorry, but not today. The captain and I have important matters to attend to," Bowden said.

I feigned a smile. "It's good to see you again, Captain."

He inclined his head. "And you, Mrs. Armstrong."

I quelled the disappointment at the lukewarm welcome and focused on the men's hushed conversation, curious. "I didn't mean to impose. However, seeing—"

"As you're here, you'd like to know what we were talking about." Bowden shook his head, with a trace of a smile pulling at his mouth.

The captain stifled a chuckle, and Bowden sent him a look of bewilderment. Captain Gillies's laughter erupted, and he looked at me with fondness before turning to clap my husband on the shoulder. "If you thought you were marrying a lass without a mind of her own, you thought wrong." His face red with merriment, he winked at me on the way to the door. "Good day, Mrs. Armstrong."

I inclined my head. "And to you, Captain."

After he departed, I turned back to Bowden and found him half sitting and half leaning against the desk with arms folded and a look of amusement on his face. I released a breath. Perhaps he wasn't too upset at the disruption.

"You know how to clear a room, don't you?" he said.

"That was hardly my intention." I walked to him and peered up into his jewel-toned eyes, and the look of devotion and admiration I found set my heart to fluttering. "Is it a crime to want to catch a glimpse of my husband?"

"Hardly." He gripped my shoulders. "I spend my days with crude sailors and menfolk. We all could use the entertainment of a beautiful lady." He nodded toward the door, and I followed his gaze to find the men in the warehouse had paused to steal a peek at us. He took my hand and led me to a corner of the office, out of sight to the workers and the windows overlooking the pier.

"What are—" He pressed me against the wall and covered my mouth with his. Delight and desire coursed through me as I became lost in the passion of his kiss. My fingers tangled in his hair, and I eagerly invited the attention I craved. When our lips parted, he didn't step back. Instead, he stood gazing at me with eyes speaking to the depths of how he'd missed me as much as I had him.

Before coming to the office, I'd considered asking him to take a moment away from the busyness of the pier to join me at a coffeehouse. But after discovering him and the captain engrossed in what appeared to be a serious conversation, it left me wondering if something troubling concerned them. "You and the captain seemed to be discussing something of great importance when I arrived." Avoiding his gaze, I traced the buttons of his white cotton shirt with a finger.

"Always down to business," he said. "You know I could take offense to this."

I tilted my head back to look at him. "To what?"

He ran a finger over my lips. "It's been weeks since I felt the embrace of my wife. And when I finally get a few moments with her, her brain is elsewhere."

"Not true." I feigned a pout. "I long for these precious moments as much as you, but I was just curious, is all."

"Willow Armstrong, curious? I would never have guessed it." He laughed and released me. "Very well, my darling. Come, sit, and I will tell you what the good captain and I were discussing." He took my hand and led me to the chair behind the desk.

Once I was seated, he perched on the edge of the desk in front of me and leaned forward with one elbow resting on his thigh. "Last week, before my return, he found a slave woman, battered and bleeding, seeking shelter on the *Olivia II*. When he questioned her on why she'd come here, she said that her mistress brought her."

"Who was the mistress?"

"Josephine." Concern flickered in his eyes.

"Josephine?" My heart beat faster. "But...why would she suggest she come here?"

"It appears she must think you got someone out once, and you will do it again. Maybe telling her of the boy's whereabouts was a mistake."

I chewed on the corner of my mouth.

"The more folks that know of our aiding slaves to escape, the more risk there is to our whole operation. You must speak to her and let her know that you will care for her son, but you aren't going to help her every time she gets in a bind."

"But to turn someone away who is in need isn't right."

"Should we risk all the others we can save for one?"

"Yes!" I stood, indignant. "No one who comes to us should be turned away." How could he suggest such a thing?

"I couldn't agree more." He grabbed my hand as I pushed by him. "The passion in your soul is the reason I love you, but we can't save them all. Is your parents' work to be for nothing?"

"Of course, not." My tension eased as I understood the intent behind his words.

"If I could turn back time, you know I would. But it is impossible. Going forward, I want to make sure I don't make mistakes that'd cause undue harm." Weariness lined his face, and he used his thumbs to rub the sides of his temples. "I hear him, you know."

My stomach dropped at the haunting tone of his voice. "Who?"

"Gray." He swallowed hard. "In my dreams. I can never see his face, and he never speaks. His guts are mangled, as they were that day, but the most troubling thing is how he just stands there pointing at me."

Tears gathered in my throat. "Bowden, it is the devil's torment. Gray wouldn't want you to blame yourself or relive the past."

"I know." He stood and paced the room with his hands resting on his waist. "But it's not only in my dreams. I see him in the streets."

"It's your mind playing tricks on you."

"I know," he said again. "At first I thought he was blaming me, but now I feel it's a warning."

"Warning?"

"Yes, like something is coming."

I strode to him and wrapped my arms around his middle, resting my cheek against his chest. "You work too hard."

His arms enveloped me.

After Gray's death, Bowden had become bent on changing a country's mentality. Then, after our union, he'd thrown himself into learning about our involvement in the Underground Railroad and my family's businesses, leaving me to the operations at the plantation. After the loss of our son, he spent his time in the North, in Canada, and at the docks. I believed it was his way of burying his grief.

I tilted back my head to peer up at him. "Let's take a stroll. A breath of fresh air would do you good."

He regarded me with pained eyes, and after a moment his face softened and he nodded.

We strode along the boardwalk, pausing from time to time to greet acquaintances before continuing, finding solace in our togetherness. I stopped to admire a hat in the window of the milliner's shop.

"Surely you wouldn't wear the likes of that." Bowden looked from the hat to me.

"Why not?" I asked.

"It looks like the designer plucked an ostrich and put every last feather on the hat. Not to mention it looks like a wig worn by the English."

I laughed and turned my attention back to the hat, trying to see it through his eyes. Perhaps he was right. The hat did have a "look at me" appeal and was sure to be a conversation piece. I turned away from the window, and he released an exaggerated sigh of relief.

"I'm glad you agree. I wouldn't want to be subjected to folks' looks and the tittering behind hands as I accompany you."

"Since when do you care what others think?" I said as we strolled along.

"If it saves me from purchasing that hat, I will develop such a concern."

I loved us most when we could forget the burdens of life and get lost in each other's company. But the lightheartedness of the afternoon was disrupted by a commotion across the street.

"You can take your business elsewhere. I won't sell to you today or any other," a man said.

I stopped when I saw Mr. Nelson, the miller, poking his finger against the chest of Mr. Barlow.

"Remove your hand, sir," Mr. Barlow said with firm politeness.

"Nigger-lovers are bad enough, but a Christian man who'd marry one of the demons is lower than the darkies themselves."

Mr. Nelson and my father had been longtime acquaintances. Surely a quick reminder of Southern hospitality would ease the passion of his prejudice. I stepped forward, bent on assisting Mr. Barlow, but Bowden clutched my forearm.

"Calm yourself," he whispered through gritted teeth, for my ears only.

"But—"

"You will not insert yourself. Let Mr. Barlow handle things."

"It's unjust!" I said under my breath.

"And there isn't a thing you can do about it. You marching over there isn't going to change his views. He can sell to who he wants."

At the commotion, people paused on the boardwalk and stepped out of stores to watch. Out of the corner of my eye, I saw Isabella and Callie exit the general store.

Mr. Barlow stepped back, putting distance between him and Mr. Nelson. "Your opinion holds no weight with me. As you stated, sir, I will take my business elsewhere."

"You will be lucky if you find any decent man willing to do business with you." The disgust hung heavy in Mr. Nelson's voice.

"We shall see, won't we? Good day, sir." Mr. Barlow tipped his hat with more refinement than the finest of gentlemen.

The calmness of his demeanor only seemed to further agitate Mr. Nelson, and he reached out and smacked Mr. Barlow's hat from his head. Both men turned to look at where it lay in the street.

To my right, I saw Callie step forward. Isabella clutched her arm, pulling her back. Some words passed between them, and the agony on Callie's face as she shot a look back at Mr. Barlow contrasted with the unshakable composure of her mother.

"It appears there are a few things you and Miss Barlow have in common," Bowden said in a low voice. I frowned at him. He returned my gaze. "Passion for right and wrong without the sense to control it."

My body temperature rose as adrenaline pumped through my veins. "Do you wish to anger me?"

"Of course not. I'm merely suggesting that if you act on all the emotions pounding in your chest, you will cause more harm than good."

I clenched my jaw, annoyed at him, Mr. Nelson, and the whole situation. I didn't care to hear the truth when all I wanted to do was march over to Mr. Nelson and give him a piece of my mind. I heaved a sigh as the sensible part of me knew Bowden was right, which only infuriated me more. Why did he always have to be right?

My eyes went to Mr. Barlow's hat as a passing buggy crushed it into the dirt. Wincing, I stood rooted on the boardwalk and suppressed tears of frustration. Every nerve in me rebelled against this wrong.

Mr. Barlow squared his shoulders and walked into the street to retrieve his hat. It was too ruined to wear. He carried it back and joined Miss Smith and his family.

"And you!" Mr. Nelson's voice boomed. He struck at the sky with a fist. "We should have run you out of town when you first arrived. Northerners thinking they can come down here and take over our businesses. What next? You damn Northerners need to be taught a lesson, thinking you can stick your noses into how we run things in the South." Tightness gripped my chest as I realized he had turned his contempt on Miss Smith. "I'll see every Northerner's flesh melt from their body before I let you question our way of life."

Miss Smith turned her back on him. The Barlows exchanged a few words with her before stepping off the boardwalk and crossing to their carriage.

Mr. Barlow helped his wife in before turning to assist Callie. His eyes fell on us and Bowden and he exchanged a look before he climbed into the carriage and instructed the driver. Settling back in the seat, he smiled at Isabella and wrapped an

arm around her shoulders. His display of pride in his wife before Charlestonians struck me with an abundance of guilt and
shame.

Isabella and Mr. Barlow rode past with their heads held
high, while Callie sat with her head lowered to hide the tears
dampening her cheeks.

My hands flexed into fists at my sides, and an ache for the
injustice of their suffering beat in my chest.

"Whites mixing with darkies," a man behind us scoffed.

"It isn't Christian," a woman said.

I bit down hard to stifle a remark as we turned to find Mr.
and Mrs. Jefferson gawking after the Barlows. When their carriage disappeared, Mr. Jefferson, an undertaker and a man of
seventy years or so, twisted to face us. He looked through us as
though we were the dead walking. A river of deep blue veins
branched beneath his parchment-thin skin. At the sight of his
perpetual scowl I felt my heart thump faster, as it had when I
was a little girl. Yes, I decided, he could indeed be responsible for
a child's nightmares.

"I offer you my condolences, Mr. Armstrong," Mr. Jefferson
said.

Bowden's brow furrowed. "What for?"

"When you sold your plantation, I'm sure you never imagined an Englishman and his nigger wife would be the owners."

"And so nearby." Mrs. Jefferson lifted a hand to her throat
and offered me a look of sympathy.

"What the Englishman does is of no concern of mine."
Bowden's fingers pressed into the small of my back.

The lines in Mr. Jefferson's forehead deepened, if that were
possible. "No?"

"Mr. Barlow's lawyer offered me a fair price." Bowden
gripped my elbow and tipped his hat at Mrs. Jefferson. "Ma'am."

He eyed her husband, his face a blank. "Good day, Leroy." He guided me around them and down the street at a pace that had me half running to keep up.

When we had turned off the main street and were headed in the direction of the harbor, he slowed. Jaw twitching, he remained silent. I eyed him in admiration. Although the poor treatment the Barlows had suffered bothered him as much as it did me, he'd remained in control, and because of him, our alliance with them would remain intact.

∾ CHAPTER ∾
𝒯𝒽𝒾𝓇𝓉𝑒𝑒𝓃

I ACCOMPANIED THE BARLOWS ONTO THE BACK GALLERY OF THEIR home one evening, some weeks after the incident in Charleston. On the horizon, the sun touched the riverbank and blazed a crimson and magenta mural across the sky. Somewhere in the distance, the soothing vibrato of an owl's call harmonized with the low country creatures of the night and the steady flow of the river. The plummeting evening temperature licked the air from my lungs and snatched our breath, drawing elongated billows before evaporating into the night.

The butler strode the gallery, lighting the lanterns posted on columns, and soon the soft glow from the flames cocooned us.

"It's too bad prior obligations kept your husband from joining us this evening, as I do enjoy his company," Mr. Barlow said.

I pulled my shawl tighter. "Yes, he was disappointed he couldn't attend and told me to offer his deepest apologies."

Magnus lowered himself into a freshly painted rocker. "I hope you won't find my question intrusive, but I'm wondering about the whereabouts of Mary Grace's husband."

"How did you know about him?" I walked to a nearby rocker and sat down.

"When I visited your plantation some time back, she greeted me on the front veranda. We shared a few words before her mum joined us and was quick to let me know her daughter was married." I heard disappointment in his voice.

Good ol' Mammy, I thought, smiling to myself before studying Magnus. He was of average height with a boyish face and earnest, pale blue eyes. In the months since his arrival, he'd proven himself to be a gentleman in all regards.

"Well, do tell us. Where is this mystery man?" Callie said.

I looked to the river, and the image of Gray's smiling face entered my mind. After a moment, I heaved a sigh and said, "He's dead."

Isabella sucked back a breath, and the Barlow men gawked at me.

"Dead?" Callie's voice sounded hollow. "He wasn't the victim of a slave catcher, was he?"

"But Miss Rita didn't act like he was dead," Magnus said.

"That is because she has spent her whole life protecting Mary Grace. She and the children are all Mam…Miss Rita has left."

"How many children does she have?" Callie asked, but I got the feeling it was more for her brother than out of her own curiosity.

"Two. Well…one, really."

"Which is it?" Callie pressed.

"Gray, her late husband, and she share a daughter named Evie. Some years ago, there was a massacre out in the swamps," I said. "A Northerner by the name of Barry purchased a plantation. Savagery ran deep in his veins, and his foreman was no different. There was no end to the depths of brutality he unleashed on his slaves. One night, his slaves rebelled and burned down the plantation with Mr. Barry and his men inside. A posse gathered soon after to seek revenge for their deaths, and tracked the slaves deep into the swamps." I shivered at the memory of the wasted lives. What I'd seen was a nightmare that would stay with me forever.

"Against Father's orders, my friend Whitney and I went out into the marshes to aid anyone we could. The slaves were defenseless, so it was over before it had barely begun. We found a survivor in the bodies, a young boy named Noah, and he was traumatized by what happened out there. We brought him back to Livingston, and he became taken with Mary Grace. She took the boy under her wing and nurtured him. Mary Grace and Gray adopted Noah, and with their love and commitment, he came out of his shell.

"When Gray was gutted by a man out for vengeance against my husband and family…" I glanced at my cold fingers lying in my lap.

"Dear God," Isabella said.

"Old Mr. McCoy and his eldest son Rufus are responsible for my mother's murder," I continued. "Rufus died in a plantation fire. Reuben, the youngest son, murdered my father. He tried to kill Bowden. We succeeded in capturing him, but he escaped. Despite the wanted posters and the rewards for his capture, he hasn't been spotted again. He is a mastermind unlike anyone you've ever seen before." I informed them of his alias, Silas Anderson, and of his crimes.

"A monster!" Callie gasped when I'd finished.

"Yes. A brilliant one, and someone to be wary of. He is always two steps ahead. I'm relieved; I've managed to put behind me the nightmares of him coming back to finish what he started."

"You've suffered so much." Callie gripped my hand. "Your strength is admirable. I'm glad we are here to offer our support and protection."

I smiled at her. "I'm grateful for your kindness."

"We are family." She returned my smile.

"Callie speaks for all of us in our dedication to you and all you love," Mr. Barlow said.

My eyes welled with tears. "I can't tell you how that warms my heart."

"Let's hope the future will be kinder." Mr. Barlow rose. "If you will excuse me, I will retire to my study." He leaned down and kissed his wife's cheek. "My dear."

She smiled up at him with reverence and affection.

After his footsteps had faded inside, Magnus rose, his expression troubled. "I will let you ladies continue your evening without me. I think I'll take a stroll."

Once only womenfolk remained, Callie glanced at her mother and said, "What is it, Mum?"

"It's been a long time since I saw that look in your brother's eye." Her expression grew tender.

Callie peered into the dark where Magnus had disappeared. "Since Charlotte."

"Charlotte?" I asked.

"The woman he was to marry. She died five years ago," Callie said. "Run over in the street by a runaway carriage."

"How dreadful." My stomach dropped at the news.

"After her death, he swore off love. But Mum and I held onto hope that eventually someone worthy would catch his eye."

"And you believe he has become smitten with Mary Grace?"

Callie bobbed her head.

"Well, I see Miss Rita has reasons to be concerned—"

The pounding of horses' hooves cut me off. Loud voices pierced the peaceful evening. A glow of light came from the front of the house. We jumped to our feet, and the panic surging through me was reflected in Isabella and Callie's eyes.

Mr. Barlow charged out onto the gallery, his eyes large with concern. "Inside, now!" He looked past us. "Where is Magnus?"

Isabella paled. "He went for a stroll. What is it, Daniel?"

"Barlow!" a man shouted.

My heart stuck in my throat.

"Men. Several of them. Come, come, inside." He gestured urgently.

"Barlow." I recognized the voice of Lucille's father. "Come out here, or you will leave us with no choice."

Callie clutched my arm as we raced for the door.

Inside, the butler met us with a rifle. Mr. Barlow took the weapon. "Gather all the rifles and arm all of the house staff capable of firing. Take up positions at doors and windows, but stay out of sight. Seal up all doors with whatever furniture you can. And for God's sake, extinguish the lanterns."

"Yes, sir." The butler raced off.

"But what about Magnus? He is out there." Worry pleated Isabella's brow.

Mr. Barlow gently gripped the nape of her neck and pulled her forehead to meet his lips. "Don't worry about him; he and the ground staff will know what to do."

"They've surrounded the house," one servant said as lanterns throughout the home were extinguished. The glow of torches reflected in the windows. Mounted men were at the back entrance. Footsteps pounded in the corridor and upstairs as anxious staff hurried to fall into position. The Barlows and I ran to the front of the house.

I halted a passing servant. "Here, give me that." I gripped one of the rifles in his hands. He released the weapon without hesitation before racing off, and I dashed into the darkened parlor after the Barlows.

"You know how to handle one of those?" a wide-eyed Callie asked.

"You bet I do." I looked at Mr. Barlow for instruction.

"Isabella, I want you and Callie to stay low and out of sight," Mr. Barlow said.

"Barlow, this is your last warning," Mr. Carter called again.

"No, we will stand with you," Isabella said stubbornly. Mr. Barlow started to protest, but Isabella shook her head and said, "If we are to survive in this new land, we must let them know that we won't be threatened."

Through the parlor window, I glimpsed the same scene at the back of the house—men on horseback holding torches. From the corner of the house stablemen and groundskeepers raced into the front yard, armed with pitchforks and axes.

"I must address them. They won't stop until I do, and I'm not willing to risk anyone's life." Mr. Barlow placed a kiss on Isabella's lips and bolted for the front door.

"We will go together," Callie said.

"No." Isabella held out an arm to stop her. "You're to remain inside. I have one child out there, I don't need another. Willow, you mustn't be seen, or they will know where you stand."

"But I can't hide in the shadows like a coward too afraid to speak up," I said.

"You can, and you must," she said firmly. "Sometimes it takes more courage to be silent. You must think about what is at stake."

I nodded and shelved the conflict inside me.

Isabella grabbed a gun from a servant.

"But Mum, you don't know how to use a rifle," Callie said.

Isabella looked to me, and I cocked the hammer of the rifle and propped it against my shoulder as though to shoot. She followed suit, then nodded at me and disappeared.

"Seal this behind us. Defend the women as you must." Mr. Barlow's voice echoed from the foyer.

"But, sir, what about you and Mrs. Barlow?" the butler said.

"Do as you're told. That's an order." The crisis had made Mr. Barlow's tone harsh.

From the shadows of the drapes in the parlor, I observed Mr. Barlow and Isabella as they stepped out on the front gallery. I counted seven men altogether, guessing there had to be at least that many at the back of the house. I recognized Mr. Nelson, the miller, Josephine's husband, her father, Mr. Thames, and Mr. Carter, but I couldn't place the other two.

"Gentlemen, what can I help you with?" Mr. Barlow aimed his rifle at the chest of the speaker, Mr. Thames.

"Mr. Nelson made it very clear we don't want your kind here. No decent gentleman would wed a Negress and give her and her bastards his family name."

Callie stood beside me, her hot breath on my neck. "Look, there's Magnus."

I squinted into the dark behind the men, where Magnus crept forward with a rifle in his hand.

"I'm very aware of your views. Nothing can undo what has been done. You men needn't concern yourselves," Mr. Barlow said.

"Ain't there?" Mr. Carter pointed his pistol at Isabella. "We could teach all darkies and white nigger-lovers what happens if they get to thinking we'll condone such an abomination."

Mr. Barlow pulled Isabella behind him. "You've made your point; now I suggest you ride on out of here." He nudged his head toward the lane.

Magnus lifted his rifle and fired into the air. The horses stomped at the ground as their riders fought to control them. "Men like you are what's wrong with the world," he said with more grit than I'd witnessed in him. Keeping the rifle aimed at the men, he circled them, making his way up the front steps one at a time, never taking his eyes off the men until he joined his parents. "Such irony you spew," he said. "Hypocrites, the whole lot of you. You lie with your Negresses and breed children of your own, but come here acting as though you are above my father, who married a woman he loved and who loves him."

"Love?" Mr. Carter's face looked like it would combust. "The demons aren't capable of love." He spat in Isabella's direction before nodding at the man next to him. They exchanged words before the man broke off and guided his mount around the house.

"Get off my land, or I will be in the right to drop you where you are," Mr. Barlow warned.

Everything that happened next was a blur.

There was the sound of breaking glass at the back of the house, and someone down the corridor screamed, "Fire!"

I raced from the room. "Where is it?" I shook a servant girl standing in the hallway in shock.

"In the library." She pointed in that direction.

I recalled where the library was and broke into a run, but a hallway stand yanked the hem of my dress and pulled me back. I fought to free myself, and when the material gave way I dashed to the library and entered. The breeze from the broken window flapped the drapes, fanning the flames engulfing them. In the center of the rug, a fire burned where the torch had landed.

A servant skidded to a stop beside me. "Quick, you see to the drapes," I said. I grabbed a blanket folded over an armchair, dropped to my knees, and worked to smother the flames. Smoke burned my nostrils and lungs as the heat of the fire's rage seared my flesh. I heard tearing material, then a clattering crash as the curtain rod and drapes fell to the floor. The man fought to gain control of the blaze. Above, the fire raced across the wallpaper.

A servant girl hovered in the doorway with a bucket of water. She stared in terror as the room rapidly became engulfed in flames. "Bring that water," I called.

Her gaze turned from the walls to me, and she held out the pail. I pushed to my feet and grabbed it from her and splashed at the flames as gunshots sounded outside. Fear gripped my chest as my thoughts turned to the Barlows.

I pushed the pail at the girl as a manservant raced into the room with a bucket. Behind him came another man. "We ain't got no more water. We need to get to the well," one said.

"Use blankets or whatever you can find to smother it before the whole house goes up in flames," I said to them before pushing the fool girl in front of me through the door. "For the love of God, move, girl!"

She took off in a run, and I sprinted toward the front door. I had to reveal myself to save the Barlows. Perhaps if the men saw I was present, they'd cease their attack.

I threw open the door and bolted out onto the gallery to find only the Barlows and their yard workers. I looked to the lane and the retreating backs of the men. "Is everyone all right?" I asked between breaths.

"We will be." Magnus pushed past me into the house.

"What happened?" I asked. "Why did they retreat?"

"Because they came here to intimidate us, not to kill us." Mr. Barlow guided Isabella inside, and we dashed down the hallway to the library.

In a joint effort, we got the last of the flames put out. Sometime later, I collapsed to the floor in exhaustion, wheezing from smoke inhalation.

"This will take us months to repair." Magnus stood observing the smoldering walls, burned through to the framework, before taking in the charred floorboards exposing the cellar.

"Willow, your hands." Callie gently took my wrists and turned my hands over to inspect them. "You're injured."

I peered down at my hands. "It's nothing Ben can't see to," I said. "I'd best fetch my driver and return home."

"We can't have you out there alone with those madmen

roaming about. I will accompany you." Magnus strode toward the door.

"They will not harm me." I rose to my feet with Callie's assistance. "When it's light, I will see that supplies are brought to begin the repairs."

"Please gather Mrs. Armstrong's things and inform her driver she's ready," Mr. Barlow instructed a servant.

"Yes, sir." The man darted off to do as instructed.

Soon I stood outside the private enclosed carriage. "Carlos?" I said to the driver.

"Missus?" The glow of the carriage lantern gilded his dark skin gold.

"Keep your eyes sharp. We don't want to be running into trouble."

"Yessum." He took my elbow to help me in, careful of the makeshift bandages covering my hands.

As the lights of the plantation disappeared behind us, I contemplated what I'd do if we encountered the men on the road. Regardless of Isabella lending me yet another dress and quickly sponging off the soot coating my skin, I reeked of smoke, and the bandages would be a sure giveaway.

My nerves hummed until we rode up the lane to Livingston, and I released a breath. I pulled back the curtain and saw Mammy bounding down the front steps. Jimmy raced around the side of the house into the yard while other concerned folks filled the veranda.

"Missus Willie, you all right?" Jimmy's keen eyes ran over me before pausing on the bandages.

"I'm fine," I said.

"You don't luk fine." Mammy's bosom heaved as she halted beside me. "We saw smoke 'bove de trees. Masa Ben took off on horseback to see what gwine on." She gestured at a shortcut through the trees that would cut off a few minutes to the Barlows' estate.

"Some men set fire to the Barlows' place."

"What for?" Jimmy asked as the driver drove the carriage around back.

"Because they loathe the union between a black and white. 'An abomination,' I believe Mr. Carter called it." I walked up the path to the house.

"Did dey catch sight of you?" Mammy hurried to catch up.

"No, I stayed hidden," I said over my shoulder.

"Et a good thing. Masa Bowden won't be happy." Jimmy puttered along beside me.

"He hasn't returned home yet?"

"We 'spected him by now. Must have gotten caught up in town," Mammy said.

I paused; my heart thumped faster. What if the men had cornered him on the road? What if—*Calm yourself. They have no cause to harm him.*

"He be here shortly," Jimmy said, as if sensing my worry. "I sho' of et."

"I believe you're right." I climbed the steps and twisted on the landing to regard them.

"You be all right, Missus Willie?"

Looking down at him where he stood at the bottom of the stairs, I offered a tired smile, hoping to ease the wrinkles charting his brow. "I'll be fine."

He pressed his lips together and walked off into the night.

"Now you go on up to your chamber. I have your bath drawn and send Tillie to help you." Mammy gripped my elbow. "I inform Masa Ben of your hands as soon as he returns."

"Thank you."

I made the climb to my chamber. Though depleted of

energy, and that my body and lungs ached, something more significant strained my spirit. Something told me the troubles had just started for the Barlows. What if the men sought to copycat the violence that had happened in Kansas, and returned? I questioned how long Bowden and I could stand quietly by before our hands were forced.

∽ CHAPTER ∽
Fourteen

Winter of 1858

THE NIGHT TILLIE WENT INTO LABOR, BEN AND I SAT IN FRONT
of the fire in the house he'd built not far from the
quarters. Although I'd argued that there was plenty of
room for us all in the big house, he'd said he wanted something
of his own. But I often wondered if it was more because the
house held too many painful memories. The home he'd built
suited him. It was small but comfortable, something one might
expect of a bachelor. A layer of dust coated the dark furniture,
scattered newspapers, and medical books.

"You know, I could tidy the place up for you if you'd like."

He narrowed his eyes. "Don't you have enough responsibilities at your own? You needn't concern yourself with mine. I will
tend to it when I get a moment. Besides, I don't need someone
in here messing around. Everything has its place."

"How is that possible?" I swept a hand toward the books
and papers spread on a nearby stand.

"Because I know exactly where everything is." He registered a look at me that said, *don't push the matter.* "And don't you
be saying anything to Miss Rita, either."

Mammy would be fit to be tied if she walked into his place.
"Fine." I lifted my hands in surrender.

Like Ben, Bowden had been a bachelor that needed a

woman to manage his household, but at first learning to live together had proved trying. I thought of our library at the big house, and how books lined the floor-to-ceiling shelves in alphabetical order. And how Bowden used to grumble when he came home to find all the papers and ledgers on the desk in the study rearranged and stacked neatly and the surface polished and gleaming. I strove to keep the home in order and to be a wife Bowden found pride in.

If Ben had a wife, she could take care of him. When he returned from the quarters at the end of the day, a hot meal would be waiting. I worried if he'd ever find someone to spend the rest of his years with. Did it matter if he loved the woman as he did my mother? Or did people sometimes marry for companionship, too? I regarded him, thinking about approaching the subject, but then thought better of the notion.

My attention moved to the branch of an eastern redbud clawing the windowpane as the howling of the wind picked up. I had leaned back in the rocker to ponder what life held for us all when there came urgent pounding on the front door, followed by a muffled voice that drew us to our feet: "Masa Hendricks, you in dere?"

Ben glanced at me with a knitted brow before whirling and marching to the door, with me close on his heels.

"Masa Hendricks," the panicked voice called again.

Ben threw the door open to find Pete, Tillie's husband, without a coat and the wind snapping at his trousers and shirt.

Concern shone in his dark eyes. "I sorry to bother ya, Masa, but I think de baby is comin'. Tillie's hurting awful bad."

Ben clasped Pete's shoulder. "All right, you get back to her. I'll get my bag and be there shortly. Get the water heated."

"Yes, sah." He turned and raced back in the direction of the quarters.

I was wiggling into my coat when Ben shut the door and turned to me. "I could use your help," he said.

"Me?" My voice hitched. "I don't know the first thing about delivering a baby."

"I'm not asking you to deliver a baby, only for your assistance."

I didn't like the idea, but I knew there was no time to waste.

Minutes later, Ben and I fought the wind as we hurried down the path leading to the line of trees shielding his property from the view of Livingston. He made a quick stop at the sick hospital to gather clean cloths before we continued to the cabin Tillie and Pete shared with a father and his three children.

"Evenin', Joe," I said to the man sitting at the table in the three-room cabin. His daughter of five or so, and two sons some years older, sat on either side of the table. The influenza outbreak had taken their mother last year.

"Evenin', Missus," Joe said, then gestured to the children. "Go on now, say evenin' to de missus."

A chorus of "Evening, Missus" followed. I smiled at them, but the tension I felt was reflected on their faces as wails came from the next room. My abdomen clenched as I recalled the excruciating pain of labor.

"Willow, I can't have you freezing up. Get those cloths ready and bring me a basin to wash up." Ben pushed past me and strode into the next room.

My nerves hummed as I slipped Kimie's apron, which I'd retrieved from the hospital while Ben got his bag, over my head. I tied the strings with clumsy fingers.

"De loudest I ever heard de 'oman." Joe clutched the pipe between his teeth. "Got herself a set of lungs after all."

Pete came through the door, breathing heavily and carrying a bucket of water. Joe's daughter, despite being but a babe herself, jumped up and brought a pot to heat the water while one of his sons stoked the fire.

Ben's soothing words drifted out to us. "You will be just fine. Deep breaths."

After the water was heated, I filled a basin and entered the room.

Pete sat by Tillie's head, mopping pearls of sweat from her brow. She was propped in a half sitting, half lying position, with her head pressed against the wall, her eyes wide with fear. "Missus, you came?" Her voice hitched.

"I was visiting him when Pete arrived." I nodded at Ben as I walked to the stand under the single window in the room and set the basin down. "I told you when your time came, if you needed me, I'd come."

Ben rolled up his sleeves and moved to the basin.

"I awful grateful, Missus." I moved to the side of the bed and perched on the edge, taking her sweaty hand in mine. Pain glazed her eyes, pulling at her face, and with a clenched jaw, she said, "I glad you here."

I released her hand and rolled back the light gray blanket until her lower body was exposed. Wiping his hands with a cloth, Ben returned, and I switched places with him. He stared at the plank-board wall as he checked her cervix.

Tillie winced, and tears glistened on her cheeks. "I can't do dis." She peered up at Pete.

I'd made the same announcement during the hours I labored. "You will get through this. And the pain will fade from memory," I said.

"I wish Mama was here." Her hands twisted the blanket. Sara had passed on last year; died in her sleep.

"It appears this baby is determined to come tonight." Ben removed his hand. "It will be crowning soon." He fumbled through the medical bag at his feet.

"So soon?" I gawked at Ben, then at Tillie. "How long have you been having contractions?"

"De pain started dis mornin' when I was down at de river, washing." Tillie gritted her teeth and pushed her head back against the wall to brace herself.

"This morning?" I said, flabbergasted. "And you never said anything?" I recalled how, after her return from the river, she'd seemed pale and winded, but I'd chalked it up to the journey back. "You should have said something, but instead you spent the afternoon in the washhouse." I balled a fist on my hip. "Did you seek to give birth on the washhouse floor?"

Tillie shook her head. "I don't reckon so. I thought de pain would pass. Masa Hendricks said I ain't due for another few weeks."

I bit down to keep the rebuke at her foolishness on the tip of my tongue. We didn't need any more deaths at Livingston—we'd suffered enough loss. "Babies don't abide by anyone's timing—"

Tillie opened her mouth and screamed as another contraction hit.

I took the cloth from Pete and dipped it into the pitcher of tepid water on the floor by the bed before handing it back.

Tillie's contractions came harder and closer together, and soon the wail of a babe filled the cabin.

"You have a healthy boy." Ben wiped a hand over the baby's face to clear the birth matter, then gave him a quick but thorough check-over before laying him on Tillie's breasts.

Tears pooled, and my chest rose and fell with an outpouring of happiness. The babe was healthy, and I'd wanted nothing more.

After the pulsation of the umbilical cord ceased, Ben tied a small strip of cloth to the navel rope. I handed him scissors, and he cut the cord. While he attended Tillie and the afterbirth, I took the babe to cleanse the vernix from his body.

As I bathed his tiny, slippery body, I marveled at the warmth and velvety feel of his flesh. An appreciation for life and its frailty stirred in me. "I wish you had been born free," I whispered to the child. "May you grow into a man who recognizes your worth. I pray that one day you'll know freedom. And may your children and grandchildren be born into a world where slavery is only something historians write about." I wrapped the babe in a clean white blanket and kissed his forehead before handing him back to Tillie. "He's perfect. I'm delighted for you both."

Tillie beamed. "Many thanks, Missus."

Ben and I finished caring for mother and babe, collected our things, and exited the cabin. As we walked along, I looked at the glittering grains embellishing the dark velvet draped overhead and thought of Tillie's blessing. Although I'd tried to control my emotions all evening, I ached for the loss of my son. My thoughts turned to Bowden's and my future. Would life grant us a child of our own?

Ben broke through my thoughts. "You did good tonight."

"You did all right yourself," I said as we came to the fork in the path that led to the main house. "Hopefully I'll see you tomorrow?" He nodded. "All right, good night." I kissed each of his cheeks and turned to leave.

He clutched my arm. "Willow."

I hesitantly turned back. I'd noticed him contemplating me all evening, and dreaded what he was about to ask. I looked up at him.

"Are you all right?" He searched my face for answers.

Was I? No. I'd spent months pretending for those around me that I was healing from my loss—not for my sake, but theirs. The birth of Tillie's baby expanded the gap of loss in my chest.

I failed to stop the tears that came next as he gathered me into his arms. Burying my cheek into his shoulder, I sobbed, soaking up the comfort of his embrace. He allowed me to cry without the need to soothe me with words, and for that I was grateful. When I pulled back, I blotted my face and patted his chest. "Thank you."

"Get some rest. If you are up to it, I will meet you on the back veranda before the house rises for a morning coffee."

My heart danced, and the sadness departed for now. "Truly? But...your responsibilities."

"Helen's rheumatism isn't going to change in an hour of quality time spent with my favorite person."

"The only person you give a moment of your time to," I said with a laugh.

He rolled his eyes toward the heavens. "Don't start. I'm perfectly content with the way things are."

"If you say so." I waved a hand in the air and marched on toward the house, all the while contemplating what type of woman would shake him out of the complacent life he'd fooled himself into believing made him happy. I'd tired of Bowden's and Ben's whining over my intruding into his private affairs. What did men know about love, anyhow? A wife was just the thing he needed.

"I mean it, Willow!" he shouted to be heard above the wind.

I grinned. *We'll see about that!*

CHAPTER
Fifteen

"GET YOUR PAPER." THE NEWSBOY WAVED A FOLDED newspaper in the air. "Runaway arrested in Oberlin. Read all about it."

Whitney and I exited our carriage, and at the news, we regarded each other with concern. Every time I heard a fugitive had been apprehended, I feared for those who had passed through our hands.

"Here, boy, I'll take one," Whitney said.

The freckle-faced newsboy stopped and held out a grimy hand, awaiting a coin. Whitney withdrew a coin from the drawstring purse hanging from her wrist and shoved it into his hand. "Enjoy your paper, ma'am." He handed her the newspaper and bounded off. "Get your paper. Runaway…"

"Does it say who it is?" I asked as she flipped open the *Charleston Mercury* and I regarded the bold heading: *Fugitive Apprehended in Oberlin.*

It went on to say a federal marshal had captured a runaway named Henry from Kentucky, who'd taken on the alias John Price.

"Isn't Oberlin an abolitionist town?" Whitney asked.

"Yes." I thought of our contacts in nearby Wellington, a farmer and his wife.

Whitney folded the paper. "To think what one must feel to have a taste of freedom only to be plucked back into bondage. I can't begin to imagine."

How could we relate? We witnessed slavery every day; slaves working in our fields and managing our homes was the backdrop of our reality. Although sentiment for the rights of the Negroes thumped in our breasts, we couldn't begin to comprehend a life of being prodded into position or beaten into submission until your intelligence became stagnated—all because a master prohibited you from thinking for yourself. Your voice snuffed out. Hope extinguished. No, as much as we tried, all we'd witnessed, and the stories told to us, we could never truly understand the horrors and grievous treatment inflicted on the Negroes, or the discrimination shown to freed blacks. As a society, we'd become numb to the audacity that characterized our world.

Hadn't history spoken of humans' desire for supremacy over the weak? Humans had enslaved the vulnerable for thousands of years: the Greeks' preference for women and child slaves to perform domestic work; the Hebrews, Rome's gladiators killed in the arenas; their slaves worked to death while mining gold and silver. Vikings raiding Britain and auctioning off their captives. The Aboriginals. Irish immigrants. The Atlantic Slave Trade. Would I ever behold the dissolution of humanity's need to hold people in bondage?

"Willow?" Whitney snapped her fingers in front of my face.

I shook my head and focused on her frowning face.

"Are you all right? You seemed to be on a journey of your own."

"I'm fine."

"Well, if we are to meet Julia and her husband at the train station, we must make haste." Whitney popped open her parasol.

Despite my delight in seeing Julia, my mind lingered on the captured slave. He'd been free, only to be dragged back to the plantation of his master. I thought of the utter despair he had to have felt. I recalled Eliza's escape in *Uncle Tom's Cabin*, a book I'd read some years prior, and the risk she'd taken to gain her freedom. And Harriet Tubman, the Negroes' Moses, and her persistent bravery in raiding plantations to free her people. Then I thought of the lives enslaved at Livingston. Like the slave masters before me, would I, too, be remembered throughout history as another human who thirsted for power? Such depressing thoughts were suffocating.

News spread of John Price's rescue by a group of abolitionists who barged into the hotel in Wellington and found him in the attic. They returned him to Oberlin, then on to Canada. Two men named Bushnell and Langston were charged with violating the Fugitive Slave Act and would soon face the federal courts for their involvement in the incident.

"What has captured your thoughts?" Mary Grace asked as she entered my chamber with a freshly pressed gown.

I closed the book I'd been trying to read all morning; I'd turned only a page or two. "It's nothing."

She arched a brow as she walked to the bed and laid the plum taffeta gown across it. "It didn't appear to be nothing."

I stood and pulled back the curtain to look down over the grounds. "We all envision a day when slavery is part of the past, but I fear at what cost freedom will come to those I love, both black and white. Politics have divided our nation and placed invisible borders between us, and there isn't a thing we womenfolk can do about it."

"Mr. Barlow says if it continues this way, there will surely be a war."

I surmised she referred to the younger Barlow—I'd witnessed several interactions between them since his arrival a year or so ago.

I released the curtain and turned to examine her. "I can't help but notice how Magnus seeks you out when he comes to Livingston, and the humming that follows you the rest of the day."

She lowered her gaze and turned to busy herself with smoothing the fabric of the gown on the bed, but not before I saw the rosiness creeping into her cheeks. "You imagine things."

"Do I?"

"Yes."

"And I thought we were friends," I said with a huff.

"We are."

I walked to the seat. "True friendship is built on transparency and trust, no?"

"All right, yes, on Mr. Barlow's visits, we have had conversations."

"About courtship?" I sat taller, my body leaning toward her as I sought to pluck every last delicious detail from her.

"Have you lost your mind?" She feigned a scowl, foreign to her gentle spirit.

I rolled my eyes at her endeavor to mask the seriousness of their relationship. My eyes hadn't deceived me. There'd been a particular incident I'd spied on from the music room window. Magnus had come to see Bowden about obtaining bricks to replace crumbling ones in the laundry house. That day, Mary Grace strolled up the path from the river with a basket of wet linens balancing on her head. Noah and Sailor had accompanied her that morning to play in the river. They skipped along beside her, lost in happy chatter. Magnus dismounted, wearing a grand smile, and strode to greet them.

At the sight of him, Mary Grace stopped in her tracks, appearing flustered. She spun and hurried to the veranda, leaving him to gawk after her. Not to be dissuaded, he hurried forward, halting her at the door.

"Good morning, Mary Grace."

She closed her eyes and heaved a sigh before swinging to face him, resting the basket on her hip. "Good morning to you, Mr. Barlow."

"Mama." Noah clambered up the steps. "Sailor and I want to go fishing. Grandpa is busy with his tasks, and you said yesterday when your tasks were done you'd take me." Sailor looked on with anticipation.

Mary Grace wiped a hand over her brow. "I know. Perhaps this evening. I've got plenty to do today." Disappointment had shone in Noah's face. "I'm sorry. I promise I'll do my best." She tried to sound cheerful, to no avail.

"Maybe someone else can take us?" Noah brightened at the thought.

"Everyone is busy with the harvest. Fishing will have to wait."

"I could take them." Magnus rested his boot on the bottom step.

The boys spun to look at him before exchanging a glance of pure delight.

"No," Mary Grace said a bit too loudly, then softened her tone. "What I mean to say is, we appreciate your offer, but we can manage. Boys, go play with the other children."

Heads hanging and arms slack at their sides, they obeyed. Mary Grace bid Magnus a good day and entered the house. I raced back to my chair and tried to look nonchalant.

"I mean it." Mary Grace pulled my attention to the present moment. "Save your intrusive matchmaking for Mr. Hendricks."

"Fine." I put my hands up in surrender. Mary Grace could guard her heart, but Magnus had fallen in love with her.

"I almost forgot to tell you. A letter came for you and Master Bowden." She retrieved an envelope from her apron waistband.

"I meant to give it to you yesterday evening, but I found ya'll…well…indisposed."

Heat invaded my cheeks.

I recalled Mary Grace as a girl of eight or so, relating to me what occurred between lovers. She had witnessed two slaves copulating in the barn and raced to my chamber to describe the ghastly sight. After she'd finished, we sat together on my bed and made a pact that we would never disrobe in front of a man or let them touch our bodies. Nor would we giggle and carry on as shamefully as the woman had, acting as though the deed gave pleasure. I smiled at our innocence.

"I thought it best to wait for morn." Merriment danced in her eyes. Gentle spirit? I think not! My dearest friend didn't always play fair.

I snatched the letter from her outstretched hand and tore it open. It read:

My dearest brother and wife,

I hope this letter finds you well. I believe it's been far too long since I've seen you both and I've decided to come to Charleston for a visit. If I can tie up my affairs here in Texas, I hope to join you this Christmas season.

With greatest affections,

Stone

I folded the letter and held it to my heart.

"What does he say?" Mary Grace eyed me with curiosity.

I smiled. "Look who's guilty of intruding now."

She laughed. "Fine, you win. But I still want to know."

"He says he's coming to Charleston and will be joining us for Christmas." My mind raced with excitement. All thoughts of pairing up Mary Grace and Magnus were swept away by hope for the holiday season.

⌒ CHAPTER ⌒
Sixteen

THE JOY OF CHRISTMAS RANG FROM EVERY CORNER OF Livingston, and with the social season upon us, preparations for our yearly banquet had begun. The aroma of roasting venison and baking pies wafted from the kitchen house, where Mammy and Mary Grace carried on the mother and daughter tradition of weeks of cooking for the upcoming festivities.

The scent of evergreen drifted through the house from the cedar boughs, bayberry, and holly draping mantels, tables, and doorframes. In the front parlor, I hummed "Jingle Bells"—a new Christmas carol—as I balanced on a chair, decorating the tree with the dried-fruit garland Tillie held. Her son sat on a blanket on the floor, grunting, a chubby hand outstretched, trying to reach the popcorn, lemon, and orange garlands slung over a nearby chair. Weeks prior, Tillie and I had painstakingly threaded each piece.

"Sho' is a big tree," Tillie said.

I straightened and regarded the tree with satisfaction. "Isn't it perfect?"

"I wonder ef other white folkses got one so grand."

"Bowden said it takes up too much space, but he resolved in our first year of marriage to let me be in charge of the season."

Tillie laughed. "I reckon dat ain't de only thing de masa let you be in charge of."

"I've settled into marriage quite well, don't you think?"

"Got more say den most white 'omen I seed. But Masa Bowden got a special love for you lak he did his mama. Got to admire a man dat speaks of his mama so highly."

I paused and thought about what she said. "Yes, it is an admirable thing, isn't it?" I leaned forward and wrapped the garland around the tree.

"Makes me miss my mama when he git to talkin'."

I glanced at Tillie and noticed the tears pooling in her eyes. I stepped down from the chair. "I know you miss her. We all do."

She glanced at the babe. "I sho' would have loved for her to meet her grandbaby."

I bent and stroked the baby's wooly crown. "She would've loved him. He is such a delightful baby."

"Pete and Davis all de family I got now."

"You always have a family here. I've never had much family myself, but I believe that loved ones don't have to be blood, they can be grown in your heart too." The statement sounded hypocritical to my own ears. After all, family didn't keep each other in bondage.

"Sometimes, Pete gits to talkin' 'bout his pappy, and I wonder 'bout mine. Is he still alive? Mama would never speak of him. Pete says his pappy is a medicine man and dat he made de long journey across de Atlantic from Africa."

I walked to the armchair and picked up the popcorn garland and held it out for her to take an end before returning to my position on the chair. "Does he ever speak about his mother?" I asked.

"Said she died some time ago."

The thought of death soured in my mouth. When a loved one dies, it's the ones left behind who endure the void of their departure. I often thought of my son and pictured him alive and healthy, and at times when life seemed impossible, I daydreamed of him roaming in a beautiful place with my parents, happy and full of life, blond and blue-eyed, with the deep dimple etched into his cheek like the one his father bore. Believing in something more after death, and faith that one day we'd be together again, gave me the courage to endure.

A quietness fell between us, and I reached to loop the popcorn garland around the tree.

"Do you mind handing me the cookies?" I referred to the shortbread cookies cut into bell shapes and threaded with ribbons. Heels clicked across the floor, and from the corner of my eye I saw an extended hand. "Thank you." Without turning, I reached for the cookie, and froze as my fingers touched a hand much too large for Tillie's. "What..." I glanced over my shoulder, and my heart skipped. Standing beside me wearing a huge smile, his stormy gray eyes dancing with glee, was Stone Armstrong.

"What, sister, don't I get an embrace?" He spread his arms wide.

"Well...I—"

He wrapped his arms around me and swung me off the chair in a massive embrace. My feet dangled in midair. "It's great to see you." He placed a kiss on my cheek before setting me down.

Winded, I grinned at him. "You're here!"

"All six feet of me." He looked dapper in a tan suit with his gleaming dark hair combed back, not a wisp out of place. He was the sort of man whose good looks made a woman take a second glance.

"I'm delighted. We didn't know when to expect you. Bowden is in town, but should return in time for the evening meal." I gripped his hands, my heart soaring. "This will be a

Christmas to remember, indeed. We have so much to talk about. Won't you help Tillie and me finish decorating, and then we will have a seat and catch up? I want to know all about your travels."

"I am at your service." He bowed at the waist.

Davis started to cry. Tillie lifted the babe and bounced him on her hip to still his cries. "I sorry, Missus, he hungry."

"No worries, you go and take care of him. Mr. Armstrong and I will finish up here."

"Thank you, Missus." Tillie curtsied.

Stone offered her a half bow. "Pleased to make your acquaintance, miss."

She blushed. "You too, sah." Her words were barely audible. She whirled and hurried silently from the room.

Stone and I continued trimming the tree with cookies before attaching candles.

"No plans to settle down?" I said.

"None yet. There's a whole world to see out there." He gestured at the window. "With my profits from the sale of the plantation I hope to expand my travels, now that I've tied up my affairs in Texas. Enough about me. Bowden wrote that you've found your sister and that her family owns our old estate."

"Yes, you must meet her. She's lovely. We are very different, but—"

"I don't think the world could handle another Willow Armstrong." Merriment reflected in his eyes, reminding me of my husband. "Not the meek and obedient sort of woman, now, are ya?" A grin spread.

I jutted my chin out and playfully glowered at him. "And thankfully I have a husband that admires me for my opinions."

"I don't think he had a choice. The fool has been in love with you for as long as I can remember."

I smiled. "You oppose?"

"On the contrary, I think you make a great companion for him. You have a smart head on your shoulders."

His view that intelligence was not the sole territory of men was one of the things I admired in my brother-in-law. Along with his love for adventure and his mission to live a life free of the strictures placed on gentlemen of the South.

"Your business sense in running this place frees him to make amends for what eats at his soul. I've never agreed with Grandfather's and Bowden's views on slaves, or the South as a whole. It is the reason I left here to start with. Christian folk manipulating scripture in a way to make owning slaves right." He shook his head in disapproval. "One man shouldn't tell another man where he can go. It is a human's right to feel the ocean breeze on their face and to wander the beauties of the world. Each time I return here, I'm reminded of why I left."

His bold viewpoints remained as harsh reminder that Bowden and I defined what he detested about the South. Livingston was my home, my heart, and deeply intertwined with my essence. If war did come and the people of Livingston scattered, a piece of my soul would go with them—a reality I wasn't sure I could face. Despondency settled in me.

"I didn't mean to upset you." He gripped my shoulders, compassion alight in his eyes.

Intent on focusing our time together on more civil matters, I placed the last ornament. "If you don't mind, I'd prefer not to speak on the flaws of the South."

"As you wish." He inclined his head.

"Will you join me for some fresh air in the garden? Mammy makes the most delicious lemonade. Perfect tartness with a hint of honey and spiciness."

"Spiciness?" he said, intrigued.

"A secret she threatened me with."

"Oh, well, then, we can't have that." He smiled and offered an elbow. "It sounds splendid."

"What part? Spending time with me, or the lemonade?" I said, slipping my fingers into the curve of his elbow.

He chuckled. "Why, the lemonade, of course."

I laughed and said, "It's good to have you home."

The promise of a memorable Christmas season hung in the air.

᧞ CHAPTER ᧞
Seventeen

M ISS SMITH STOOD BEHIND THE COUNTER, PEERING AT A
ledger with a pencil gripped between her teeth. She
glanced up as Bowden and I walked into the general
store.

"Good afternoon, Miss Smith," I called out cheerfully.

She removed the pencil from between her teeth and regarded us over her spectacles. "Mr. and Mrs. Armstrong." An
awkward smile registered on her usually stern face.

I strode to the form showcased in the storefront window—
which held the most exquisite ruby gown I'd ever laid eyes on—
and removed my glove to touch the fabric with appreciation.

"I compliment you on your admirable marketing skills, Miss
Smith," Bowden said. "This gown caught her eye from across the
street."

Ruddiness brushed Miss Smith's pale cheeks and throat at
the compliment. "I purchased it from a designer in New York. I
thought the ladies of Charleston might enjoy it for the social season. Perhaps for the Livingston banquet. As usual, all the ladies
are whispering about the event."

"Whispers of excitement, I hope." I ran my fingers over the
wide lace cuffing the extravagant puffed three-quarter sleeves.
The holiday frock was lovelier than it had been in the catalog.

"Oh yes, an event Charlestonians look forward to." Her
shadow overtook me as she walked to the window. "Isn't the

shade extraordinary? A rare color to find, but perfect for the banquet."

"And you're not lacking in your sales pitch, either, I see." Bowden shook his head with amusement before walking off to meander around the store.

"I sent you an invitation," I said, "but I haven't received your reply. Won't you join us this year?"

"No, no. I thank you for the invite, but crowds and feigning cheerful greetings to the uppity folks of Charleston isn't my idea of enjoyment. I'd much rather spend my evening reading about Mark Antony and Cleopatra," she said. Then her eyes widened. "P-please don't take any offense. Sometimes the words come out before I can catch them."

I laughed. "No offense taken." She looked out over the busy streets, and I wondered if underneath all the frostiness lay a woman yearning for love. "Very well, but won't you join us Christmas morning for breakfast? No one should be alone on Christmas."

Uncertainty flickered on her face. "Perhaps. I'll think about it and let you know."

"I hope you do." I glanced at the gown. "It is beautiful." I turned over the price tag.

"Should I wrap it for you?"

"Not today." I walked away from the gown before weakness took over. "I'm looking for a gift for a small child. A boy. Nothing too elaborate, but something special."

"I think I may have just the thing." She marched to the back of the store, where a small selection of toys lined one shelf. Rising on tiptoes, she reached for a box of tin toy soldiers with painted red trousers and blue coats and hats. She handed me the box. I looked at the little soldiers and smiled as I thought of Sailor playing on the parlor floor.

The chime over the door signaled the arrival of a new customer. I didn't look up, my attention fastened on the gift.

"Please excuse me." Miss Smith touched my arm before moving off to greet her customer. "Hello," she called out.

I'd walked a step or two, eyeing the limited options on the shelf of toys before I stopped at the sound of Lucille's shrill voice. "Why, Willow, is that you?" Lucille said, blatantly ignoring Miss Smith's greeting.

I squeezed my eyes shut and compressed my lips before pivoting slowly to face her. "Lucille, how are you?"

At her side was not Edwin Meyer, her fiancé, but none other than Corwin Peacock, the son of a wealthy rice planter from Beaufort and the sole heir of his parents' fortune—the man with whom she was having an affair, a behavior that was no longer a rumor but a fact. I'd witnessed the pair locked in a kiss after Sunday service. Corwin peered down at her with sickening admiration, like she was a possession he'd sought to acquire all his life. Had she no shame? Parading around town as though she wasn't promised to another...why, she had more guts than a wanted man strolling into a sheriff's office.

She was adorned in tiers of ruffles and lace, and her head bobbed like a chicken's as she walked toward me. *Lucille Peacock.* I rolled the name on my tongue. Yes, satisfactorily fitting indeed.

Lucille's gaze moved from me to Bowden, who squatted beside a burlap sack of brown sugar. "Bowden! Why, I didn't even see you there." She smoothed the bodice of her gown and veered toward him.

Bowden rose and backed up slightly. "Miss Carter. How do you do?"

"Fine, thank you." She regarded him through lowered lashes, all the while leaning in to enhance the low cut of her bodice. "I wanted to ask you why I hadn't received my invitation to attend the Livingston banquet." Her exaggerated pout sickened me. She had no self-respect and, indeed, no respect for others. Her lover stood back, watching with the gaze of a lovesick buffoon.

"Well, I don't know. That's women's business." Bowden glanced at me over the top of her head, his eyes pleading for rescue.

My eyes burned into the back of her head. Why, I'd slap the flirtation right off her pretty face.

"But don't you have the final say?" she said, her voice heavy with seduction. "You're just what Livingston needed after poor Mr. Hendricks died." She rested a gloved hand on his arm. "A gentleman who's man enough to oversee the place. With women, hired hands, and a slew of niggers running the plantation, they were sure to run it into financial ruin."

Bowden straightened to his full height, and his expression turned angry. "My wife managed quite well. Her skills at running a plantation have proven to be outstanding, and give me leave to attend to affairs at the docks."

I strode to my husband's side and glared at the woman.

"Oh, Willow," she said with a smile that never went past her lips. "I'd forgotten about you."

I bet you did, you two-bit harlot. My hands balled into fists in the folds of my gown. "Are we done here?" I looked up at Bowden.

"Indeed." His voice was deep with relief as he encircled my waist with his arm.

"Good day, Lucille." I swerved to get by her gown and we said goodbye to Miss Smith.

"Why, I ought to pluck every hair from her head," I fumed as we stepped out onto the boardwalk.

Bowden nodded at passersby. "Don't let her get to you.

Women who behave in as poor taste as Miss Carter does are hardly worth getting riled up about."

He was right. I inhaled, trying to shake off the exchange with Lucille. The spirited singing of nearby carolers helped quiet my agitation. A crowd had gathered to listen to them. "Let's join them, shall we?"

"Must we?" Bowden groaned.

"What better way to rid ourselves of the stench of Lucille?" I gripped his hand and pulled him to the edge of the street, waiting for an open carriage to pass. The passengers drew my eye. Mr. Barlow tipped his hat as he, Isabella, and a woman I'd not seen before rode by with trunks strapped to the back of the carriage. The lovely blond woman, with delicate features and high cheekbones, captured my attention. She had arrived. Miss Pippa, Isabella's friend from England.

"Will we be crossing today?" Bowden asked as we stood unmoving on the edge of the street.

"Did you see her?" I gawked after the carriage.

"Mrs. Barlow's friend?"

I nodded, excitement pounding in my chest. "Wasn't she lovely?"

He frowned. "I know that look. Need I remind you—"

"No, you don't," I said, cupping his elbow as we crossed the street.

"Women," he grumbled to himself.

But I didn't care. Not even Lucille could dampen my mood or the plotting in my head.

As I joined in the contagious euphoria of the carolers, I schemed how I'd meet Miss Pippa and get a feel for her. If she was as beautiful inside as she was on the outside, I'd ensure Ben took his head out of his work long enough to notice her too.

CHAPTER
Eighteen

As Mary Grace buttoned the back of the muslin gown we had chosen for the evening, I listened to the sound of carriages arriving and the chatter of guests. In previous years I'd dreamed of the banquet and awaited it with anticipation, but guests at Livingston no longer filled me with excitement. My stomach had churned all day.

After discussions with Bowden on the wisdom of withholding Lucille's invitation, I'd grudgingly delivered an invitation myself. She had squealed and danced about before showering me with unwanted kisses. I bristled at the memory.

"All finished." Mary Grace stood back.

I turned to inspect myself in the looking glass. The blue gown nipped my waist and emphasized my cleavage, leaving me feeling exposed and uncomfortable.

"Always a vision, but I had something else in mind for the evening," Bowden said.

Surprised, I turned to find him standing on the threshold with a large white box in his hands.

"Too revealing?" I said self-consciously. "The trendsetters of Europe are wearing this design."

He strode to the bed and set the box down before opening it and peeling back the parchment inside.

My heart jumped as I caught a glimpse of the ruby fabric. "You, didn't!"

He smiled, pleased with my reaction, and removed the jewel-toned gown that had been displayed in the window of Miss Smith's general store. Mary Grace released a breath of excitement.

"But won't people think it's too extravagant in times like these?" I inched forward to touch the fabric.

"This is an evening of celebration. Besides, can't a husband spoil his wife?"

"A deed you're guilty of more often than not." I peered up at him with teary eyes. "Thank you." I rose on my toes, and he threw the dress on the bed and captured me around the waist. We shared a tender kiss.

"You'd best hurry and get into it. We don't want to keep our guests waiting." He cupped my cheek in his hand. I smiled and dabbed at my tears. "I'll be right outside." He strode to the door and left the room.

Mary Grace squealed and raced forward to feel the dress for herself. "Magnificent. I bet Queen Victoria doesn't have one so grand."

I laughed, turning for her to unbutton me. "I doubt that. She probably has so many that the appreciation for beautiful things becomes dull."

Once dressed in the new gown, I spun to look in the looking glass, and happiness strummed in my chest. The neckline rested just above my cleavage and provided a peek-a-boo effect with the modesty I preferred. Tilting my head, I ran my hands over the skirt of the gown. The richness of the color and the grand sleeves were decadent, while the simplicity of the embellishments gave the gown a classic feel. The dress would certainly receive Whitney's approval, and I delighted in the fact. I slipped on elbow-length gloves and walked from the room with a quick goodbye to Mary Grace.

Bowden was pacing the corridor and spun around at the clicking of my shoes. He froze, eyes wide, and stared in admiration. "You look as beautiful as I'd imagined."

I grinned and twirled in a full circle for his inspection, the rustling of the fabric filling me with pleasure. Bowden laughed at my delight. I walked to his side, and he held out an elbow. "Shall we? I can't wait to show off my wife to our guests." The gold flecks in his blue-green eyes gleamed in the light from the corridor chandeliers.

As we made our descent, he asked, "Are you happy, my darling?"

I smiled at the guests filtering into the foyer from the parlor. "Why do you ask?"

"I haven't seen you glow quite like tonight in some time."

"Perhaps I'm feeling loved."

A light chuckle came from him. "Is that all I have to do to make you smile?"

"It isn't just the gown. At least for the next few hours, we can put business and pressures aside. If the evening must be spent admiring you from across the room, I'll enjoy it. I find I'm the happiest when you're near."

At the bottom of the stairs, he spun me around and tipped me back, placing a light kiss on my lips for all to see before pulling me upright. Flustered, my heart racing, I felt my cheeks warm. He winked as murmurs of delight—and a few of judgment—rose around us at his disregard for proper etiquette in public.

"Good evening." He looked around at our guests with a courteous smile.

Peering up at him, I felt my love overflow. He was my security. My hope.

As guests pulled us away, I shared in small, polite conversations until a blond in a silver gown who stood off to the side, observing the people around her, caught my eye. "Will you all excuse me? There's someone I must speak to."

I wove between guests toward the blond woman, and as I approached, her face brightened. "I'm pleased you decided to come," I said.

"Mrs. Armstrong, it's a pleasure. You look stunning." Philippa Buxton's smile reflected in her blue eyes.

Soon after her arrival from England, Isabella had invited me over to formally introduce us. A private conversation between Isabella and I had included her plan to persuade her friend to attend the banquet in hopes Ben would make an appearance.

"Thank you," I said. "Please, you can call me Willow."

"Yes, let's forgo formalities, as I much prefer Pippa to Miss Buxton anyway. Much too stuffy for my liking." I recalled from our first meeting how she'd put me at ease almost right away. She had a calmness about her, and self-assurance.

As a servant carrying a tray of champagne walked by, I stopped him and retrieved two glasses. Handing her one, I moved to stand beside her as the band changed songs and couples began to dance. I overheard some ladies next to us whispering.

"Who is she? Sounds like an English accent to me."

"I heard she was staying with the Barlows. I wonder why the Armstrongs would invite her?" another said.

"From what I hear, she isn't married and therefore isn't guilty of the sins of the Barlows."

"But doesn't she condone it by befriending them?"

"Clearly, the Armstrongs had the good judgment not to invite the Barlows. Can you imagine them mingling with decent Christian folks? My condolences go out to the Armstrongs. Dealing with the Barlows as neighbors is one thing, but having to live with the guilt over Mr. Armstrong's part in bringing such ghastly concerns to us all is another. Why, Mr. Armstrong must be beside himself with regret for selling out to nigger-lovers. The last thing we need is abolitionists living amongst us."

I bristled, keeping my back to the ladies. Pippa surreptitiously placed a reassuring hand on my wrist. I wondered if anything in life riled her. Taking a lesson from a *proper* lady, not the gossips of Charleston, I released a weighted sigh, attempting to shake off the naysayers.

Whitney's voice carried from the entrance to the parlor, drawing my attention. Looking especially striking in the dove-gray dress she'd worn on her wedding day, she was conversing with Julia and Lucille. Julia, always a delight and exuding cheerful energy, laughed and carried on the chatter while Whitney tried to get a word in edgewise. Lucille glowered at Whitney, the distaste at her presence evident on a face that could be attractive if it wasn't for her personality.

Whitney's eyes met mine, and she exchanged a few words with the ladies before leaving them to head our way. She took a full look at Pippa. "Good evening."

"Whitney, I'd like you to meet Pippa. She is joining us from England."

"You don't say?" Whitney said.

"Whitney is married to Knox Tucker, a good friend of my husband's. Her sister Kimie helps us here in the quarters and at the plantation hospital."

"She has the stomach for nursing. That's admirable." Pippa's dewy flesh paled. "The sight of blood makes me squeamish."

I felt a twinge of disappointment as I considered Ben's profession. What would it mean for my hopes that she'd be the one to sweep him off his feet? "Ben—my uncle—is our doctor. He speaks highly of Kimie."

Whitney moved out of the way as a dancing couple jabbed her from behind. "She's quite taken with him as well."

"A courtship in the making?" Pippa asked.

"Oh, no," Whitney and I said together.

"My sister is way too young for Mr. Hendricks."

"An older gentleman, this uncle of yours?"

"No, Kimie is Whitney's younger sister." I pointed to Kimie in the arms of Wyatt Harris as he swung her around the dance floor, her cheeks rosy from exertion, and a look of distress on her face.

"I see," Pippa said. "Quite a pretty little thing. Is the young man her beau?"

"Hardly," Whitney said with a snort that had Pippa looking at her with shock, but then a small smile escaped as she considered her, intrigued. I recollected my similar befuddlement upon meeting Whitney for the first time, and how I'd been drawn to her unrefined ways.

Whitney continued, "Although he'd like nothing more, he has a reputation with the ladies. My sister shows no interest in him, so it makes him try that much harder. But her ambitions go much deeper than Wyatt Harris. She's eager to learn from a doctor as highly sought after as Mr. Hendricks." A gleam shone in her eyes as she looked from me to Pippa. "The ladies of Charleston would love to snare him, but so far, none has caught his eye."

"Perhaps he is happy with bachelorhood." Pippa took a sip of her champagne. "Not everyone is meant to marry."

Whitney stood taller and took a second gander at Pippa, as though her words had sung to her soul. "You aren't married?"

"No," Pippa said. "Life never granted me the opportunity."

"Have you ever been in love?" I recalled the stable boy she'd run away with, only to have cholera take him. I pondered on the similarity between Ben and Pippa's love stories, the passion and commitment to love that forced them to make unthinkable choices. She'd given up her title and family. He'd given up my mother and his child, so no reproach befell us. Were there two people more deserving of a chance at happiness?

"Oh, I was in love once, but it was a long time ago." I appreciated her willingness to be forthright over something that'd caused her immense pain. "Because of that love, I've always longed to find love again, but as I said, life hasn't given me the opportunity."

"I guess I will continue to be the anomaly," Whitney said with a shrug. "Marriage is something I never sought."

Pippa's brow pleated. "You aren't in love with your husband?"

Whitney studied Knox, where he stood a few feet away. He chuckled and clapped an elderly gentleman on the back, causing him to cough and choke on his drink. "Like friendships, there are many types of love. Of course I love him, but marriage was never a dream of mine. I aspired to be like my Aunt Em. To travel the world and make money of my own, to not be defined by a man."

Again, a look of intrigue flickered on Pippa's face. "Such women are definitely an oddity."

"I'm all right with being different." Whitney picked at the cuff of her glove.

"I, for one, admire that Whitney doesn't care what society thinks, and that she stands up for what she believes in."

"A true friendship." Pippa smiled warmly.

Across the room, Mary Grace was in her position by the punch bowl. Ben stood in front of her as she filled a glass and held it out for him. "If you will excuse me, I will be right back." I left them and hurried over to Ben before someone pulled him away.

He turned as I approached, and a broad smile spread across his face. "My darling." He kissed each of my cheeks.

"I have someone you must meet," I said, pulling him back the way I'd come.

"Who?" he said, moving reluctantly. "This isn't another one of your schemes, is it?"

"This person is a friend of the Barlows." I avoided using "she" to keep him from retreating.

"Oh?" he said.

Pippa and Whitney saw us coming. I noticed how Pippa's gaze slid past me to Ben. Her eyes widened, and a hand went to her throat. A smile danced in my heart.

"Pippa, I'd like you to meet my uncle, Benjamin Hendricks."

"H-how do you do?" Ben said politely, but his hand squeezed my elbow. I knew I'd get an earful later, but I believed Philippa Buxton was worth his rebuke.

"Quite fine." Pippa held out a hand. "I'm pleased to make your acquaintance. Your niece and Mrs. Tucker were just telling me what an accomplished doctor you are in these parts."

"I'm sure they did." Ben winced, aware he'd been set up. "How long do you plan to be in South Carolina?"

"Until spring," she said.

I spoke to Whitney with my eyes, and she nodded minutely and said, "Willow, can I speak to you privately on a matter I've meant to discuss with you?"

"Oh, well, yes. If you two will excuse us." I hurried away before either of them could stop us.

In the crowded corridor, I gripped Whitney's forearm and giggled. "We're going to be in trouble for this."

Tucking against the wall, we peeked around the corner to spy on Pippa and Ben. "Well, you may, but I'll be long gone. I'm all for helping a friend in need, but I don't understand why you insist on him finding someone. It may be as he said, he's comfortable with being alone and married to his practice."

"Nonsense." I glared up at her as she hovered above me. "Most men are unaware of what they want."

"Says who?"

"Every woman that has ever persuaded a man and won in the end."

"Are you referring to Bowden and yourself? If so, your union worked out for the both of you, but it doesn't mean it's for everyone."

I waved a hand to silence her while taking in the smile on Ben's face as Pippa chatted and laughed.

"Mission accomplished, I see," Bowden said behind us.

We jumped, and I smacked my head on Whitney's chin. She cursed under her breath, lifting fingers to rub the area. My heart thumped faster as we whirled to face him. He stood with an arched brow.

"I-I—" I said.

"No mission on my part," Whitney said.

I glowered at her. Clearing my throat, I moved to his side to slip my arm through his bent elbow. "Can't you see I was right? Look how well they are getting on." I nodded toward the pair.

"Don't seek my help when he comes looking to reprimand you when this evening is over," Bowden said, and he and Whitney shared a look of camaraderie.

"You two are impossible!" I said. "What's wrong in wanting him to find happiness?"

"Nothing. But let him decide what makes him happy."

"I second that," Whitney said.

Annoyed at Whitney and Bowden's joining forces, I turned to focus on Ben and Pippa and found them engaged in what appeared to be a more serious conversation. I presumed those moments were minutes more than Ben had given a woman in some time.

We'd see who was laughing when I proved to be right! I stormed off to get some fresh air.

CHAPTER
Nineteen

New York, 1859
Reuben, alias Oliver Evans

THE MONOTONOUS SOUND OF MY BROTHER AS HE DRONED ON and on grated at me. The offensive, yet familiar, odor of sweat and ale that I associated with him permeated the study of the townhouse I'd purchased under the alias Oliver Evans. Leaning back, I peered across the desk at Rufus, lending an ear to his chatter while focusing on his shirt, where a beating heart lay just behind a ribcage. I imagined the sound of the vital organ—*thump, thump, thump.* Then the scraping of a blade as it peeled back the flesh and sawed away the bone, exposing the throbbing organ within. My chest heaved as I imagined severing each artery, one by one.

In the hallway, the grandfather clock struck noon, and I shook my head free of the enthralling vision. I struck a match and lit the cigar clenched between my teeth, inhaling deeply before releasing a satisfying cloud in his direction. "Are you sure your plan will work?"

Rufus's intoxicated eyes gleamed as he regarded me from beneath his wide-brimmed hat he never removed—it concealed the mark of the masked men of Charleston. "The man knows what is at risk. He will do as he is told to clear his debts, or his wife will pay the consequences."

"One would think, with your distaste for the South, you would have had your fill of Negresses," I said dryly. "Who's to say he won't get to Charleston and run straight to the authorities? Your neck may not be on the line, but do remember I am a wanted man."

"You forget, brother, in your raving, you revealed my involvement in the Hendricks woman's death. If someone were to discover I'm alive, I would swing from a noose next to you," he said. "The nigger doesn't know you're a wanted man. You saw to that." Bubbles of saliva pooled in the corner of his mouth as he waved a hand at our surroundings. "Your brilliance in this last escapade of yours worked quite nicely. Reckon it's time I took a lesson from my little brother."

I studied the pathetic waste of flesh before me. As a child, I'd trembled at the sight of him, aware that he took great pleasure in torturing me. But as a man, I saw the frailty of his existence.

Kill him now. The constant humming in my head howled with the appetite for torture and suffering. It had been months since I'd felt the glorious rush from ending a life. My gaze held his throat, and I contemplated the crunching sound his windpipe would make as it collapsed beneath my fingers. The thumping in my chest sped up, and euphoria blanketed me. No! I dropped my gaze. His time would come, but for now, there was a bigger plan in motion.

Together we'd take care of Bowden and Willow Armstrong, and only then would Rufus get what he deserved. When my brother least expected it, I would make the last move and end his miserable life. There was but one person I hated more than the Armstrongs, and he sat before me. A man assumed dead in the Barry fire some years ago couldn't be murdered, and certainly wouldn't be missed. Yes, killing my brother would be the easiest of my tasks.

Until that day came, I savored an agenda vastly more satisfying. My chest rose and fell with ecstasy as I envisioned Livingston and Hendricks Enterprises lying in ruins. Death would come, and I'd paint my body in a river of blood. Glory would be mine.

"Our informant says Armstrong visits the auctions regularly. And once the time is right, and the man is in place, I will see to the rest," I said as Rufus lifted the whiskey bottle on the edge of the desk to fill his glass.

The sour taste of revulsion coated my mouth. Like our old man, he'd become a drunk, which only spoke to the weakness that lay within him. No substance or person would have power over me. I had castrated the craving embedded in the McCoy men for booze and women.

Rufus grinned. "It will give me enormous satisfaction to look into that nigger-lover Willow Armstrong's eyes when her niggers lay slaughtered, and her beloved Livingston is no more. And revisiting the delicacy of her handmaiden's body is something I've dreamed about for too long." He squirmed in his chair, appearing aroused.

A noise outside the door silenced our discussion, and I gestured for Rufus to check it out. He walked with weightless footfalls to the door and threw it open. He glanced up and down the corridor before turning back to me with a shrug and closing the door. "Ain't nobody there." He strode back to his seat and plopped down.

"Every move needs to be precisely planned out."

"It will be," he said.

"I thought I'd done that before, and she outwitted me. I won't allow it to happen again."

"Very well," he said. "We will do this your way, but remember the slave girl Mary Grace is mine."

My stomach convulsed at the notion of bedding a Negro.

Memories of my childhood rose in my mind. From my prison in the shed, I'd heard the cries of the darkies Pa and Rufus had brought to our homestead. Later they'd release me to bury the women's battered corpses. I didn't like the coloreds any more than they had, but I would never lie with one. Whereas Pa and Rufus had found pleasure in victimizing the weak, I'd found gratification in taking down the strong.

I recalled the day Rufus had thrown open the door of the shed, carrying a plate of food...

He gasps and lifts a wrist to his nose to block out the smell of my feces and urine as he stands over me. "She insists I bring the dog his food."

Mother. I yearn for her gentle touch.

Chained to the floor, I crouch with my knees drawn up to my chest, shivering from the cold, stomach burning with hunger and my tongue thick and dry from thirst. I eye the food.

He glances at the plate and laughs. "Is this what you want?"

"Please," I beg.

Grinning, he drops the plate, and its contents scatter on the ground. I scramble to grab the food and shove a handful into my mouth, the grit of dirt and the pungent taste of my waste coating my palate. Then warm liquid splatters me in the face. Using the back of my hand, I wipe the burning moisture from my eyes and look up at him. His glee nearly euphoric, he urinates on me, then every morsel of food to humiliate me.

The memory fed my hatred. *He must die!* the voice shrieked.

CHAPTER
Twenty

Amelie

THE CONVERSATION INSIDE THE ROOM CEASED. HEARING footsteps, I quietly ducked into the next room and pressed myself against the wall, my heart pounding in my ears.

Who was this Willow Armstrong Oliver mentioned? The darkness I'd glimpsed in Oliver's eyes had colored his voice as he spoke about the woman. He and his friend had declared their desire to harm her and her slaves, but why?

I'd come to know him as a passionate and fierce man. His lovemaking was the strangest I'd ever encountered, sometimes tender and gentle, other times intense and confusing, stirring unsettling memories of my past and leaving me frightened.

I was born and raised in a San Francisco whorehouse. After Mother had offered me as a young girl to her gentlemen callers, I'd sworn no man would ever touch me again. But circumstances had led me back to a life I'd tried desperately to wash away.

Where other mothers were nurturing and possessed of the maternal instinct to protect their children, mine had seen me as a way to make a profit. *"Two for the price of one,"* she'd often laughed, pulling me from the shadows of the room, her nails digging a warning into my shoulders, her body warm as she pressed me to her side. She'd peer down at me, her eyes glistening with intoxication, a forced smile on her rouge-stained lips.

The first time she'd clutched me for a suitor's inspection, I'd stood trembling. As his hands ran over me, and I relived the movements and noises between Mother and her lovers, my bladder released. Appalled, the man stepped back and Mother, seeing the puddle on the floor, struck me across the face and shoved me back into the corner. I was ten at the time.

Life had proven to be hard and miserable in my few years on Earth. I'd witnessed far more than a child ever should. My cleverness and sharp mind had gotten me through the months that came. Each time she would decide to offer me up, I would relieve myself to escape until a caller came who enjoyed such things. I was powerless to stop what happened next.

"Wipe your tears, girl." Mother regarded me with a look of disdain before walking naked to the door to let the suitor out. After the door closed behind him, she turned to me. "A woman was made for one thing, to pleasure a man." She stroked her curves and private area, pulling her bottom lip between her teeth and releasing a sound similar to the noises that had come from her earlier. "Use your God-given weapon—your body— and secure their wealth. Learn their weaknesses and secrets, and in the end, you will have ultimate control."

My insides burned from the violation. I sat curled against the headboard with the sheets tucked up under my neck, the scent of urine, sweat, and the release of the man pungent. That day I was forever changed. I learned to trust no one, least of all the woman who'd borne me. And hate for men wove into every fiber of my body. That night I would recollect as the milder of the assaults I would endure, but it was the rape that took everything from me.

In the years she prostituted me, something changed in her.

Now at six and twenty, I recognized the look as hatred. Her visitors had come to her room seeking me—the younger version of the once-striking Madeleine Rougeux.

It was around my thirteenth year that life would change.

My throat tightened, and a shiver ran through me as I recalled how the summer breeze had ruffled the curtains of the open window. The commotion from the streets of San Francisco drifted into the room: the clop of horses' hooves and the rumble of carriages, the curses and the dull smacks as two men fought, the laughter of a nightwalker as she tried to lure her prey, and a steam whistle blowing in the distance. However, it was the image of Mother and the scent of her cigar that are embedded so profoundly in my memory. Wrapped in a silk robe, she sat in a chair with her legs open to reveal the darkness between her thighs. In one hand she held the cigar, in the other a bottle of whiskey, and her eyes held a hard glint as she regarded me.

I held out a hand for the whiskey. She smiled and held the bottle out to me. I stepped forward to take it, but she snatched the bottle back, placed it to her lips, and took a large swig before her unnerving gaze returned to me.

"No, whore," she said between clenched teeth. "Tonight you will forgo the habit of numbing yourself with drink. I have a surprise for you." There was a knock on the door. "Ah, just in time."

As she walked to the door, I caught a glimpse of myself in the looking glass. My hair was styled in two plaits, and a simple cotton dress concealed the curves transforming my body. Mother had insisted I forgo the usual provocative lingerie, ensuring I resembled a child, except for the rouge aging me beyond my years.

As the door opened and he strode in, my stomach revolted. It was the man who'd robbed me of my innocence years prior.

Sweat beaded his brow and dripped into a white beard that swallowed up his face. The buttons of his cotton shirt fought against his massive belly. He was an important man—a congressman.

After taking what he'd come seeking from me, he rolled over and fell asleep with a satisfied look on his face. Mother lay on the bed, passed out from drink. Wiggling from between them, I slid off the bed. The cotton dress lay in a heap on the floor, the buttons scattered. I walked to the small closet, removed one of Mother's dresses (too large for me), and clothed my bruised body before slipping on a pair of her boots. I retrieved the congressman's felt hat, piled my waist-length curly red hair on top of my head, and pulled the hat low over my ears.

I stood over him. For a long moment, I looked at him and the naked form of my mother—the woman who had played a significant role in stealing my youth. My virtue. My innocence. A tear fell as the yearning to be loved by her swelled, but I quickly pushed it away.

She had held me down while the man crushed me beneath him. I'd called to her in desperation, but she'd stroked my hair and cooed, "It will be over soon. Be a good girl and lie still."

"No," the congressman had said between panting breaths. "I like the fight."

At his words, I slumped face-first into the bed, my tears soaking into the sheets as I fought to calm the fight within me, seizing the only control I had. I wouldn't add to his pleasure.

In a drawer under Mother's lingerie, I found the blade she kept for suitors who attempted to cheat her. Pulling open the bottom drawer, I retrieved a tin can holding all the money she had and emptied the contents. I removed the man's pocketbook from his discarded clothing.

At the bedside, I pressed the knife to his throat, barely visible between his broad shoulders and his jowls. Stirring, he blew out a weighted snore. Taken by surprise, I jerked, scraping his flesh with the blade. My heart pounded in my ears, but he never woke. Hatred bubbled within me, and before I lost courage, I made one quick swipe with the blade.

His eyes flew open. He gurgled and grabbed at his throat as the blood oozed over his fingers and melded into his white chest hairs. Fear, pain, and bewilderment flashed across his face, his body flailing as he fought against a fate deemed his from the night he had chosen to take my innocence. Then his body ceased thrashing and his hands fell away, and his lifeless eyes gazed at the ceiling.

Mother moaned and turned onto her side, revealing perfect curvy buttocks embellished with a single mole on her left hip. At one time in her life she had been beautiful, with her mane of dark hair, her blue eyes, and flawless ivory skin.

I moved to her side of the bed and let my gaze run over her. A life of fornicating with hundreds of men had given her the disease. Years of drinking had also taken its toll on her. At scarcely thirty, her face was a map of the life she had led. Soon the disease would kill her, and regardless of the torment I'd lived at her hands, I wouldn't be responsible for her death. No, she would suffer soon enough.

I wiped the blade on the sheets before slipping from the room and out into the corridor, hazy and stinking with cigar smoke, cheap perfume, and copulation. The gleeful laughter of patrons and their ladies echoed up from below, melding with the lively thumping of the piano. I slipped out unnoticed.

For the next several years I wandered from town to town, taking on the alias of Amelie Laclaire. I'd come across the last name in a newspaper clipping I'd found in the streets, and the name Amelie had sounded French enough. I hitched rides in the back of wagons and stowed away on a steamer headed to Georgia.

It was there that I met a runaway who lived in the swamps. He went by the name Big John—an African prince and medicine man. He'd trudged all the way from Alabama on a hunch that his son Pete had been sold to a plantation in South Carolina.

He found me in the backcountry, lost and near death from starvation. Lethargic and dazed, I lay on the ground, petrified, as he towered over me. He stretched as tall as the highest building in San Francisco, and he had glistening, dark flesh like that of a prized black stallion. But the way his shoulders slumped as though life had defeated him, and the emptiness in his eyes gave me pause. Hoisting me into his strong arms as though I was no more than a small child, he said in a low voice, "Ain't nothing to worry 'bout. Name's Big John." He carried me to a stolen boat and gingerly lay me down on burlap sacks of food before clambering in and rowing us deep into the swamps.

For the next year, we lived in a hut he'd built like the ones in his homeland in Africa. At night, his chanting in his mother tongue and the harmony of the swamp creatures lulled me to sleep. He taught me to fish, live off the land, and create medicines from plants and herbs. Conversations about his motherland, family, and mission to find his son revealed this ex-slave's gentle spirit.

"We can't hide out in the swamps forever," I said one evening as we sat by the fire pit inside our hut.

He crouched beside the open flame, scooping stew into a bowl he'd carved from a fallen cypress tree. Keen, dark eyes met mine over the fire as he handed the bowl to me before resting against a log and stretching out long legs. "You right," he said, the deep, soothing sound of his voice calming. "Only planned to lie low for a few weeks, till de slave catchers moved on, but den you came along, and I reckon you needed me, so I stay. Bin thinking 'bout moving on soon."

I felt a twinge of sadness. I slurped back a spoonful of stew, and it burned all the way down. I suppose I'd always known the day would come when he'd move on, but I never expected to feel a sense of utter loss. "You risk your life to find him. How do you know he is still at the plantation in Charleston? He could have been sold again. I've heard stories of how Negroes are sold off, most never seeing their families again."

"I find him, or I die trying." He stared into the coals. "He my son." The pain in his voice made my throat tight. "I his pa."

His yearning filled me with envy. If only my mother had cared for me with such passion. As for my father, I would never know which one of Mother's...or her...suitors had created me.

"Dis life ain't worth living widout him," he continued. "When de whites sold my Rita and her baby seeded by her masa's rapes, dey sold my heart wid her. After dat, de masa decided I be a good breeder, and I seeded many of chillums. Pete de boy by my second wife. I raised him. He de only good I have left in dis world."

"Tell me about her."

"Who?"

"Rita."

He sat quietly for a moment, staring into the flames before releasing a deep sigh. "She de purtiest 'oman I ever saw. Dat what I notice 'bout her first," he said with a chuckle—a sound that hadn't come from him often, and it delighted me when it did. "She had de spirit of a lion. I never forgot her, but I suppose she done found a new man and has a family of her own."

He rose, and from beneath a blanket removed a pouch before turning and presenting it to me in his outstretched hands.

"For me?"

He nodded, his dark eyes intense with anticipation.

As I took the offering, I recognized the leather scabbard of a dagger. Glancing at him, I furrowed my brow. He gestured for me to continue. I removed the blade he'd fashioned from scraps of metal in the past weeks. Intrigued, I had watched him make it, never once suspecting that he was constructing it for me. The side profile of a woman of strength, her face tilted to the stars, had been carved into the wooden handle. Tears pooled. "Thank you," I said, my voice ragged with emotion.

"I give you de African name, Otobong."

"Otobong." I rolled the name on my tongue. "What does it mean?"

"From God," he said.

I swallowed the tears building in my throat.

"You are strong in spirit. May dis dagger protect you from dose who seek to harm you."

That night marked five years and three days since I'd murdered the congressman. I recalled it because it was the next day that Big John didn't return from venturing out to obtain supplies. Three days later, I knew something was wrong and set out to find him. I waded through the alligator-infested swamps until I reached the road and made the long journey into town.

I spent the next days inquiring about him until a newspaper boy said, "Yeah, I seen him all right. He a runaway. They got him locked up in the jail until they can transport him back to his master."

When it grew dark, I crept along the outer wall of the jail and peeked into the dimly lit cells through the barred windows. Then I heard him. The light chanting in his native tongue gripped my heart. I found him sitting on the edge of a cot with his head buried in his large hands.

Lying flat on my stomach in the grass, I hissed, "Big John."

Dropping his hands, he squinted up at the window. "Dat you, Miss Amelie?"

"Yes." I cast a look over his shoulder to the sleeping officer I'd scouted out earlier, sitting with a hat shielding his face and boots propped on the desk.

He moved to the window in one quick stride and slipped his hand through the bars. I slid my hand into his, soaking in the warmth of tenderness I never thought I'd feel again. Tears spilled over my cheeks. "How are we gonna get you outta here?"

"Don't worry 'bout dat. I bin mighty worried 'bout you, out in dat swamp all by yourself wid no boat or food and thinking I done run off, leaving you." His eyes glistened.

"We need to get you outta here," I said again, reefing on the bars in frustration. "I'll find chains or a rope, and maybe we can pull these bars off."

"No," he said in a voice filled with defeat. A sound that frightened me. "Ain't no use, gal. Ef we could git dese bars off, I too big to fit through."

"We have to try." I blinked back tears of desperation and panic.

He shook his head. "Et over. In de morn, I go back to my masa. But you free. A gal lak you too smart and young to live a life on de run. Et dangerous out dere and et ain't no place for a gal. Reckon et time you put aside what hurt you so bad. Folkses will continue to do unthinkable things to each other, and we never gwine to understand why. Dey seek to shatter our spirits, but you de keeper of dat flame inside you," he said with a sad smile.

"No, I can't lose you. I won't." Determination swelled in my chest. "I will get you out." I scrambled to my feet.

"Where you gwine?" He pressed his face to the bars.

"To get you out." I raced to the front door of the jail.

When I threw open the door, the officer leaped to his feet, his face heavy with sleep. I took in the three jail cells, all empty but the one holding Big John.

"Something I can help you with, miss?" the officer said.

I closed the door behind me and walked to the room's window and drew the sun-bleached gingham curtains shut.

"Excuse me, what are you doing?" His voice hitched.

As I turned back, I looked at Big John, who stood gripping the bars of the cell, his eyes filled with concern, his expression perplexed. I swallowed hard and blocked him from my mind. What I was about to do would've been impossible if I allowed the knowledge that he was watching me take precedence in my mind.

I turned my alluring smile on the officer as I undid the top button of my dress. "Why, I saw you sitting in here all alone, and a man can get lonely cooped up in a place like this."

"No!" Big John cried, his voice agonized. He shook the bars of his cell. "Don't do dis."

The officer sent a confused glance his way but swung back to look at me as I moved closer.

Narrowing my focus to the officer, I allowed everything else in the room to fade away, blocking all sounds around me as I'd so skillfully learned to do in my life. It became only the officer and me in the room.

His eyes widened with surprise as I wiggled my arms out of the sleeves of my dress, allowing it to slip to the floor, revealing my full breasts and the curves I'd inherited from *her*. "It must get lonely here at night with nothing but the chanting of that nigger to keep you company." I jutted my chin toward Big John, a blur in my vision.

He shrugged. "It's my duty." Gray eyes trailed over my body, and he released a sigh of appreciation.

Though I'd successfully seduced him, nausea swirled in my belly. *I can't do this. No, you must.* Now that he was distracted, I glanced at the keys dangling from his belt.

I sucked in my bottom lip as I'd seen *her* do, and sashayed toward him. When I felt the heat of his closeness, I ran my fingers down his chest, playing with the brass buttons on his coat. A groan escaped him.

"Do you like what you see?" I fluttered my lashes as I'd seen *her* do.

He swallowed and bobbed his head. I felt the hardness of his manhood press against me. Pushing down the bile threatening to erupt, I unbuttoned his coat before removing his belt, and he hurried to help me. I noted the clang of the keys hitting the floor. The officer's thin lips curved in a grin almost hidden under a blond mustache bearing traces of his last meal. He smelled of garlic and sweat. Dropping his trousers, he turned me around. Gripping the edge of the desk to steady myself, I eyed the pistol lying unguarded.

His desire made the act fast, and when it was over, I laughed as flirtatiously as *she* had. He stepped back, and I turned around. He eyed my nakedness with satisfaction, as though I was a prize a man like him was usually incapable of winning.

My fingers gripped the cold metal of the pistol, and without hesitation, I swung the gun up and pointed it at him.

"What the hell?" he gasped.

"Stay where you are," I said with disgust. Keeping the gun pointed at him with surprising steadiness, I darted for my dress, and with some effort, slipped in my legs and an arm before he crept forward. "Not another muscle, or I'll paint these walls with your brain." My hard tone sounded foreign.

He froze.

I knelt by his belt, never letting my eyes leave him as I searched for the keys. My fingers touched them and I pulled, but they wouldn't budge. Frowning, I glanced down to see one key had become stuck in the floorboard. Before I could free it he lurched at me, knocking me backward. My head struck the floor, and pain radiated through my skull.

"The nigger's lover, are ya?" His spittle speckled my face as he straddled me. "Come in here thinking you can seduce me and free him."

Fear kept me silent.

He grabbed the gun where it lay next to us and yanked me up by the hair. "Sit down now!" He threw me against the desk. My hip caught the edge, and excruciating pain caused me to cry out. He swiftly pulled up his trousers and marched forward to shove me into the chair.

What have I done? It had all been for nothing. Shame oozed through me. This time, Mother hadn't forced me. No, I'd lain with the officer of my own accord. But I blamed her as much as myself. I hated her, but more than anything, I hated myself.

I heard weeping, and without looking, I knew it was Big John. I had failed to free him and disgraced myself in the process. Weighted with grief and self-loathing, I wept that day harder than I'd ever cried before. Big John had been the one person whose opinion had ever mattered to me. Our odd companionship—a slave and a whore—had meant more to me than anything had in my life.

The officer ordered me to finish dressing. "Now get out of here before you humiliate us both. If I ever see you around here again, you won't be let off so lightly."

When I sat without moving, he leaped forward and hauled me up and dragged me to the door. He threw the door open and hurled me out into the street, where I landed on my backside.

A couple walking by gawked from me to him.

"Whore has taken a liking to a nigger prisoner. Came here attempting to seduce me," he said before slamming the door.

The gentleman glowered and pulled the woman in to his

side, as though protecting her from a leper. The woman spat on me as they continued down the boardwalk.

The next day I watched from the alley as Big John was loaded into the back of a wagon. I wanted to run to him and confess my love for the man who'd been father and friend. The internal flame of a child's spirit had been snuffed out by the abuse of my childhood, but during my time with him the kindness and compassion he'd shown me had ignited my spirit. Now, as I cowered in the alley, watching, it flickered and died.

I never went back to the swamp. It would've reminded me of him and how he'd seen me for what I was…wasted goods.

I made my way to New York, and shortly after, Madame Fleurine's and my paths would cross.

In the slums of Five Points, I found odd jobs to keep the hunger pangs at bay. Corruption ran rampant in the place. Murders happened in broad daylight while the emaciated bodies of the young and the old lay in alleys and streets. Thievery and prostitution were commonplace; at first it had seemed unusually blatant, but soon it became normal to me.

When I heard about a widow seeking to hire a woman to do some mending, I thought, *How hard could it be?* I visited Mrs. Turner to inquire about the job, and to my surprise and relief, she was blind. I delivered the speech I'd fabricated on my expertise as a seamstress, and when she asked for a sample of my work, I provided her with a handkerchief I'd taken off an unsuspecting wealthy woman.

Her brow had puckered, and with experienced fingers, she studied the quality of the handkerchief. After her inspection, she'd remained silent for several unbearable moments, until she smiled, and said, "Magnificent. I see you're indeed talented."

I released the breath gripping my chest.

I found myself employed, which included room and board.

Mrs. Turner earned a living by mending for the men of the slums and sewing handkerchiefs for brothels. She had been kind to me, and periodically guilt plagued me for taking advantage of her vulnerability. But as with most things in life, I learned to shuffle such feelings into the part of my soul I'd labeled "Forgotten." It was the place where I kept the painful memories of my childhood and the image of Big John's face that night at the jail.

"You get those over to Madame Fleurine," Mrs. Turner said one day, tilting her head at the sound of my movements.

I concealed the pitiful handkerchiefs I'd sewn in the bottom of the basket, under the beautifully crafted ones she'd made. I'd never developed the necessary skills of most women, and the tedious tasks of housework, sewing, and cooking proved to be challenging.

"Yes, Mrs. Turner. I'll take them straight away."

"Good girl," she said with a smile.

Over the weeks I was in her employment, I'd skimmed coins and hid them under my mattress. I'd removed things from her home and sold them, knowing sooner or later, customers would show up with complaints about the workmanship, and I'd be out on the street again.

Survival was my greatest talent. At the time, I'd been unaware I was becoming a replica of the woman I loathed. No matter how far I'd run from *her* and my past it was always there, shaping me. On rare moments when I reflected on my start in life, I wondered if I'd ever stood a chance.

I walked through the front door of Madame Fleurine's cathouse, and the mingled scent of perfume and cigars, and the thumping of a piano and laughter, sent me reeling back to my past.

"Can I help you, miss?" A brunette woman dressed in a

yellow frock with a neckline scooped low enough to reveal most of her ample breasts strode toward me.

I stared through her, tuned in to the haunting sounds of the place. Lightheadedness enveloped me.

"Are you all right?" she asked.

I shook my head and blocked out the noise, focusing on the base of her throat. *Breathe*, I prompted myself. "Yes, I'm looking for Madame Fleurine."

"State your business. Madame is a busy woman."

I visualized what sort of busyness that meant. "Mrs. Turner sent me to deliver her sewing."

The woman eyed the basket I held out for her inspection. "Wait here." She turned and strode across the dark wooden floor to the far end of the main room. She approached a blond woman enrobed in green silks who sat at a table, writing in a ledger. The brunette whispered something to her, and she glanced in my direction before summoning me with a hand.

I made my steps quick, to not keep her waiting. The brunette took her leave as I stopped in front of the table.

"Don't dally, girl. Show me what you've brought." She held out a dainty hand accessorized with a large sapphire ring.

My heart thumped as I pulled back the fabric concealing the cloths within.

"Yes, these will do." Her intense dark eyes roved over me, and I felt myself freeze under her inspection. "You are quite striking. Are you of Irish descent?" She picked up a lock of my hair and stroked it between two fingers.

I removed myself from her grasp and shook my head.

"Do you speak?"

I nodded.

"Hmm," she said. "What happened to the other girl that used to work for Mrs. Turner?"

"She died."

Taken aback by my bluntness, she frowned, but after a moment, she stood. "What do they call you?"

"Amelie."

"Well, Amelie," she circled me, "if you ever find yourself in need of lodging and a way to make a living, do come back." She stopped in front of me.

I bristled. "No, ma'am. I will never work in a place like this."

She lifted a brow. "I see; too good for my establishment."

No, quite the opposite. I'd felt a sense of belonging when I walked through the doors. I understood what was expected in an establishment like hers, and that much hunger and need for shelter would never befall me. But I said to her, "Yes, ma'am. As I said, I will never be part of this world."

Her blues widened. "This world?" she said. "My, you're quite sure of yourself, aren't you?"

I squared my shoulders and left minutes later. As I stepped out on the front landing of the establishment, I reflected on her words and said aloud, "I will never be *her*."

Days later, I returned from making a delivery to find Mrs. Turner waiting for me.

"You are a cheat!" She was red-faced with anger.

I didn't need to hear any more to know I'd been caught.

"A supply of handkerchiefs have been returned." She dangled one, my pathetic attempt to cut straight edges and my lopsided stitches obvious to even me.

I found myself on the streets again. A week later, in the shelter I'd built with crates, I was robbed and gang-raped. Left for dead, I lay naked and battered, staring up at the night sky. My vision distorted by a swollen eye, the taste of blood on my lips, I concluded I'd been born for one purpose in life—to fulfill men's desires.

Determined to survive, I promised myself to never allow my body to be used against my will. I would mold men's emotions in the palm of my hand, and take everything from them, as they had from me.

I returned to Madame Fleurine the next day.

Seeing my condition, she pressed her lips together. "Come, let's bathe you and tend to your injuries." The warmth of her arm around my shoulders gathered tears in my throat.

Under Madame Fleurine's tutelage, I became known as the Jezebel of New York City. Men from states away arrived at the doors of the establishment she'd bequeathed to me upon her tragic death. Stories fed men's desire to lie with the woman rumored to be of striking beauty and the greatest of lovers. Skilled at heightening my suitors' sexual desires, I only gave of my body, and only as much as necessary to bleed influential gentlemen of every ounce of their wealth.

The day Oliver Evans walked into the brothel, I looked up from my position at the bar. My breath caught, and I found myself enthralled by the dark and handsome gentleman clothed in a beige tailored suit.

"Have you seen that man in here before?" I said to the bartender.

He glanced in Oliver's direction. "Don't believe so."

I frowned. Why did the man look familiar?

Oliver looked around the room until his gaze settled on me, and his tightly composed expression faltered for a brief second, a look I'd witnessed on men plenty of times. He strode to the bar and sat down several seats away. For the next few days he returned, never seeking the warmth of a woman or touching a drink, but to sit at the bar.

One evening I approached him. "What brings you in here, stranger?"

He never looked up.

"You hard of hearing?" I said.

His jaw tensed, but he maintained his composure.

"You don't require a woman to satisfy your needs?"

"Never have," he finally said.

I gulped. "Never?"

"I won't pay a woman to lie with me."

"Then why come here?"

He turned and his cold eyes regarded every inch of me. My heart beat a little faster under his examination. "Women are men's weakness. But I am a man not molded by the need for a woman."

"Really?" I said with a laugh. *You'd be the first.*

"I've heard of you," he said. "And I've come to see for myself the great seductress of New York."

"Well, here I am." I twirled, my burgundy taffeta gown swishing as I made a full circle and delivered my most winning smile. "Was it worth the trip?"

He grunted, lit a cigar, and eyed me, his expression unreadable. My inability to evoke any sign of desire in the man grew infuriating. Oliver Evans was a challenge I wouldn't back down from. Each time he came back, I worked on him.

When he finished with his business in New York he left, but he returned a year later. Evidence my endeavors had paid off.

"So, you return." My tone was silky and alluring as I lightly rested a hand on his shoulder.

He tensed before twisting to face me. "I have. But don't get your hopes up that it's you who brings me back."

"Why would I?" I said.

"Because I see the way you look at me. Like a challenge you haven't yet defeated. A man who isn't so easily manipulated." His eyes gleamed with pleasure.

"Don't flatter yourself, Mr. Evans." Inside I bristled, but I made sure not to reveal the emotions he stirred in me. "Basil," I said to the bartender, "see to it that Mr. Evans has all he needs." I looked back at him. "Enjoy your evening. Please excuse me." I turned to go, but he grabbed my arm and swung me around.

Before I could respond, he crushed me in his arms, covering my mouth with his. Hungrily he forced my lips apart, and his tongue moved inside my mouth. I felt the passion burning in him, a yearning that stirred my own.

Later we lay naked, breathless, and tucked in the sheets of my bed. Never had I experienced such ecstasy.

Over the last year, he had become my poison and I, his. However, what I'd overheard from the study gave me grave concern. What was he up to? And who were these people he sought to harm?

CHAPTER
Twenty-One

WHITNEY AND I BALANCED ON LADDERS, PLUCKING APPLES from the orchard's weighted canopy. A gentle fall breeze rustled the branches, scattering leaves and sending the odd fruit bouncing on the ground. Beneath us on a bed of fallen leaves, Evie and Sailor played, and the innocence of their happy chatter placed a smile on my face.

"When we grow up, we're gonna git married." Evie propped her doll against a rock.

"Married? Lak Missus Willow and Masa Bowden?" Sailor said.

"Yes, and we gwine to live in a big house jus' lak dem."

"I don't want no w-wife."

She scowled. "Why not?"

"'Cause I lak fishing, and Jimmy says a wife jus' gwine stop you from doing what you lak."

Whitney and I exchanged a smirk.

"So young and they have it all figured out. Marriage is a snare." She placed an apple in the basket hanging from her forearm.

"It is not," I said.

"Is too."

I placed the last apple that would fit in my basket and started my descent. "Knox is a good man," I called up to her.

"No one is disputing that," she shouted back.

"Do you not love Knox?" I asked as she joined me on the ground.

"I do, but not the same as you do Bowden." Her gaze rested on the children. "Knox has been good to us, and I know he loves me, but sometimes I think I'm incapable of love."

"That isn't true. I've seen what you sacrificed for Kimie and Jack. If that isn't love, what is it?"

"That's a different kind of love. I'm referring to the love between a man and a woman. I find I'm the most at peace when Knox is in the fields or off with Bowden. I rather enjoy being alone."

I couldn't comprehend her desire for solitude. Although I relished the quiet of the morning before the house and ground folks rose, I loved it when the house was alive with the movement and voices of the house staff, the squealing of children at play, and the melodies of the quarter folks. Whereas Whitney claimed contentment in solitude, I yearned for people and family to occupy my days. Fear of abandonment and loss of those I loved had shadowed most of my life.

"Sometimes, I feel as though I cheated Knox." She regarded me with watery eyes.

"What do you mean?"

"I feel I've been selfish. I married him because I was exhausted from caring for the twins and myself. I grew tired of responsibility. In the end, marrying him only added to the burdens forced on me before my time. Since I can remember, I've been taking care of people—nursing a sick mother, worrying if there would be enough food, or if Father would return home drunk and hurt her or me. Then Father came back, and I found out I had a brother and a sister. I wanted to save them from Father's cruelty. But, on reflection, how could I save them when I was incapable of saving myself?" Her voice shook.

I touched her arm, tears gathering in my throat. "Whitney…"

She continued. "I knew I was fond of Knox, but I had doubts that I loved him as a wife should. But I wanted so desperately for the twins to have a good father and a proper home. All things I never had. I knew I wasn't the romantic type. Women like you dote on your husbands and take pride in caring for a home, but that isn't me. I'll never be that woman. Perhaps because I've played the role of both mother and father for so long, I dream of something more. A life without the burden of endless responsibilities."

It was unconventional for women to think of a life outside of marriage and raising a family, but Whitney wasn't so easily molded into society's views on women.

She looked to the field spotted with slaves at work. "I envy them, you know."

I frowned. "The slaves?" I questioned the stability of her mind. "What in heaven's name for?"

"Not the ones that remain behind, but the ones who take their freedom, have the courage to break from a life of bondage."

"I didn't realize you hated marriage so." I failed to see the similarity between marriage and a person born into slavery.

She nodded at the children playing on the ground. "Look at Evie. She's just a child, and she speaks of marriage." She heaved a sigh. "I don't recall as a child ever thinking of my wedding day—or playing with dolls, for that matter."

I thought of my own childhood; I'd loved dolls. Caring and nurturing came easy to me, but like Whitney, I hadn't thought of marriage until Bowden moved to town. After Knox and he had humiliated me that day in the outhouse, I'd sworn off men forever. However, imagining life without him now seemed unfathomable.

"Sometimes people marry out of convenience," Whitney said.

"And you think there is happiness in that?"

"Certainly. Everyone's destiny isn't the same. What works for one doesn't necessarily work for the other."

"You are proof of that," I said, trying to lighten the mood.

She smiled, but the sadness that had overtaken her remained. "Now that the twins are capable of caring for themselves, I long to set out on an adventure."

I stiffened, my fingers tightening on the basket. "Adventure? What rubbish do you speak?"

"I've been thinking about it for a while. I want to see what is out there, and Aunt Em has suggested I come to stay with her for a while. To clear my mind and find myself."

Find herself? I bristled. Did she forget she was a woman? A man may make such a statement, but not a woman, and indeed not a married one with responsibilities. The selfishness she displayed made my chest tighten. "What is brewing in that head of yours? You aren't thinking of leaving, are you?"

When she leveled her gaze at me, I saw it in her eyes. "B-but what of Knox and the twins? You can't do that to them." *Or to me.* Panic thumped in my chest.

"Knox and I have talked about it, and he's resigned to the matter."

"But you can't leave!" My temples pulsed and fear guided the words I spewed next. "How can you be so selfish? What will people think? Not to mention what they will say about Knox. People will laugh behind his back."

Hurt flickered across her face before she shuffled it away, and with an intense gaze registered on me, she said, "I'll admit I'm rather disappointed in your reaction. You of all people."

"I don't care!" I waved a hand of dismissal at her and

marched back and forth. "I usually sit quietly through most of your antics, but not this time. You have a duty to your husband."

Whitney untied the pinafore I'd given her and thrust it at me. "I have a duty to myself first. I think it's best I take my leave before you say too much more."

"Leave then!" I gestured down the row of apple trees to the lane.

"Very well." She whirled and stomped away, apples spilling from her basket as she went.

Go, I care not! I fumed. *How dare she just pick up and leave? To abandon us all.* My core shook, and tears rimmed my eyes as I stared after her.

Later, I stood in the orchard with tears of frustration streaming down my cheeks as she rode out of Livingston. When her buggy disappeared, I crumpled to the ground and sobbed.

"Missus Willow?" a soft voice said, and I twisted to find Sailor standing next to me.

"Yes?" My voice trembled, and I quickly brushed away the tears.

He searched my face. "You all right?"

I gathered him into my arms, clinging to the comfort he brought me. *Please, don't ever leave me.* "I'm fine. You needn't worry," I pulled back and held him at arm's length. "See? Nothing to worry about."

He frowned as if he wasn't so sure.

"Let's head back." I took his hand. "Come, Evie, gather your things."

CHAPTER
Twenty-Two

GUILT OVER HOW WHITNEY AND I HAD PARTED CONTINUED TO eat at me in the weeks to come, and when Bowden returned home and mentioned he'd seen Knox and Whitney on the road heading to town, I'd frowned.

"At this time of the day?" I gripped the hat and coat he'd handed me upon entering the house.

Weariness dragged at his face. "She's to catch the evening train," he said over his shoulder as he strode down the corridor to the study.

I'd chosen not to inform Bowden of the argument we'd had because more pressing concerns controlled his days. Besides, he'd probably have considered our disagreement a trivial matter.

At his mention of Whitney leaving, I froze, panic surging. Leaving? Without as much as a goodbye? Had our years of friendship meant nothing to her? But all the while I chastised her, I felt a pang of regret. Hadn't I been just as stubborn? I should have ridden over to her place and made things right between us.

I couldn't leave things the way they were. "Take me to the station." I chased after Bowden.

He paused on the threshold of the study and swung back to face me. "What for? Surely you two have said your goodbyes. It will be night before we reach town, and I've just returned."

"Please," I begged, thrusting his hat and coat at him. "I've been horrible. Shamefully so. I must make right the dreadful things I said to her."

He closed his eyes and pressed his index finger and thumb to the bridge of his nose. "What are you talking about?"

"Some weeks back, she and I had an argument."

"And you wait until she leaves town to make it right?"

"I know." I stepped forward and gripped his arms, the ache of my regret heavy in my voice. "I beg you. If you do not, I will find someone to accompany me." Determination swelled in my chest.

He sighed and gripped my shoulders. "Very well, I will request a carriage readied. But pack an overnight bag; we will have to stay at the townhouse for the night."

I squealed and planted kiss after kiss on his lips. "Thank you."

"I wonder about this thing called love," he grumbled. "It makes you do things when you least want to."

"Isn't it grand?" I said, racing from the room.

At the staircase, I gathered the sides of my frock and darted up, the hoop of my crinoline swaying to and fro.

"You owe me," he called after me.

I smiled—my heart had steered me right when it had fallen for the mischievous Texan boy of my youth.

By the time we entered Charleston, darkness had fallen. I sat on the edge of the seat, clutching my handbag and tapping my feet repetitively on the carriage floor. "I hope we aren't too late." I sent a nervous glance at Bowden.

He turned the carriage down the last street to the station. "Wearing out the floor won't help us arrive any faster."

I scowled into the darkness, biting back the sass on the tip of my tongue. Too often, I was driven to prove my point, but I was learning silence was sometimes the most suitable option, and a gentler approach more effective than my passion of past days. After all, the anxiousness consuming me was hardly his fault, and he'd been kind enough to bring me.

We reached the station, and he had barely stopped the buggy before I stood and disembarked.

"Willow, be careful. We don't need you breaking a limb," he called after me, but I was already advancing down the boardwalk.

I pushed my way along the congested platform, taking a few knocks from passengers' satchels and suitcases. Searching faces for Whitney, my gaze paused on a woman clad in a black silk gown with auburn curls peeking out from beneath a matching hat and veil. *Whitney.* My heart leaped. I dodged trunks piled on the platform and wove through the crowd to get to her. Bowden called out to me, but I ignored him and pressed on as she started to move away.

No, wait!

"Excuse me. Sorry," I said to passengers as I elbowed my way through. When I was within reaching distance of Whitney, I grabbed her arm.

"Whitney, wait."

She turned to me, her face concealed by the veil, and tilted her head to look at my hand gripping her arm.

"Listen, I'm sorry. I was wrong. I wanted to come and apologize sooner, but I was stubborn."

She stood silent, withholding her forgiveness.

"Please, say something," I said in desperation. Tears welled, prompted by the fear that she'd leave without saying she forgave me.

She cocked her head as if to regard me with interest, and said, "I'm sorry, miss, but I'm not the one you seek."

I released her and placed a hand at my throat. "Pardon me." Heat flushed my cheeks.

"It's quite all right," she said, her voice soft and sympathetic. "I hope this Whitney is smart enough to accept such a sincere apology."

"Me too," I said, my words barely a whisper.

The woman continued down the platform, and I removed a handkerchief from my handbag and blew my nose. Heavy of heart, I spun to look behind me and smacked into someone. "Excuse me. Please accept my apologies," I said, tears of panic overtaking me.

Firm but gentle hands gripped my shoulders. "You mustn't get yourself in such a panic," my husband's husky voice soothed.

"Oh, Bowden," I sobbed, burying my face in his chest. "It's hopeless. I can't find her."

"It's only as hopeless as you make it." Pulling back and holding me at arm's length, he used a thumb to dry my tears. "When did all the common sense I admire about you take wings?" Merriment shone in his eyes.

I glowered at him. "Why would you seek to tease me at such a moment?"

"Because"—he turned me to face away from him—"See there?" His warm breath tickled my neck and I followed his finger to behold Whitney sitting on a bench outside the ticket office. "I spotted her right away, but you were in such a panic that when I called out to you, you didn't hear me."

The conductor called "All aboard" and passengers started forming lines.

"We'll lose her," Bowden said. "Come." He laced his fingers in mine, and used his body as a shield to plow through the crowd.

Through gaps in the crowd, I saw Whitney rise and step

into line. "Whitney!" I shouted, but she didn't seem to hear me. "Whitney," I called again as Bowden guided me closer.

Recognition shone on her face, and she turned her head to scan the passengers. Bowden removed his hat and waved it in the air to get her attention. Her eyes locked on him and then me. "Bowden, Willow, what are you doing here?"

Bowden released me, and I rushed forward. Caring not how she responded, I crushed her in my arms. "I'm sorry, so sorry."

She stood like the emotionless ice queen so characteristic of her, but I didn't let go. I couldn't. As stubborn as Whitney Tucker was, I too could be stubborn. I'd cling to her like a child does a parent's leg if need be, until she accepted my apology. And I resolved to do just that before I'd let her leave with the distance that had grown between us intact.

Hope buoyed as her arms encircled me, and she patted my back with the customary stiff awkwardness she demonstrated when uncomfortable. "Now release me before you make more of a spectacle," she said.

I stepped back and found her eyes misty. "I should have come sooner, but I let my stubbornness get the better of me. I behaved poorly because I didn't want you to leave. I was selfish… and scared of losing you."

I'd been so busy being upset, I'd not processed the inner struggle pulling at my soul. Did I regard people in my life as possessions to be placed neatly on a shelf? To provide me with comfort and security until the thoughts of losing them left me feeling vulnerable, scared, and alone. I did not know.

"I forgive you. Now stop blabbering," she said firmly, but a twinkle danced in her eyes.

"All right." I blew my nose and dabbed the corners of my eyes before looking up at her. "And it's all your fault."

Her mouth unhinged.

"I refer to me chasing you down and making a complete fool out of myself. Can you believe I offered a complete stranger an apology?"

Satisfaction settled on her face. "If only I could have witnessed it. What a delight that would have been."

I smiled sheepishly. "I suppose I deserved it."

"Yes, you did," she said smugly, her chin jutting.

I giggled.

"All aboard," the conductor bellowed.

"I must be going," she said.

"I shall miss you."

"And I, you."

I leaned in to embrace her, and to my utmost joy, she returned the embrace with tenderness. "No adventures without me," she whispered.

"Promise." I gave her an extra squeeze before we parted.

She hurried to slip into line with the last passengers boarding. When she stepped onto the train, she swung back and placed fingers to her lips, then held them out to me. From my position, it appeared that she was on the verge of tears, but I wondered if it was my heart longing for her to miss me as much as I'd miss her, or if she'd genuinely been welling up.

An arm encircled my waist, and without looking, I melded into Bowden's side. The scent and warmth of him consoled my melancholy heart.

My gaze followed Whitney as she walked down the aisle to find her seat. Once seated, she searched for me as the train started moving down the tracks. When our gazes met, she pressed a palm to the window, and I lifted a gloved hand and waved as tears spilled over my cheeks.

I would miss her terribly.

Captured in the loving embrace of my husband, I stood

there until the chugging of the train and its billows of smoke faded on the horizon.

"Let's get you home," Bowden said. "Maybe we'll find someone still up, as the staff wasn't expecting us."

I glanced one last time at the horizon before allowing him to lead me across the vacant platform to the carriage.

CHAPTER
Twenty-Three

Mary Grace

M AY YOU SOAR WITH NEWFOUND WINGS.
I read the script Masa Bowden had engraved into Gray's tombstone, and my eyes misted. Dropping to my knees, I paused a moment before leaning forward to brush away the soil and debris littering the stone. I placed the wildflowers I'd picked on the way up to the family plot. Today I'd accompanied Willow to the old Armstrong Plantation, and Mrs. Barlow had granted me permission to visit the cemetery.

For years, "if only" had plagued my thoughts. If only I'd sought Willow's help in liberating Gray, or suggested he and I run away together, maybe he'd be alive, and we'd have a new life in a land of promise. If only I had considered leaving Mama behind—a thought that sickened me. Maybe if I'd approached the subject of her coming with us... But as I'd reflected on such a notion, I'd understood Mama would never have left the daughter born of Olivia Hendricks's womb.

Gray had been a dreamer, and I'd laid in his arms, becoming lost in his fantasies. We had sought a life of our own, free of our masters' control. I imagined owning a piece of property with a small homestead, some cows and chickens, and a garden of my very own. I would wash the evening dishes while watching from the window as our children played in the front yard with no overseer in sight. For hours we'd indulged in hopes for a future beyond the plantation grounds, but as the sun came up and the reality of our duties to our masters returned, all thoughts of leaving Livingston faded.

I traced the words etched into the headstone with fondness for our aspirations for a brighter future. "Oh, how we dreamed."

I'd once thought happiness and a life of our own as foolish as Mama had, but I missed living inside Gray's head, and the blink of hope his notions had provided.

Lately, I'd come to consider how deeply ingrained Mama and I had become. I loved her and admired her strength and spirit, but I didn't want to become her. I wouldn't be controlled by fear as Mama was. After the rape and Gray's death, I'd spent years governed by the same fear and numbness. But something had changed in me…an awakening of sorts. Some days I became a prisoner to my love for Mama and Willow, and other days by the fear of the unknown in a foreign world. I wasn't the property of Livingston, but I may as well have been a slave. I acted and performed my daily tasks as a slave would. My daughter had been born free, but she knew the life of a slave child. All were considerations that weighed on me. Was I doing right by my children? Or did I rob them of a life and their future? Did life hold purpose for me in a world where equality didn't exist for the blacks? I was a mulatto, but the white blood I bore meant nothing. In people's eyes, I may as well have been full-blooded Negro.

As the questions and considerations had mounted, the desire for more in life pulled at my soul. In recent months, the possibility of a new existence beyond the gates of Livingston occupied my mind—a life without dreams of old. However, to venture out on my own, a free black woman alone with two children, was insanity.

"I miss you." Resting back on my heels, I breathed into the

peacefulness of the afternoon. "Noah speaks of you often, but no longer asks when you're to visit—understanding has stolen the words from his lips. Evie is growing so fast." I smiled, envisioning my daughter as love expanded in my chest. "She becomes more like Mama each day. But in her eyes I see you, and the spirit of a dreamer."

I reflected on the reason I'd needed to visit his grave. "There is something I must tell you, and I hope you can forgive me." I paused, trying to conjure the words and voice them aloud. "My heart awakens with an awareness that leaves me confused." Tears welled. "I've strived to fight off such thoughts, but I'm weakening to the matters of the heart. Am I wrong to care for him as I do?" I waited, as though expecting to hear Gray's words of wisdom rise in the afternoon breeze. And when only the knocking of a red-cockaded woodpecker perched on the ancient live oak—the graveyard's warden—answered back, I stood and placed my fingers to my lips, and touched the tombstone. "Goodbye, my love."

Strolling the path leading back to the big house, I thought of the one who captured my days. *His persistence has worn me down,* I lied to myself, to displace the guilt of caring for another besides my husband. Magnus Barlow had shown more refinement and consideration than I considered plausible for a white man toward a woman of color. Self-assured and bold in his intentions, yet respectful and attentive.

The day he'd come to see Masa Bowden there'd been a fluttering in my chest as his skin brushed mine when he passed me in the foyer. In the days since, I found myself sweeping the balcony and pausing to glance down the lane in hopes of seeing him riding up. The way he looked at me told me that he regarded me as a man does a woman; not as a white does a Negress he seeks to bed, but like a proper gentleman with the desire to court a lady. But I was no lady. He didn't know of the shame I bore.

The past summer, while the masters spent the hotter months in Charleston, I'd been working in the front garden when he'd ridden up to Livingston. Grinning, he'd leaned over his mount and held out a succulent peach, picked from the Barlows' orchard. His blue eyes had sparkled like the sun glistens upon the water, and the fondness of the memory made my heart race.

"If only I could behold that smile every day," a voice said, interrupting my reminiscing and making me jump. Magnus stood a few feet in front of me. "My apologies, I did not mean to startle you."

"I did not see you," I said without stopping. "You have a habit of showing up out of nowhere, Mr. Barlow."

He fell into step beside me. "Do I? Perhaps I should have pursued a career as a detective." He chuckled.

I glanced at him. "Did Missus Willow send you to fetch me?"

"No. I was unaware she was here. I've just returned from a ride and thought I'd take a walk along the river. Imagine my delight in seeing you."

The pattering of my heart quickened at his words. "You're too kind."

"A stroll to clear one's thoughts?"

"In a way, yes."

"Tell me of him."

I stopped. "Who?"

"The man who had the privilege of winning your heart." He turned to glance down at me.

I frowned.

"Are you not coming from visiting his grave?" He swept a hand in the direction I'd come. "I've wandered these grounds often, as I much prefer the sounds of nature to the chattering of people. In my wanderings, I noticed your husband's final resting place lies in the family plot amongst the previous masters of this estate. A gesture and risk taken by Bowden, no?"

I studied his face for any objection to laying a slave to rest amongst the whites. "Does it displease you?"

"Certainly not. From time to time, Bowden speaks of your husband with fondness and a yearning to see his face again."

I continued to walk. "Gray was a good man, and I loved him very much. We dreamed of freedom and a life of our own."

"Understandably so," he said. "It weighs the heart, the loss of a loved one. I, too, know the pain of such a loss."

Again I stopped, as did he.

A flicker of pain crossed his face as he lowered his gaze. "I was to marry some years before coming to America. An unfortunate accident took her from me."

A sense of connection forged by grief kindled in me. The death of a loved one changes a person. It carves out a piece of your heart, never to be filled again. You continue on in life because the human will to survive demands it, but the world around you is never the same. "I am sorry for your loss."

He inclined his head. "As I am for yours." When he elevated his gaze, the tenderness and love I saw in his blue eyes caught at my heart.

I looked away as fear and panic rose. I fought against the swell of emotions he had awakened. Was it madness to open my heart to another, let alone a white man?

"Did I say something that offends?" The tenderness in his voice only plagued me more.

"No, you've been most kind," I said in a morose voice.

He stilled his footsteps and took my wrist, pulling me to a stop. I flinched at his touch, but he never let go. And, oddly enough, I didn't pull away. Instead, I peered into his eyes, my heart striking in my throat.

"I am no threat to you," he said.

"It's not that. It's…"

"What? Tell me what grips the heart and makes your body tremble so." His eyes revealed his desire to understand.

The day in the field when Rufus and his men had raped me flashed through my mind. I trembled at the memory, and hugged myself to quell the tremors. "Some years back, Missus Willow and I were attacked by the overseer and his men from the Barry Plantation." My voice shook. "And…well…the men raped me."

He inhaled sharply. I searched his face for any understanding of the shame I carried like a parasite, always feeding on me. He shifted his feet and looked away.

Would he think less of me, a woman handled and broken? I hadn't wanted to be regarded in such a way, especially by him. But the need to be forthcoming had pushed me to speak of the past.

He returned his gaze to me, and compassion poured from his eyes. "I have no words. I—I…" The ache in my soul was mirrored in his eyes. "I have no words."

"There is no need for any. I wanted you to understand the reason I've regarded you with leeriness."

"Rightfully so." His voice was hard, but then softened. "I imagine it takes great courage to speak of unbearable afflictions. And I do not wish to cause you more pain. The honesty of your heart is an attribute most attractive in a woman."

Appreciation at his response heightened my sense of trust. After the rape, all men, aside from Gray, had become Rufus and his men, seeking to harm me in the way Mama had warned me about since I was small. Harm she had also suffered—which only intensified our bond as mother and daughter.

"I best get back. Missus Willow will wonder where I am." I turned to go.

"Mary Grace." His fingers touched mine.

I paused and turned to look at him. "Yes?"

"You must know I've come to care for you."

The pounding in my chest accelerated.

"I hope you will consider allowing me to visit you," he said.

I thought of Mama and the way she eyed Magnus with leeriness every time he visited Livingston. At night she knelt at her bedside in prayer, sending up requests for me to come to my senses and turn my eyes and heart from such thoughts. Mama's free time would be spent on her knees once I told her of Magnus's request. I could withhold it from her, but I'd learned at a young age that there could be no secrets from Mama. She always found out. Even when Willow had been able to convince me otherwise, it had never turned out in our favor.

"You need not answer now. Please think about it."

"I will do as you ask," I said softly.

"I await your answer." He bowed at the waist. "Good day." He turned and strode back the way I'd come.

I stood watching him, warmth swelling my heart—before Mama's taut brow and her fist-on-waist stance came to mind. I heaved a sigh and tilted my face to the heavens. "Perhaps you can tame the tiger?"

I continued down the path toward the house, contemplating how I would break the news to Mama, and conjure the courage to tell her the condition of my heart.

CHAPTER
Twenty-Four

Bowden

RYAN'S AUCTION MART HUMMED WITH THE HUNGRY excitement of purchasers. Once I had visited slave markets with the same eagerness, but in recent years, entering such establishments evoked an abundance of shame and remorse.

As I often did when attending auctions, I stood in the shadows to observe. In my hand I clutched the advertisement listing the day's stock. Another sleepless night had left me weary and questioning my decision to attend the auction. Leaning back against the high brick wall, I rested my eyes. But my ears couldn't shut out the chatter around me.

"He and his men overran the arsenal," a fellow said, annoyance in his voice.

I tensed at the reference to John Brown's recent arrest after his attack at Harpers Ferry. I had attended one of Brown's meetings and recalled the unnerving way his piercing eyes roved the crowd. How he'd rocked on his heels and spewed hatred, stoking passions and eliciting a hankering for retaliation on slave owners.

"No match for the US Marines," another man said. "Colonel Robert E. Lee and Lieutenant J.E.B. Stuart are applauded for taking the abolitionist bastard and his men out. Rumor states that they killed two of Brown's sons in the attack. The sooner he stands trial, the sooner we will be rid of the likes of him. If only we could rid the world of all abolitionists."

I eyed one of the men, recognizing him as the renter of the warehouse next to Hendricks Enterprises.

"I concur. Brown will swing from the gallows before you know it, and I intend to be there to see it."

The men's conversation shifted to other topics and my awareness traveled to the auctioneer, who stood to the side of the auction block, in what appeared to be an in-depth discussion with another man. As I studied the men they looked in my direction and, upon catching me watching them, hastily turned away. I frowned at their behavior but pushed it from my mind as someone collided with me on their way by.

I gripped the cloaked woman to keep her upright. "You all right, ma'am?"

She used a gloved hand to pull her hood closer, attempting to shelter her face. An endeavor that failed because I caught a glimpse of her hazelnut flesh and green-hued eyes.

"Are you mad? What are you doing here?" I hissed.

Her gaze flitted around us before she leaned closer and whispered, "Curiosity has gotten the better of me. Such places don't exist in England."

I pulled her into the shadows and said through gritted teeth, "This is no place for you. Does your father know you're here?"

She regarded me with the level stare of Charles Hendricks, and the stubbornness of my wife was reflected in the jutting of her chin. She pulled her arm free. "I'm a grown woman. He doesn't need to know my every move."

My jaw twitched. Oh, how I'd witnessed that same defiance before. The Hendricks women were a rare breed—not the meek and obedient type. I dipped my head and said, for her ears only, "Then you must know the kind of men slave traders are.

Free or not, they would corner you in an alley, and you would be standing on that block. One can never be too careful. Especially a woman of your parentage." I stole a look around. "Stay in the shadows and out of sight."

Concern flashed in her eyes, and she nodded as the auctioneer's voice rose and the sale began. Chains rattled as the first line of slaves were moved into position. I stood beholding the robbing of humans' fundamental rights and considered how I could have been so blinded by a system.

As a child, a black mammy had dried my tears, slaves tended our home, and their children had been my playmates. It had all seemed normal. I analyzed how society and parents wove into adolescent minds the morality of slavery. Weren't children merely victims of circumstances, without a choice of the life assigned them? Then they grow up, and although wholly competent in shaping their own decisions in life, they're so dulled by a system that they find no fault in its methods. Had I not been so? Deaf to Willow's pleas to recognize the error in my ways, I'd had to reach my own understanding, but the circumstances that prompted that still haunted me.

Gray had been a man of honor, and I'd held him in high esteem. He lived his life seeing beauty in a world saturated with pain and ugliness. The man had offered grace and forgiveness to me when I was undeserving, serving me more ably than any hired hand. After his death, I'd resolved to live each day with purpose. To look at life through his eyes and dedicate my life to honoring a man far superior to me and those around me. I sought to end the practice of slavery.

"Why do you come?" Callie whispered.

Without turning, I said, "Because it reminds me of the man I once was and the man I refuse to be again."

"But why torture yourself?"

"Whether here or out there," I nodded toward the exit, "it does not stop the cries of the past that pursue me."

She gulped, but never said another word.

The next hour passed, and I stood spectator while men dictated people's lives, selling slaves to new masters, and with each transaction an invisible grip squeezed my chest.

A slave of smaller stature, with delicate features for a man, was shoved up onto the auction block. The auctioneer began rattling off his sales chatter. "A favorite with his master. Not a mark mars his flesh. Get yourselves a look at his teeth." He pried open the man's mouth with a wooden rod. "Have you ever seen a nigger with such a fine set of teeth? He'd make a nice accompaniment to a master's bed. Or perhaps a butler or a personal driver. A man with such beauty would be the perfect embellishment atop a carriage, and he'd look mighty fine in your estate's garb." The auctioneer pulled down the slave's trousers and used his stick to prod the man's genitals for the crowd's observation. My fists balled at the gesture. Behind me, Callie gasped.

The auctioneer instructed the man to turn, giving the audience a complete view of the stock. My belly tightened and churned as the slave received the same consideration a customer seeking to purchase a horse for the Charleston races would give.

"He acts as though the man is merely a piece of artwork," Callie whispered with revulsion as the auctioneer rumbled off bids.

"And as such, he will go to the highest bidder," I said. "I've had enough. Let me walk you out." I stepped from the shadows, removed the hat from the crook of my arm, and sat it atop my head.

"Sold! To Mr. Bowden Armstrong," the auctioneer's voice boomed.

What? I gawked at him. "You're mistaken, sir," I shouted to be heard over the murmuring of the crowd. "I did not offer a bid."

"But you did. Your arm went up."

"I was merely replacing my hat."

He looked at his assistant. "Is it not so?"

"Saw it with my own eyes," the man said.

"And there you have it; my associate bears witness. An offer is an offer, and you're bound to it," the auctioneer said with a cunning grin. "I was unaware of your taste in slaves, Mr. Armstrong. Nevertheless, you're now the lucky owner of number fifty-one."

Hands clenched at my sides, I pushed my way through the crowd. Standing in front of the platform, I glared up at the auctioneer. "I will have your tongue for such slander. I do not require any more slaves, and as I said, I did not bid on this man or any other here today."

The auctioneer grinned and spread his arms wide, making a spectacle. "Are the good people of Charleston to believe that Mr. Armstrong is not a man of his word?"

My jaw clenched, and I glanced from him to his accomplice. The way he stood regarding me, as though pleased with himself, left me baffled. I pushed it from my mind and turned back to the auctioneer. "I've made myself clear," I said with purpose. "I do not require another slave."

The auctioneer stepped forward on the platform, towering over me. "The slave is yours. Now I must move on." He glanced over the crowd and broadcasted, "I won't keep the people waiting."

My patience growing thin, but aware of the murmurs around me, I said firmly and loud enough for all to hear, "You are a cheat, but to keep you from making a fool of yourself, I will give you a quarter of the price you called and nothing more." The auctioneer would not be able to accept a rate lower than the price the slave's master desired. I would end the debate and be on my way.

Again the auctioneer turned to his accomplice, and the men shared a few words. I eyed the slave on the block, and when our gazes met, I caught the plea in his eyes. I frowned.

"We will make an exception this time. It appears, in these trying times, his owner is in desperate need of the money."

Bewildered at the auctioneer's agreement to my pitiful offer, I swung my gaze back to him. "But—"

"All right, let's move on, shall we? Bring up the next one." He turned his back on me.

Grumbling under my breath, I wove through the crowd and staggered outside. As the light afternoon breeze hit me, I released the breath pressing at my chest. Removing my hat, I swiped a hand over my sweaty brow before kicking the ground. "Dammit!"

"A shady business, indeed," her soft voice said behind me.

I spun around to find Callie standing nearby. I'd forgotten about her. "Indeed." I focused on the street. "Did you come to town alone?"

"No, Magnus is at the bank, and I thought I'd take a stroll."

"Unchaperoned?" My jaw twitched with agitation at what could have transpired. "You had better curb your free-spirited ways before someone finds reason to do it for you." My tone sounded harsh to my own ears.

She turned and regarded me, looking bewildered and hurt. "It's time to take my leave and go find my brother," she said. "Good day."

"Callie," I called after her, but she hurried to put distance between us and soon disappeared around the corner of the mart. "Dammit!"

Muttering in subdued rage, I swung around and marched back to the office.

Hours later, I was still going over the accounts of Hendricks

Enterprises. The numbers were down again compared to the prior month. I rubbed my temples and peered out over the dock, where unsold cotton bales, rice, and tobacco accumulated. Our fleet of ships sat in the harbor, where they'd been moored for far too long. Captain Gillies and Captain Phillips had taken leave until operations picked up again.

A knock on the door shifted my gaze, and at the sight of the auctioneer I cursed. Scraping back my chair, I rose and strode to the door. The headache that had chased me all morning throbbed with each step.

"Did you forget something?" The auctioneer studied the office before peering up at me. A fresh shirt and pressed suit failed to conceal the lingering perfume of the prostitutes he frequently visited at Charleston's waterfront brothels.

"Do you make reference to a slave I didn't bid on?" I returned his hard gaze. "I have all the mouths I need to feed." I spotted the slave standing some feet away, his eyes downcast.

"What will your competition say when they hear of your unwillingness to pay?"

"I care not."

"I will take the matter before the courts."

"Do as you must. I won't have my hand forced. You know I didn't bid on that slave. Your shady dealings are no secret. I will not be your victim today or any other day."

His face reddened, and his spittle speckled my face. "You will pay for this. I will see everyone knows that you, Mr. Armstrong, aren't a man of your word."

"Says he who doesn't have an honest bone in his body," I said. "Your threats have no weight on me. I have a long enough standing in these parts to be known as a fair man."

The man bounced on his toes as his finger jabbed at my chest. "You will never be Charles Hendricks."

Unwilling to be cornered by the likes of him, I stood my ground. "Nor do I intend to be."

"Sir, please," a voice said.

I glanced over the head of the auctioneer to the slave, who'd stepped forward. "What is it?"

"If you don't mind me saying, I'd like to take my chances with you." His plea and his beseeching gaze left me dumbfounded.

In my peripheral vision, I glimpsed the relief that flashed on the auctioneer's face. I regarded the slave with skepticism, but the urgency in his gaze gave me pause, and I sighed. "Very well." I reached into my pocketbook, removed banknotes, and thumped them against the auctioneer's chest. "Take it and get out."

"Splendid!" The auctioneer swept a hand of triumph through the air, and without a moment's delay, strode out of the office.

I glared at his retreating back and cursed before turning my attention to the slave. "You sound like a Northerner."

"Yes, sir." The man looked me straight in the eye. "Born free as you."

My suspicion rekindled. "And how did you end up in chains?"

"Well," he said, "I was coming home from my job at the factory, and three men nabbed me on the street. Next thing I know, I wake in chains on a ship headed south."

I believed his story. It was one I'd heard too often. The injustice of the crime inflicted upon him dispelled the anger I'd felt when the auctioneer had pushed me into a corner. "For the time being, you will come home with me, and from there, I'll figure out what to do with you. As I stated to that slimy bastard," I nodded toward the door the auctioneer had taken, "I don't need another mouth to feed."

"Yes, sir." He bobbed his head eagerly.

I stepped forward and undid the ropes securing his wrists. If the man ran off, I cared little; it would save me the trouble of figuring out what to do with him. "In the meantime"—I gestured to one of the hired men—"if you could make yourself of use, I'd be obliged."

"As you wish, sir." Gratitude shone in his black eyes.

I grunted and returned to my office.

CHAPTER
Twenty-Five

Willow

F OLKS IN THE SOUTH CELEBRATED WHEN JOHN BROWN, CHARGED
with treason, murder, and insurrection, was put to death
by hanging. In the North, people viewed every Southerner
as Preston Brooks, and in the South, every Northerner became
John Brown. After his death, Brown was exalted as a hero in the
North.

In the South, threats of secession rang from taverns, mar-
ketplaces, and social gatherings, and became newspaper head-
lines as worry mounted over the Republicans attaining the White
House. Contempt for Abraham Lincoln and his ambition to run
for president cloaked the Southern states.

Months had passed since Bowden had returned home with
the man he'd purchased at the auction. His explanation of how
he'd become his master caused us both unease. Bowden had instructed Jones to keep an eye on the man claiming to be Burrell
Rawlings. Mr. Rawlings appeared genuine enough, and proved to
be a hard worker. His story pulled sympathy from the quarter
folks, and they quickly embraced him.

One afternoon I stood on the back veranda, leaning against
a column while watching folks in the work yard performing their
daily tasks. I noticed Burrell standing near the corner of an outbuilding, observing Bowden and Jones in a conversation several

feet away. Something about the way he craned his neck in an attempt to eavesdrop raised my suspicion, and I descended the stairs and trudged across the yard and around the outbuilding to approach him from behind.

"Is there something about my husband and Jones that interests you?"

He jumped and spun around, fear evident in his dark eyes. "I-I—no, ma'am. I will get back to my tasks." He whirled to dash off.

"No!" My interactions with the man had been limited, but on that day, I felt compelled to know more about him. "Do stay," I said in a gentler tone.

He froze with his back to me for several moments before turning to face me. "Is there something I can help you with?" He kept his gaze downcast, and his voice quavered.

"Tell me, Mr. Rawlings, do you have family in the North?"

"Yes, ma'am."

"Children?"

He screwed up his face, but continued to answer my questions. "No, ma'am."

I drew closer. "A wife, perhaps?"

He nodded.

"Surely she is concerned about your disappearance and has reported you missing."

"I'd guess she has, but I hold no confidence in the authorities caring to locate me."

Like him, I doubted the authorities would put much effort into locating a man missing from Five Points. They'd most likely put him down as dead from disease, murdered, or he'd set out for a chance at a better life without the burden of a wife. "How long have you been married?"

"Just over a year."

"Newlyweds," I said with enthusiasm. "How nice. Do you mind me asking what your wife's name is?"

"Rose."

"Ah, what a pretty name. I'm sure she is lovely."

The trace of a smile formed on his lips. "She is. Her skin is the prettiest you ever saw. The color of the woman I see with you."

"What woman?" I arched a brow.

"The slave woman?"

"Tillie?"

"No, the other one."

"Mary Grace?"

"Yes, I believe that is what I heard you call her."

"Your wife is a mulatto?"

"Yes, ma'am. And she is as lovely as a painting. Don't know what she saw in me." His shoulders slumped.

I regarded the handsome man before me. If his wife were the superficial sort, his looks alone would have turned her head.

"I always knew she deserved a man who would do right by her. But the fool woman loves me."

"And I can see you love her too."

He lifted his head, and I saw the pain in his eyes. "More than life itself."

"Such love is a rarity." The tension in my shoulders dissolved, and I smiled at him. "Mrs. Rawlings is lucky to have a husband that loves her so."

He dropped his head. "If only that were true."

"You are too hard on yourself," I said. Instead of prying further, I bid him a good day and returned to the house.

In the study, I sat at the desk and retrieved stationery from a drawer. Lifting a pen from its holder, I dipped it in the inkwell and began a letter.

My dearest friend,

I hope this letter finds you, Saul, and your sweet girl in good health. I wish with all my heart that I could have accompanied Bowden and your father to New York to share in the joy of her birth.

I'm writing to ask you for a favor. I request that you inquire about a Burrell Rawlings and his wife, Rose. Mr. Rawlings worked at an iron factory in Lower Manhattan and claimed to reside in Five Points. Again, I find myself with few details and request much from you.

As always, I appreciate all the help you can provide.

Sincerely,

Willow Armstrong

I folded the letter, slipped it into an envelope, and sealed it with the Armstrong family crest.

"Tillie," I called.

"Yes, Missus?"

"See to it that someone delivers this letter to Mr. Sterling, so it can go out on tomorrow's train."

She had taken the letter and turned to go when I stopped her. "Has Pete said anything about Burrell Rawlings?"

"No, Missus." She regarded me with inquisitive eyes.

"Ask him to keep his ears and eyes open and report back to me."

"I do as you ask." She curtsied.

I followed her from the room. As she walked down the corridor to the back door, I brushed away the troublesome suspicions of Mr. Rawlings and went to see if Bowden had finished up with Mr. Jones.

For now, I intended to keep my investigation into Mr. Rawlings' origins to myself. If it proved he was indeed who he claimed, then I would set my mind to the matter and ensure he and his wife were reunited.

CHAPTER
Twenty-Six

"M ISSUS." BREATHLESS, TILLIE RUSHED INTO THE MUSIC room, where I sat for afternoon tea with Callie. I glanced in her direction. "Yes, what is it?"

She held out an envelope. "Mr. Sterling brought de mail. Dere a letter from Missus Sparrow. Maybe she sends word 'bout de Rawlings fellow?"

"Yes, yes, bring it here." I waved my fingers eagerly. Regardless of any news Ruby sent, Bowden had set plans in motion to have Rawlings returned to his wife, but I tore the letter open and skimmed the script.

"What does she say?" Callie leaned forward to get a peek.

My shoulders relaxed, and I regarded her over the letter. "She says that Mr. Rawlings is who he claims. She checked into him, and all seems to be in order."

"She spoke to his wife?"

"No, she said she was unable to contact her, but others confirmed Rawlings' story."

"There you go. All is as it seems. Soon he will be returned to his wife," Callie said with satisfaction. "The poor man has been through enough. You should have seen how they prodded at him while he stood on the auction block. Why, it was ghastly and downright disgraceful." Her upturned nose curled in disgust.

"And you expected to see something different?"

"Well, no. But I suppose I wasn't prepared for the indecency of them dropping men's britches and lowering women's frocks, exposing their bodies for all to see. Not to mention the prodding and jabbing as though they were beasts being led to slaughter." Her voice quavered. "And the heartbreak as they tore families apart—why, it is something I'll never forget. To think Grandmum and Mum suffered so. Such barbarity is unfathomable." Despite her origins, Callie was as kept and as privileged as I had been. Although the Barlows had suffered their fair share of prejudice in England, and since their arrival in America, she had much to learn about the ways of the South.

"Barbarity the Hendricks family helped bring to this country," I said despondently. "We can't change the past. All we can do is continue with our united efforts."

"Agreed." She brightened, and the creases in her forehead softened. "I'm glad there's nothing to worry about with this Rawlings bloke. At least you can remove that concern from your mind." She bent forward and touched my hand.

I smiled. "I believe you're right. Trouble is the last thing we need. Our stresses only mount with the menfolk's controversies—the possibility of war and secession."

Tillie cleared her throat, and Callie and I looked at her. She stood with hands clasped in front of her and eyes downcast.

I frowned. "What is it, Tillie?"

"I...et jus' dat Pete say dis Rawlings fellow bin askin' lots of questions."

"About what?"

"'Bout de comings and goings of folkses here. And what kind of masas you all be. Always sneaking 'round, Pete say."

Callie and I shared a look. "He is a free Northerner. Perhaps he's curious, is all," I said.

"Don't know, Missus. Pete says he holds back and watches evvyone. Real creepy lak."

I considered her words. "I will have Bowden take up the matter with Jones. One can never be too cautious. Thank you, Tillie."

She curtsied and dismissed herself.

I stared after her, worry painting Mr. Rawlings as a villain sent to spy on us, but realizing the idiocy of my paranoia, I laughed. The sooner Mr. Rawlings left Livingston, the better.

"What is that look that tugs at your face?" Callie asked.

"It's nothing," I said.

"Hardly nothing," she said with a snort. "You've turned ashen."

"Have I?" I patted my cheeks. "As you are aware, the risk of outsiders at Livingston comes at a high cost. The circumstances around Bowden being forced to purchase Mr. Rawlings make me nervous. But if Ruby says all is well, I will have to believe it is so." I feigned a smile for both our sakes, but the knots tightened in my stomach. For a brief second, Reuben McCoy and his schemes came to mind, but I shook the image away. *Calm yourself, Willow,* I soothed. *Everyone is not* him *and bent on pursuing your end.*

The next morning, Bowden put Mr. Rawlings on a steamer headed for New York. We both breathed easier for it.

As we lay in bed a few nights later, I scooped into the curve of his arm.

"Willow?" Bowden said, sounding serious.

"Mmm." I lay with my eyes closed and in pure bliss, listening to the beating of his heart while soaking in the warmth of his naked chest against my cheek.

He lifted my hand and laced his fingers with mine. "I hope, in time, we will have another child."

I tensed, opening my eyes. My heart beat faster. Over the last years, we'd avoided speaking about having another child, and I'd managed to put such thoughts from my mind. To conceive a child meant the peril of facing more pain and loss. "I'm not ready," I said.

"But when?" He slipped my head from his arm and propped himself up on an elbow.

"I don't know." Tears welled. I'd expected the subject would eventually arise between us.

"Stone shows no intention of settling down, and I wish for a son to carry on the Armstrong name. With our families so small, I think it would be wise to add to it."

"But with the uncertainty in our country, do you think it's wise to want a child?" I used the same excuse I'd applied to myself for endless months. The very one I'd plotted to offer him if he came asking. Time hadn't mended my heart after the loss of my son. Most days, I merely suppressed thoughts of Little Ben.

"I won't force you to do anything you aren't ready for. But please tell me you will consider it. I wish to hear the laughter and pattering feet of our own children roaming these halls."

I heard the whisper of disappointment in his voice, and guilt and shame at my shortcomings ran rampant in me. He deserved more, but I couldn't give him what he asked. At least not now. "You aren't angry with me, are you?" I peered up at him.

He played with a lock of my hair. "No." A flicker in his expression gave me reason to believe he lied.

"In time, we will try again. I promise." I reached up to kiss him before sinking back against the pillow.

He searched my eyes for affirmation. "That's all I ask." I heard a teasing tone in his voice as he said, "Perhaps Stone is the wisest of the Armstrong men."

"How so?"

"He guarded his heart." He chuckled and blocked my hand from its playful attack. Pinning my wrist to the bed, he rolled and straddled me.

The weight of his body on mine filled me with desire. His eyes grew intense as he peered down at me and proceeded to untie the strings of my night shift. "You, my darling, become more beautiful each day."

I laughed. "Are you trying to flatter me, Mr. Armstrong?"

"Perhaps." He placed a kiss on my lips before trailing his down my neck.

My body arched and molded against his. He slipped a hand inside my gown, sending goose pimples over my flesh. My desire surged. "Bowden," I whispered.

"Mmm," he said, his voice thick.

"I love you."

He covered my mouth with his and muffled his affections.

In the heat of our passion, my ears tuned to the pounding of horses' hooves. Bowden tensed and broke away. Tilting his head toward the sound, his expression grew concerned. He scrambled to his feet and moved to the chair under the window, pulling on a shirt.

I kicked back the covers and hurried to redo the laces of my shift. "Who do you think it could be at this time of night?" I asked.

"No idea. But they are in a rush. Stay here." He marched to the door and exited.

I rose, grabbed a robe, and slipped my arms into it as I raced from our chamber. Bowden bounded down the stairs with me on his heels.

Mammy stumbled out of the parlor, sleepy-eyed and dressed in a nightcap and shift. "Et four riders, from what I can see," she said, her eyes flitting to the front windows. "And dey got a nest of wasps after dem by de sounds of et."

"Thank you, Henrietta." Bowden gripped her shoulder as his bare feet hit the floor of the foyer. He glanced back up at me and shook his head, but didn't bother scolding me for dismissing an order to stay put.

He lit a lantern before racing to the door and stepping out onto the front veranda. Mammy and I traded a worried look and followed behind him.

Bowden held the lantern high as the riders reined in their horses at the bottom of the staircase. Someone broke into a coughing spell, and my breathing stopped when I caught sight of Rawlings in chains, forced to run behind a horse. His right eye was swollen shut, and the blood from a gash on his mouth had dried, streaking his chin.

"You Armstrong?"

"I am," Bowden said.

"Name's Ardy Baxter—"

"I know who you are."

Baxter, a free black, lined his pockets by preying on his own kind.

"Well, then." He hunched over his saddle horn with a leering grin that sent chills scurrying up and down my spine. "The bes' damn nigger catcher you will ever find."

"Is that so?" Bowden cocked a brow.

"Got something that belongs to you." He yanked the rope, and Rawlings stumbled forward. "Said you sent him on an errand, and he got lost." His eyes moved from Bowden to me, and he tipped his hat. "Ma'am."

I nodded, unnerved by his chiseling stare.

"I sorry, Masa Bowden. I guess I lost my bearings," Rawlings said.

I stifled my surprise at his willingness to conceal our aid.

"Does the darkie speak the truth?" Baxter asked.

"He does." My chest tightened at the bite in his tone. "You in the business of returning slaves half dead to their owners?"

Out of the corner of my eye, I saw Jimmy entering the yard.

"I reckon we got a li'l excited in the chase. Ain't that so, boys?" he said over his shoulder.

"That's right," several said.

Baxter's grin was menacing. "The damn fool wouldn't stop. We had to 'bout run him to death."

I gritted my teeth to stifle a vile response.

"Release him at once," Bowden said.

Jimmy darted forward to help Rawlings.

"Henrietta, see to it that his wounds are tended."

"Straightaway, Masa," Mammy said.

Baxter released the rope, and I watched as Mammy and Jimmy disappeared around the corner of the house with Rawlings.

"Took me some time to figure out the nigger belonged to you. Had to ask around town till I found someone who said you recently purchased him at an auction in town."

"And I thank you," Bowden said. "State your price, and I will see you rewarded."

Baxter eyed us with suspicion and spat tobacco juice from the corner of his mouth. "Something funny about the whole matter."

I heard a low rumble in Bowden's chest, and he squared his shoulders and glared at the slave catcher. "Oh? What's that?"

"I saw no reward posted for your runaway."

My heart froze.

"Are you questioning my methods?"

"Reckon I am."

"Did your informant also state that I paid barely a fraction of the slave's worth? Or that I didn't need another mouth to feed?"

"Come upon hard times, have ya?" he said with a smirk.

"As much as the next planter. A problem we have all felt."

Baxter straightened in his saddle and took a look around. "Maybe it's nature's way of evening the score."

"Make yourself clear," Bowden said in a tone that indicated his tolerance of the man was coming to an end.

"A balancing of the scales," he said. "If there is a war, then maybe the rich can finally feel what it's like to go hungry. Maybe it's time they work their own fields. I hope ruin rains on you all."

"And if war comes, and the North succeeds in abolishing slavery, it won't only be slave owners that will lose, but you *too* will find yourself crippled of profit," Bowden said.

Baxter snarled like a rabid dog and spat on the bottom step. I crept closer to the protection of Bowden's side. Amusement flickered in Baxter's eyes. "You scared, ma'am? Or is it the darkness of my skin that causes you to tremble?"

Fire heated my veins. "It is not your skin that makes you a monster, but the vile acts of your life and the fool words that spew from your lips."

Bowden gripped my arm to silence me. "State your price and be gone."

Perhaps realizing his attempt to intimidate us had failed, the man declared his price.

"Come." Bowden clenched my elbow and led me inside.

Without a word, he retrieved the funds requested and blew past me with the rage of a bull, returning outside to pay the man.

On the threshold of the open door, I stood until the pounding of the horses' hooves grew distant. Bowden bounded down the stairs, and I chased after him as he rounded the house and marched toward the quarters.

My bare feet padded against the cool ground as I hurried to catch up with him. "Bowden, wait up."

He swung around and held the lantern aloft. "You will catch your death." He looked at my feet.

"Then we will die together." I pointed at his naked feet.

"Come, let's make haste." He gestured a hand, and I raced forward, slipped my hand in his, and we hurried to the quarters.

"Where did James take Rawlings?" Bowden questioned some menfolk sitting around an open fire, engaged in stories of the day.

"I saw dem enter James's cabin."

Bowden mumbled a thank you and pulled me in the direction of the cabin.

As we mounted the stoop, Mammy's voice drifted from inside. Inside we found Jimmy sitting in a rocker by the fireplace and Rawlings at the table, where Mammy hovered over him with a needle in hand.

"Sit still, ya fool. I 'most done," she said.

We stood back, allowing her to finish up.

"Dere. You ain't gonna be as purty as you once were, but I reckon you will heal jus' fine," she declared before looking at Bowden and shaking her head. "Fool is all yours. De thrashing dey give him save me de trouble. Gitting himself caught and putting evvyone in danger. Dey did you wrong when dey makes you buy dis one." Mammy nudged her head at Rawlings.

Bowden regarded her with a small smile. "Thank you. Now, if you will see my wife to her chamber, I will finish up here."

I started to protest, but Mammy stepped up. "Yes, Masa," she said. One glance at my bare feet, and she clucked her tongue and took my arm as though governing a child. "Land sakes, Missus Willow, what you doing wid no shoes. Bes' git you home and in bed 'fore you come down wid a bout of pneumonia." She rambled on, but as we stepped out onto the stoop, my ears tuned to Bowden's inquiry of Rawlings.

"Why do I find you back here? You should be on your way to New York by now."

"The blame lies with me. The steamer was yet to leave, and

I spotted a peddler selling trinkets, and foolishly left to purchase my wife a gift. But I hardly made it off the ship before Baxter and his men cornered me. He wouldn't take my word that I was a freed black in town visiting family. Pulled me into the shadows of a warehouse and roughed me up. When I awoke I found myself in chains again. They tied me to the back of a horse, and here I am." His shoulders slumped. "I'm right sorry for the trouble. You've been kind enough to take my word and risk reproach by returning me to my wife."

I turned to look back into the cabin, but Mammy inserted herself and closed the door before turning and leveling a look of warning at me. "Masa Bowden say bed for you."

I scowled but allowed her to pull me toward the house. "I am not a child."

"No matter how big ya git, you always be my angel gal. And de temperature is too cold for you to be gwine 'round in dose flimsy night clothes and no shoes."

"Says *she* who is in the same state," I muttered.

"Your Mammy is tough."

"And I am not?" I scoffed.

"You tough all right, but et my job to see no harm come to you."

I knew there was no use arguing with her.

In my chamber, she tucked me into bed as she had so often when I was a child, and the nostalgia of the moment filled me with a yearning for the years when the trials and afflictions of adulthood seemed distant. She had a way of calming your worries with a gentle touch or words of wisdom. Each day, as her rich contralto voice rose in song, it was a balm to all who heard it.

She peered down at me, as though trying to dissect my thoughts. Concern glimmered in her eyes, as it had the day she'd raced into my chamber when I changed from child to woman with the arrival of my first bleed. I lay splayed across my bed, weeping inconsolably, for death had indeed come for me. She clambered onto the bed next to me, and I rose and slung my arms around her neck, soaking her blouse with my troubles and tears. After hearing what troubled me so, she released a low chuckle. Insulted, I pushed back to search her face. But she swiftly stifled the laugh and dried my tears before informing me that I would live, but face the agony month after month and for years to come.

She smoothed the blankets around me. "What be troubling you, angel gal?"

"Nothing." I knew better than to try and hide my distress because, like a proficient detective, she had a way of plucking information and emotions from me I wasn't aware of at all.

She tipped her head and narrowed her eyes. "Ain't no use. Tell your ol' Mammy and see ef I can help sort et out."

"Well, it's just that Bowden desires a child."

Her fingers paused in smoothing the blankets. "And what you feeling 'bout dat?"

"I'm scared."

"Oh, angel gal." Her brow furrowed, and she lowered herself down on the edge of the bed. "Life ain't easy, dat for sho'. But you can't fear dat evvy baby gwine be born wid de trouble Li'l Masa Ben had. Your babe wasn't long for dis world 'cause de Lard need him for somepin' special. Yes, sah. And de li'l masa wouldn't want you suffering none. He'd want you to be happy."

Tears pooled as misery twisted my soul. "Sometimes I fear that God punishes me for the sins of me and my family against the folks enslaved to Livingston."

"De Lard don't work lak dat. No matter de fear Christian folkses tries to put in others," she said. "You a good woman. You do de bes' you can by de folks here. And I know ef'n you could, nobody be property of Livingston."

"You think too highly of me. You're blind to who I really am."

"Whatcha mean?"

"I'm a wicked person. I may as well be Baxter and his men."

"Dat no-good slave catcher? De black demon goes around scooping up his own kind and dragging dem back to deir masas. You ain't Baxter, and you never could be."

"I may as well be."

"You speak of your worry to be left wid nobody?"

"Yes." Tears marred my response, and I pounded the linens with a fist. "It is selfish of me, I know."

"Ef'n a war come, dere no saying what gonna happen to any of us." I saw the uncertainty in her eyes before she pushed it away. "Dat why having a babe would give you what you seek."

"But what if…"

"De babe dies again?"

I nodded.

"No use thinking lak dat, 'cause dat kind of reasoning ain't nothing but torment bent on keeping you a prisoner. Ain't no way to live. Hopes and dreams are what keeps a body alive." She gave me a comforting smile and patted my hand. "You want ol' Mammy's advice?"

"Yes."

"You jus' let nature take et time, and when de time is right, your womb will swell again." She patted the blankets and pushed to her feet. "Rest now, angel gal. Ain't no use worrying 'bout things you can't control."

"Night, Mammy."

She turned the lantern down and whispered good night before her weighted treads faded down the corridor, trailed by a sweet, hummed melody.

CHAPTER
Twenty-Seven

A MORNING RIDE LEFT ME REFRESHED BUT FAMISHED, AND UPON my return to Livingston I was eager for breakfast.

"Please see that he gets extra today. I rode him hard," I said as I handed my mount's reins to the stable hand and dismounted. I rubbed the muzzle of the gray Andalusian I'd insisted Bowden purchase at the Charleston races last year. After the horse had suffered an injury and was no longer deemed fit to race, his owner had sought to sell him. I'd begged my husband to purchase him, and I'd been right in doing so, because with Jimmy's expertise, the horse had healed remarkably. Although he'd never return to the races, he was as fine a horse as his competition.

"You can't nurture every creature back to health," Bowden had said the day at the races, only to come back some months later and admit, "You and James have done well with the horse. I'd never have thought it possible."

I smiled at the recollection as I wandered down to the kitchen house to get something to nibble on and to sit and talk to Mammy for a spell. However, upon my arrival, I found the place washed and tidied, but no sign of her or Mary Grace.

"Must be at the house," I mumbled as I scoured the shelves and counter for something to satisfy the beast within me.

Securing a small wedge of cheese, I cut a slab of bread and slathered it with butter before seeking a piece of dried meat.

Unearthing none, I took a bite of the cheese, and with a blade in hand, I left the kitchen house. Following the path to the smoke-house, I responded to the "Afternoon, Missus" that folks offered along the way. Their gazes locked on the blade I carried in front of me. I laughed, and sheepishly lowered it to my side. I suppose I looked a sight, with wisps of hair hanging in my face from the ride, cheeks stuffed with food, blade in hand, and eyes on the bounty—the smokehouse.

Inside, I cut a link of dried sausage hanging from the rafters before walking out and securing the door behind me. As I took my leave, I caught a glimpse of a human form sprawled in the grass in the lee of the back wall of the smokehouse. It was a Negro man, lying facedown and shirtless. His back was scarred with old lash wounds and an R branded his shoulder, labeling him a runner. I couldn't recall anyone at Livingston with the mark.

Keeping the knife ready, I nudged at his leg with my shoe and got no response. After prodding him a time or two, I moved in closer and dropped to my knees before struggling to turn him over. He was a brute of a man, and perhaps the tallest I'd ever seen, with flesh as dark as a starless sky.

As I rolled him over, I gasped, then gagged at the stench coming from a gaping wound in his thigh, visible through a rip in his trousers. Maggots crawled from the injury, which he'd attempted to pack and tend. Gray threads dominated his hairline and time had carved deep channels in his face. Dried blood stained the cloth he'd wound around his feet as makeshift shoes, probably constructed from his shirt. I studied the ownership brand on his palm, and couldn't place him or the mark from neighboring plantations. I believed his master a fool and unwise to blemish his property with an estate brand and identify the man as a problem-atic slave. Both practices had gradually fallen out of use.

From the corner of my eye, I caught movement and glanced over my shoulder. Jones was walking by. When he saw me, he paused and frowned. "Mrs. Armstrong, what are you doing?"

"Help me get him to the hospital."

"Him?" he said, hurrying forward.

"He is wounded."

Jones hovered over me and gagged before blocking his nose with his wrist.

"Do you recognize him?" I asked.

"No, ma'am. Don't reckon I do."

"He's marked as a runaway," I said.

Jones scanned our surroundings for prying eyes. "Best get him out of sight then."

We managed to get him half up, but I stumbled under his weight.

"The man is built like a bull," Jones wheezed.

"Hold on, I'll go fetch some help." Pushing to my feet, I hurried away.

A familiar, whistled tune drew my attention. "Jimmy!" I called out as he exited the stables.

"Ah, Missus Willie. What can I do for you today?" He grinned.

I beckoned him with a hand. "Hurry, I need your help."

His smile evaporated, and he bounded forward without a moment of hesitation. "What is et? Somepin' wrong?" Concern creased his dear face.

As he reached me, I turned and hurried back the way I'd come, and he quickened his pace to catch up. "I found a slave sprawled on the ground by the smokehouse. He's gravely wounded, and Jones and I need help getting him to Ben."

"He not from here, I take et."

"He bears a brand I'm not familiar with. He most likely isn't from around these parts."

We returned to Jones, and Jimmy dashed forward to prop himself under the man's arm. Together the men hoisted the slave up.

"Comes from good stock," Jimmy said with a groan as they marched down the path to the sick hospital with the slave's bent legs dragging behind him.

I gathered the sides of my skirt and ran ahead to warn Ben.

Reaching the hospital, I bounded up the steps and threw open the door. Kimie jumped, and the bottle of alcohol she'd been placing on a shelf shattered on the floor.

"Willow, what in heaven's name—" Ben rose from his perch on the bedside of Codjo, the plantation's potter.

I leaned on a bedpost to catch my breath. "I found a slave. He is wounded. Jimmy and Jones are on their way with him now."

"Kimie, prepare the table." Ben waved a hand at the examination table before walking to a shelf and retrieving fresh bandages. He was calling out orders to Kimie while lining a tray with required instruments when Jones and Jimmy clambered up the steps.

"Get him on the table," Ben said.

Once the slave lay on the table, Jones and Jimmy stepped back.

"All right, thank you, gentlemen. I need room to work, and this place can barely fit a few patients and Kimie and I."

I stood to the side as the men hurried from the room and closed the door behind them. Folks strode by and cast curious glances through the windows.

As Ben and Kimie worked to clean the wound, I stayed back to give them space. The sick hospital held but two beds, and Codjo lay sleeping in one. "When do you expect him to be back on his feet?" I strode to Codjo's bedside and adjusted the sheet to cover his bare shoulder.

"The tumor is only a small sign. I believe the disease has spread to his vital organs. I've done all I can do. Now it's up to the Almighty if He will take him or not," Ben said over his shoulder.

I covered the man's hand with mine, regarding the hollows in the once full cheeks and listening to his ragged breathing. Last spring, Bowden and I had purchased him at an auction in New Orleans. The man was half dead as he stood on the auction block, looking like he cared little of what became of him. The urge to add some quality to what was left of his life had pressed me to buy him. Other purchasers had eyed us with suspicion and whispered behind their hands at our foolhardiness in purchasing the walking dead. In the months since his arrival, with Ben's care and proper nourishment, he had started to thrive, until he'd recently taken a turn for the worse.

"That should do for now," Ben said. "We'll have to keep a close watch on him, that he doesn't open the wound. Now we must get the fever down and hope that he awakens to tell us who he is."

"Let's hope no slave catcher or his master tracks him here," I said, joining Kimie and Ben.

Ben wrapped the slave's thigh with fresh bandages. "Kimie, if you don't mind, will you go and fetch someone to help me get him into the bed."

"Yes, Dr. Hendricks." Kimie hurried to the door and was gone before we could barely blink.

Ben peered after her.

"She is a godsend, isn't she?"

He broke his gaze to look at me. "Indeed, she is."

"Tell me," I said, distracting myself with the unnecessary tidying of items on a shelf. "I couldn't help but notice in recent months that you and Miss Pippa engage in afternoon rides." I kept my back to him to avoid encountering his disapproving gaze. Only a clod would miss the budding relationship between them, and I had delighted in spying on them from behind the drapes. Pippa's light chatter and infectious laughter would leave me bursting with happiness as Ben helped her onto her mount, a soft expression on his face. Call me a romantic, or an interloper, it didn't matter. I'd been right, and Whitney and Bowden could eat their words. I smiled, reflecting on the Christmas banquet some years ago, before yearning to see Whitney again took precedence. I longed to find an escape from responsibilities and linger a moment or two in the madness that often blossomed in her head.

"I enjoy her company," he said.

"As she does yours." I turned to face him. "So, is there anything more you'd like to share?" I had learned that getting any information from my father was like asking an animal to speak, and I wondered why he relished making me suffer so.

"I'm uncertain where you come by such intrusiveness into others' affairs," he said, lips twitching with a smirk.

I scowled. "Is it so wrong for a daughter to want to see her father happy? Should I not have an opinion of a woman who has caught his eye?"

"Of course," he said with amusement, crossing his arms and leaning back on the edge of the room's small desk. "Am I to assume I have no choice but to hear these opinions?"

I smiled. "I approve wholeheartedly of your choice. Miss Pippa is genuine and lovely. All the traits I'd imagined you'd seek in a wife."

"Wife?" He straightened. "Aren't you getting ahead of yourself?"

"Perhaps." I shrugged, and my mind moved to another thought. "Have you stolen a kiss?"

He lifted a brow. "And why would I reveal such things? Have you forgotten all manners?"

I released a huff and moved to stand in front of him. "On the contrary. I'm invested, is all. Say you and Pippa were to marry. She would become my stepmother, and it is only fitting that I would be interested in knowing about the relationship developing between you and her."

He smoothed back a lock of hair that routinely slipped over his forehead and sighed. "All right, yes, my darling daughter, I care very much for Pippa."

I squealed and crushed him in a hug. "Splendid. I just knew she was the one."

He hugged me back and kissed the top of my head. "You may have got this one right. But don't expect me to allow you to continue to pry into my affairs in the future."

I stood back, grinning, and crossed my heart in a promise. "I swear."

"That's hard to believe," he said with a laugh as the door opened, and the weaver's husband and Kimie entered.

After the runaway was settled into the bed, Kimie and I covered him with blankets, and soon after I left, with instructions to summon me when he woke.

In an armchair in the parlor, I read a short story in an issue of *Atlantic Monthly* titled *A Modern Cinderella: or, The Little Old Shoe* by Louisa May Alcott. I considered the knowledge of the writer's abolitionist parents and the family's efforts in the Underground Railroad. Would future written works tell of her experiences, or perhaps childhood memories? I sat engrossed in her words until my lids grew heavy and I dozed off, only to awaken to a gentle nudge some hours later.

"He is awake." Kimie peered down at me.

I laid the magazine aside and retrieved a shawl before following her to the sick hospital. I found the runaway propped up against pillows and eyeing us warily.

"Hello," I said. "It's good to see you've awakened." I walked to his bedside, where Ben sat offering him spoonfuls of broth. Pulling up a chair, I sat. "You have nothing to fear. You're safe here."

He stared at me, not as a man seeking to flee, but as someone exhausted beyond measure. "You don't seek to turn me in?" He frowned, perplexed.

"No," I said. "My name is Willow Armstrong. Can you tell me where you come from?"

"I am a prince of de Yoruba people. Taken from my home in West Africa along wid many others from my village and surrounding villages. Held prisoner by too many white masas. De last one from North Carolina." His voice was deep, and unyielding pride arched back strong shoulders while years of slavery kept his eyes from meeting mine.

"You've traveled far. What do they call you?"

"In my country, dey call me Ojore." He held his head high. Then his tone grew bitter. "In dis country dey call me John."

"Why come deeper south when freedom lies in the opposite direction?" Ben asked.

"I seek my boy."

"A son," I said. "And you believe him to be in Charleston?"

"Yessum." He slurped back another mouthful of broth. "I lost track of him for a few years, but last I knowed he sold to dis plantation here."

I straightened. "To Livingston?"

"Yessum."

"What's his name?"

"His name is Pete."

"Tillie's Pete?" I shared a glance with Ben.

He shrugged. "How old would your son be?"

"Twenty, or one and twenty, I reckon," he said, hope alight in his eyes.

"We do have a young man by that name living here. He is married to my handmaiden."

I sent Kimie to fetch Pete, requesting she say nothing about why, and she hurried to do as instructed. A short time later, Pete and Kimie entered, and he froze in his tracks just inside the door.

The wounded slave gasped, and a low moan rumbled in his chest.

"Pappy?" Pete gasped. "Dat you?"

"My boy." The slave's voice was thick with tears before he rattled off in a dialect I recognized as Lukumi. In years past, I'd encountered a slave passing through our hands who'd spoken the same dialect.

Pete bolted across the room and flung his arms around his father's neck.

I sat back in astonishment. I wouldn't have connected the bulky John and the lanky Pete as father and son. My chest swelled with glee at the reunion.

I glanced up at Kimie as she placed a hand on my shoulder. She smiled happily down at me as tears dropped on her cheeks, rosy from running. I covered her hand with mine.

"Blessed be Orisha to bring you to my arms one last time," John breathed, but Pete tensed, and his father cast a worried glance at us. "Apologies. In my excitement, I forgit de forbiddance of gods foreign to dis land."

"A glorious day, indeed," I said, brushing off behavior that would be punishable by most.

"Dat et is, Missus Armstrong. Dat et is." Pete beamed. "Pappy, I got me a wife and a boy."

Tears streaked John's face. "Dat mighty fine, son."

"I feel there's much cause to celebrate. After all, this is a rare and seemingly impossible reunion." My mind spun to the reunion between Jimmy and Ruby, and my heart swelled at the memory. "I am curious about how you found out where Pete had gone. I mean, it's been so many years, has it not?"

"Slave folkses talk," he said. "After my boy was sold de first time, I asked 'round 'bout where de masa sold him. Slave tell me he was sold to a white man in town. When I got a chance to go in to town, I go, and found dat man's house. Only my boy warn't dere. De butler said he had bin, but de masa sold him to a plantation in Georgia. Before I got a chance to find him, dey done sold me to another masa, but I still hold on to hope, and when I got de chance, I set out to find him. And I 'most find him, but dey found me and drag me back. Spent de next years trying to find a chance to run again, but already marked a runner dey watch me close. When I got free, I made et back to de plantation. But dey told me he was sold to an estate in Charleston. I bin asking slave folkses along de way, and deir help led me here."

"And where did you come by your injury?" I asked.

"It appears to have come from a dog attack," Ben said.

"Dat right. Slave catchers came upon me some weeks back. I escaped dem at first, but one of deir bloodhounds sniffed me out and got me real good. But I wasn't 'bout to go back. I got free, but de dog warn't so lucky. Den I hid my tracks by following de river."

"In Africa, my pappy was a warrior of his tribe." Pete sat straighter, giving his father a doting look. "Ain't nothing stopped him 'fore. Ain't dat right, Pappy?"

I smiled at the pride on Pete's face.

"I wish et were so," John said with a grave sadness.

Pete frowned. "What eating at ya?"

His father's eyes misted. "Long 'fore you come into dis world, deir be someone I would travel all dis land to find. Somepin' I always regretted."

"Who you talk 'bout?" Pete's brow puckered.

"De 'oman I always loved. De one I love to dis day, and 'til my soul joins my ancestors."

"You mean 'fore Mama?"

John's expression grew dreamy. "She be de purtiest li'l thing you ever saw. Gentle and hardworking. She caught de masa's eye and, well, he do things to her dat left her broken. Changed her forever. She got wid chile by de masa, and sought to end ets life, but I told her I love any babe of hers as though et my own."

My heart struck harder at the similarity of that woman's story to Mammy's. Wishful thinking, I told myself, and turned, intending to give the men some much-deserved privacy. John's next words made me pause.

"Soon after, de missus sold her and de babe—"

"Did she have a name?" I waited, my heart thumping in my ears.

"Missus?" John's deep voice asked.

I spun around, and with more harshness than intended, I said, "The woman. Her name." Tears made my voice tremble.

"Her name be Rita—"

I bolted for the door. *Oh God in heaven. Big John. Mammy's Big John.* I lifted the sides of my skirt and raced, weaving along the paths to the main house. Dashing through the back door, I almost collided with Mammy.

"Heaven's sake, gal, whatcha be doing? I 'bout to send Tillie out to find ya. Masa Bowden home and supper's 'bout ready."

I grabbed her hand and pulled her toward the door. "I have something I must show you."

"Right now?" she protested. "I ain't 'bout to let de food git cold."

"The food can wait." I closed the door behind us without releasing her. "Let's make haste."

"You skeering me. Why you got dat strange luk in your eyes?"

"You'll see soon enough."

"You and your secrets. Always conjuring up somepin' in dat purty head of yours," she muttered as she trailed behind me.

"Oh, hush now." I forced myself to keep from running and dragging her behind me as excitement beat in my chest.

"Gal, you bes' slow down. My legs ain't as young as yours."

I stifled a giggle as urgency pushed me forward. When we reached the corner of the sick hospital, I came to a sudden stop, and she plowed into the back of me.

"What in de—"

I caught my balance and swung to face her. "Mammy." Love swelled in my heart as I looked deep into her eyes. She'd suffered in the worst possible ways, but strength and resilience were hers. She'd raised me to become a woman of purpose, and from her I'd gathered courage, heart, and hope. She and the folks of the quarters had provided me with a sense of family and belonging I'd so desperately craved. Admiration for the beloved woman before me flowed into every part of me as I gathered her hands in mine.

Her brow furrowed as she studied my face. "What is et? Evvything all right?"

"Someone is here that wishes to see you."

"Who?" She looked to the hospital.

"John. Your Big John."

She pulled away, hurt and insult playing on her face. "Why you do me lak dat? Don't play wid me, angel gal."

"I'd never do that," I said. "You know that runaway I found early today?"

"De one passed out by de smokehouse?"

I bobbed my head. "He came here looking for his son, Pete."

"Tillie's man?"

"Yes."

She stumbled back. "He my Big John's boy?"

I nodded, my vision blurring.

"No." She shook her head, tears in her voice. "Ain't possible after all dese years." She turned pain-filled eyes on me. "Why you be so cruel? Telling me dese lies."

I stepped forward and clasped her upper arms. "I would never hurt you so. If I wasn't certain, I'd never tell you."

She glanced at the hospital. "But how you know he mine?"

"Because he spoke of a striking woman that he yearns for." I swallowed back tears. "He referred to her as 'my li'l Rita.'"

She trembled under my hands. "Can et be true?"

"Come see for yourself." I turned to pull her toward the stairs, but she stood rooted to the ground, and I swung back. "What is it? Isn't this the day you've dreamed about?"

"Et jus' dat...I skeered." She looked at me with wide eyes. "Plumb skeered. Et bin so long since he seed me. I changed."

"I'm sure he has also changed," I said.

"He may not see me as purty no more."

Her troubled expression and her admission gave me pause. "Here, turn around."

She frowned at me but did as instructed, and I untied her dirtied apron, removed it, and bundled it in my arms. "Now, look at me."

She again obeyed. I tucked a few wisps of hair underneath her scarlet head rag and straightened the collar of her floral cream cotton dress. "One last thing."

"What?" She eyed me eagerly.

I leaned in and gave her cheek a hard pinch.

"Gal, what ya doing?" She lifted a hand to soothe her cheek as I gripped the other.

"There, that should do." I stepped back and smiled. "A little color in your cheeks is all you need. Let's go." I urged her toward the stairs, and to my delight, she moved with me.

We paused outside the door and she looked at me, again worried. "It will be all right. I promise." Before she could flee, I opened the door and stepped inside, pulling her along behind me.

John tensed in his bed, and I glanced at Mammy, who stood with her head lowered, too afraid to look.

"Rita?" Emotion clotted John's voice.

Mammy jerked at the sound of his voice, and slowly lifted her gaze. She froze as she beheld him.

"De gods be praised," John said. "My Rita, jus' as purty as I recalled."

A sob came from Mammy. "Is et you?"

"Et me." He threw back the blankets in an attempt to rise.

"No!" Mammy said, rushing forward. "Dey say you injured. Stay put," she ordered.

John's brow dipped before he broke into a grin. "You bossier dan I 'member. I reckon wid good cause."

She inched toward the bedside, coming to a stop just out of reach, and looked down on him. "Et is you," she whispered in disbelief.

"Yessum." He held out a hand. She studied it a moment and then slipped hers into his. He stroked the top of hers with a thumb and pulled her closer.

"I can't believe et you," she said, dropping to her knees beside the bed.

He cupped her cheek in a large hand. "Et me, Rita gal. I come to find my boy. After losing you and our gal, I never thought I'd see you again. But I never stop loving you."

"Da Lard be good." Mammy laid her head in his lap and wept.

Tears streamed over my cheeks, and with a full heart, I departed with Ben, Kimie, and Pete.

As we stepped off the stairs, Pete turned a troubled gaze on me. "Missus?"

"Yes."

"What we gwine do ef his masa tracks him here?"

"We follow protocol," I said firmly. "I will never allow him to be parted from Mammy's side or from yours, for that matter."

"I awful grateful. I never thought Pappy would ever meet my chile. But dis night de impossible *is* possible." He smiled.

I clasped his arm and squeezed gently. "Go find Tillie at the house and rejoice with her over the good news. Tell her I've dismissed her for the evening."

"Many thanks, Missus." He grinned and darted off.

"Won't you both join Bowden and me for the evening meal?" I said to Ben and Kimie. They agreed.

Kimie and Ben entered the house before me, and I turned and rested my hands on the veranda railing. Tilting my face to the heavens, I whispered my gratitude for bringing Big John back to Mammy's loving embrace.

CHAPTER
Twenty-Eight

Mammy

AS I LAY AGAINST HIM, MY TEARS FADING INTO THE LINENS, I inhaled his medicinal scent. My John. The ocean of pain within me receded, and I found refuge and comfort in the gentle touch of my man's hands as he stroked my head and back, offering hushed words of solace until the weeping subsided. Rocking back on my heels, I used my sleeve to dry spent tears.

Under my weight, the grooves of the plank boards dug into my knees, and I stumbled to pull myself up, biting back the wince from the constant pain that hummed in my hip. An ache I dared not reveal to Mary Grace or angel gal, because Lard knows what schemes they'd unleash upon me. I recalled the evening when they dragged Crazy Henry from the quarters to extract my tooth—a night I wasn't keen on revisiting. No, sah! Catching those gals with their heads pressed together was a sure sign of trickery and scheming. And I warn't about to let them fool me again.

I dropped into a chair, and the grinding of my knees screamed of a life spent scrubbing, cooking, and cleaning for white folk.

John beheld me with a strange look in his eyes, and I dropped my gaze, growing self-conscious of how I'd changed. Why, it was just that very morning while cleaning the bed chambers that I'd caught a glimpse of myself in the looking glass—something I had avoided for decades—and the person staring back at me, I failed to recognize. My body was plump and ample, a shield I'd unconsciously forged to ward off men's lustful appetites. However, it wasn't the disappearance of the sensual curves or the wobbly, fleshy bits that consumed the figure of my youth that left me pondering. No, I was all too conscious of that forged protection I carried—I was reminded each morning as I hauled myself out of bed and heaved to catch my breath while climbing the staircase. But Lard help me, when had I gotten so gray? If I hadn't known better, I would have thought my mama was in that room, peering back at me. I'd smiled fondly at the brief glimpse before it faded, and my focus shifted to the deep grooves in my forehead. And the jowls, where had they come from? Foolishly, like a woman filled with vanity, I'd lifted a hand to smooth away the telltale signs, but as I studied the peculiar woman before me, my hand stilled and dropped. Tilting my head, I had viewed the woman with a new reverence. Eyes lacking the glow they once held but replaced by the wisdom only age could bestow. Eyes that told a tale of survival and perseverance—my story and my truth.

As I regarded John, I noted the same wisdom in his eyes, the channels etched into his face as though chiseled by a master carver. Years and slavery had claimed our youth, but was it possible the future wouldn't be so bleak?

"Why you luk at me lak dat?" I said.

He smiled, his teeth gleaming against dark flesh. "You a fine sight."

I waved a hand at him. "Reckon I changed. Ain't de gal you 'member."

"We all change. Dat what years do," he said. "You still my 'oman, and I love you jus' de same."

I smiled and placed a hand on his, finding solace there. The same strong hand that had explored my body with passion and tenderness, removing the filthy touch of Masa Adams. Healing had trailed from his fingers as he'd held my trembling form until sleep overcame me.

When Missus Adams sold me, I'd never thought I'd find comfort again, but I had. Not in the loving ways of my man, but in my daughter, her children, and angel gal. They had given me a reason to rise each day, breathing life into a soul depleted. Gratitude at the blessings bestowed upon me swelled in my heart.

"Pete your boy?" I asked.

"He be."

"You love his mama?"

"She was a good 'oman." His dark eyes rested on mine. "But she never filled de void in my heart after you left. Dat a place dat lay empty till now."

I glanced at my chapped and dry hands as worry gnawed at me. "Hearts mended, only to be split open again."

"What you mean?"

"Ef'n your masa comes luking, what den?"

"We face dat day ef et comes. De white 'oman say she help me."

"Angel gal be a good woman."

"You speak of her wid fondness."

My bosom heaved as love and devotion warmed my heart. "She lak my own gal. I raised her. I de only mama she ever knowed."

"Such consideration be dangerous."

"She mine," I said hotly. "She white, but she mine. I die for dat gal."

He raised a brow. "Only one white person I ever cared a smidgen 'bout." His gaze drifted, as though traveling back in time. "Went by de name Amelie. Reminded me of an injured cub, yearning for love and acceptance."

The tenderness with which he spoke of the white woman stirred a twinge of jealousy in me. "You speak of her wid admiration. Who be dis woman dat turn your head?"

John chuckled and leaned forward to pat my hand, then winced, gripping his wound.

I tensed and stood, gently pressing him back in the bed and tucking the covers around him. "Be careful. We don't need you opening your wound. Masa Ben won't be happy."

He smiled, weariness pulling at his eyelids. "Ah, my Rita." He lifted a hand and cupped my cheek, and my tears flowed again.

I pulled my chair closer, and when seated, I said, "Tell me more 'bout dis white woman."

Leaning his head back against the metal headboard, he peered at the whitewashed rafters. "She was but a child. I reckon eighteen or so. De first time I set out to find my boy, I came across her in de woods, half starved. But et wasn't jus' de body dat was starved of nutrition, but a soul needing healing. I never intended to stay so long in dem swamps, but somepin' 'bout her reminded me of you. A dim glimmer of de spirit left in her from de harm she'd come to at men's hands…" His jaw quivered. "Our time together was too short. But I luk back at dat time wid fondness. I often wonder where she be now."

Pride replaced all jealousy as I beheld him. "Maybe she better off for meeting you."

He shrugged, and as though putting thoughts of the woman from his mind, he said, "I afraid to ask, but I must know. Where is my gal?"

His reference to my daughter seeded by Masa Adams expanded the love I held for him, and I leaned forward and kissed his weathered cheek before pushing to my feet. In my excitement and doubt that it wasn't all a dream, I'd forgotten about Mary Grace. "She up at de big house." I smiled down at him.

"She here?" His eyes widened.

I bobbed my head eagerly. "After I was sold by Missus Adams, de Hendrickses buy me and bring me here. I lived a good life here at Livingston. Better dan any slave ever hope for, and when Missus Hendricks died, she freed me and my gal."

His mouth dropped open, then he mumbled a few words in his native tongue before saying, "May de gods rain blessings upon dis house."

God be praised, I thought. The one true God. John was like most slaves plucked from their countries and forced to shed their gods and convert to the Christian faiths of their masas. But I had been born in America and believed in the God my mama and pappy had taught me about from the time I was knee high. John had kept his gods alive by giving them the names of the saints from the Catholic faith, a disguise often used to preserve beliefs and culture in the new world. My faith had been the anchor that had gotten me through the years since I was parted from John's arms. The Calm in the storm. The Comforter of the nightmares and fears that often became smothering. Without my faith in Him, I'd be a weak vessel, and in the Creator I found my strength.

"I go git my gal, and tell her de good news." I turned to leave, but swung back. "John?" Joy beat in my chest.

"Yes?"

"I a grandma." I beamed. "Got two grandbabies to fill my days. A family of my very own. Right here on dis land."

Tears misted his eyes. "Many nights as I thought of you and our gal, never could I have imagined dat life be so good to you. Et makes our years apart worth de longing and hurt."

I frowned at the thought, and for a moment reflected on how I'd yearned for him, never once thinking our separation was for the greater good. As I left to retrieve my gal and grand-babies, I offered thanks to God for the blessings He continued to shower on me and mine.

CHAPTER
Twenty-Nine

Reuben—alias Oliver Evans

THE RIGORS OF THE NEW YORK WINTER AGGRAVATED THE familiar throbbing of my foot, where toes had been lost to frostbite in earlier years. The stinging cold burned the tips of my ears, and I pulled up the fur collar of my coat as I turned to glance through the hatter's frosted window. Amelie browsed inside the shop, stopping to admire a green velvet bonnet.

"Dammit, woman, hurry up." I lifted numb fingers to my mouth and blew into them to warm up. *Tick, tick, tick,* the pounding in my head ignited and raised my awareness before the words took form.

Become an attendant to a woman, have you? the voice taunted. *Have you forgotten they're the bane of men's existence? You must rid yourself of her, or she will surely become your successor. She is too close. Too smart.*

Silence. I gritted my teeth and rubbed my temples to block out the nattering before turning from the window. Thoughts turned to Rawlings's revelations on Livingston. The man hadn't been eager to report until Rufus and I resorted to extreme measures to pry it from him. It was as I'd suspected: Willow and her husband were involved in aiding fugitives. Rawlings had exposed their illegal activities, including an impressive operation in which they taught their niggers how to read and write, and marketable skills, in the hope that one day liberation would come to all darkies. I grinned, relishing an image of a rabid Charlestonian mob bent on destroying the Armstrongs. However, I couldn't arrive in Charleston and reveal my discovery because doing so would see me in a jail cell next to them. No, I would use the knowledge as a weapon against them, in my time and for my benefit. The Armstrongs' and Ben Hendricks's deaths would rest at the feet of a cause more fitting, and Rufus and I would be exempt from the crime.

I lit a cigar and inhaled in rapture, its effect soon smothered as I observed the bustling New Yorkers, their continuous rambling and gaiety.

Imagine a world where no human existed. The carnage that would annihilate them, wipe them from existence, the voice cajoled with feverish ecstasy.

Adrenaline coursed through my veins. What an incredible rush. An end to a world congested with humans, inventions, turbulence, and their repulsive scent. A universe vacant of life, sound, and movement. An end of nature in its entirety. Freedom from the voices prattling around in my head from morning till evening. I inhaled deeply, expanding my lungs. Yes, I could visualize and crave a world where silence reigned, and with it, perhaps some sort of peace.

The boisterous voice of a woman set me on edge, and I stiffened at its familiarity and scanned around me until my gaze locked on the owner. Whitney Tucker. My chest tightened, and I snuffed out my cigar and took a second look to be certain. Indeed, it was none other than the hag herself. She strolled toward me, engaged in conversation with a well-tailored older lady.

I cursed under my breath, and swiftly grabbed the doorknob of the hatter shop and ducked inside out of sight. Hidden behind a wooden form adorned with a ridiculously huge hat, I observed the women as they approached.

"Shall we try the hatters before finding a coffeehouse to warm our bones?" Tucker's companion said.

Discovery would ruin everything. I glanced around for an escape, my gaze pausing on the back door to the shop as my ears tuned in to Whitney.

"I appreciate everything you've done, but honestly, Aunt Em, I can't accept anymore. I'm a grown woman and can purchase my own things."

Kill the woman, the voice urged. *In doing so, you will send a blade into Willow's heart.*

"No, the time isn't right," I said as the women walked by. "Soon enough, Willow will die, and all she loves."

"Oliver?" Amelie's voice seized me, and I shook my head to gain focus, fighting against the power of the voice. "Who are you talking to?"

My vision cleared, and I forced a smile. "Amelie, darling."

Confusion pulled at her face, and she glanced at the large storefront windows before shifting her attention back to me. She tilted her head as though trying to read me.

"What is it?" I pushed down panic. I feared no person, and especially not a woman.

Her face softened, and the grandeur I'd come to relate to Madam Amelie returned. She had become the one human I found tolerable—for the meantime, anyhow. "It's nothing." She smiled and swept toward me, a vision in furs and silks. Slipping her hand in the crook of my elbow, she said, "Shall we leave?"

"Did you find what you were looking for?"

"Yes. I asked the shopkeeper to have my parcels delivered."

"Very well, let us go then."

The memory of Whitney and the woman she referred to

as Aunt Em fresh in my mind, I stepped out onto the street and collided with a woman weighed down with parcels. "My apologies, ma'am," I said, careful to keep my alias, the respectable and dapper Oliver Evans, intact. Inside, I seethed with annoyance and wanted nothing more than to kick her parcels into the street. Instead, I bent and retrieved her packages.

As the woman continued down the street, I glanced at Amelie, who stood peering away from me. "Are you ready, my dear?" I claimed her elbow.

She swung to face me, looking dazed, but as before, she pushed it away and beamed. "What do you say we sit for a bit?"

"I'll hail a cab, and we'll return home," I said.

She peered up at me through thick lashes. A gesture that failed to deliver the impact she had intended, but I smiled benignly regardless. "Not just yet. I'm not ready to return home." She returned a hand to my elbow, and I permitted her to guide me down the boardwalk until we reached a coffeehouse.

"They have the best pastries," she sang as she pulled open the door and, without waiting for me, strode inside.

I grumbled and followed after her. The low drone of patrons made me twitch, and perspiration beaded on my brow. I glanced back at the door.

"Oliver?" Amelie's voice rose above the rest.

To my approval, she'd chosen a table in the far corner. One that provided a clear view of the door and the comings and goings of people. Eagerly she motioned for me to join her.

After I'd seated myself and an attendant brought our steaming cups of coffee and pastries, for which Amelie offered a gushing thank you, she lifted the mug to her lips and, eyes sparkling with delight, peered at me over the rim.

My fingers froze halfway to my coffee mug as I heard Whitney Tucker's voice. I tensed and looked around the shop to locate her. Not finding her face amongst the patrons, I assumed that she sat behind me.

"What is it? You appear to have seen a ghost." Amelie's warm fingers touched mine.

"Mindful not to reveal myself, I looked askance and found the Tucker woman and her companion seated behind a tall plant. She sat with her back to me. The grip on my chest loosened, and I turned back to Amelie. "A bit faint, is all." I took a rather large bite of the sickly sweet pastry in an attempt to avoid answering her.

"Perhaps some food will clear the lightheadedness," she said in approval.

I swallowed the mouthful and took a long sip of the coffee. The next twenty minutes passed with light conversation, and as usual, I let Amelie take the lead. As she spoke, I tried to keep my foot from tapping the floor as the need to flee raged within me. If the Barry woman noticed me, my plans would go up in smoke. It was best if Willow Armstrong and her acquaintances had forgotten about me.

As Amelie took her last sip of coffee, I asked, "Well, should we go?" Not giving her the option of an answer, I rose.

Wrapping furs around herself, she stood and followed me out of the coffeehouse, but a short distance down the boardwalk, she halted. "How could I have forgotten?" She stamped a foot and placed a hand on her forehead in exasperation.

"What?"

She pointed across the street. "I just recalled that I have a meeting with Mr. Curtis about the purchase of the property in Five Points."

"Right now?" My muscles tensed in agitation.

"I'm afraid so." She looked apologetic as she withdrew a timepiece from her velvet satchel. "You mustn't wait for me.

I will see you at home in an hour or two." She rose on tiptoe and kissed my cheek, and without waiting for a response, she swerved and stepped into the congested street.

Baffled at her lapse of memory, I regarded her as she wove through carriages, peddlers, and hansom cabs. After traversing the street, she opened the door to a brownstone building with a sign overhead, clearly stating it was indeed a lawyer's office. However, suspicious, I darted into traffic and succeeded in crossing without incident. In a window of the office, I saw Amelie greet a man, and he thrust out his hand and clasped hers before gesturing for her to take a seat.

So she spoke the truth. I cranked my neck to ease the tension before hailing a hansom cab. As I entered the carriage, I took one last look at the coffeehouse and set my jaw as my thoughts returned to savoring the demise of the Armstrongs.

Behold, their blood will rain like mana from the heavens, the voice sang.

I sank back into the seat and lit a cigar, allowing all pressures to dissolve.

CHAPTER
Thirty

Whitney

ABRAHAM LINCOLN'S ELECTION AS THE SIXTEENTH PRESIDENT OF the United States and the first Republican to win the presidency left New York streets, shops, cafes, and restaurants buzzing about the recent debates by Mayor Woods and his officials and their ambitions to leave the Union. New York relied heavily on the Southern states, and without them, the city would suffer financial ruin.

"I do miss the warmth of the South," I said to Aunt Em as we strolled the boardwalk, our hands weighted with parcels. The frosty air nipped my nose, and the relentless chill seeped through my furs and wool.

Aunt Em laughed. "Too many years away has lowered your resiliency in a proper winter. In the North, we can withstand what Mother Nature sends our way."

My teeth chattered like they were carrying on a conversation of their own. "It is a season I could do without." I pulled the new cashmere shawl that I'd fashioned into a scarf, and brilliantly so, closer around my throat and wished I'd purchased the heavy knitted scarf instead. Pretty or not, the one I'd chosen had been more of a fashion choice, and perhaps a little vanity as I'd imagined Charleston's ladies eyeing it with envy. While standing in the store, marveling over the piece, it had seemed like a splendid idea, but now in the cold, I recognized how pride had led me astray. I'd been downright foolish, in fact.

Aunt Em's merriment faded. "A little meat on your bones would help. You've become much too skinny, my dear. I wonder if the heart longs for something once questioned."

My heart skipped a beat, but I kept from meeting her inquisitive stare and focused on the snowflakes dropping on my woolen mittens before they melted.

The relationship between my mother's sister and I had been one I treasured, and her perception of the emotions I strove to keep hidden always caught me by surprise. She understood me as so few did, and in her presence I didn't feel like an outcast. She allowed me to be myself. I'd idolized her all my life, and envisioned having a life as grand as hers. But recently, thoughts of my quiet homestead pulled at the heart, throwing me into a flurry of confusion.

Jack had gone off to West Point, and although I missed him terribly, I hoped his training would calm the rage inside him. He wrote often, and I cherished every word, but the love and passion in my little sister's letters filled me with a yearning to see her again. I smiled. Sweet, sweet Kimie. Although I was older, it was *I* who looked up to *her*. Often, she'd stumbled in at night, weary from the hospital but kindled with infectious joy and enthusiasm. I craved the happiness that she exuded. The joy I witnessed in Willow and Bowden. Like Kimie, my friend's work for the cause gave her purpose and a fire in her bosom.

My heart clenched as I thought of Knox, and how I missed the safety of his love and attentiveness. Although I'd written several times, no word came from him. I took the silence as his displeasure with me, and rightfully so. Would he ever forgive me? He had every right to take a new wife. Many times, I'd wanted to ask Willow if he had found comfort in the arms of another, but stubbornness and shame stilled my pen. Then nausea surfaced before the ever-pressing guilt that had accompanied me since I'd left. During my time away, I'd blamed my confusing emotions on Willow and what she'd said in the orchard that day, deluding myself into believing it had played with my mind. But in all honesty, her words had only magnified the guilt and the questions I'd attempted to evade.

I had never intended to stay away for so long, abandoning Knox with no answers or certainty. I'd gotten too caught up in Aunt Em's showering of luxuries and the warmth of her love and acceptance, which had filled the void for a time.

Sharing in her life, my days and evenings were occupied with the theater, luncheons, traveling, and social engagements—all activities I'd dreaded in Charleston. It proved no different in Paris, London, or New York. Our outings left me more miserable and confused than before I'd left the quietude of my homestead and the simple life I shared with my husband, and I began to wonder if the source of my dissatisfaction lay within me.

The twins no longer needed me. With Jack gone and Kimie's time occupied with Parker and Livingston, I'd been left to question what purpose life held for me. My whole existence had been based on raising my siblings when, in truth, I'd never regarded them as my brother and sister, but as though they were my own children. Except I'd forgone the dreadful birthing process, and I was grateful for it. I shivered at the thought.

A trip to New York would alleviate the melancholy, Aunt Em had insisted, but as pleasant as our time had been together, my thoughts turned toward home. The pull had changed as of late— becoming more pressing, almost daunting, like a weighted shawl I couldn't shed.

"Shall we try the hatters before finding a coffeehouse to warm our bones?" Aunt Em suggested, pulling me from my thoughts.

"I appreciate everything you've done. But honestly, Aunt Em, I can't accept anymore. I'm a grown woman and can purchase my own things." I withheld the truth that I could hardly afford the cashmere shawl, and with Knox's silence and my extended time away, I'd run out of funds.

"Very well, let us duck in here and sit for a spell." She gestured at a coffeehouse, and her eyes sparkled as she said, "Perhaps a coffee will stop the chattering of your teeth."

Oh, how I loved her. As a child, she had been my savior and the last piece of my mother I'd clung to, but as an adult, she was my confidant, friend, and a soft place to fall. As I wrapped my arm around her frail shoulders, my throat thickened as I recognized her fragility. She was a woman energetic with spirit and life, but age had started to pursue. One day death would take her from me, and I didn't know if...

Shaking such troubling thoughts away, I feigned a smile and peered down at her to see admiration mirrored in her eyes.

Inside, we found a seat at the back and settled next to a window. After ordering, I regarded Aunt Em as she sat studying me. "What?"

"Let us speak about what troubles you."

"It's nothing—"

She scoffed and shook her head. "You can't fool me, so you may as well not try. You've been present in body, but your mind is far removed."

I played with the crystal sugar bowl. "You know me too well."

"That I do."

Certain she would get to the bottom of my problems or we'd turn to corpses where we sat, I sighed. "I thought by coming to stay with you, I'd finally feel better, that time with you was what I needed to fill the void. But it hasn't." I sat back as the waiter placed a black coffee before me. I inhaled its heavenly aroma, and it soothed me for a moment. Lifting a spoon, I scooped sugar into my coffee and stirred. "Why can't I just be happy with what life has given me? I have a husband who works hard, is kind and funny, and loves me. Everything a woman could dream of in a husband. I tried to be a good wife; honestly, I did. And I was happy for the most part, but with the twins no longer needing me, it left me, well, questioning where I go from here."

Her warm hand covered mine where it lay on the white table linen. "Perhaps children of your own. You are so young."

I held her gaze. "No, that isn't for me. Knox knew this when I married him. I did what needed to be done for Kimie and Jack, but I do not wish to be a mother. All women aren't destined to be mothers. Look at you. You never married."

She lowered her gaze. "But it's not that I didn't wish for those things."

I frowned. She'd never mentioned a desire to have a family or a husband.

"To get to my age and be alone is not something I wish for you." She brushed a tear streaking her pale flesh and looked at me. The emotions I read in her eyes clotted my throat. "What is it you wish for, my dear?" she asked.

"To be happy."

"Happiness is not obtained by a chase. It comes from within."

I threw my hands in the air. "Yes, yes. I've heard such babble before."

She lifted a brow.

I calmed my antics and, pressing my elbows on the table, leaned forward. "Be clear, Auntie Em. What does it mean?"

She eyed my elbows with a stern look, and I removed them from the table and sat back, resting my hands in my lap. Her chin bobbed with approval.

"It means that no amount of time spent with me will make you happy, nor will the twins or Knox. Until you fill the gap and look inward, you will continue looking for happiness in all the wrong places."

"The gap as in the loneliness?"

"As in what was broken inside you years ago."

"And how does one do that?" I pulled for answers, desiring to feel whole.

"By being conscious and embracing the pain."

She had lost her mind. I knew she meant well, but memories of the past were best left there.

Sensing my unease, she turned the conversation to pleasant matters, and soon we were laughing.

"I've enjoyed our time together," I said.

"As have I, dear." She dabbed at tears spent on laughter, and her expression grew serious. "I'll miss you dearly, but you've been gone too long from your husband's side, and I think it's best you return home. Maybe this time away will have stilled the mind's pondering of what lies beyond your homestead."

"But I don't know if I have a home to return to."

Wrinkles pleated her brow. "Whatever do you mean?"

I glanced down to avoid her stare and twirled the spoon on the tablecloth. "I've written to Knox several times, but he doesn't reply. I fear he is very cross with me."

"He may be, but it is something he may get over if you return to waiting arms."

"I don't know…"

"You, Whitney Tucker, are no coward. You are boisterous, and at times crude, but you've got more backbone and grit than most. If your heart pulls for home, then you'd better pay heed."

A shadow fell over us, and we glanced up to find a red-haired woman clad in silks and furs. The woman's gaze shifted to the door and back, and worry dipped her brows as she looked from me to Aunt Em. "Whitney Tucker?"

Aunt Em nudged me.

"Who is asking?" I straightened and regarded the enticing creature before me. Her glorious mane lay in precise, lustrous ringlets beneath a velvet winter bonnet. Rouge highlighted dewy flesh and high cheekbones, and her perfume had a lure of its own. Men at nearby tables had stopped conversations to admire the woman. I, too, sat intoxicated.

"My name is Amelie Laclaire. I must ask you, do you know a Willow Armstrong?"

I tensed. "I do."

She gulped, and fear appeared on her face. "I-I have reason to believe she may be in grave danger. If you wish to help your friend, meet me at the corner of Baxter and Park Street."

A lump lodged in my throat and adrenaline raced through my veins as I started to rise, but she lifted a hand to stop me.

"Please don't cause a scene." Again, her troubled gaze turned to the door. "I feel what I have to say is most urgent. If you care for this Willow, you will meet me at the named spot at seven." She whirled and hurried to the door.

I searched for her through the window, but she had vanished as quickly as she'd arrived. The hairs stood up on my neck. I looked back at Aunt Em, whose eyes revealed concern.

"It's dangerous to go to the Five Points in broad daylight, let alone at night," she told me. "It isn't safe. Besides, how would that strange woman know anything to do with Willow? And moreover, how did she know you're an acquaintance of hers?"

I trembled from the encounter, and I sat numbly, taken off guard by the woman. "I don't know, but I can't ignore a claim that Willow is in danger. She is my dearest friend, and I would not see harm come to her."

She sighed. "Then, if you must, I will see you're accompanied."

"What are you referring to?"

"Hired help."

The stubbornness that had steered me wrong before told me I didn't require help, but Willow's and Ruby's stories of Five Points left me nodding my head. Again I'd be indebted to Aunt Em with no means to pay her back, but at the moment, Willow's well-being was all that mattered.

❧ CHAPTER ❧
Thirty-One

Amelie—Thirty minutes prior

I N THE LOBBY OF THE LAWYER'S OFFICE, I GLANCED OVER MY shoulder and caught a flash of Oliver darting through traffic to cross the street. My pulse raced with the chance of him discovering my lie, but his actions and the words he'd spoken in the hatter's shop had snatched the breath from me: *"No, the time isn't right. Soon enough, Willow will die, and all she loves."* He had stood as though in a trance.

His strange behavior and his obsession with the woman had amplified over time, and his reaction to the two women he'd spied on from the hatter's shop left me frightened yet inquisitive. His response resurrected the memory of a night soon after I'd overheard him and his friend, Michael, in the study. Gasping, I'd awakened, clawing at the restriction around my neck, to find Oliver's hands clutching my throat, his teeth bared, eyes feverish but unseeing. *"You must die. I will end the curse and take my revenge,"* he had said.

In recent months, it was as though he'd become possessed— during conversations, he fell into tangential rants that held no rhyme or reason. Then there were moments when he addressed me, but as though he was speaking to someone else. Other times I would catch him alone but holding a discussion as though someone was in the room.

As he continued to unravel, my wariness intensified. All was not as it seemed with him. The man I'd known had been calculating and brilliant to the point of genius. I'd attributed his intelligence to the infinite encyclopedias and documents analyzing army strategies and battles he feasted on, and the hours spent staring at a chessboard before making a single move. I'd decided that his parents had purchased the best education money could buy—an assumption, because he never divulged anything about his family or his past.

One afternoon, I'd turned onto the street to his townhouse as a private carriage pulled up out front, and Michael stepped out. The eerie man of inadequate stature sent shivers through me whenever I encountered him in his visits over the years. Each time, he disrobed me with a single glance and left me feeling defiled and handled without lifting a finger. When I broached the subject to Oliver one evening, he'd laughed and stated that a woman like me should be used to the lust of a man, and then went on to say that he posed no threat.

On that particular day, Michael turned and yanked a black man from the carriage who appeared to have been roughed up. I darted out of sight and observed the struggle between the pair, quickly recognizing the black man, as he had been summoned to the townhouse before.

The men climbed the stairs, the black man limping, and Michael pounded the brass knocker and stepped back to wait, never releasing his grip on the man. Soon the door opened, and Oliver ducked his head out and looked around before gesturing the men inside.

I raced to the back alley and entered the home from the back door, making sure not to draw attention to my arrival. Slipping off my shoes, I crept down the hallway and into the parlor, where a painting of me in a navy silk gown hung. My nerves vibrating, I carefully removed the painting and set it down without a sound. Behind the painting was a peephole I had carved into the wall while

Oliver had been in Maryland on business—an act that could mean my life if he found out, but as my mistrust rose, so did my anxieties about the secret I'd carelessly revealed to him. The murder I'd committed as a young girl. A deed a man like him, I'd come to believe, would use to see me rot in a prison cell before I hung from the gallows if it suited him.

I rebuked myself for the senseless way I had allowed myself to soften my heart for the man, believing I loved him. The thought soured my stomach with self-disgust.

Rising on my toes I peered through the hole, which provided a clear view of the study.

Michael shoved the black man forward, and he fell to his knees. "It took me a while to find him. He went into hiding after Armstrong put him on a steamer back here. My sources managed to locate him, and after a well-deserved thrashing, he admitted to trying to find his woman instead of coming to us with information. It gave me great pleasure to take my anger at his disobedience out on his pretty wife's voluptuous backside." He thrust his hips forward as if in final release inside a woman's warmth. "Ain't that right, Burrell?"

A harrowing moan came from the black man referred to as Burrell.

I trembled with memories of the men of my adolescence, who'd used my body without my consent. Big John's gift had never been far removed from my flesh, and my fingers pressed against the dagger strapped to my inner thigh under my gown. The urge to slit Michael's throat where he stood nearly overwhelmed me. His type, who found pleasure in taking what wasn't theirs for the taking, fed my hatred for men.

"It is as we thought, the Armstrongs are neck-deep in aiding niggers. The plantation is a facade to hide their operations." Michael looked as though someone had handed him a goldmine rich with glimmering veins.

Burrell's shoulders slumped further as Michael shared this information.

Oliver circled the desk to loom over him. "Is this so?" he asked in an emotionless tone.

Burrell didn't answer, and Michael stepped forward and struck him on the temple. "Answer, you black demon, or I'll be sure your wife pays for your failures."

Fury reared in me. *And I'll see your guts unravel.*

"She has unjustly paid for my shortcomings. I beg of you, let her go," Burrell sobbed.

Emotion clotted my chest at the agony in his voice and the injustice of what the couple had suffered.

"But I've become rather fond of her. The depths of her warmth have proven to be quite exhilarating." Michael patted Burrell's cheek.

"Very well, you have done as requested, and you shall be rewarded with her release," Oliver said.

Michael's head snapped up. "But—"

Oliver held up his hand to silence Michael's protest, and Burrell fell forward and kissed his shoes. "Thank you." He wept shamelessly.

Tingles chased up my spine as Oliver craned his neck side to side and stared blankly, the way he had the night he tried to strangle me.

"Tie him down," Oliver said in a heavily accented voice that was neither his nor any I recognized.

With his derangement exposed, my heart pounded in my ears, and I fought the urge to flee. What the hell was wrong with him? I frowned and pressed my face tight against the wall to get a better look.

"We will see to it he never speaks of this," Oliver said.

Burrell blubbered in panic. "I swear I won't say a word. You don't have to do this!"

No!

"Gag him," Oliver said.

Michael regarded him as though uncertain of his sanity. "Are you sure this is the place? Someone may hear."

"Amelie isn't due to visit until tonight, and I sent the staff on errands, mindful that we might need to take care of matters here and now," Oliver said in his own voice.

I peered from one madman to the other. Michael never blinked at Oliver's bizarre behavior, but did as instructed. He gagged Burrell and threw him into a chair and bound him with ropes.

Oliver retrieved a saw lying on the desk and held it up for inspection. Burrell's eyes widened with terror. Oliver ran his finger along the teeth of the saw, then quickly pulled it away and placed it to his lips, sucking the blood drawn by the saw. A sinister smile twisted his handsome face.

Fear strummed in my chest, and I stumbled backward, perspiration dampening my flesh. I couldn't let this happen. I had to stop them! But, as the screams rose, understanding filled me. If I barged into the room, I too would become a victim to the animals within. I replaced the painting and crept back down the corridor and slipped on my shoes before exiting the townhouse. Gathering the sides of my gown, I raced down the alley, putting distance between me and the horrors happening inside. As I ran, I felt invisible fingers pulling at my dress, seeking to expose my knowledge of the atrocities inflicted upon Burrell.

Several minutes later, I stopped as my stomach revolted and spewed its contents into a nearby honeysuckle bush. Swiping the back of my hand across my mouth, I paced the alley, keeping my eyes keen for the men's appearance. Guilt and remorse washed over me as I realized the depths of the monster I'd bedded, believing he'd brought me happiness. I was such a fool. I anchored a hand on my waist and rested another on my forehead. What could I do? I couldn't just stand by and do nothing. But I couldn't risk the men identifying me as a spectator to their depravity.

After lengthy consideration, I returned to the townhouse to wait for Michael to leave. If by chance Burrell still lived, I'd figure out what to do then. From the shelter of a parked private carriage, I watched the townhouse, and an hour later, Michael and Oliver hauled an unconscious, bloody Burrell out and put him in a coach. The fact that he yet breathed filled me with determination, and after the carriage moved down the street, I hailed a hansom cab and instructed the driver to follow before climbing inside.

Michael made a stop at a building outside of Five Points, and he disappeared inside and returned with a black woman dressed in a yellow taffeta gown fit for a woman of luxury. Her hair had been styled with care, but how she regarded Michael like a caged animal validated what I feared: she had suffered at the man's hands. My core heated with anger, and I struck the seat with my fist. I envisioned my hands around his throat, relishing the life draining from his eyes—an end too lenient for a man of his depravity.

My driver followed the other carriage to a shack in Five Points, where the carriage door opened and Burrell landed in the street in a motionless heap. Then the woman was shoved out to sprawl on the muddy ground before the carriage carried on down the road. I watched the weeping woman crawl to her man's side.

Onlookers stood back, watching, but no one moved to aid the woman as she labored to haul her man from the street and oncoming traffic. Long after they disappeared inside, I sat numbly in my seat.

"Ma'am?" The driver slapped the window.

I leaned forward, cracked the door, and gave him the address a few blocks from the brothel. I couldn't risk the driver discovering who I was, and I didn't know how deep Oliver's ties ran and who he kept in his employment. As the carriage pulled away from the curb, I took one last look at the shack the couple had entered and offered a prayer to Big John's gods that Burrell would survive.

Since that day, I found every excuse not to visit Oliver, but regardless of how hard I tried, all could not be avoided. And on the occasions when we copulated, I lay on my side afterward, trembling, long after he slept. When sleep did come, my dreams were haunted by what had transpired inside the study, or that Oliver had discovered I knew of his plans, and he was blackmailing me with my murder of the congressman. Upon waking, my mind raced with ways to even the score. I was at a disadvantage, and it made me ill at ease. I had to find out who Oliver Evans was, to gain an equal footing.

So far, the private investigator I'd hired had failed to bring me any information, and my patience dwindled. Thoughts of spending another moment in the company of a monster roiled my stomach. But I could surpass any actress on Broadway with my performance skills. When Oliver and I lay together I turned off the emotions, as I had as a girl, and to my advantage, he didn't require coupling as often as most men.

"Good day, Miss Laclaire." Mr. Curtis pulled me from my thoughts as he rose from his chair. In my peripheral vision, I caught Oliver standing on the boardwalk, observing through the large windows. "What are you doing here? Our meeting isn't until next week."

At fifty or so, he was a respected lawyer and a family man. I sashayed forward, and his blue eyes widened as he relished the calculated sway of my body. So easily molded. Mentally, I smiled. He offered an outstretched hand in which I lightly placed mine. I lowered my gaze, peering at him through thick lashes. Ensuring

I stood front and center in the window, I said with a flirtatious laugh, "Oh, foolish me. I must have gotten the dates wrong."

His fingers lingered. "No need to worry. Please have a seat." He gestured at a leather chair in front of the walnut desk.

I obliged, and he rounded the desk and sat. "I won't have the papers for the property drawn up until Friday, but we can discuss anything that may concern you."

His voice trailed off as I watched Oliver climb into a carriage, and as it pulled away from the curb, I leaped to my feet, almost kicking over the chair. He gaped.

"Miss Laclaire?"

"I'm sorry for the mix-up. I will return next week as scheduled."

"Are you certain?" He followed me as I hurried from the room.

"Yes," I said over my shoulder as I gripped the doorknob.

Glancing up and down the boardwalk before stepping outside, I wove back across the street to the coffeehouse. My stomach knotted. *Please still be here.*

The aroma of fresh coffee beans and sweet pastries tantalized my senses as I entered. The man who'd served Oliver and me came to greet me. "You've returned. Did you forget something?" His sparse brows lifted.

Dismissing him with a hand, I searched for the women, and to my relief, they remained, engaged in conversation. I approached the ladies, and as they glanced up, I cast a look at the door, half expecting Oliver to walk in and drag me off to the warehouse where Michael had kept the black woman, never to see the light of day again.

Fear whispered its warning but I suppressed it as Big John's face flashed before my mind's eye. I envisioned him in the aftermath of whatever Oliver and Michael schemed against

Livingston. Life would never cross the slave's and my paths again, but if I could help one of his people, my pathetic existence wouldn't have been in vain. Willow Armstrong and her slaves would suffer terribly if I didn't warn of the threat awaiting them. My courage ignited, and determination pushed me forward.

I regarded the ladies' confused faces and looked at the auburn one wearing an outdated and somewhat tired outfit, though she exuded an admirable sense of fashion. The other lady seemed to have been strikingly attractive in her day. Although time had wrinkled her flesh and silvered her once-blond tresses, her eyes were wise and her beauty had only been transformed with age. I addressed the older woman. "Whitney Tucker?"

She nudged the younger woman, who straightened. "Who's asking?" Her voice echoed like a train leaving the station. I cringed at the attention she attracted.

A callous glint shone in her eyes as they roved over me. I responded with my own examination, and on closer inspection, I sensed that, stripped of prettiness and the fashionable facade, this was a woman of fortitude and grit. However, I detected what I'd observed in many of the women who entered my brothel looking for work—an unpolished gem, damaged by life. In Tucker's eyes, though, flashed an inner spirit that yet survived. A disposition that jived with mine.

"My name is Amelie Laclaire. I must ask you, do you know a Willow Armstrong?"

The woman tensed. "I do."

I gulped, and warnings scurried. *Are you sure you should do this?* The wrath of Oliver would see me vanish. "I-I have reason to believe she may be in grave danger. If you wish to help your friend, meet me at the corner of Baxter and Park Street."

Tucker's fingers gripped the table, and she started to rise, but I lifted a hand to stop her. "Please don't cause a scene." Again I glanced at the door. "I feel what I have to say is most urgent. If you care for this Willow, you will meet me at the named spot at seven." I whirled and bolted for the door.

ⳡ‿ⳡ

Later that night, wrapped in a simple dark cape, I waited for the Tucker woman in night's shadows, and with each carriage that approached my heart hammered faster. When a buggy stopped down the street, I squinted to inspect who stepped out. A man disembarked and turned to offer a hand to a woman, and in the dim street light, I recognized Tucker's auburn mane.

What was she doing? Hadn't I said to come alone? I thought back and couldn't recollect if I had, but surely she had understood the risk of bringing a spectator. Perhaps it was her husband, I consoled myself before setting my jaw. Even so, she risked my involvement by including someone else.

As they drew closer, I stepped from the shadows. Tucker jumped and released a string of curses.

"Who is this?" I pointed at the man.

She placed a hand to her throat before her green eyes flashed with annoyance. "You about plucked the heart from my chest. Is it you?"

"Yes, it's me. You should have come alone."

"That may be so, but my auntie wouldn't hear of it. So here we are."

"Who is he?"

"Protection," she said sharply. "Hired by my aunt. Now let's not waste time. Why did you request that I come? Tell me what danger you speak of."

I glanced at the man, who stood back, surveying the street

and passersby. "Come." I clutched her hand and ducked back into the shadows.

Once out of sight, I glanced around for prying eyes before lowering the hood of my cape and lifting the veil concealing my face. "Do you know someone by the name Oliver Evans?"

She shook her head. "Not to my recollection."

"A Michael?"

"I've known a few in my time. What's the man's surname?"

"I'm afraid I don't know."

"Well, that's splendid," she scoffed, throwing her hands in the air. Sarcasm and Tucker appeared to be well acquainted.

I gritted my teeth. "They speak of a place called Livingston and a woman by the name Willow Armstrong."

"And?" She rolled her hand in midair as if to pluck my words at a speed of her own.

"I've heard them plotting to harm them."

"Harm them? How so? And why?"

"Some time back, I overheard the men discussing a plan to establish a spy at Livingston. They sought information concerning their suspicions that the Armstrongs were involved in the aiding of fugitives."

At that, she stiffened, and her face blanched. "A spy?"

"Yes, and when the man returned after time away, Michael brought him to Oliver, and the man confirmed the men's suspicions. Whatever it is your friend is involved in, they know, and they intend to use it against her."

Hands anchored on her waist, she paced in a small circle. "How can you be certain?"

"I told you what I heard."

"Scarcely anything to go on," she said in a curt tone.

"I feared my word wouldn't be enough. That is why I've brought you here."

She glanced around. "Why?"

"To speak to the man himself."

"The spy?" Her voice clanged like a church bell.

I yanked her arm and said through clenched teeth, "Where did you learn to whisper? In a gunfight?"

She pulled her arm free and glowered at me, but managed to whisper, "Where is he?"

I lowered the veil and concealed my hair under the hood before gesturing for her to follow. She turned and belted out a loud whistle. I halted in my tracks, the sound pinging my nerves and alerting those around us. I glowered at her. What was wrong with the woman? She appeared intelligent enough, but my God, had she been hung from her toes and shaken of all common sense?

"Perhaps more discretion would be best." I strode by her.

The streetlights caught the flush in her cheeks. "I'm sorry."

I thought it best to keep conversation to a minimum. We walked back the way we'd come, and the hired man joined us. Taking a good look at him I realized I didn't recognize him, and I was grateful for that. "Let's go."

I led the way down the boardwalk, keeping to the shadows of the buildings until we reached the shack the black couple had entered that day. I hoped the man yet lived and wouldn't run squealing to Oliver and Michael about our visit. I turned to Tucker and the man. "He stays outside. If something goes awry, then he can aid. Understood?"

Tucker went to instruct the man, and he glanced at me with an emotionless but professional expression. When she returned to my side, I took a deep breath in hopes of stilling the pulse hammering in my head before knocking on the door.

Footsteps shuffled inside, and a few moments later the door squeaked open a crack. "Who goes there?" a woman called out.

"Ma'am, I need to speak to your husband," I said.

Her eyes flashed with fear. "He isn't taking visitors."

As the door moved to close, Tucker kicked out her leg to stop it, and before I knew what was happening, she bolted forward, and the woman stumbled back. The pitiful door grumbled and moaned on its hinge as Tucker stepped over the threshold of the couple's home.

"What are you doing?" I grabbed at the back of her cape.

She shook me off. "I have no time for niceties. We will get to the bottom of this, and quickly."

I'd been a fool to bring the woman. What had I been thinking? Heat radiated on my face, but my attention fell to the woman's hand, combing the corner for a stick that lay just out of reach.

"Ma'am, we mean no harm. We came here seeking answers," Tucker said, seeming unaware of the woman's intent.

Before I could warn her, the woman gripped the stick and charged, cracking Tucker in the temple. She stumbled back from the blow and let out a scream. Behind me, the hired man charged in, and the woman came at us again before he bounded forward and pinned her wrists at her sides before she could strike again. The frightened woman kicked and fought.

"Easy, now," I said to the woman while glancing at Tucker, who stood stunned and rubbing the egg-sized welt forming on her temple. "It is as she said, we aren't here to harm you. I know what you have suffered, and I'm here to help. We have reason to believe a lot of lives are in danger, and your husband could help us stop a massacre of innocent lives." I crept forward and placed a gentle hand on her shoulder. "Please."

She ceased her struggling, but her gaze flitted between each of us. "I can't help you. I know not what you speak of."

"Where is your husband?" I gestured at the man to let her

go. "We'll handle it from here. Wait outside." He released her and departed, pulling the door shut behind him.

The woman rubbed tender wrists. "Who are you?" She directed her question at me.

My brain told me not to reveal my identity, but I knew if I intended to win the woman's trust, I had to be transparent with her. I lowered the hood and lifted my veil. "I am Amelie Laclaire."

"I've heard of the name somewhere," she said.

"I was there the day your husband was brutally attacked."

She cringed and stepped back to put distance between us. Her gaze flitted from Tucker to me, then the door.

I held out a hand, hoping to ease her panic. "I also saw the man take you from the building. I'm not sure I have all the details, but I believe the man that took you used you as blackmail to make your husband do his bidding. Am I right?"

Tears welled as she stood trembling like a foal on newfound legs, but she remained silent.

"I promise you will not see harm for what you reveal. I've made arrangements for safe passage for your husband and you out of New York this very night."

A flicker of hope shone in the woman's eyes.

"What name do you go by?" I asked.

"Rose," she said.

"Rose, do you know why they chose him?" Tucker asked.

Leery, the woman regarded her. "Because he—"

There was the noise of a struggle outside, and the three of us exchanged looks of panic. Tucker strode to the door and peeked outside. Mumbling something inaudible, she stepped back as the hired man pushed into the house, dragging a black man by the collar.

Rose gasped and raced forward and threw her arms around

his neck, clinging to him as though he were a lifeline. The man stood with his head lowered and face hidden beneath a worn felt hat.

"Is this your husband?" Tucker asked.

Rose bobbed her head, tears streaming down her cheeks.

"Release him." Tucker gestured at the hired man, and he obeyed and returned to his post.

"Sir, we come in peace. I can help you, but I need your help first," I said.

The man lifted his head and looked me in the eye, and for the first time, I got a clear view of him and what lay hidden in the shadows of his hat. Gruesome slashes from a blade, raised and still healing, scarred his cheeks. He stood regarding us blankly.

"Come, sit. Let us hear what they have to say." Rose led him to a chair at a small table that looked as if it would topple over if any weight were put on it. He allowed her to guide him and sat down. She took a position at his side with a hand resting on his shoulder. It was then I noticed that nothing protruded from the cuffs of his coat.

I waited for the man to speak, and when he didn't, I said, "Sir?"

"He cannot speak." Rose squared her shoulders.

But I had heard him speak in the study. I gawked from Burrell to Rose. "But—"

"They ensured he would never reveal what he knows." The woman's voice trembled. "They took his tongue so he couldn't speak of their tyranny." She leaned forward and lifted a cuff of his coat to expose the bandaged knobs beneath. "And his hands so he couldn't write it."

I stifled a cry as the man's screams reverberated in my head. They had to pay. Somehow, someway, as God as my witness, I'd see to it.

Tucker gasped and lifted a hand to shield her mouth, her face white in the lantern light.

"Monsters!" The venom spewed from me when I saw the man's suffering, and bile rose in my throat, but I forced it down and paced the floor. The depths that Oliver and Michael would descend to in order to see harm come to Willow Armstrong and Livingston was evident in the man's torture.

I stopped and swerved back to face the couple; heat flared in my belly, as it had the night I took the congressman's life. I looked the man square in the eye. "I am Amelie Laclaire. Oliver Evans, one of the men that did this to you, was my lover."

Burrell tensed, and Rose's mouth unhinged as she eyed me with a look of betrayal.

Tucker sent a glance my way. "Lovers? Perhaps not the best piece of information to provide."

"If I am to win your trust, I must be forthcoming with you," I said. "I have seen you visit his townhouse. Some years ago, I overheard their plans to insert you as a spy at a plantation in the South called Livingston. Am I correct?"

He nodded.

"I assume they took Rose as leverage to make sure you came through with the information they wanted."

"My husband's appetite for gambling left him indebted to the man who showed up here one day," Rose said. "By taking me, they wished to force his hand, but it did not matter what my husband did. He could have sold his soul, because it didn't stop the man's lust for a Negress. He used me like a Southern masa would a quarter slave. Defiled me in ways"—her voice quavered, and her expression was bitter—"one can never erase from memory."

My own haunted memories rent at my heart, and I found an unwanted commonality with the woman.

Burrell lowered his head and silently wept.

"You are wasting your time here. They secured his silence. You will not receive any more information than you already have. I've tried. It's impossible to get information from my husband in his condition."

"We must try," Tucker said with a gentleness I hadn't witnessed in her so far. "I am Whitney Tucker, and Willow Armstrong and her husband are my dearest friends."

The man lifted his head and regarded her. Opening his mouth, he tried to speak, but his words came out as agonizing moans.

"Have you been to Livingston?" She pulled up a chair and sat.

He nodded.

"To spy on them and report back to this Evans and his man?"

Guilt flooded his face, but again, he nodded.

Rose stood by gawking as though it were the first time she'd received the information.

"Why do these men seek to harm them?" Tucker asked the question I'd wondered over the years.

The words Oliver had spoken when I'd awakened to his hands around my throat came to mind. "To lift a curse," I said.

Tucker's brows dropped before her eyes widened, and she went as white as fresh snow. "What did you say?"

"One night I awoke to Oliver choking me and saying something about taking his revenge and ending a curse."

Tucker leaped to her feet, and her chair toppled over. "Silas!"

"Who?"

"Silas Anderson. No, I mean—" She stopped as if searching for something in her mind. "Reuben McCoy."

Reuben McCoy. The name sounded as familiar as his face had the day he walked into my brothel. But why?

All eyes fixed on her as she placed a hand to her forehead and paced the room. "It has to be."

I stepped forward and gripped her arm, halting her pacing. "Please tell me what you know."

Avoiding my question, she peered at me with a look of debilitating fear. "Describe this lover of yours."

I frowned but complied. "He is dapper, handsome, and for the most part, charming. However, lately he has seemed to unravel, and his behavior has become most troubling."

Tucker clutched the table to steady herself. "Does he walk with a limp or a shuffle?"

"He does."

She slumped forward with both palms on the table, and it creaked and leaned under her weight. In a drawn-out breath, she said, "It is he."

Rose left her husband's side to escort the woman into a chair. "Sit before your legs give way." Her gesture of kindness took Tucker by surprise, and she obeyed.

After a pause and a lot of confusing facial expressions, Tucker said, "I believe your lover is the man I mentioned. He's responsible for the murder of Willow Armstrong's father, and his family murdered her mother, Olivia Hendricks, when he was but a small boy. The man is controlled by demons and obsessed with the belief that Olivia cursed his family with her last breath. He is crazed, not right in the head. He sweeps from town to town, taking on aliases and murdering anyone to further his purposes and to satisfy a need. You're not the first to become a target of his derangement." Tucker's shoulders slumped. "His slave, Caesar, lost his tongue to ensure he never reported Willow's mother's murder."

If he was a wanted man, was that why he seemed familiar? Perhaps I'd seen him on a wanted poster. I cringed at the thought of the man I had bedded. How could I have been so blind? Had he not been calculated and charming? "Your friend has suffered greatly," I said.

"And his accomplice," Rose said in a low tone. "What about him?" Her eyes were wide with the need to know.

"I do not know." Tucker shrugged but offered a look of sympathy. "Perhaps a hired man he acquired to aid him in his mission to see my friend dead." She stood. "We must go. We have to inform the authorities, and I must return to Charleston at once to warn my friends."

"Swiftness in alerting the Armstrongs is of great importance—"

Rose's voice hitched with panic. "You promised you would help us."

I turned to her. "And I will." I took her hands in mine. "I will return within the hour. Be sure to be ready, with only what you can carry."

We took our leave.

Sometime later, outside the police station, I stopped. Tucker shifted to face me. "What is the holdup?"

"I can't go in there."

"Why not?" She grimaced.

My pulse raced in my ears. "Because, like Oliver…or Silas or whatever his name may be, I may have a bounty on my head."

She crept forward and, to my surprise and relief, looked around before whispering, "What do you mean?"

I quickly summed up my childhood and the life I'd taken. "So you see, if I go in there, I may not be coming out."

She straightened, and with a look of compassion and understanding, said, "I will do this alone. Take him." She nodded at the hired man standing some feet away. "Get the Rawlingses out of New York and away from McCoy."

Tears welled. "You have my gratitude."

"You risked much to help. We are indebted to you."

"There is no debt to repay."

"Very well, but I have one question." She held my gaze.

I inclined my head out of reverence. "Speak it, and I shall answer."

"Why jeopardize your own life to save people you don't know?"

I swallowed back rising emotions. "B-because some years ago, a runaway slave saved me from starvation. Not only of the body but the heart, and I owe him my life." I dipped my head. "Maybe in saving *his* people from a sure fate and aiding the Armstrongs, I can ease a guilty conscience and honor a man who gave me something I needed."

"What?"

I brushed a tear trickling down my cheek. "Worth."

Big John would never know he had been my saving grace. I pushed the vision of his grief-stricken face inside the jail cell from my mind. Even after all these years, the despondency and disgrace were too much to bear. That night had become equivalent to my childhood of horrors—another memory I strove to strike from my mind.

"I must go," she said. "Be safe." And with that, she spun and marched up the steps and into the brownstone building.

From the shadows of the boardwalk, I stood wondering if I'd ever see her again, and I felt a deep respect for the woman.

The hired man and I returned to the Rawlings' shack, and I froze when I saw the door ajar. In a flash, the man stepped in front of me and moved me behind him before flinging back his coat to grip the pistol holstered at his waist. We crept forward, and on the threshold, he halted. I peered around his broad frame and saw blood pooling on the floor.

No! I pushed by him and charged into the shack. And gasped. I stopped and raised a hand to cover my mouth. Burrell's lifeless body sprawled on the dirt floor, gutted from sternum to spleen. Next to him, Rose lay gasping for air with a knife in her chest. Beneath the blade, like a flower pinned to a frock, was a folded piece of parchment. I gulped, knowing without asking who was responsible.

I raced to her side and dropped to my knees, cradling her head in my lap. "No, no, no," I moaned, sobs clutching at my chest.

Blood bubbled from her lips and trickled down her chin as she fought to speak. "H-him. It was…" Her fingers dug at my wrist as she fought for life, fear contorting her features.

Tears blurred my vision. I brushed back her blood-soaked hair. "I-I am sorry I could not save you."

Her body arched and thrashed. Then, as the spirit left her body, her face softened, and she lay still.

A shadow loomed over me, and I glanced up at the hired man. He squatted beside me and plucked the blade from her chest and unfolded the note, and glanced at it before handing it to me. I scanned the words scribbled for my benefit.

Do not forget I know what you've done. You will pay with your life.

Numbed, I sat unaffected by Reuben McCoy's goodbye…for now.

"Come," a husky voice said. A gentle hand rested on my shoulder and I glanced at the man, who leaned forward and offered a hand. I peered into his eyes, regarding me with empathy and concern. Tilting my head, I gazed into their light brown warmth before searching his face. He had an ordinary face with a strong jaw and scars from too many brawls, but his eyes hauled me back.

"We must bury them," I said.

"It isn't safe." He pulled me to my feet in a single attempt in a way that didn't instill fear, but a sense of security. "If your enemies return, I will have failed my client. And I want to get paid."

As we walked from the shack, he wrapped an arm around my waist. Embracing the offered support, I leaned into his body. "Perhaps you might seek new employment."

He paused but soon continued. "Am I to believe you want to hire me?"

"Yes, but on more permanent basis."

"As your personal bodyguard?"

"I have the means to see you well paid."

"Very well, Miss Laclaire, I am open to discussing the matter."

CHAPTER
Thirty-Two

Willow—December 20, 1860

THE SOUTH'S AMBITION TO SECEDE FROM THE UNION intoxicated those out on this December afternoon. Marching bands, fireworks, and rallies congested with citizens echoed from every street in Charleston. Flags hung from balconies, and hotels were packed to capacity with the delegates for the Secession Convention.

"Do you think they will be successful in their mission to secede?" I asked Bowden from my seat in our open private carriage. I was observing the festivities with apprehension.

"The South's very civilization was built on the unwavering belief in the benefit of slavery. President Buchanan's position is that we have no right to secede. With him supporting his oath during his inauguration to not run for reelection, and with Lincoln's recent election, I fear he is powerless to stop South Carolina from seceding. Heaven help us all if they do."

I regarded my husband's rigid form as he watched the gunboats patrolling the harbor, assigned by Governor Pickens to ensure Major Robert Anderson didn't receive reinforcements or move his garrison to a stronger position at Fort Sumter.

"Pastor Abel joins others in Preacher Palmer's view that the South must defend the foundation of God and religion by supporting the institution of slavery," I said.

"Men putting themselves into positions of power to impress their ideas on their parishioners. I don't condone such antics."

As we rode along, concern over what was transpiring inside St. Andrew's Hall weighed heavily on our minds, and our conversation ceased.

Bowden turned the buggy down Broad Street, where a crowd waited outside the hall for news of the pending decision. Amongst the crush of silken gowns, tailored suits, parasols, bonnets, and top hats of high society folks mingled farmers, bakers, dockhands, blacksmiths, and street cleaners, blacks and whites alike. The congestion prevented us from getting closer. Bowden pulled to a stop. After securing the team, he reached for my hand and helped me from the carriage, and we joined the crowd.

"Willow," a woman called, and I spotted Josephine pressing through the crowd toward us.

"How are you?" I smiled when she joined us.

"As well as can be expected." She leaned in and embraced me before kissing each of my cheeks. "I've meant to stop by," she whispered in my ear, "but with the heightening of the vigilante patrols on the roads, seeking to oust abolitionists harboring slaves, I thought it best to stay away." She stepped back.

"I'm grateful," I said.

Our relationship since her discovery of her son's whereabouts had deepened immensely. She continued to put Sailor's well-being first, and in doing so, Livingston and our assistance to fugitives continued undiscovered, unbeknownst to her.

"If you ladies will excuse me, I believe I see Knox," Bowden said.

Holding him within my sight, I asked Josephine, "Are you here with your husband?"

"I am, but he left me to gain a closer view. I have no mind or care for political matters. My husband insists on hosting his political friends in our home, and I've become quite bored in the process."

"But what secession would mean for the South must give you cause for concern?"

"Of course. I look out my parlor windows and behold the gunships coasting the harbor. It's an eerie feeling for me, as it is for most. But a woman has no say in the actions of the men who rule our country. So why concern myself with such tiresome matters?"

"But their ambitions are sure to bring war," I said for her ears only.

"There is a possibility." She wiped an invisible chill from her arms. "I, for one, don't wish to think about such matters. But I—"

Lucille's high-pitched voice drew our attention to where she stood, clad in a pale pink gown embellished with all the bolts of lace and accessories once available in Charleston. Her husband was stationed at her side, and some feet away, her lover stood eyeing him with malice. Always the spectacle. I compressed my lips but kept my opinions silent.

"Shall we avoid the exhibition?" Josephine nodded in Lucille's direction, smirking.

I struggled to keep from bursting into laughter and looped my arm through hers. We strolled in the opposite direction, fading into the crowd. Through gaps in the assembly, I noticed the Barlows and Callie, and when Magnus spotted me, he nodded his acknowledgment but refrained from attracting attention.

"Have you heard from Whitney?" Josephine asked.

"She writes."

"Any mention of returning home?"

"I'm afraid not."

"She has been gone so long," she said. "I do hope she plans

to return regardless of the slander others have fixed to her name. And Knox..." I followed her gaze to where Knox and Bowden stood absorbed in what appeared to be a serious conversation. "He tries to hold his head high and only speaks warmly of his wife. A man of rare character. Perhaps if I had paid him more attention before she moved to town, I wouldn't find myself trapped."

"I know he misses her. He has had a terrible bout of melancholy since her departure."

I had resolved myself to Whitney's decision to leave, and with her failure to return, I wondered if she might never return home, but I hadn't broached the subject in our correspondence. Bowden and Ben had teased me about my restraint in the matter, but I wouldn't be so readily taunted. Hasty words conjured by despair that day in the orchard had caused enough unhappiness. I'd set my mind to keeping concerns about Whitney and Knox's separation private.

"I'm sure you miss her too," Josephine said.

"I do. But a good friend must support another. Regardless of the difference in our views—" My words were drowned out as a resounding call made the crowd erupt with delight.

"Secession!"

A multitude of hands thrust into the sky in triumph, and my legs trembled.

"A glorious day!" A woman shoved past me.

Smiling womenfolk embraced, and men shook hands and clapped each other on the back.

"The South is purified!"

I glanced from Josephine, who seemed dazed by the roar of the crowd, to my husband. He searched the faces before our eyes locked, and the concern on his face was akin to the pounding of my heart.

"Now what?" Josephine clutched my arm.

"I don't know, but it can't be good."

"My husband says the Northerners have turned from God, and in doing so, we had to rid ourselves of them. I guess choosing this secession will see to that. He said that if this resolution was successful, other states would soon follow."

"A clear divide from the rest of the Union can only mean one thing."

She gulped as realization flickered in her eyes. "I suppose I had foolishly hoped that if I blotted out all discussions of the South's withdrawal from the Union, as well as my husband and others fanning words of war, I could extinguish the certainty."

The victory for South Carolina could only mean one thing… war waited in the aftermath of this day.

CHAPTER
Thirty-Three

THE WARMING KITCHEN DOOR SWUNG OPEN, AND MARY GRACE stormed in, her features pinched with anger. "She is impossible! Simply impossible." The door groaned shut behind her.

I halted the fork of sweet potato pie halfway to my mouth and eyed her, frustrated. Lowering the bite of temptation that had beckoned to me since Mammy brought its steaming goodness from the kitchen house, I forced back the moan of disappointment and set the fork down, hoping for a swift resolution. I turned to give her my full attention.

Although she rarely came untangled, when she did, her mama's fiery spirit appeared. On such occasions, all who stood by would be wise to flee. I glanced at the door, blocked by her tense body, and resolved myself to defeat. "Who?" I said.

"Mama." She flung her hand in the air as though I should already know.

Mary Grace and Mammy had faced their share of differences lately. I figured the dynamics of their relationship had changed with Big John's arrival last spring, and Magnus and Mary Grace's blossoming affections.

"Care to tell me what happened?"

She dropped into a chair at the small table under the window overlooking the work yard and sat silently for a moment, her attention seized by something in the yard. I lowered myself down across from her and followed her gaze. Outside the kitchen house door, Big John stood with his arm resting against the exterior wall, and Mammy stood peering up at him, both lost in chatter and smiles. Each month that passed, the renewed love between the pair was endearing to see and much deserved. I had delighted in their happiness and the love and joy that seemed to radiate throughout Livingston.

"She has Big John now, and I don't begrudge her." She turned to regard me with misery in her eyes. "I love Mama. You know I do."

"Of course." I covered her hand with mine where it lay on the table, and felt it tremble. "What has you so upset?"

"I'm afraid to tell you because I fear you may react like Mama."

She could tell me but one thing that would strike fear into me. I had attempted to conceal the abundance of emotions that created, but to no avail. Before she spoke what was in her heart, I knew what was coming, and my stomach churned. "Tell me." I swallowed the lump in my throat, willing the threatening tears away.

"Magnus has asked me to marry him, and I've accepted."

"That's wonderful news!" I said with as much enthusiasm as I could muster, yet part of me braced, because my heart told me there was more.

Her half smile revealed her uncertainty. "I'm glad you approve."

"Of course. I've come to care about the Barlows dearly, and a union between you and Magnus would practically make you blood." I smiled.

"You know I hold much love and respect for you, but the time has come that I wish to leave Livingston."

I attempted to freeze my smile, but it slipped with the

announcement. So it was as I had feared. Their love would take her on a new journey. She deserved happiness more than anyone, and as Magnus's wife she would truly be free. He could provide a better life than the one she had at Livingston. All facts that resonated, but a grave sense of loss hollowed my core. I had learned a lesson in my poor behavior with Whitney's departure, and I promised myself I wouldn't hurt Mary Grace when the day came upon us. "I expected you would eventually come with the news of your desires."

Her jaw dropped. "You knew?"

"One would be blind not to see how much you and Magnus love each other. You're a free woman and should live your life as such. However," I lowered my gaze to my hands lying in my lap, "I would be lying if I didn't tell you the ache of knowing this day was coming hasn't tormented me. With Whitney still gone, I'd tried to work on my fears of loss and wanting to keep my loved ones tucked away in a trunk for safekeeping. You aren't treasures to be held hostage for my comfort." Tears came, and I failed to stop them. "You're my dearest friend and like a sister to me. I want your happiness more than anything. Not that you need it, but I give you my blessing. It is past time you have your own life."

I just hoped it wasn't too far away. My mind clutched at a vision of my own creation—Mary Grace and the children would move to the Barlows' plantation, where we would visit often. The heart could handle that distance.

Uncertainty shone in her eyes, but she didn't divulge anything further. "I accept your blessing, and your consent of my wish to leave warms the heart."

"Good." I scraped back my chair and retrieved an extra fork and the piece of pie. I returned to my seat and handed her a fork. "For old time's sake."

She laughed. "I suppose it won't be often that we can sneak the first slice."

"A moment for memory." I forked in a mouthful and moaned with delight as its creamy decadence danced on my tongue. I silently sang Mammy's praises.

"I will need to enlist your help." Mary Grace swallowed a mouthful, and brushed pie crust crumbs from her lips.

"In what?"

"In obtaining Mama's blessing."

I paused in chewing and said with a full mouth, "Have you lost your mind?"

She grinned.

"Getting on Mammy's bad side is a fate I don't wish to face."

"Together, we have always fared better at winning Mama over."

"I don't know…" Mammy's feistiness could intimidate most, and her disapproval cut to the heart. I played with the last bite of pie on the plate, my appetite dispelled by the thought of the task.

"Please, you must help me." She gripped my hand. "I know you can convince her."

I heaved a sigh. "Very well. I will conjure the courage to face the wrath of the beast."

She squealed and bounced in her chair before pitching forward to peck my cheek. "I knew I could count on you."

I arched a brow. "May I suggest you contain the excitement. I've yet to approach her, and the outcome could be disheartening."

Her smile faded, and her jaw set. "Then I will do what I must. Blessing or not, I will marry Magnus." She pushed back her chair and marched from the room, leaving me gawking at the protest of the swinging door.

"Heaven help us all," I whispered in the wake of her retreat.

CHAPTER
Thirty-Four

LATER THAT AFTERNOON, I TRUDGED DOWN TO THE FORGE TO VISIT Jimmy and found him hovering over a broken wagon wheel. He looked up and straightened, wiping his hands on a leather apron. "Ah, Missus Willie, whatcha be needing?"

"Must I need something to pay you a visit?" I said with a laugh.

"Reckon not, but by de luks of dose puffy eyes, my guess would be you bin crying."

"That obvious?" My shoulders slumped.

"Reckon so. What be troubling ya?"

I leaned against the worktable and used my shoe to draw in the soot and grime blanketing the floor as thoughts centered on the changes unfurling around me. "It seems silly," I said.

"Sometimes troubles of de mind jus' need sorting."

Embracing the sadness that had enveloped me since Mary Grace's revelation, I said, "I suppose I fear change as much as the next person. You and the folks of Livingston moving on causes me great distress, but who am I to stop them from pursuing their lives? I admit I'm guilty of using you all as a false sense of security. Change is happening across our country and here on this very plantation. Regardless of how we push for liberty for all Negroes, selfishly, I can't help but dread the emptiness that would ensue. I am the biggest hypocrite of all." Shame heated my cheeks at the inner battle that had roiled within me for years.

"Some of us folkses feel de same. We yearned for freedom so long, but now dat dere be a taste of et in de air, et leave us wid concern of what price we pay for what be 'round de bend."

"Bowden believes revolution is coming for the South, and I'm inclined to believe so as well. We, like many Southerners, seek to trade with Europe. Our relationships in Europe continue to be crippled by Northern manufacturers and politicians endeavoring to exploit and control the South's goods with tariffs that prevent European merchandise from being cost-effective. They continue to prevent our wares from ever reaching Europe, and all of this keeps Bowden from my side. Lincoln's attempt to resupply Major Anderson and his garrison and the rebels shooting at *Star of the West* does not bode well. And it appears the negotiations between the major and General Beauregard are going nowhere."

"Dat be so." His face grew taut. "Wid war comes death and suffering. Reckon et de aftermath we need to fear most."

A chasm opened in my stomach. "One moment I dream of a new Livingston where free blacks are employed on their own accord, and in the next, I envision the plantation a shell reduced by the devastation of war and folks' desire to break the chains that have held them here."

"Your concerns are fair 'nuf. I suppose I feel somewhat de same."

I craned my neck to look at him. "How so?"

"When your pappy purchased me, I was a dead man walking. Dis place breathed life into me, and gave me purpose. Dis been my home for so long; I reckon et hard to imagine de change you speak of. Et only human to want to hold onto dose you love."

I envisioned the beloved faces of those who roamed the grounds, making Livingston all it was, and the passion in my heart for each of them. Nightmares haunted me of racing to the quarters to find cabin doors slung open and no one to be found. What would become of Livingston if such a thing were to happen? What about Jimmy, Mammy, Tillie, Pete, and even Jones? Where would life take us all?

"Bowden says together we will face what comes."

"Dere be wisdom in de masa. He steer you right."

I chewed at the inside corner of my lip. "I hope he returns soon. His extended bouts away fill me with the same loneliness as when Father would leave on business, but greater, of course."

"Masa return to waiting arms soon 'nuf," he said with a knowing smile.

"Missus Willow!" a panicked voice called.

I swung and marched to the doorway as a house servant raced into the work yard, her eyes scanning for me. "Here, Bella." I stepped outside. "What is it?"

Eyes wide with concern, she said, "A carriage approaches and et coming fast."

"Send up the call." I gripped her arm.

She bobbed her head. "Yessum."

I hoisted the sides of my skirt and sprinted for the front yard. The slave spiritual lifted, warning all of the possibility of impending danger.

Pausing to catch my breath, I squinted at the open carriage spewing dust as it charged up the lane. Whitney? Goosebumps puckered my flesh. I raced to meet her, my thoughts reeling with the urgency of her approach. She hadn't mentioned her return in her last correspondence.

Upon seeing me, she reined in the team. I glanced from her to the frail man next to her. The fellow sat gripping the side of the carriage to keep from being launched overboard. He scowled at her. "You are insane, woman."

"Hush." She returned his glare. "We would never have

reached here at your speed." She clambered down. "Make haste and remove my trunk."

"Here?" His brow wrinkled.

"Yes, here," she scoffed. "And make it quick."

He grumbled and hopped down.

"Whitney, what is it?" I gripped her arm and pulled her aside.

She glanced at me, her eyes never gaining focus. My insides churned with the sense that something was gravely wrong. "Is it Jack?" I placed a hand to my chest. "Don't tell me. Aunt Em?" My mind whirled with possibilities for what might be frightening her.

She craned her neck to look at the driver, and I suspected she had seized his carriage to make it to Livingston. "Hold on," she said. Turning, she strode to the man and removed payment from her handbag.

His scowl never subsided as he grabbed it and clambered atop the seat. Without a word, he turned the carriage and headed back down the lane. Most likely seeking to put distance between himself and her.

Her bizarre behavior ate at me. "Whitney, what is it?"

"Come." She took me by the arm and hurried toward the house.

"What about your trunk?"

"We'll send someone for it." She marched on.

I yanked my arm from her but it didn't stop her, and I found myself racing to keep up with her longer gait. "For God's sake, tell me what has you charging in here as though death is on your heels."

"If Reuben McCoy has his way, it will," she said without missing a beat.

Reuben McCoy. Invisible vines rooted my feet to the ground. "What are you talking about?" I shouted after her.

She paused before whirling and marching back to me. My heart hammered at the look in her eyes. Fear. Unadulterated, irrefutable fear. "Whitney? You're trembling. What is this about McCoy? Do you have information about his whereabouts?"

"Aunt Em and I were in New York, and a woman by the name of Amelie Laclaire sought us out in a coffeehouse. She claimed that you were in grave danger." She quickly told me about the woman and what had transpired in New York.

My legs buckled and I dropped to the ground, thrown into the sea of nightmares that had persecuted me for so long. "Bowden," I said. "We must get word to him."

"I checked at the warehouses before coming here. But I was informed he is in California."

"He isn't to return for another week or so." I looked up at her. "What will we do?"

"What we've always done." She offered me a hand and I took it, allowing her to haul me up. "Long before you had a husband, it was women who ran this place. We will put plans into action. Come." She steered me toward the house.

Yes. Think, Willow. Think.

"We have no idea what he has planned or when. Jones and his men are here. Though they are few in number, we will arm anyone else we must. I will send someone for Knox; we could use his help," I said.

"Good. I'm glad to see the old you still lives in there somewhere, and marriage hasn't stolen your courage." Her sarcasm reigned, and instead of extending criticism, I anchored myself to the strength in her demeanor.

I scrambled up the front steps and barged into the house. "Tillie."

"What is et, Missus Willow?" She descended the stairs with a chamber pot in hand.

"Go fetch Ben and Jones. Tell them to come quick and run like all hell has unleashed."

She set the pot down and charged off.

"Land sakes, Missus Willow, what be all de trouble?" Mammy darted out of Tillie's path as she raced by before proceeding purposefully down the corridor. Her forehead creased with concern as she glanced from me to Whitney.

"Reuben McCoy has resurfaced with a plan that could see all we love vanish before our eyes." As I uttered the words, I cringed.

Whitney gripped a house boy's arm on the way by. "Head over to my homestead and bring my husband here at once."

"Yessum!" The boy dodged out the door.

"What you mean by dat?" Mammy stood awaiting an answer, her brow glistening with sweat.

Whispers and murmurs overtook the main floor and the balcony above as house folk listened.

"Everyone gather in the backyard. Quickly," I said. "Whitney, gather guns and ammunition."

Without a moment's pause, she sprinted down the corridor.

"Missus Willie." Jimmy called behind me. "What gwine on?"

I spun around to find him standing on the front veranda, taking a gander at the scurrying house servants. "Reuben McCoy. He's coming." Relieved at his arrival, I flung my arms around him. He stumbled under my weight before catching his balance. "He seeks to harm us with his bloody obsession with the curse." My chest heaved with unraveling panic.

Warm hands patted my back. "Dere, dere, Missus Willie, we figure dis all out. Gather yourself." Pulling back, he stared into my eyes, and for the first time, he cupped my cheek with a tender hand—before a cold glint appeared in his eyes and his shoulders rolled back. "I give my own life 'fore I let harm come to you. Black or not, I take up arms to defend dis plantation, and all dat call et home."

"No white man stop me from shooting him dead where he stands," Mammy said with conviction as she encircled my waist with an arm. "Wipe dem tears, angel gal. We bes' do what needs doing."

You must be strong. If you crumble, what then? I brushed away the tears and cleared my throat before eyeing Jimmy. "Ready a horse, and ride to the Barlows and tell them of our troubles."

"Yessum."

"But, Missus Willow, ef'n someone catches a black man on a horse, dey hang him for sho'," Mammy said.

Mary Grace appeared. "She is right. I'll go."

Mammy's head cranked around so fast, she probably pulled muscles. "You will not. I forbid et." Fire spit from her eyes. "De white blood in you and de fact you to wed a white man don't make you any less black dan James. You still black. No amount of whiteness you surround yourself wid gwine to change dat."

"Yes, I'm black." Mary Grace glared at her. "How can I forget, as it's something you remind me of daily, lately. I'm proud of the Negro blood I bear. But that is neither here nor there and is insignificant in the current circumstances." She eyed me. "James doesn't venture far from the plantation. You and I have wandered these woods and trails all our lives. I can ride. I'll be back with help as quickly as possible."

"We have no time to stand here and argue," I said. "Go. And be careful."

She nodded, sent a glance at her mother, and bolted out the door. Mammy lunged forward and grasped the doorframe to steady herself as a guttural wail rose from her.

"Fetch Big John," I said to Jimmy.

"Straightaway." He departed.

"She will be fine." I spoke an assurance I had no right to say. What did I know about what lay in wait? "Magnus may be white, but he is a good man, and he will see no harm comes to her."

"He can't stop what happens between here and his plantation." She lifted her head to reveal tear-stained cheeks.

"Trust in God." I pulled on her faith to instill strength. "Did he not return Big John to you?" When her sobs continued I looked helplessly around at the house, emptied of scuttling servants.

"Willow!" Ben burst through the back door and rushed toward us. "What is wrong?"

Mammy ceased her weeping and whirled to face him. My muscles eased ever so slightly with his arrival, and I strode to meet him. He clasped my shoulders and peered from a distraught Mammy to me.

"It's Reuben McCoy," I said.

His eyes widened. "What about him?"

"Follow me. I will inform everyone at once. Come, Mammy." After she joined me, I looped an arm around her waist and guided her out the back door.

Outside on the back veranda, I waited until the murmurs died down. Joined by Whitney, Ben, and Mammy, and with all eyes on me, I addressed the people.

"It appears the freed man by the name of Burrell Rawlings was placed here as a spy by Reuben McCoy."

A gasp went up, and folks gawked at neighbors.

I rested my hands on the railing. "He knows of our involvement in the cause and seeks to disarm us, and we remain uncertain what that all entails. But we must prepare for whatever is coming. It is with regret that I must call on you to help me defend you all."

Mothers clutched their children, and husbands wrapped arms around their wives' shoulders. Friends swapped frightened glances before a profusion of questions and concerns erupted.

"What are we to do?"

"How do we defend ourselves?"

"Et mean death to lift a hand to a white." Pete pulled Tillie closer to his side.

"I understand your concerns, and they're valid. I ask much of you, but you each have a choice—to stand and defend or seek protection. In his derangement, McCoy has proven not to see reason. With the notion that he can harm me by getting to you, I believe he will stop at nothing. Unfortunately, the truth he holds over us leaves us unable to call on neighbors for aid because, if we come out of this victorious, we can't risk them knowing of Livingston's operations."

Murmurs rippled amongst them.

"The decision is up to you. If you choose to leave, go with God. If you stand with Livingston, may He protect us all."

I exchanged a few orders with Jones as people departed. Some darted for the quarters; others stood in discussions, their gazes on us as though contemplating their chances.

"Ben, will you join me inside?"

In the study, I spun to face him, wiping sweaty palms on my skirt. "What are we to do? We have no idea when he will show up. It could be any moment, or months down the road."

"You do what you have done," he said. "Enlisting our friends' help and putting people on watch is all we can do for now."

I paced the floor. "But is it enough?" I stopped to look at him, worry and misery eating me up. "What if he harms the folks here? It could be a bloodbath. He is capable of such things," I reminded him. "Whitney says he has taken on another alias. The man is a mastermind, and insane. He will stop at nothing to end this concept of a bloody curse. What if he enlists every supremacist vigilante from New York to here in his need for our end?"

"Until then, we will secure the plantation and be on guard." He opened the bottom drawer where my father had kept his pistol and holster, which he removed and strapped around his waist. Then he strode to me and kissed my forehead. "You aren't alone."

I molded in to him. "But what if—"

He rested hands on my shoulders. "You will drive yourself mad. We will place guards at the front and back of the house. No one will get in or out. Men will be stationed at the gates and by the river. I'll enlist any willing black." With that, he hurried from the room.

That night, and the next week until Bowden's return, we took up posts around the plantation, but Reuben never came, and anxiety pursued me with every sound or movement. I envisioned him like a hawk gliding overhead, waiting to pounce.

❦ CHAPTER ❦
Thirty-Five

April 11, 1861

A S FORESEEN, A NATION DIVIDED INFLUENCED THE BROILING frictions of our country. Jefferson Davis had been elected as the interim president for the Confederate States of America. In the months following South Carolina's secession from the Union, six other states seceded, forming the confederacy of states. The Kentucky self-taught lawyer Abraham Lincoln was inaugurated as the sixteenth president of the US.

Months had passed since Bowden and I had attended the Charleston races—a record-setting, four-mile competition Albine, a South Carolina filly, won against the Virginia stallion, Planet. Governor Pickens had attended the races. He had also commanded all batteries on the seawall to prepare, in anticipation of a forty-eight-hour bombardment.

Although the looming threat of war weighed profoundly on our minds, as it did many, the threat of Reuben McCoy waiting and plotting our undoing became paralyzing. Like a tornado, the news of his intent had swept me back to a time when he had plagued my nights and days. The expectation of his arrival, and the unpredictability of the crazed individual we were dealing with, riddled me with fear.

Bowden had taken all precautions possible, but our

country's unraveling stability and the South's enlisting of able-bodied men took precedence. Home guards formed, composed of older men and boys too young to join the Confederate cause. Clad in long, homespun gray coats, they policed Charleston streets and the countryside with the objective of maintaining the Negroes. Each day fathers and sons, with military skills or without, said their goodbyes and set out to aid the South Carolina militia.

It was early afternoon when Bowden loaded our satchels into the carriage for an overnight trip to town. The next day, Ben, Knox, and Bowden would set out to join the other men.

"Do you think it is wise to leave for the night?" I asked.

"I hear your concern, but I can't leave *them* in the warehouse another day."

His reference to two of Thames' slaves left me pondering on the impossible task at hand. "With soldiers roaming the streets and the harbor heavily guarded, any chance of getting them out seems improbable."

"I concur, and I've been considering what I'm to do now." He turned, and I noted the lines of weariness etching his face. "They have to remain in Charleston. We have no other choice."

"And put them where? We can't risk having recognizable fugitives hiding at Livingston, and we don't know who is watching us. Look how easily McCoy contrived the purchase of Rawlings. God rest his soul."

"I know." He hung his head. "The fault lies with me for endangering all your parents and we have accomplished."

"Don't." I stepped forward and rested my hands on his chest. "It isn't your fault. It could have happened to any of us. The pressure on our shoulders has been great."

He lowered his head to stare into my eyes. "As obscure as it may sound, the distraction gave me purpose—salvation if you may. But it has kept me from your embrace." He lifted a finger and brushed my cheek. "Life without you and this place is one I can't imagine."

Despite my melancholy, I forced a smile. "I don't know how we'll manage without you."

"Like you've always done." He wrapped an arm around my waist and drew me to him. "Unfortunately, we've delayed long enough in involving ourselves in the inevitable. We're left with no choice. It's a matter of home and country now. And all must do their part to defend our homes, lands, and families."

"Then let us go and tend to matters in town. And, afterward, allow ourselves the enjoyment of one last evening together. We can return at first light."

He placed a kiss on my lips. "Then say your goodbyes, and we will be on our way."

He released me, and I walked the path to the front veranda, where dear faces waited, and my eyes welled with tears at their smiles.

"No tears, angel gal. We be jus' fine. You enjoy some time wid de masa," Mammy said with a toothy grin as I came to stand in front of her. Hand clasped with hers, Big John was stationed dutifully at her side. The sight brought renewed tears. Love had returned him to her side, and I hoped fate would not see it undone despite what was to come.

"We will return swiftly," I said.

"And we stand guard till den." He inclined his head.

"And ef'n dem damn Northerners git to thinking of invading, well, only de Lard can help us den," Mammy said matter-of-factly and squared her shoulders.

Her bluntness had a surprisingly calm effect. She was right. Fearing something one had no control over almost felt worse than looking death in the eye.

I moved down the line to Tillie. "As you know, I don't require your assistance in town, so if it suits you, you can take to Pete's cabin with the babe for the night."

Her eyes gleamed. "You sho', Missus Willow?"

"Yes." I winked.

"Thank you kindly."

Mary Grace waited with an arm around Evie's shoulders. Noah, almost a young man, stood on her other side, standing nearly as tall as his mama. "Take care of each other," I said. "Noah, you're the man of the family, so I expect you to keep an eye out for your mama and sister."

He saluted me. "Yessum."

Goodbyes completed, I descended the stairs and walked to where Bowden waited, speaking to Ben. Ben opened his arms, and I walked into his loving embrace.

He kissed the top of my head and gave me an extra squeeze before holding me at arm's length. "You leave matters here to us."

"There have never been more capable hands." I glanced at the people of Livingston.

"Missus Willie."

Warmth wrapped my heart, and I turned to find Jimmy arriving. I smiled with delight.

"I know et jus' for a night, but I wanted to wish you a safe journey. And I reckon I see you when you git back."

"You can bet on it." I patted his arm.

Bowden spun to look down the lane at the sound of an approaching carriage. "It looks like Lucille," he said.

I circled our carriage to get a better look. I grimaced. Lucille, indeed. What in heaven's name did she want? The last time I'd endured her company had been the evening ball after the races. I'd spent the night avoiding her prying questions about Bowden's and Ben's negligence in assisting their countrymen.

I heaved a sigh as her carriage rolled to a stop, and opened my mouth to question her, but she spoke before I could get a word out. "Do accept my apologies for coming unannounced." She lowered her lashes, attempting to convey vulnerability, something that may work on her lovers, but it proved ineffective on me. "I come out of concern."

"Oh?" I raised a brow.

"Yes. You see..." She drew out her words. "I do consider you one of my dearest friends."

Oh, lucky me. Shading my eyes with a hand to block the sun, I peered up at her, pondering how I could remove myself from her "dearest friends" list. I suspected I wasn't alone. "You're too kind," I said.

She sat twirling her parasol. "You must know what people are saying."

No, but I'm sure you are going to tell me, I fumed inwardly. "Is this why you've come calling?"

She paid me no mind but glanced at Bowden, who stood some feet away, observing us. In a hushed tone, she rushed to spew her assumptions before they devoured her. "Some are speculating that your husband may be a Northern spy."

"You don't say." I anchored my fists on my hips. To say I was surprised would be a lie. As I'd assumed, Lucille's feigned act of goodwill had been instigated by a need to get a closer look for herself.

She gawked at me. "Well, are the rumors true?"

"Are you oblivious, or complete fool?" I threw my hands in the air.

"Pardon me?" She pulled back and placed a hand to her chest.

I pointed in the direction of Charleston. "Anderson moved his troops to Fort Sumter. The militia occupies Fort Moultrie,

Castle Pinckney, and the US Arsenal. Defenses are being constructed around the harbor where gunboats patrol the waters. And you question me about how my husband seeks to defend our home and land." She blurred in my rising fury.

"But everyday men are willingly leaving their lands and homes in the care of their womenfolk to aid in the Confederate cause."

"And our hired hands have already left to join. If you must know, my uncle and husband are set to leave in the morning."

"But why the delay?"

I rubbed my temples. "I grow tired of your intrusive ways. Must you always spend your days interfering and gossiping about others?"

She glared at me. "I'm offended by your hostility."

"And I'm offended that you spread rumors about the ones you call friends. Not to mention the time you wasted riding out here to investigate."

She gasped. "I did not. I-I came out of con—"

"Save the falsehoods for someone that isn't wise to your ways. I've tried with you; honestly, I have, but we are just two vastly different people," I said. "I believe a time is coming when we women will need to stick together more than ever before, and I do not wish to make an enemy out of you, but you must keep your nose out of my affairs."

She appeared shaken and on the verge of tears. "So you believe it too?"

"What?" I dropped my hands to stare at her in confusion.

"That war is coming?"

Oh, for the love of all that is holy! Breathe. "Look," I said more gently, "it's coming, regardless of whether we are ready or not."

Her face twisted with an unbecoming pout. "My husband believes, if it does come, it will be swift and over before we know it. But it doesn't make all this talk of war any less terrifying. Why must we women deal with such things? Shouldn't it be the menfolk's duty to keep trying times at bay? Besides, they are the ones that got us into this mess."

And in her declaration, she presented a significant moment in our history. For once, Lucille and I agreed on something.

The leaders responsible for our nation's decisions had delivered war, rabid and snarling at our heels.

CHAPTER
Thirty-Six

Reuben—April 12, 1861, 4:25 a.m.

THE DAWN WAS UPON US, AND THE SWEET PERFUME OF RECKONING hung in the air. Inhaling a long, invigorating breath, I exhaled gray billows that were embraced by the fading mist of the night. I extinguished the cigar on my mount's side. The beast stomped and whinnied in protest, heightening my anticipation of what I would soon unleash.

I relished the screams I imagined, and the looks of terror as the people of Livingston scrambled for their lives. Death would charge the morning air as I released the Northern wolves on the unsuspecting folks nestled in their beds.

Amelie's betrayal had failed to hinder my plans, and I would deal with her soon enough. I stifled the ache that tried to twitch in my chest at that. *We warned you,* the voices pealed. *A woman is the devil's temptation.*

Silence. The voices had retreated, and I was grateful for it.

I leaned over my mount, beholding from the ridge the sleeping plantation in all its vulnerability. Positioned at my flanks were Rufus and a posse of Northern militia thirsting for Southern blood. Chaos and destruction would unfold; blood would pool in the low country, from livestock to slaves. Once and for all, we would cleanse the earth of the Hendricks bloodline, end Olivia's curse, and see Livingston in ruins. And in Charleston, men lay in wait, and it was with regret that I knew I wouldn't behold the splendor as their mission ignited the skies.

Twisting in my saddle, I observed the gleaming eyes of the men next to me, each eager to dirty his hands on his terms, not governed by military protocols. We had recruited them from taverns, farms, and roadsides as we rode south toward the conclusion that had warmed my gut for far too long. I had delivered them a new religion. The tenet that below lay one of the wealthiest and most influential families in the South, who traded their raw goods across the ocean, employing all tactics to circumvent the North while cultivating the belief in the South that Northerners were an affliction that needed extracting. The tensions overtaking the country had played out brilliantly, and like children eating from my hand, the wolves fed.

"Ripe for the picking. Our time has come, brother." Rufus clapped my back.

I pulled away from his touch. *Yours will be the final blood to spill.* I masked the thought even as I savored it. My focus remained on the manipulation of my plan—strategies I'd spent far too long constructing, while patiently waiting to execute them at the appropriate time. The Northern militia would take the fall, and no one would be the wiser.

My brother directed his frenzied gaze at me before rotating in his saddle to address the men.

"Remember, the slave girl is mine. You can't miss her. She's the exotic-looking mulatto with curves and breasts that will seize your manhood with one look. If you see her, bring her to me. As for the rest, do as you will."

Grins flashed.

They will curse the day they drew breath.

We will pluck the bodies of the woman's loved ones from their graves and leave them scattered amongst the rubble, the voices crowed.

I hadn't considered that. Brilliant. I smiled. The desecration would be the ultimate blade in Willow's heart. First I would behold her face as she observed the collapse of her beloved Livingston. Then I would slit her man's throat and savor the thrashing of his body as he fought to live, and the departure of his spirit from this world. "Then she will meet her fate," I said.

"I too want to see the wench die. She has always been much too high and mighty on herself." Rufus straightened in his saddle in preparation. "Shall we?"

I dipped my head in response.

A cannon thundered in the distance. Startled, I craned my neck in the direction of Charleston, visible on the horizon. Color painted the sky.

Oblivious, Rufus struck the air with a fist and released a war cry, drowning out whatever was occurring in Charleston. "Revenge is ours!" he screamed, and charged.

Twenty-two militiamen followed him.

I whipped the reins and raced toward my impending salvation.

ᔐ CHAPTER ᔐ
Thirty-Seven

Mary Grace—Thirty minutes before

THE SYMPHONY OF KATYDIDS AND CRICKETS CEASED AS DAWN drew near. Croaking bullfrogs and the boisterous harmonies of Carolina wrens and robins took center stage. Sitting in the rocker on the back terrace, I sat reflecting on the conversation between Mama and me last night.

She had kept her back to me as she roamed the house, turning down lanterns and preparing to retire for the night.

"Mama, please." I stalked behind her. "You must understand. I'll be forever grateful to the Hendrickses, and, like you, I hold them dear in my heart. I honor the sanctuary Livingston has provided for you and me. But I hold no love for this place. It has taken much from me, and most of all...my freedom. No matter how hard Willow's parents before her, and she and Masa Bowden try, they can never eradicate the lamentations and suffering of the hundreds of slaves whose lives started and ended in bondage to this place."

"You got a lot of hate brewing in your belly, gal." Without glancing in my direction, she waved a hand in dismissal. Disapproval soured her tone, and her stubbornness took charge of all sense. The spirit that had kept Mama alive often became the very trait that made her obstinate and grueling to deal with.

Trembling inside, as I often did when trying to make her see reason, I refused to allow her anxiety and fear—or mine of cross-ing her—prevent me from speaking what was in my heart. "Not hate. Passion," I said. "Olivia Hendricks gave me my freedom, and I intend to accept that gift."

"I knowed Mr. Barlow take you from me soon as he started hanging 'round de place. Should have run him off a long time ago." Glaring, she whisked past me and marched down the cor-ridor to the library. "Ef et warn't for de good deir arrival bring to Missus Willow, I wish dem back to England where dey come."

Roiling inside at her disregard for all reason, I staked heated words into her retreating back. "How can you be so selfish? Does my happiness mean nothing to you?"

Her footfalls ceased, and my breathing caught.

She gasped before her shoulders slumped.

Pain slashed through my heart. "Forgive me," I whispered. "I don't mean to hurt you." I crept forward and placed hands on her shoulders. "Mama?"

She turned slowly to face me, and tears marked her cheeks.

Regret staked my heart. "I'm sorry—"

"No." Looking at me, she smiled sadly as she raised her hands and adjusted my frock's collar. "Bin luking 'round evvy corner so long, suppose I failed to see you grown. Reckon I bin acting a fool. You right, gal. I got a whole lot of selfishness too. A parent got a vision for deir chillums, and I reckon I saw you and my grandbabies staying wid me till de Lard takes my spirit home. But I wrong in holding you here. I ain't no better den a slave masa." She dropped her head and released a guttural sob as she shook with unmasked grief. "I sorry, gal, real sorry."

"I understand, Mama. I dread the day Noah or Evie seek to part from my side. But we must do what's right by our children. If you cage a bird for too long, eventually they will seek flight."

"Dat be so. Guess I figured when you 'ccepted Mr. Barlow's

proposal dat you only be a carriage ride away. But dis plan to leave Charleston for good be hard to take. But, in time, I adjust lak any mother does."

"I never expected love would come my way again, and certainly not with a white man. Nor could I imagine a day I wouldn't be at your side. But he has renewed my spirit in humanity and given me a desire to live a life that has purpose. To give my children more."

"And for dat, I owe him," she said.

"In time, I hope you will come to see what I love about him."

She balled a fist on her hip and regarded me as though I'd lost my mind. "And how you reckon I do dat ef ya'll plan on hightailing et outta here?"

"Mama!" I glowered.

She shrugged before a cheeky smile appeared on her face. "Folkses from England sho' do talk funny. Don't reckon I ever git use to dat."

"You're impossible." I threw my hands in the air.

She turned and occupied herself with gathering books before walking to the wall-to-ceiling shelf and placing them in their assigned spots. "Does angel gal know of your plans?"

I strode and removed a book from her hand and placed it on the shelf she struggled to reach. "No, she has too much to worry about. I feared the news would cause unneeded grief."

"You right 'bout dat. But ef not now, den when?"

"Soon."

After she had retired, I wandered out to the terrace, where Magnus waited on the porch swing. He stilled its movement and patted the seat beside him.

"Tell me, what does Miss Rita say this time?"

I walked to him and sat. "You know Mama, she can be as calm as a morning breeze one day, and a charging bull the next."

He laughed and set to tracing the top of my hand where it lay in my lap. The delight of his laughter calmed my nerves, and I relaxed back against the swing, observing his face as he concentrated on his finger's movement. Goose pimples scurried over my arms and my heart skipped a beat or two, as it often did in his company. He was so tranquil, a trait apparent from the beginning. Despite the many times I'd pushed him away after he'd made his intentions known, he had proceeded with patience and the integrity I needed. In time, he had earned my trust, and even in our lovemaking, he had been tender but passionate.

"I will miss her," I said. "It's always just been Mama and me. She did what she thought was best, and I don't fault her for it. If the Hendrickses hadn't purchased her, then we would never have come here, and Missus Olivia wouldn't have given us our freedom. I will forever be grateful to them, and it's because of this place that I met you."

"Indeed." He lifted his gaze. "And if it wasn't for my mother's love affair with Charles, we would never have ended up here. Our lives will always be deeply intertwined with the Hendrickses."

I laced my fingers with his. "I worry what Willow will say when she discovers our plans extend beyond Charleston."

"I've come to know her as a reasonable woman, and one who cares deeply for others. She will come to accept you're leaving, as your mother will. Besides, it doesn't mean we will never return. I wish to show you and the children what lies beyond this plantation. There is a whole world out there to be discovered."

I looked into his eyes, seeking comfort for the worries plaguing me. "A world I've learned to fear."

"A fear that can be extinguished." He stroked my cheek.

"But it's not only my fear of being outside the protection of masters, it's the reactions to our union. Are you willing to spend your life being ridiculed for marrying a mulatto and becoming a father to Negro children?"

"I've witnessed my parents' struggles over their union, and I know the hardships they've faced. But I also see the love they hold for each other. If they had paid heed to the alienation of friends, family, and strangers, they would have missed out on a lifetime of happiness that fate deemed was theirs." He captured my chin with his fingers and lowered his lips to meet mine.

Placing my hands on his chest, I welcomed his kiss. The desire to pull him closer arched my body, and I wrapped my arms around the nape of his neck, drawing him nearer. His lips smiled, and I melted into his embrace, my heart singing to the melody of his.

In his arms I had found refuge, the sense of wholeness and security I'd felt before Rufus and his men had raped me. Back when naivety had me regarding Mama's fear of men and their intentions as her paranoia. He had provided me with a sense of safety I'd never felt with Gray. Although my husband would have given his life to defend me, he was but a slave in a system that left him powerless.

When he released me, I scooted into the warmth of his side and rested my head on his shoulder. "Thank you."

"For what?" he whispered into my hair.

"For choosing me."

"It is I who should offer gratitude. After Charlotte died, I didn't know if love would find me again. The promise of a new life in America, where I wasn't reminded of her, was a needed escape. From the moment I caught a glimpse of you in the wagon, I was smitten. Although you had no eye for me," he said with amusement. "There was a hunger to know you better. I'm thankful that, eventually, you came to your senses and realized my intentions were pure."

Some time later we moved to the rockers, where we sat talking for the next several hours, lost in our dreams and aspirations until he fell asleep. Soon after, I dozed off, but awakened some hours later, my mind troubled with how I would tell Willow of my upcoming departure. Although I considered her easier than Mama, I didn't want to see the pain in her eyes that I'd seen in Mama's. The thought sickened me. But she had Bowden now, and Mama had Big John. The time was right. *It couldn't be better, in fact*, I consoled myself.

I glanced at Magnus, slumped in a rocker to my left with is hand hanging limply over the side. His chest rose and fell with sleep, and the peacefulness of his face and his soft breaths lulled me. Entwining my fingers with his, I relished the warmth of his flesh against mine. His love had been the cure I'd spent years seeking, and I needed him more than I had needed anything in a long time. My eyes teared up with love and gratitude for his appearance in my life.

I peered into the twilight. Soon the plantation would shake from its slumber, and cabin doors would swing open as folks wandered out on their stoops to stretch and behold the start of a new day. Short of sleep, the day promised to be long for me, but the bliss enveloping me would give me vigor for the day.

I pulled to my feet, rubbed the ache in my neck from a night of improper sleep, and looked down at Magnus. I smiled and leaned to kiss his cheek.

He stirred, and his lids fluttered open, confusion in his eyes. Glancing around, he sat up. "Fell asleep, did I?"

"It appears we both did," I said.

"It's almost dawn. Mum has probably been pacing the floors with worry." He stood and pulled me into his embrace. "I shall blame you for my disappearance," he informed me, amusement in his voice. "'Intoxicated me with her company' is how I'll start off."

I laughed and pushed back to look at him. "Blame I will gladly—"

We jumped as a terrifying cry broke the silence. Magnus gripped my arm at the thunder of approaching horses. He bolted across the wraparound terrace toward the front, and I followed close on his heels.

"God in heaven!" he said.

"What? What is it?" Fear gripped my throat and hammered in my chest. I peered around his shoulder at the glow of torches and horses plummeting down the ridge.

He pushed me back in the direction we'd come. "Quick, send up the signal. Go quick."

I charged back to the bell hanging from the rafters on the back veranda, and rang it with all my might. Tears blurred my vision as the thought of my children asleep in the quarters.

Mama, groggy from sleep, stumbled outside, and several house slaves followed after. "What is et?"

"Men. Lots of them. Get the rifles and prepare to defend as Masa Bowden showed us," I shouted in panic.

"De babies." Mama bolted for the steps, but I pulled her back.

"No, Mama. Stay inside." I bounded down the back steps.

"Mary Grace!" Magnus's voice struck at my back.

I flew across the work yard as if terror itself were at my heels. *Not my babies. Please, God, help us!*

"Mary Grace." Someone grabbed my arm and reeled me back.

"Let me go." I clawed at my captor. "My children. I must get to them."

"What is happening?" I recognized Masa Ben's voice.

I ceased my struggle for a brief moment. "T-they're coming."

"Who?" He shook me with urgency.

"I don't know." My chest heaved with sobs. "Riders coming from the ridge. Lots of them."

Behind him, wide-eyed quarter folks spilled into the work yard.

Masa Ben released me, and I bolted as his voice carried behind me. "Mothers, get your children to the river. Everyone else, fall into position."

At the cabin I shared with my children and another family, I threw open the door and collided with someone. My head spun from the impact, and hands gripped my arms to keep me from falling.

"Mama?" Fear strummed in Noah's voice.

My gaze focused on my son. "Noah," I sobbed. "Oh, my baby." I clutched him to my chest and kissed his face repeatedly.

"What is it, Mama?" He trembled.

I broke away and looked at the gawking faces of the family. "Trouble. And lots of it."

On the cot I shared with my daughter, I noticed her sleeping form. I raced to the bedside, threw back the blankets, and attempted to jostle her awake, but she slept on without flinching. "Evie!" I screamed, glancing over my shoulder as the family raced from the cabin. I nudged her harder, and she stirred but turned on her side, facing away from me. I scooped her into my arms and staggered under her weight.

Noah dashed forward to assist. "You're scaring me, Mama," he said.

"And with good cause." I pushed his sister into his arms. "Take her and go to the river with the others. Stay there until I come for you."

"But what about you?" Terror gleamed in his eyes.

"I will be fine." I kissed Evie's cheek as she awakened.

"Mama." Panic clotted her voice. "What is happening?" She scanned the door hanging ajar and the empty cabin before throwing her arms around my neck. Her nails bit into my flesh.

"Evie, listen." I pried her off me. "You need to run. Run as fast as your legs will carry you. Do you hear me?"

She bobbed her head as Noah lowered her to the floor. He clasped her hand tight in his.

"Good girl. Now do as he instructs—"

Gunshots cracked. One shrill reverberation after another.

Evie screamed and cupped her hands over her ears.

"Go now!" I shoved them toward the door. "Stay put until I come to you."

Noah rushed out the door with Evie struggling to keep up.

From the stoop, I watched them join the women and children fleeing for the river until they disappeared over the bank. "Watch over them," I said into the chill of the morning.

All around me, harrowing screams reverberated, mixed with horses whinnying, the crack of gunshots, and wafting smoke. I twisted to look back in the direction of the big house, but it was blocked by outbuildings and cabins. My heart hammered harder at the sight of flames stretching above the rooftops. I craned my neck in the direction of Charleston as cannons thundered in the distance, and the sky radiated shades of crimson, orange, and mauve. My limbs shook, threatening to crumple beneath me. Was the town under attack? Had war finally erupted? Perhaps Lincoln had commanded Major Anderson to set his men on Southern plantations. My mind raced with possibilities.

Howls of exhilaration rose three cabins down, and I crouched low as men kicked open cabin doors; inhabitants' shrieks followed. Tears of pure panic streamed down my cheeks as I gripped the hem of my dress and ran back toward the main house.

I found the work yard overrun with riders, and slave folk armed with rakes and hoes and some with guns. I scanned the chaos for Magnus and Mama, to no avail as horses blocked my view, and I pressed my hands against their chests to avoid being trampled. I ducked when I felt the breeze of a rider's hand as he tried to grab me on his way by. Evading his grip, I darted around a fallen horse, lying injured, its lifeless rider pinned beneath its weight.

Glass shattered as a rider launched a torch through an upstairs window. *Mama!* I leaped over wounded slaves and riders as I pushed on. Then I froze as a rider's face snatched the very breath from me.

No! It's impossible. But as I got a full look at his face, my own screams joined the nightmare unfolding around me. The man twisted in his saddle at my cry, and Rufus McCoy's eyes widened before a devilish grin broke across his face. Kicking his heels into the sides of his mount, he charged toward me.

Snapped from my trance, I fled. As the back steps came into view I pumped my legs faster, glancing over my shoulder to find Rufus advancing. I burst into tears at his sinister grin. He kicked vigorously at his horse's flanks to gain speed. I looked back at the house, tripped over an object, and struck the earth so hard my teeth rattled and pain shot through my body. Looking at the lump responsible for my fall, I recognized the dead form of Parker's pappy. Next to him lay the lifeless body of the weaver woman's husband, a rake still clutched in his hand. *This can't be happening.* My mind raced to the children. Had they made it to the river? What about Mama and Magnus? Where were they?

I saw Jimmy, a short distance away, as he dropped to his knees. A uniformed white man towered over him. *No.* Grief crushed my chest.

A shadow loomed over me, and I swung back as Rufus reined his horse to a sudden stop to avoid crushing me. I felt the draft as the beast reared up on its hind legs.

"We meet again, my little pet," Rufus said.

Using my elbows and heels, I scooted back before twisting onto my side and pushing to my feet. He dropped to the ground behind me and seized my ankle. The smell of his stagnant breath revolted my nostrils and flooded my memories with his mouth seeking pleasure from my bruised, naked body. *No, no, no!* I twisted and kicked with all my strength, jabbing the heel of my shoe into his shin. Again and again, I kicked until his wails rose, and I broke free. I scrambled to my feet and sprinted away.

The massive body of a horse blocked my path, and my heart skipped when I looked up into the unsmiling face of Rufus's brother, Reuben McCoy. A shot rang out, and he jerked as a bullet struck him in the head, but instead of falling, he slumped forward, gripping the mane of his horse.

I swerved around the beast. Fingers seized the back of my dress, and I screamed and twisted to free myself, feeling the fabric give as my dress ripped.

"You can't run from me." Rufus's fetid breath heated my neck. "I will bed you this night."

"Duck, gal!" Mama's voice rang loud and clear.

I gawked at the lower step, where she stood with a rifle at her shoulder. I dropped to my belly, and the crack of a gun rang in my ears.

I heard a gasp behind me, and I turned my head to see Rufus clutching his chest, blood oozing through his fingers. Mouth agape, he sank to his knees.

Mama marched across the yard as though the chaos around her had evaporated. Eyes fastened on Rufus, she advanced. Passing a dead slave, she swooped with astounding swiftness and retrieved a hoe from his grip without so much as a glance sideways.

A thump made me whip my head back to Rufus, who had collapsed face-first.

"You never hurt my gal again." Mammy swung the hoe high above her head and brought it down into Rufus's skull. "Never again."

I lay unmoving, dumbfounded as she struck again and again, the warmth of his blood speckling my face. "Mama," I whispered, but it fell on deaf ears in the heat of her determination.

Energy spent, she dropped to her knees beside him, and a sob escaped her. I crawled to her and wrapped my arm around her shoulders, gaping at the brain matter oozing from Rufus's skull. I gulped. "He's dead for good this time."

"And I would kill him again. He ain't de first I killed for thinking he gonna take something dat ain't his for de taking."

My brow puckered at her statement, but there was no time to ask questions. "If we don't find cover, we're as good as dead out here." I hauled Mama to her feet and, crouching low, we dashed toward an old wagon engulfed in high grass and weeds.

"Get in." I pushed her down and, with effort, she scurried under on her belly.

There was a scream, and what sounded like a struggle.

"Tillie?" Mama said. "Et me, Rita."

I sank to my belly and scrambled to get out of sight, coming face-to-face with a wide-eyed Tillie clutching her shrieking son. Tears and sweat dampened the boy's face and blended with his mother's.

"Why aren't you at the river with the others?" I asked.

She tried desperately to soothe the child. "Got cut off."

I turned and tussled the grass behind me, attempting to conceal our entry point.

"De babe give us away as sho' as anything," Mama said.

"I don't know what to do. He plumb skeered, Miss Rita." Tillie's voice trembled.

Mama patted her shoulder. "I know, chile."

I reached into my pinafore pocket, recalling the sugarcane I'd taken from the kitchen house for Evie. I had planned to surprise her with the treat when I retired to the quarters last evening, but with Magnus's unexpected arrival I had hurried to say my goodnights and left the children with the promise of my soon return. Only I never had until I charged into the cabin to rip them from their beds.

I removed the sugarcane and handed it to Tillie. "This may soothe him."

She took the sugarcane and chewed it to soften the end before placing it to the child's lips, squeezing the sweetness over his tongue. His screams turned to whimpers as his chubby fingers stretched for the treat.

Tillie looked at me with a look of gratitude and relief as the boy pacified himself with the sugarcane before she buried her face into the curve of his neck, sobbing softly.

Mama rubbed Tillie's back in gentle circles and whispered a prayer.

We sprawled there until the pounding of horses' hooves faded, and an eerie stillness fell over the plantation. Although our immediate surroundings had calmed somewhat, I heard the crackling of flames, and the booming vibration of cannons continued in the distance.

As I stretched to part the grass to investigate our surroundings, Mama caught my arm. "You don't know what waits out dere, or ef et safe."

"Mary Grace!" Magnus's voice shouted.

My heart leaped, and tears gathered in my throat. He was alive. I parted the grass and scooted from beneath the wagon and clambered to my feet.

Before us, Masa Ben, Magnus, and others moved across the work yard, examining the dead and wounded. Jones and slaves raced with slopping water buckets toward the big house. The fire had collapsed outbuildings and cabins, and the rubble lay smoldering while flames still chewed through the main house. With effort, it might yet be saved.

"Mary Grace!" I heard the panic in Magnus's voice as he rose to stand over a woman's corpse. He scanned the bodies around him, terror evident on his face.

"We are here," I said before turning to help Mama up, then Tillie.

"Tillie, dat you?" Pete bounded toward his family, and Tillie melted into his protective embrace.

Magnus crushed me in his arms. His heart hammered against my ear. "I thought I'd lost you," he whispered.

"Are they gone?" I muffled into his chest.

"For now." He pulled me back to inspect me for injuries.

"Where my John?" Mama tugged at his arm.

"Sorry, Miss Rita, I lost track of him in the chaos," Magnus said, sympathy in his blue eyes.

"I got to find him. I lose him once; I not see et happen again." She marched off.

"Be careful," I called after her.

At the sound of approaching horses and wagons, Magnus pushed me behind him and hoisted the rifle. Everyone froze, terror on their faces as folks readied for a second attack. But as neighbors crowded onto flatbeds and on horseback poured into the work yard, Magnus lowered the gun.

Masa Ben sprinted to greet them.

"What happened?" Mr. Sterling, a neighboring farmer and constable for the area, jumped down.

"We must help get the fire out," someone said, and people raced to the well to join the assembly of slaves already in action.

Masa Ben nudged his head at the horizon. "It appears

Northern militia thought to take advantage of whatever is befalling in town and hit us before the US Army got a chance."

"Militia?" Mr. Sterling eyed the collection of bodies. "You may be right. It appears they don states' militia garb." He rubbed a hand over his face and pulled down, weariness and concern on his face. His gaze turned to the horizon, as did those of several other men.

I listened to the men's conversation as daylight revealed strangers dressed in various uniforms, as well as simple clothing.

"Your plantation sits midway in both directions. Why did they choose to attack ya'll first?" a farmer asked.

"Good question, and one I may have an answer for." Masa Ben gestured for them to follow.

He stopped at Rufus and, with the toe of his boot, rolled over the corpse. The thumping in my chest beat faster as I half expected him to stir. But Mama had finished him good. I shuddered, recalling the splitting of his skull and the taste of blood on my lips. The bandana he had worn to cover the word Willow had carved in his forehead as a warning to all had shifted, revealing his offense against me. "Gentleman, here lies one of the McCoy brothers."

A man crouched down to get a better look, covering his mouth and nose with a handkerchief. "Wasn't he the overseer at the Barry Plantation?"

"That's correct," Masa Ben said.

"I thought he died in the fire." Mr. Sterling cocked his head to look at Masa Ben.

"The McCoys are not to be underestimated. The lengths the brothers will go to to see my family in ruins is not to be taken lightly. They're masterminds bent on ending a damn curse the fools believe Olivia placed on their family. One can only assume they wove some kind of lunatic tenet into their misguided belief." He swept a hand over the dead. "Nothing they spew can be trusted."

I stood in awe as Masa Ben shrewdly painted the McCoys in a light that would deflect the brothers' attempt to expose Livingston's operations. Rufus lay dead, but I'd seen his brother Reuben, who posed a more significant threat—he had the genius intellect of a calculated killer. He too may have ceased breathing, or lay injured with breath enough to reveal his findings. And what of his acquaintances and the men who had attacked, now scattered?

Mr. Sterling pointed at the markings on his forehead. "It appears someone wanted the world to know the nature of the man." He gritted his teeth. "There is no end to the McCoys' crimes. What of the younger brother? Any sign of him?"

"He was here. He may be among the bodies. I fired a shot at his head and saw him fall forward, but lost sight of him in the chaos."

"We will get the fire out in the main house while you tend to your wounded," Mr. Sterling said. "Then we must return to our homes." His eyes turned to the horizon.

"Mary Grace." Magnus shook my arm. "We must check on the children."

The children. I gulped, and without waiting, I whirled and raced toward the river, not slowing until I reached the bank. Magnus offered me a hand, and we skidded down the edge onto the rocky waterline.

"Et Mary Grace," a woman called out.

Women and children stepped from their hiding places.

"Et safe?" someone asked.

"Yes," I said.

"Mama!" Evie and Noah dashed toward me.

"My darlings." I stretched out my arms to scoop them into an embrace.

Evie dampened my dress with her tears. I kissed Noah's cheek and pressed him close to my side. Clutching my children to my breasts, I sent a prayer of gratitude as the warmth of Magnus's arms encompassed us all. The children clung to him and he regarded me over their heads, tears glittering in his eyes.

Soon after, we walked back toward the work yard, and I beheld the entirety of the destruction to the plantation, and the horror of what had transpired. Quarter folks and house slaves had given their lives to defend a place that had claimed their liberty, but as the thought hit me, I knew it went deeper. They had offered their lives for their belief in a more favorable tomorrow, placing their faith in Livingston's owners and their passion for the cause.

CHAPTER
Thirty-Eight

Willow—4:30 a.m., April 12, 1861

THE BLAST OF A CANNON BOLTED BOWDEN AND I UPRIGHT IN BED, and instinctively I dropped to the floor as screams and shouts reverberated in the aftermath. Bowden raced for the trousers draped over the armchair by the window overlooking the harbor. He pulled back the thin white sheers, and I gasped as I caught a glimpse of the flames engulfing the sky.

"They're firing on Fort Sumter," he said. "Get dressed!"

Pushing myself up from the floor, I hurried to don a night robe as he hopped about trying to wiggle into his trousers. My trembling fingers fumbled with the robe's tie. My heart hammered as if trying to escape my chest, and I jumped when urgent pounding rattled our chamber door.

"Mr. Armstrong!" Our butler's voice rose. "The warehouse and ships are on fire."

Bowden grabbed my hand and we dashed for the door. He threw it open and on the other side stood our winded butler, with sweat beading his upper lip and forehead. Beside him, a heaving Captain Gillies gripped the door frame, trying to catch his breath. He stood sopping wet from head to toe, pooling water over the recently refinished floorboards.

"Gillies?" Bowden's brow furrowed. "Why are you in such a state?"

"Someone set fire to the *Olivias* and the warehouse."

My blood ran cold.

"Are you saying Major Anderson's troops have made it ashore? Then why are the Confederates unleashing on Fort Sumter?"

"I don't believe it was Anderson's troops. The culprits were militia."

"Militia? How can you be certain?"

"Got a gander at them before I was forced to abandon ship."

We all ducked as another cannon cracked.

"Hell has been unleashed!" groaned Jane, the butler's wife. She crouched in the corner, her gaze fixed on the corridor window at the end of the hall.

"I couldn't prevent the spread on my own." The captain's face twisted with remorse.

Bowden pushed past the men and darted down the corridor, dragging me along with him. He slung open the door to stairs leading to the rooftop, and we raced up. The treads of Captain Gillies and the servants thundered behind us.

As we stepped out onto the rooftop, I beheld the bleeding sky. All around us, Charlestonians stood on rooftops and balconies with their eyes trained on the harbor. Bowden released my hand and stumbled forward until he stood at the far corner of the roof, his gaze concentrated on our ships and warehouse immersed in flames. Horror gripped me at the destruction unfolding at the docks and the harbor.

"Armstrong, isn't that your ships?" Mr. Hewett, our neighbor, called from his balcony.

"It appears so," Bowden answered, his voice hollow. He slumped forward, resting his palms on the railing.

"Caught in the crossfire, I assume. Damn Lincoln and his ambitions!" Mr. Hewett called back.

As though walking through a nightmare, my footsteps leaden, I moved to my husband's side, and Captain Gillies followed. I touched Bowden's shoulder, and he straightened and glanced at me.

"All *they* fought for, gone!" Tears welled in his eyes.

I gulped as grief filled me. "We will rebuild," I said, my words sounding vacant and unpromising.

As the three of us stood beholding the harbor Bowden pulled me tight to his side, and drew a ragged breath. "Only God can help us now!"

PREVIEW OF

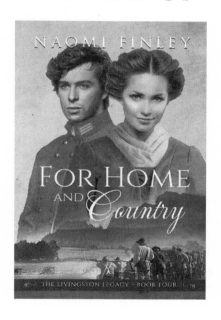

CHAPTER
One

Charleston, April 12, 1861

ANNON-FIRE WHISTLED AND CRACKED, AND WITH EACH EXPLOSION, I jumped, my nerves spun tight since the onset of the battle taking place in the harbor. The roar and thunder of shells unleashed on Major Anderson of the US Army and his garrison at Fort Sumter had been going on for hours. The South Carolina militia, led by General Beauregard, controlled the beach and the surrounding forts. Citizens remained on rooftops and balconies, and gathered at the Battery and in the streets to witness the bombardment. Older men, and boys too young, patrolled the streets, intent on protecting the city and keeping the Negros under control.

I paced the foyer of our townhouse, awaiting Bowden and Captain Gillies's return with news on the damage to our warehouse and ships. The muscles in my neck and shoulders ached from the tension, aggravated by the relentless thundering of cannons.

Jane, the butler's wife and our housekeeper, walked down the hallway with a silver tray rattling in her hands. She and her husband—freed blacks—had managed the townhouse for as long as I could remember. "Missus Willow, you must rest. I've fixed you some coffee and breakfast."

I eyed the lanky woman of sixty or so. "I can't possibly eat at a time like this."

She strode into the parlor and set the tray down on the sofa table. "You look ready to drop where you stand. Running to the window in hopes Mr. Armstrong and the captain have returned won't make their arrival come any faster."

"The wait is unbearable." I chewed on the corner of my mouth, now raw from gnawing.

Another crack ripped through the morning, and I ducked as though expecting the shell to land in the room. Jane gripped the doorframe, her wide eyes flitting to the window.

"I must return to Livingston at once." I straightened and eyed the small retinue of house staff hovering in doorways and at the top of the stairs. "Folks would have heard the ruckus and concerns will be high."

Jane released her hold on the doorframe. "What do we do if the army takes the city?"

The hissing of cannon-fire was loud in the silence as I thought. "Although Major Anderson seems to be at a disadvantage, circumstances could change. When Bowden and Captain Gillies return, we'll know more of what is to be done—" The boom of the rapid firing of shells lodged my heart in my throat, and Jane and I clung to each other.

"Fort Sumter returns fire," shouted an informant, a boy of nine or ten clad in a long gray coat, as he raced through the street.

"Anderson has finally shown up," a man shouted in his wake.

I gawked at Jane, and we rushed to the parlor window and drew back the dark blue velvet drape.

Atop his mount, Josephine's husband, Theodore Carlton, garbed in a similar homespun coat, addressed the citizens. "This war will be over before you know it. General Beauregard has the advantage."

In the North, men had joined the US Army, while in the

South, capable men formed militias and aided in the Confederate cause. Like Mr. Carlton, those too old took up policing and were accompanied by boys too young to fight.

"The South will persevere, and our menfolk will return." He thrust out his chest. "Lincoln and his ambitions will fail to take hold. Let the North be reminded that the South won't be defeated." He struck at the heavens with a fist, and the citizens erupted in cheers.

"There is no certainty in what you say." Bowden's voice rose, and I pressed my cheek against the windowpane to find him in the crowd. Locating him standing some feet from the front steps of our townhouse, I released the drape and raced for the door.

Stepping outside, I descended the stairs to join him. He looped an arm around my waist without looking sideways. Soot and grime covered his face and hands, and the odor of smoke wafted from his clothing.

"Providing hope for the people is one thing, but offering false hope is a pitfall." He glanced at Theodore and the two young boys on his flanks. "If you intend to man the city and country-side, ensure your efforts are to the benefit of those needing it. Our womenfolk need men they can count on."

Carlton turned his intense blue eyes on Bowden, and the men engaged in a standoff of glares until Theodore broke focus and turned an uncanny look of open fascination on me. My legs trembled under a gaze that defined me as the prey and he the hunter. He had earned a reputation for pressing himself upon women and quarter slaves. His attention unsettled me. With our men away, men like him would seek to rise in power.

"And what the South needs is decent menfolk who are willing to defend our cause. Yet you're still here, while the good men have already left. Why is that?" He leaned forward, resting an elbow on his thigh.

Bowden tensed. "I will be gone soon enough."

Carlton smirked. "And, in your absence, I will see that your lovely wife is well cared for."

At that, Bowden gripped my elbow and turned to climb the steps. He hurried me inside and shut the door.

"Jane."

"Yes, Mr. Armstrong?" She came forward.

"Pack our things. We leave at once for Livingston."

She bowed and hurried away.

"Uriah?"

"Right here, Mr. Armstrong." The butler held out a glass of whiskey, which Bowden took without hesitation and drained.

The windowpanes vibrated from the impact of cannons.

"In my absence, I hope that I can keep you employed to care for the place. Of course, until the threat to your safety makes that impossible."

Years had hunched Uriah's towering frame; no longer did he have to duck to walk through doorways. "We stay as long as needed. Don't have no place to go anyhow. We talked 'bout staying with our boy in Georgia, but don't reckon any place is going to be safe after this." Concern pulled at his face.

"I fear you are right. I will leave a stable boy to tend the animals." He glanced around at the staff, all waiting for answers on the upstairs landing and the main floor. "All other employees are to return to your homes and family until we can bring you back. If there is a place to come back to."

Murmurs lifted.

"Come, come." Bowden made a brushing gesture with his hand. "We mustn't delay."

The staff scurried to do his bidding.

"Bowden?" I gripped his arm. "What is the situation at the docks?"

He turned, and the look in his eyes hollowed my stomach. "Not good. The *Olivia I* has capsized, and all but one of our fleet is engulfed in flames. The warehouse remains, but the damage is severe. Our goods are ruined and unsellable."

I gulped, afraid to ask the question that had been governing my thoughts. "Is it as Captain Gillies said?"

"You refer to Northern militia?"

I nodded.

He shrugged. "If so, they are long gone."

"And with what is unfolding in the harbor and your leaving, there is nothing we can do about it," I said.

"I'm afraid not. Now I must leave, and all of the madness is left in your hands." He rested hands on my upper arms and held my gaze.

"We will manage." I offered reassurance while my insides roiled with uncertainty and fear. Reuben McCoy was out there, scheming, and with Ben and Bowden away, it would be up to Jones and me to manage and protect Livingston.

"I will have the carriage readied, and we will return home," he said before brushing my lips with his.

As our carriage rode along I sat closer to Bowden, enjoying the warmth of his side as the battle in the harbor faded behind us. My ears continued to ring from the hours of explosions. The uncertainty of what was to come had stolen our thoughts, and we sat in silence. The scent of smoke never faded as we rode on toward Livingston, and when we were a few miles from home Bowden's body tensed.

"Do you see that?" I looked to where he pointed. Smoke was rising above the trees.

My heart thudded. "Livingston!"

He lifted the reins to urge the team to greater speed, but paused at the sound of approaching horses. In one swift movement, Bowden grabbed the rifle under the seat.

Two riders came around the bend, and I quickly recognized Mr. Sterling and a neighboring farmer.

"Sterling, where does that smoke come from?" Bowden asked as the men reined in their horses.

The look in Mr. Sterling's eyes confirmed our fears. "Your place. Northern militia attacked about the same time as the sky lit up in the direction of Charleston."

"No!" I wailed.

Bowden didn't wait to hear more. "Out of the way!" He slashed the reins, and the team charged forward, forcing the men to heel their horses to clear out of our path.

Please, God, no. The team's manes and tails snapped in the wind of our passage.

"Dammit!" Bowden cursed.

I clutched the side of the carriage to avoid being launched overboard as we charged toward Livingston at a bone-jarring speed. An invisible weight compressed the air from my lungs. We should never have left. Never. I eyed Bowden askance, and the panic clear on his face made my heart beat harder. Images of what we would find upon our arrival swarmed my mind. Whisking away blinding tears, I forced down the bile burning my throat. *Please, God, I'll do anything you ask of me.*

The next miles seemed to move at a painstaking crawl. As we reached the main gates, I glanced over my shoulder to find Mr. Sterling and the farmer on our heels. As our buggy charged up the lane, I fought to clear the relentless tears obscuring my vision.

"Good God!" Bowden leaned forward and whipped the reins harder.

A wail escaped me as I beheld the smoldering main house, still standing, but its windows shattered and the exterior scorched. Our chamber and the nursery located on the left side of the house sat exposed to the heavens.

Bowden slowed the team as we rounded the house to the work yard.

"No!" My agonized wail echoed off the ruined buildings as I viewed the rows of bodies covered in blankets.

"Willow," someone called, and hands reached for me.

I sat numbly in my seat but turned my head to stare at the speaker. In my daze, I couldn't make out their face or voice.

"Come," they said.

My body moved, but I wasn't sure if I'd been lifted from the carriage or advanced of my own accord.

Somewhere Bowden conversed with someone, but I couldn't make out his words.

"Willow." Hands shook me.

I turned my head, frantically trying to concentrate on the person's face. "Magnus?" My vision cleared as I came to my senses. "What happened?"

Dried blood, soot, and grime marred his face. "They came out of nowhere."

"Mary Grace and the children. Are they…" Fear snatched my words.

"We are fine." Mary Grace rushed toward us and crushed me in her arms.

My legs buckled, and I clutched her for support. "Why? Who?" I muffled into her shoulder.

"It was as we feared. The McCoys advanced just before dawn."

I stiffened at the reference before withdrawing from her arms. "McCoys?"

She bit down on her lip. "You need to see for yourself, or you will never believe me." She took my hand and pulled me toward the lines of corpses.

Jones stood next to Bowden, who crouched next to a body and peeled back the blanket. I frowned at the familiarity of the deformed face. It couldn't be. I glanced at Mary Grace, and she swallowed hard and bobbed her head. But how?

"It appears the bastard never died after all," Bowden said.

I gawked from him to the face and the distinguishing markings on the forehead. My hand rose to my throat. Rufus McCoy.

"Angel gal?"

I twisted, and a sob lodged in my throat as I saw Mammy grip the sides of her skirt and bound down the back steps. I rushed toward her, not stopping until we clutched each other in an embrace.

"Mammy. Oh, Mammy." The strength of her embrace kept me from crumpling to my knees. "You're alive."

"Yes, gal. I all right." She pulled me back and cupped my cheek. There was a profound sadness in her eyes. "Can't say de same for others."

My breath caught as I thought of who may lie under the blankets. "Where is Ben?"

"At de hospital, taking care of de wounded."

I glanced around at the weary folks sorting through the wreckage and ashes of outbuildings and cabins for survivors. My heart struck harder, and without looking at her, I said, "Sailor?"

"He fine. De chillum and de 'oman folkses dat made et to de river are all fine."

"And Jimmy?"

"He at de sick hospital." Her voice hitched, and I turned to look at her.

"Providing my uncle aid?"

She gripped my arm, tears welling in her eyes. "No, angel gal. He hurt real bad."

Pulling my arm free, I stumbled back, shaking my head. "No."

The concerned faces before me vanished in a river of tears, and without another word, I turned and fled. Pulse roaring in my ears, I pumped my legs faster. Pain radiated in my chest by the time the sick hospital came into view. Wounded quarter folk and Jones's men lay on makeshift beds constructed of blankets spread out on the ground. Kimie looked up at me as I slowed my pace. Blood stained her apron, and she lifted bloodied fingers to smooth back her blond locks. Tears of devastation glittered in her blue eyes. Whitney knelt beside an injured woman offering her water, and our eyes met as I grasped the magnitude of the destruction that had befallen Livingston in my absence.

"Willow," Ben said, and I followed the sound of his voice to find him standing on the hospital stoop. Face tense, he waved me forward. As I met him on the stoop, he put his arm around my waist, and I leaned on him for support.

"Is he…" Fear captured my voice.

"He is alive, but barely. If he makes it through the night—"

"No." I shook my head. "It can't be." I collapsed against his shoulder, sobbing, my fingers grabbing at his shirt. "This is all my fault."

"You are not to blame," he consoled me. "The McCoys are."

"He warned me," Bowden said, his voice grave and vacant.

Lifting my head, I located him through my tears. Face ashen, he stood observing the sea of injured people. "Who?" I said, my voice rasping.

"Gray. The dreams. The visions. All warnings." Gripping the sides of his head, he dropped to his knees and released a guttural wail.

I rushed to his side and tenderly clasped his head against my waist. Turning, he buried his face into the fabric of my dress and wept like I'd never seen him do before.

⤳ CHAPTER ⤳
Two

ENTERING THE SICK HOSPITAL, I LOOKED TO THE COT BY THE window and recognized the face of Gray's pa, who had chosen to remain at Livingston after Bowden had sold his plantation. Nausea roiled in my gut. He lay unconscious, his breathing shallow. As I turned my gaze to the other cot in the room, my body shook, and I fought back a cry as I saw Jimmy's bloody form. My feet rooted to the planks, but the gentle urging of Bowden's hand on the small of my back pushed me forward.

The warmth of his hand faded as he left me and went to kneel beside Gray's pa. "Hello, old friend," he said, his voice thick as he took the man's hand.

A sob caught in my chest, and I turned back to Jimmy. He lay shirtless, a bloodstained bandage wrapped around his torso. Elsewhere, flesh wounds had been left by a blade. His breathing was ragged, and I knew that he held on to but a glimmer of life. I knelt beside him and slipped my fingers under his hand, lying at his side.

"Jimmy, it's me, Willow." My voice was tattered. "You will be just fine. I'll see to it." I stroked his hair. Tears streamed down my cheeks and tickled my neck before soaking into my blouse. "You're too stubborn to die," I said with a laugh, blinking off tears. His eyes fluttered open, and my breath caught, but they quickly closed, as though his subconscious had reacted to me. "I need you. More than you will ever know." I closed my eyes and laid my cheek on his chest, finding comfort in the beat of his heart. "Ruby, Saul, Mercy, we all need you," I whispered.

A shadow fell over me, and I opened my eyes to find Ben standing at the foot of the bed. I pushed to my feet and walked a few feet away, and he followed.

"He can't die," I said in a low voice, my lips quivering. "He mustn't. He is like a father to me in all the ways that matter. He loved me and taught me things my own could not." Misery and fear wrenched at my heart, and thoughts of hurting him didn't enter my mind until too late. Catching myself, I gasped, "I'm sorry. I don't mean to—"

"Do not apologize for speaking the truth." I saw compassion and understanding in his eyes. "His love for you radiates, as does yours for him. Regardless of your parentage, Miss Rita and James raised you and stood in when we could not. My brother's and my failures will always haunt me, but there is no time for regrets of the past. I've done all I can for him. The rest lies in God's hands. Both men need a miracle." He looked wearily from one cot to the other.

As Bowden joined us, I said, "You all are supposed to leave today. I can't possibly manage—"

"We have no choice but to leave. We will send word of what occurred here, and hope they will grant us a few days." He strode to the door and called out to Kimie. When she entered, he gripped her shoulder. "Are you capable of caring for the wounded in our absence?"

"I-I..." She looked from Ben to him.

"The next best person to a trained doctor," Ben said.

Her expression uncertain, she gulped and then squared her shoulders. "I'll see to them."

"Good." He released her. "Willow will ensure that any capable womenfolk are put into position to help you."

I had yet to realize the gravity of the lives lost at Livingston. My pulse quickened. When I did, could I face the knowing? What of the bodies scattered across the work yard requiring burials? My gaze turned to the window, and the injured spread across the lawn. So many hurt and needing attention.

"But what am I to do?" I gawked at Bowden, dumbfounded. As I thought of the impossible task ahead, my panic mounted. Recalling the damage I'd observed upon our arrival, I pointed at the window. "Destruction is everywhere: our ships, the warehouse; the main house is partly destroyed; the kitchen house and smokehouse are gone. How can I possibly make Livingston functional again with no menfolk around? I can't do this. It's too much." Concealing my face in my hands, I let sobs rack my body.

"Come." Bowden took my hand and led me outside.

We left the quarters and strolled along the path leading to the family cemetery and the ponds.

"I know it is a lot to ask of you," he said. "Too much, really. But you will have Jones, and after we assess our losses we will know exactly what we are up against. Unfortunately, in the current times, many are forced to do things we don't want to. Not only the men who have enlisted, but the women left behind to run our lands."

I took a deep breath to relieve the tightness in my chest. Although my heart remained heavy, the numbness over what had occurred was slowly evaporating with the determination to put everything in order. Bowden needed me to be strong. The people of Livingston needed me. I couldn't possibly crumble now. "I know," I said as we stepped from the tree line and the graveyard came into view.

I froze. "No, no, no!"

"What is it…" Bowden's words faded as he too beheld the sight. "My God!" Bowden raced forward, hauling me behind him.

At the edge of the cemetery, I dropped to my knees and gawked in horror. The fence had been demolished, gravestones uprooted, and the graves of my son, mother, father, and grandparents trampled. The McCoys had sought to desecrate their very memory.

A part of my soul fractured, and with a forlorn wail I fell forward, pulling at the grass and dirt. Why? Had we not suffered enough?

Bowden knelt and wrapped me in his arms, and I lifted my head and looked at him. Silent tears stained his cheeks. Had I cursed my husband in our union? Why was God bent on unleashing pain on my family? Had I brought misery and suffering to Livingston? I collapsed against Bowden, sensing the galloping of his heart, and his trembling body.

"H-how do we go on?" I sobbed into his shoulder.

"We must." His hard voice made me look at his face. There was a cold glint in his eyes.

I gulped. "Please don't leave. I can't bear it. I can't."

"I have no choice." He hauled me to my feet and turned me in the direction of the house.

All of me wanted to curl up and die and leave the cruelty of a world I wasn't designed for. I wanted to rewind the past days—we would never have gone to Charleston, and perhaps we could have prevented the desolation that had befallen Livingston. In doing so, the slaves hidden in the warehouse would have perished in the fire.

Wait. I stopped in my tracks and turned to him.

"The men that set fire to our ships and the warehouse—do you think it was the McCoys?"

"I believe it's impossible to have been anyone else." He clasped my hand and continued toward the house.

"But how can you be certain?"

"Because amongst the bodies are men clad in states' militia uniforms," he said.

"Missus Willow, Masa Bowden." Mammy's voice drew our attention to her hurrying toward us. Big John, supporting his weight with a makeshift cane, hobbled behind her. As they got near, I noticed the bandages covering his hands and the way he wheezed.

"You all right?" I asked.

"Nothing time won't heal," he said with a bow of his head.

"He tried to save de house, and 'bout killed himself in de process." Mammy scowled up at him, and he grinned, finding amusement in her feistiness.

"Miss Rita, I need you to take my wife up to the house and give her something to calm her nerves."

"No." I pulled from him. "I will not be set aside as though I'm too weak to handle what needs doing. I—"

He pulled me to him and placed a finger to my lips, stilling my words. "Look at me," he said gruffly. I looked at him. "Do you think I don't know what you're capable of? You're capable of more than even you realize. I'm counting on you while I'm away. The people need you more than ever before. I fear the trials will be many, but together we must stand united and see this to an end."

"But what if you don't come back?" My voice trembled at the thought. "What if none of you do? Am I to have a graveyard of loved ones?"

"Missus Willow, you mustn't think lak dat. None of de misfortunes and losses dat befell dis place or your family got anything to do wid you." Mammy touched my shoulder. I pulled from Bowden to face her. "Life ain't fair. Why, et downright unjust at times, but we got to keep moving anyhow. Now come along and do as Masa says. You won't do anyone any good if you don't keep a sound mind." She took my arm and escorted me across the work yard. I glanced over my shoulder at my husband, who stood staring blankly after me.

Turning back, I considered what lay ahead, and worry gnawed into my fear. Would we survive what was to come?

CHAPTER
Three

Drifter

Y LIDS OPENED, AND I GRITTED MY TEETH AT THE PAIN RICOCHETING through my skull. Touching the damp bandage compressing my head, I frowned as the recollection of how I'd obtained the injury deserted me. Parched, my tongue thick, I licked my lips to relieve the burn of cracked skin. My hollow stomach gurgled, demanding food. Blankets soaked in sweat clung to me like a second skin, and my nostrils rebelled at the smell of my body.

Senses tuning to the musky, woodsy scent enveloping me, my gaze went to the animal pelts hanging from the plank walls of what appeared to be a one-room cabin. The door was ajar. A table sat next to an open fire where an iron skillet sizzled.

Where am I? Struggling to a sitting position, I grimaced at the ache of bruised ribs. I sensed my lack of clothing, but before I could locate any the doorway darkened. I regarded the mountainous man with silver plaits and an unruly beard who lingered on the front stoop, with a blade in one hand and a slab of meat in the other, appearing freshly carved from an animal's carcass. Blood dripped over his fingers and onto the dirt floor.

My heart beat harder. The weakness in my limbs and the awareness of my nakedness seized me with vulnerability. In a panic, I glanced around for my trousers or something resembling clothing.

"You return to the land of the living." His voice was gruff, but not unfriendly. He strode into the cabin and tossed the meat into the skillet before wiping his hands on buckskin trousers.

"How did I get here?" Thirst made my voice a rasp.

"Weeks back, I found you belly up by the river about ten miles from here." He turned to face me, and his brown eyes held a keen glint. "It appears you took a shot to the head. You're one lucky son-of-a-gun. Someone must be watching out for you, 'cause you should be dead. Fixed you up the best I could. I couldn't find an exit wound, so I reckon the bullet is still in there. If my woman was still around, she would have fixed you up good. Sickness took her about five years ago. She was one of the last of her tribe," he said matter-of-factly.

The only good woman is one that doesn't draw breath, a voice chimed.

I examined the cabin's shadows for the speaker and sensed we were alone. Gaze turning to the open door, I looked to the outside and again detected no one. Only the songs of the forest critters, and the neighing of a horse.

The grizzly fellow strode to my bed and held out a tin cup. "My name's Samson. What do they call you?"

I opened my mouth to speak, but memory failed me. What was my name? Frowning, I regarded the man as he waited for an answer.

Say nothing, the newcomer said.

Sweat beaded my brow as recollection of anything before the opening of my eyes didn't exist. Panic surged, and the beating in my chest galloped faster. Who was I?

"Well, do you got a name or what?" His eyes narrowed, and the deeply etched channels in his jowls and pocked and weathered flesh gave him an intimidating appearance.

He asks too many questions. End him before he has a chance to tell.

Tell? Tell what? I hid my hands in the blankets to conceal their tremors. My attention going to the blade he'd set on the table, I studied it before directing my eyes to the outstretched hand holding the cup. A vision of his lifeless body, gutted and splayed out on the cabin floor, flashed through my mind, and I shook my head to dispel it. I swallowed hard. The amount of damage from the gunshot was concerning.

I gawked at Samson. His penetrating eyes scoured my soul in quest of answers.

"Name's Preston Lawson," I said. The name rattled from my head as natural as a next breath. *Preston Lawson.* I rotated the name in my mind. Why did the name sound so foreign?

Yes, that will do. Glad to see you haven't lost all your senses, the voice jeered.

"Drink." Samson gestured with the cup at me.

My pulse slowed to a more calming beat. Reaching out to seize the cup, I noticed the steadiness of my hand.

"You get a look at the one who shot you? Ain't messed up with the law, are ya?"

I took the cup and drained the contents before handing it back to him. "In the wrong place at the wrong time. Rode into a meadow just as a hunter lifted his rifle to shoot; next thing I know, I'm waking up here." The story rolled off my tongue with no sense of recognition.

An uncanny chuckle made me eye Samson, but he stood with lips pressed together. I trembled at the mounting awareness that the prattle may occur in my own head.

"Got ten lives, I reckon." Shaking his head, he returned to the skillet as the odor of scorching drifted.

As I observed him, the image of an auburn-haired woman with voluptuous curves and rouge-stained lips surfaced, and my jaw gritted at the vision. Who was she? And why did I get a sense of bad blood between us?

Exhausted, I slumped back and allowed sleep to take me.

ABOUT
the Author

Naomi is a bestselling and award-winning author living in Northern Alberta. She loves to travel and her suitcase is always on standby awaiting her next adventure. Naomi's affinity for the Deep South and its history was cultivated during her childhood living in a Tennessee plantation house with six sisters. Her fascination with history and the resiliency of the human spirit to overcome obstacles are major inspirations for her writing and she is passionately devoted to creativity. In addition to writing fiction, her interests include interior design, cooking new recipes, and hosting dinner parties. Naomi is married to her high school sweetheart and she has two teenage children and a dog named Egypt.

Sign up for my newsletter: authornaomifinley.com/contact

Made in the USA
Columbia, SC
23 February 2021

33445665R00212